SUSAN MALLERY

the vineyard *at*
painted moon

CANARY STREET PRESS

**CANARY
STREET
PRESS™**

Recycling programs
for this product may
not exist in your area.

ISBN-13: 978-1-335-00640-0

The Vineyard at Painted Moon

First published in 2021. This edition published in 2023.

Copyright © 2021 by Susan Mallery, Inc.

For questions and comments about the quality of this book,
please contact us at CustomerService@Harlequin.com.

Canary Street Press
22 Adelaide St. West, 41st Floor
Toronto, Ontario M5H 4E3, Canada
CanaryStPress.com

Printed in U.S.A.

Praise for the novels of Susan Mallery

To Barbara—this one is for you.

the vineyard at
painted moon

one

"Not that what you're wearing isn't great, but the party starts in an hour."

Mackenzie Dienes looked up from the grapevine she'd been studying, her mind still on the tight clusters of small, hard grapes that would, come late September, be ripe and sweet and ready for harvest. Between now and then, she would monitor their progress, willing them to greatness and protecting them from danger, be it mold, weather or hungry deer.

She blinked at the man standing in front of her, tall and familiar, with an easy smile and broad, capable shoulders.

"Party?" she asked, letting her thoughts of the vineyards go and remembering that, yes, indeed, it was the evening of the annual Solstice Party, hosted by the Barcellona family. As she was a Barcellona, by marriage if not by name, she would be expected to attend.

Wanted to attend, she reminded herself. It was always a good time, and Stephanie, her sister-in-law, worked hard to make it a perfect night.

"The party," she repeated, her voice slightly more panicked this time, then glanced down at herself. "Crap. What time is it?"

Rhys, her husband, shook his head. "You really don't listen when I talk, do you? We have an hour. You'll be fine."

She pulled off her gloves and shoved them into the left front pocket of her coveralls, then stepped behind Rhys and gave him a little push toward the flatbed truck he'd driven out to the west vineyards.

"You say that because all you have to do is shower and get dressed. I have to do the girl thing."

"Which takes you maybe ten minutes." He put his arm around her as they hurried toward the truck. "Happy with the grapes?"

"I think so," she said, glancing toward the healthy vines growing on either side of them. "We might have to do some thinning in a couple of weeks, but so far, so good."

As they slid onto the bench seat of the old truck, he glanced at her. She smiled, knowing there was a fifty-fifty chance he would call her out on her thinning statement. He was, after all, the vineyard manager. Technically all the decisions about the vineyard were made by him with her input, but not her instruction. As winemaker, she managed the grapes from the moment they were picked until the wine was bottled.

But at Bel Après, areas of responsibility often overlapped. Theirs was a large, boisterous family in which everyone had opinions. Not that Mackenzie listened to a lot of other ideas when it came to her wines, although as Rhys often pointed out, she was very free offering hers when it came to *his* work.

He drove along the dirt path that circled the vineyard, stopping by her truck. She slid into the cab, then followed him back to the family compound. The main road leading into Walla Walla was thick with tourists who wanted to enjoy the longest day of the year. She merged into the slow-moving traffic, doing her best to keep from glancing at the clock on the truck's dashboard as she inched along.

Vineyards stretched out on either side of the road, flat on the left and rising toward the hills on the right. Bright green leaves topped sturdy trunks that had been carefully trained to grow exactly as she wanted them to. The rows were long and neat, and the spaces between them were filled with native grasses that held in moisture and protected the roots from the heat.

Looking at her healthy crop kept her mind off the fact that she and Rhys were going to be desperately late.

Twenty minutes later, she followed him off the highway onto a less crowded secondary road—a back way home. Five minutes after that, they parked the trucks by the processing buildings behind the big tasting room. Rhys had already claimed one of the golf carts the family used to get around. She slid in next to him and they took off toward the center of the property.

Bel Après Winery and the surrounding land had been in the Barcellona family for nearly sixty years. Rhys and his siblings were third-generation. The original main house had been updated several times. When Rhys and Mackenzie had married, Barbara, Rhys's mother, had suggested they build themselves a house close to hers, rather than commute from town. Eager to stay in the good graces of her new mother-in-law, Mackenzie had agreed.

A large two-story home had been built. Barbara and Mackenzie had decorated every room, the act of choosing everything from light fixtures to doorknobs cementing their affection for each other.

A few years later, Stephanie, the second of Barbara's four children, had gotten a divorce and moved back home with her two kids, requiring another house to be constructed. When the youngest of the three girls had married, the last house had been added. Only Lori, the middle daughter, still lived in the original home.

All four houses faced a huge central courtyard. Mexican pavers were shaded by vine-covered pergolas. The extended family used the space for big dinners and as a kids' play area. If one of the women baked cookies, a cookie flag was hung out the front door, inviting anyone to stop by. At Christmas, a large tree was brought in from Wishing Tree, and for the annual Summer Solstice Party, dozens of long tables were brought in to seat the two hundred or so guests.

Rhys swung the golf cart behind the large main house, circling counterclockwise. Normally he would cut across the courtyard, but with all the party preparations, he had to go the long way. He pulled up at the rear entrance to their house and they dashed inside.

Mackenzie paused to unlace her boots and left them in the mudroom. Rhys did the same. They raced up the stairs together, separating at the landing to head to their individual en suite bedrooms.

Once in her bathroom, she started the shower. Thankfully, she'd already picked out the dress she would wear. She raced through a shower. After she dried off, she wrapped her hair in a towel and dug out the scented body lotion Rhys had given her a couple of years ago. Why anyone would want to smell like coconut and vanilla was beyond her, but he liked it.

She walked into the large closet and opened her underwear drawer. To the right were all the sensible bikini panties she usually wore—to the left were the fancier ones for special occasions. She chose a black pair and slipped them on, then went to the second drawer and looked for the matching push-up bra. When it and the pads were in place and doing the best they could with her modest curves, she pulled on a robe and returned to the bathroom.

After plugging in her hot rollers, it took her only a few minutes to apply eyeliner and mascara. She was flushed from the day working outside, so she didn't bother with any other makeup.

Her hair took a lot longer. First she had to dry the dark red shoulder-length waves, then she had to curl them. While the rollers were in place, she searched for a pair of black high-heel sandals that wouldn't leave her crippled by the end of the night.

Those found, she opened her small jewelry box and pulled out her wedding set, sliding both the engagement ring and the wedding band into place on her left hand. Diamond stud earrings followed. She'd barely stepped into her sleeveless black dress when Rhys walked into the closet, fully dressed in black slacks and a dark gray shirt.

She sighed when she saw him. "See. You have it so much easier than me."

"Yes, but in the end, you're more beautiful. That should be worth something."

"I'd rather have the extra time."

She turned, presenting him with her back. He pulled up the zipper, then bent to collect her shoes. They retreated to her bathroom and together began removing the curlers.

"We're late," Mackenzie said, catching sight of his watch. "Your mom is going to be all snippy."

"She'll be too busy welcoming her guests."

The last of the curlers was flung onto the counter. Mackenzie fluffed her hair, then pointed to the bedroom.

"Retreat," she said, reaching for the can of hair spray.

Rhys ducked to safety. She sprayed the curls into submission before running into the bedroom to escape the death cloud. Rhys was on the bench at the foot of the large bed. She sat next to him and quickly put on her shoes.

"Done," she said, pausing to reacquaint herself with the seldom-used skill of walking in heels.

She grabbed her husband's wrist. "Seven fifteen. Barbara's going to kill us."

"She's not. I'm her only son and you're just plain her favorite."

"We weren't ready exactly at seven. I can already hear the death-march music in my head. I want to be buried on Red Mountain."

Rhys chuckled as he led the way downstairs. "In the vineyard? I'm not sure your decaying body is going to be considered organic."

"Are you saying I'm toxic?" she asked with a laugh as they walked toward the front door.

"I'm saying you're wonderful and I'd like us to have a good night."

There was something in his tone, she thought, meeting his gaze. She'd known this man her entire adult life. They'd met over Christmas her freshman year of college. Her roommate, his sister Stephanie, had dragged Mackenzie home to meet the family. Grateful not to have to spend the holiday by herself, Mackenzie had gone willingly and had quickly found herself falling not only for her best friend's hunky older brother but for the entire Barcellona family and the vineyards they owned. Barbara had been like a surrogate mother, and the vineyards, well, they had been just as magical as Rhys's sexy kisses.

Now she studied her husband's expression, seeing the hint of sadness lurking behind his easy smile. She saw it because she hid the same emotion deep inside herself. The days of stealing away for sexy kisses were long gone. There were no lingering looks, no intimacy. They had a routine and a life, but she was less sure about them still having a marriage.

"I'd like that, too," she murmured, knowing he wasn't asking them not to fight. They never did. Harsh words required a level of involvement they simply didn't have anymore.

"Then let's make that happen," he said lightly, taking her hand in his and opening the front door.

The sounds of the party engulfed them, drawing them into the rapidly growing throng of guests. Mackenzie felt her mood lighten as she took in the twinkle lights wrapped around the pergola, the tables overflowing with food, the cases of Bel Après wine, stacked and ready to be opened. Servers circulated with trays of bruschetta. There was a pasta bar and a dessert station. Music played through speakers hidden in foliage, and the delicious smell of garlic mingled with the sweet scent of summer flowers.

Mackenzie spotted Stephanie talking to one of the servers and gave Rhys's hand one last squeeze before separating from him and walking toward her sister-in-law.

"You outdid yourself," she said, hugging her friend.

"I'm pretty bitchin'," Stephanie said with a laugh, then waved her hand toward the twinkle lights. "Those will be a lot more effective when the sun goes down in two plus hours."

Because the longest day in their part of Washington State meant nearly sixteen hours of daylight.

"You exhausted?" Mackenzie asked, knowing Stephanie had spent the past three weeks making sure every detail of the party was perfect.

"It's been the usual challenge with a few extras thrown in," her sister-in-law said lightly. "I won't even hint at what they are, but brace yourself for a surprise or two."

Mackenzie immediately scanned the crowd. "Is Kyle here?"

Stephanie, a petite, curvy brunette with beautiful brown eyes and an easy smile, groaned. "What? No. Not that. I told you. I'm over him. Totally, completely, forever."

"But he's here."

"Yes. Mom invites him every year because he's Avery and Carson's father. The fact that he's my ex-husband doesn't seem to faze her. You know how she gets."

Mackenzie did. Once her mother-in-law made up her mind about something, she could not, would not be moved. There was no evolving of an opinion over time. Barbara was a human version of the immovable object.

"Kyle is her oldest granddaughter's father, and therefore a member of the family." Stephanie wrinkled her nose. "I deal with the awkwardness of it. On the bright side, she refers to him as 'the sperm donor,' which I like."

"If only he'd fought the prenup, Barbara would have turned on him like a snake." Mackenzie paused. "You're sure you don't want to start back up with him?"

"Yes. Totally. I'm done with that. He strung me along for years after the divorce. No more sex with the ex. It's been eighteen months since our last bump and grind, and I'm standing strong. I'm horny as hell, but standing strong." She glanced around at the guests. "Maybe I'll hook up with someone here."

"Have you ever hooked up with anyone?"

"No, but there's always a first time." Stephanie wrinkled her nose. "I just don't know how it works. Do we slip away to the barrel room and do it on a desk or something? I can't take him home—the kids are there. And a car is just so tacky."

"Because the barrel room isn't?" Mackenzie asked with a laugh.

"I don't know. It could be romantic."

"Or, at the very least, intoxicating."

Stephanie waved away that observation. "Fine. Not the barrel room, but then I'm still left with a lack of location, not to mention any prospects." She sighed as they walked toward one of the wine stations. "This is why hooking up has never worked for me. It's too complicated. They make it look easy in the movies and on TV, but it's not."

"I have zero experience. I'm sorry. I'll read up on it so I have better advice next time."

"Which is why I love you." Stephanie shook her head. "Obviously I should let the whole man-slash-sex thing go and focus on other aspects of my life."

They each asked for a glass of cabernet. While Stephanie simply sipped her wine, Mackenzie took a moment to study the color, before sniffing the aroma. She swirled the wine twice, then inhaled the scent again, liking the balance of fruit against the—

"For heaven's sake, just drink the wine, I beg you," Stephanie said with a laugh. "It's fine. It was fine when you watched the grapes being crushed, it was fine in the barrels, it was fine when it was bottled and it was fine when it won what I'm sure is a thousand awards. Okay? It's good wine. Relax and stop being a wine-maker for one night."

"You're crabby." Mackenzie took a drink and smiled. "For the record, it's much better than fine."

"You would say that. It's your wine." Stephanie looked over Mackenzie's shoulder and smiled. "Here comes your handsome husband. I'm guessing he wants your first dance."

Mackenzie turned and watched as Rhys approached. He enjoyed the dancing at the Solstice Party and took all the female guests for a turn around the dance floor, but he always saved the first one for her.

"Shall we?" he asked, holding out his hand.

She passed her wineglass to Stephanie, then followed her husband to the small dance floor. No one else joined them, but she knew that would change as soon as they got things started.

"We need to check the Seven Hills drip system," she said as they moved in time with the music. "The forecast says we're going to get hotter and drier in the next few weeks, and I want to control the exact amount of moisture."

One of the advantages of "new world" vineyards was the ability to control quality by providing exactly the right amount of irrigation. Once the fruit was established, she could stress the vines, causing them to focus more intensely on the fruit.

"I know better than to point out we walked the vineyard last month," Rhys said lightly.

"That was a general check. Now I have a specific concern."

"As you wish." He spun them in a tight circle. "Maybe the rest of the work conversation could wait until tomorrow."

"What?" Why wouldn't they talk about— "Oh. The party. Sorry."

"Don't apologize. You're never truly off duty, but if we could put it on hold for the night, I would appreciate it."

Because he enjoyed events like these. He liked talking to his friends and meeting new people and generally being social. Rhys was much more extroverted than she was. If someone new joined the tight circle of vineyard owners in the area, he was the first one to go introduce himself.

She nodded her agreement and tried to think of something to talk about that wasn't vineyard or wine related.

"I hope Kyle leaves Stephanie alone," she said, thinking that was a more neutral topic. "She's trying hard to move on."

"She has to figure out what she wants. He's always going to ask—it's up to her to tell him no and mean it."

She knew he was right, but for some reason his blunt assessment irritated her.

"That's not very understanding," she said before she could stop herself. "Kyle's a big-time Seattle sportscaster with the ability to find a different woman every night. Stephanie's a small-town single mom working at the family business. Where, exactly, is she supposed to meet someone?"

Her husband stared at her. "What does her dating someone else have to do with whether or not she's still sleeping with Kyle?"

"There aren't any other options for her. She's lonely."

"She's going to stay lonely until she gets herself out there."

"What *there* are you talking about? The giant singles scene here in Walla Walla?"

They stopped dancing and stared at each other. Mackenzie realized this was the closest she and Rhys had come to having an actual argument in years. She had no idea why she had so much energy about the topic or what was causing her growing annoyance. But whatever it was, the Summer Solstice Party was not the place to give in to unexplained emotions.

"I'm sorry," she said quickly. "You're right, of course. Stephanie has to find a way to change her circumstances so Kyle is less of a temptation."

His tight expression softened with concern. "I want my sister to be happy."

"I know you do."

"I want *you* to be happy."

There was something in the way he said the words. As if he wasn't sure that was possible.

"I am," she said quietly, thinking she was almost telling the truth.

"I hope so."

She faked a smile and waved her hand toward the growing crowd of guests. "You have a lot of women to dance with tonight. You'd better get started."

He studied her for a second, as if assessing her mood. She kept the smile in place until he turned away. When he was gone, she looked longingly toward her house. Disappearing into the quiet tempted her but wasn't an option. Tonight was a command performance and there was no leaving early. But soon, she promised herself. In the quiet of her room, she wouldn't feel the low-grade unease that had haunted her for the past few months. Alone in the dark, she would be calm and happy and think only of good things, like the coming harvest and the wine she would make. Alone in the dark, she would be herself again.

two

Barbara Barcellona observed her guests as they laughed and talked. The Summer Solstice Party was a ten-year-old tradition, and one she enjoyed. She liked being the generous hostess and being able to show off her glorious estate and her attractive adult children. She liked how everyone dressed up for the evening and how the invitations were highly sought after, and how those who were not invited schemed to be included the next year. She liked the music and the food and even the twinkle lights her daughter Stephanie always insisted on, even though the sun was still visible at seven thirty in the evening.

The large crowd was a tribute to her, but more important, it was a tribute to Bel Après. People came to show their respect for the winery and all it represented, and that was what Barbara enjoyed most of all.

Forty-one years ago, when she'd married her late husband, Bel Après had been struggling to stay solvent. She hadn't known the first thing about wine or winemaking, but she'd learned as quickly as she could.

She and James had grown the business together. Eventually she'd taken over as general manager. She'd been the one to find the winemakers who had created the wines that had slowly, oh so slowly, brought Bel Après back from the brink.

Her gaze moved across the crowd until she found her daughter-in-law. Barbara watched Mackenzie talking with some of the winery owners and she smiled as she saw how they all listened attentively. Mackenzie had been a find, she thought warmly. A shy but gifted young woman who had immediately understood Barbara's vision of what Bel Après could be. Even if Rhys hadn't married her, Barbara would have hired her. But he had and Mackenzie had joined the family.

Barbara's warm, happy feelings vanished as Catherine, her youngest, joined Mackenzie. That girl, Barbara thought grimly, taking in the flowing tie-dyed dress most likely created from a couple of pillowcases and a yak bladder. Catherine's mission in life was to not be ordinary and to annoy her mother as much as possible. Happily for her, the quest for the former naturally led to the latter.

She felt a hand on her waist, then a kiss on her bare neck. She turned and smiled at Giorgio, who pulled her close.

"You're looking fierce about something," he said, pressing his body to hers. "Tell me what troubles you, my love, and I will find a solution."

"How I wish that were true." She nodded toward Mackenzie and Catherine. "My daughter's a mess. Can you fix that? And while you're at it, can you make her stop being an artist and find an actual career?"

Giorgio, a tall man who, despite being sixty-five,

was still vibrant and handsome, said, "She's lovely. She'll never have the beauty her mother possesses, but she is a sweet, caring young woman."

"You're too kind." She smiled at him. "I mean that. Stop being so nice. What is she wearing? At least her husband had the good sense to put on a decent shirt, and the kids look fine."

He took her in his arms and spun her in time with the music. "Let her be who she is, at least for tonight. Think only of me."

She laughed as she moved with him onto the dance floor. "That's very easy to do."

As they danced, Catherine once again came into view. Her daughter smiled at her and raised a glass of wine, as if in a toast. Something really had to be done about her, Barbara thought, although she had no idea what.

"May I cut in, or would that break the mood?"

Barbara smiled at Rhys, her only son. "You may."

Giorgio pretended distress. "Fine. A single dance, but then I must reclaim your mother."

"I'll bring her back to you unharmed," Rhys promised, guiding her through a series of quick steps. "Great party, Mom."

"It is. Stephanie did an excellent job, much to my surprise. The bruschetta bar is very popular. She was right about that." She looked at her son. "Have you seen what Catherine is wearing?"

"Mom, let it go."

"She looks terrible."

"Jaguar doesn't seem to think so."

Barbara followed his gaze and saw Catherine and her husband slow dancing, despite the fast pace of the music. Typical, she thought with a sigh. God forbid Catherine should dance to the same beat as everyone else.

As for Jaguar—actually his real name. Barbara had insisted on seeing his birth certificate before agreeing to the marriage—he wanted whatever Catherine did. The woman practically led him around by the nose.

"Stop," Rhys told her. "You're getting your 'my daughter is annoying me' look. Enjoy the party."

"I am. It is a lovely night. I'll even pretend I didn't notice that you and Mackenzie were late."

"By fifteen minutes, Mom. She was in the west vineyards communing with the grapes."

"Is she still happy with how things are progressing?"

Her son smiled. "You know she is. Otherwise, she would have been in your office, telling you every little thing that was wrong."

Barbara knew that was true. Mackenzie always kept her informed. They were such a good team.

The song ended and Rhys led her back to Giorgio, who was chatting with several guests. As Barbara walked over to the bar to get a glass of wine, her youngest joined her.

"Barbara," Catherine said pleasantly. "Wonderful party."

Barbara did her best not to bristle. At the beginning of high school, Catherine had insisted on changing her name to Four, of all things. As in the fourth child. Barbara had refused to accommodate her, so Catherine had started calling her by her first name, to be annoying.

Barbara simply didn't understand where things had

gone wrong. She'd been loving but fair, had limited TV and made all her children eat plenty of greens. Sometimes parenting was such a crapshoot.

She motioned to her daughter's dress. "One of your own creations?"

Catherine spun in a circle. "It is. Don't you love it?"

"With all my heart."

Catherine grinned. "Sarcasm? Really?"

"What did you want me to say?"

Catherine's good humor never faded. "What you said is perfect."

As her daughter drifted away, Barbara moved closer to Giorgio. He put his arm around her waist, the pressure against her back both comforting and familiar. She nodded as he talked, not really listening to the conversation. Whatever he was saying would be charming. He was like that—well-spoken, always dressed correctly for the occasion. He had an enviable way with people and a natural charm she'd never possessed. She supposed that was what she'd first noticed—how easy he made everything when he was around.

This night, she thought with contentment. It was exactly right. Her children and grandchildren were around her. Giorgio was here. The vines were healthy and strong and come September there would be another harvest.

She spotted Avery, her oldest grandchild, talking to her father, Stephanie's ex. Kyle was too smooth by far, Barbara reminded herself. Their marriage had been a disaster from the beginning, but Stephanie had been pregnant, so there had been no way to avoid the entanglement or the subsequent divorce.

At least Avery and Carson hadn't been scarred by

the breakup. Barbara couldn't believe Avery was already sixteen. She was going to have to remind Stephanie to keep a close eye on her daughter when it came to boys and dating. If she didn't, there was going to be a second generation with an unplanned pregnancy, and no one wanted that.

She often told people that children and vineyards meant constant worry. Just when you were ready to relax, a new season started with new challenges.

Stephanie walked over to her. "Mom, it's about time for the toast, if you're ready."

"I am."

Barbara excused herself to follow her daughter toward the DJ and the small platform by the dance floor. She took the microphone the young man offered and stared out at the crowd. Stephanie called for quiet and it took only a few seconds for the party to go silent.

"Thank you so much for joining me and my family at our tenth annual Summer Solstice Party," Barbara said, pausing for applause, then holding up her glass of chardonnay.

"To my children—may the next year be one of happiness for each of you. To my grandchildren—know that you are loved by all of us." She turned and found her daughter-in-law, then smiled at her. "To my special daughter of the heart—the day you came into our lives was a magnificent blessing."

There was more applause.

Barbara looked at Giorgio and smiled. They'd discussed whether or not she should mention him, and he'd asked her not to. After all, he was just the boyfriend and he'd said tonight was about family—yet another reason she loved him. The man understood her and wasn't that amazing.

She waved her glass toward the crowd. "To the rest of you, here's to a wonderful summer and a happy life."

"Happy life," they all echoed.

"How does it feel to be a magnificent blessing?" Four asked with a grin.

Mackenzie did her best not to groan. "It's better than last year when she said I was a miracle brought into the family to take Bel Après to greatness. Although technically I'm pretty sure she said I brought a magnificent blessing, not that I was one." She looked at her youngest sister-in-law. "Sorry about her enthusiasm."

"Don't be. We love you just as much. Or maybe more. Our love isn't conditional."

Four was right about that, Mackenzie thought. Barbara always claimed Mackenzie was her favorite, but that affection was very much tied to her work in the winery. If she hadn't been interested in Bel Après, Mackenzie wasn't completely sure Barbara would have allowed the wedding to take place.

"She is a challenge," she murmured.

"She is," Four agreed. "She's my mother and I love her, but there is something deeply wrong with her. I can't figure out if she was traumatized as a child or if she was just plain born mean."

The stark assessment surprised Mackenzie. "You think she's mean?"

Four's eyes brightened with amusement. "Do you think she's nice?"

"I wouldn't say nice. She can be…exacting. But she's always been good to me."

"She has, and you deserve her affection." Four hugged her. "You have an open and giving heart that warms us all. You are the fairy dust that allows us to fly." She waved her glass. "Oh, and you're magnificent."

"I agree."

The male voice came from behind her. Mackenzie turned to see Bruno Provencio walk up to join them. The man knew how to dress, she thought. Like Rhys, Bruno wore slacks and a long-sleeved shirt, but somehow the clothes were more elegant on him. Barbara said his clothes were all custom—a concept Mackenzie understood intellectually but made no sense to her on a day-to-day basis. Why take the time when you could buy stuff online and have it delivered with just a few clicks?

Something she would guess that Bruno had never done in his life, she thought, trying not to smile. Bruno came from money. He was good-looking, with dark hair and brown eyes, and carried himself with an air of confidence that added to the appeal.

One day she would be confident, too, she told herself. If not in this life, then maybe the next.

She groaned. "Don't say magnificent, please. Barbara was just being…"

"Her usual charming self," Bruno said, taking Mackenzie's free hand in his and leaning in to kiss her cheek. He did the same with Four.

"Successful party, as always," he said.

"It's all Stephanie," Mackenzie told him, setting her empty glass on the passing server's tray.

Bruno held out his hand to Mackenzie. "A dance?"

She smiled and nodded. She wasn't sure if she gave off a non-dancer vibe or if it was her position as Rhys's wife and Barbara's daughter-in-law, but almost none of the men at the party wanted to dance with her. But every year, Bruno asked and she happily agreed.

They moved toward the dance floor and joined the other couples there. Rhys was dancing and chatting with the owner of a local fashion boutique. Barbara and Giorgio were wrapped in each other's arms.

Bruno put his hand on her waist, keeping a respectable distance, and they began to move to the music.

"Perfect weather for the party," he said.

She glanced toward the setting sun. "It is. We were lucky it wasn't too hot." The high eighties were manageable, but a day in the nineties would have made for an uncomfortable event.

"We're seeing more of you than usual," she added. "Do you have new business in the area?"

Bruno was a wine distributor—at least that was how he described himself. She knew he also invested in a few wineries and had more money than God, and when he flew into town, he did so on a private jet. But aside from that, he was a mystery. A handsome mystery, but still, an unknown.

"I'm thinking of buying a winery," he admitted.

"You are? I knew you were an investor, but I didn't think you wanted more than that."

He gave her a half smile. "I like being in charge."

"Can you tell me which one?" she asked, then shook her head. "Never mind. I'm sure you can't. Still, I'll have to speculate."

"Text me your guesses. I'll tell you if you figure it out."

She laughed. "There are nearly five hundred wineries in a hundred-mile radius. You'd be forced to block me before I got even close to figuring it out."

"I promise not to block you."

"Buying a winery. That's exciting. All the possibilities."

"Interested in being my business partner?" His voice was teasing.

She laughed. "You flatter me, but Bel Après is my home. So you'll be living in Walla Walla permanently? What about your family? I know your parents are still alive and you have siblings."

"They are all perfectly content on the East Coast and I like life here. I get home to see them often enough."

Now it was her turn to tease. "So you don't want to be *too* close."

"Best if I'm not. My mother likes to set me up on blind dates. They never go well."

"So distance is your friend." Mackenzie looked around. "Speaking of dates, you didn't bring anyone tonight, did you?"

"No."

She met his gaze. "At the risk of sounding like your mother, you never bring a date. Why is that?"

"I'm not seeing anyone in particular."

"Why not? I would think finding women would be easy. You're a successful, good-looking guy. I would think women would be all over you."

"Are you flirting with me?"

She laughed. "I think we both know I'm not capable of flirting." A thought occurred to her. Maybe the problem wasn't women at all. "Unless you'd rather not date women and you're concerned we'd have an issue with that. We wouldn't."

She paused, not sure how to navigate the socially awkward conversation she'd inadvertently started.

His half smile blossomed. "I'm not gay. I do like women. I'm not seeing anyone seriously because I can't seem to find someone who interests me enough to make the effort."

"Have you been married?"

"Yes."

She stared expectantly. "And?"

"We got a divorce. It was a long time ago."

"I'm sorry."

He shrugged. "I was at the time. Not anymore." He looked into her eyes. "I can't have children. We found out when she couldn't get pregnant. She didn't want to deal with that and she left."

Mackenzie came to a stop. "How could she be so awful? There are other ways to have children."

"She wasn't interested in any of them."

"I'm sorry, Bruno. For prying and for reminding you of a difficult time in your life. I should stick to small talk."

He pulled her a little closer and spun her. "I don't mind that you know."

"Still. I'm sorry."

"We'll change the subject. How much does Barbara hate what Four is wearing?"

Mackenzie looked at her sister-in-law. Her flamboyant dress was all bright colors, with an uneven hem and a short sleeve on one arm and a long sleeve on the other.

"I haven't talked to her about it, but I'm sure it's not her favorite."

"Four enjoys tormenting her. If Barbara would stop engaging, Four would stop being so outrageous."

She turned back to Bruno. "That's insightful."

"I'm a good observer."

"What else have you figured out?"

He looked at her for several seconds. His gaze was so intense, she was sure he was going to say something that would shock her, or maybe just keep her up for three days. Instead he stepped back, squeezed her hand, then released her.

"I should let you get back to your party," he said. "Have a good night."

He walked away, leaving her alone in the crowd, uncertain about what had just happened and what it had all meant. If anything.

The party was getting louder as more wine was consumed. Delicious smells from the buffet made her stomach growl. She was just about to grab something to eat when she spotted Rhys talking with a pretty blonde whose name Mackenzie couldn't remember.

As she watched, the woman reached out and touched Rhys's forearm. The flirtatiousness was clear, and she waited to see how her husband would respond. He gave the woman a brief smile and took a half step back.

Mackenzie doubted his movements were the least bit planned—no doubt he'd reacted involuntarily. Rhys wasn't the type who cheated. He was a good man who took his responsibilities, whether to her, his family or the winery, seriously. She could depend on him. She trusted him.

But they hadn't shared a bedroom in nearly five years, and it had been at least that long since they'd made love. So if he wasn't sleeping with her, who was he sleeping with? And even as she asked the question, she wondered if she really, truly wanted to know the answer.

Stephanie Barcellona wanted to state—for the record—that ex-husbands were a very bad idea. Especially good-looking ones with easy smiles and knowing glances. She'd spent the past hour ducking and weaving to avoid Kyle, but no matter how she busied herself with the party, he kept circling closer.

If only her mother hadn't insisted he be invited. Perhaps more to the point, if only Stephanie had the back-bone of a goldfish, she would walk up to him, look him in the eye and say that it was over. O. V. E. R. She was done being his booty call whenever he found himself in Walla Walla with a few hours to spare. They had been divorced over a decade. Nearly twice as long as they'd been married. They needed to be finished with each other for good. Having sex a couple of times a year didn't help either one of them. Though she was pretty sure it didn't faze him at all and only she was left feeling like an idiot.

It had been eighteen months since her last, um, encounter with Kyle. She'd gotten through last year's party and the holidays without giving in to his whispered "Hey, beautiful, let's go somewhere quiet." She told herself that if she could stay strong for the rest of the night, she would have broken free of him. She was determined, she had a plan. Unfortunately, she was also horny.

Betrayed by my hormones, she thought glumly as she circulated around the guests, making sure all was well. While she checked the flow of food and double-checked there was plenty of wine at the bar, her girl parts began to ache. Kyle always knew exactly how to make her come in, like, eighteen seconds. Humiliating but true.

She spotted him out of the corner of her eye, headed in her direction, and quickly walked the opposite way. If he got within touching distance, he would do that shoulder-to-wrist strokey thing with his fingers. The one that made her all shivery. Then he would lean in and tell her she had a great ass, because Kyle was just that much of a romantic. Then he would corner her so he could lightly brush against her nipples and she would be lost.

"Not happening," she breathed. "I can't do this anymore."

She continued the duck-and-weave dance, feeling like a character in a very badly written play, when she saw Giorgio nod at her. It was time.

All thoughts of Kyle fled as she checked her pocket for the small cloth bag tucked there, before walking directly to the DJ.

"Stephanie," Kyle said, his tone low and suggestive, as he closed in behind her.

She didn't bother looking at him as she said, "Not now."

When she reached the stage, she smiled at the DJ. "Ready."

He gradually lowered the volume of the music, then

handed her the microphone. All the guests turned toward the small platform.

"If I can have your attention for just another moment," she said, looking at Giorgio, who appeared incredibly calm, despite the momentousness of the occasion. "A certain gentleman would like to have a word with his very special lady."

She passed both the microphone and small cloth bag to him, then stepped back into the crowd that had gathered.

Avery, her sixteen-year-old daughter, slid in beside her. "What's going on?"

"Watch. It's going to be epic."

Avery sighed. "Mom, I've talked to you about trying to use slang. It's not a good look."

"I just do it to annoy you."

They linked arms and leaned in to each other. Stephanie didn't care if the word was too young for her. It was perfect—because this was going to be 100 percent epic. She could feel it in her gut.

three

Barbara had no idea what was happening, and she didn't like that one bit. She looked between Stephanie and Giorgio, hoping they weren't going to do something ridiculous like sing a duet. Stephanie didn't have much of a voice.

Still, she trusted Giorgio. The man took care of her the way no one ever had, so she should just relax and pretend to enjoy whatever silly thing they had planned.

Giorgio smiled at her as he spoke into the microphone. "Hello, my love."

She smiled back without speaking. He knew she didn't like to be played for a fool and she trusted him. Whatever misgivings she had, she should ignore.

He glanced at the circle of people around them. "For those of you who don't know me very well, I met this wonderful woman two years ago, in Italy. We were tasting wine at a little place outside of Tuscany. The day was beautiful, but the woman next to me was even more appealing. I found myself unable to look away."

"You were very charming," she said, relaxing as he spoke.

"On the outside. On the inside, my heart was beating so quickly. At my age, that can be a dangerous thing."

Everyone laughed.

"I introduced myself and suggested we share a glass of wine." He smiled again. "She agreed and I was so happy, I could barely speak. You told me about Bel Après and your children and Mackenzie, and I could hear the love and pride in your voice. Within the hour, I was smitten."

Barbara felt herself getting lost in the memories of that first meeting. He'd surprised her by talking to her. She hadn't known what to think. Handsome men simply didn't ever talk to her—not the way he had. He'd been funny and kind and the afternoon had flown by.

"I was married before," he said. "My wife passed away five years ago, and it never occurred to me that I would find love again, but I have. A great, glorious love that has filled my heart."

She placed her hands on her chest and mouthed, "Me, too."

He handed Stephanie the microphone and took something out of a small bag, then stunned her by dropping to one knee.

"Barbara Barcellona, you are the love of my life. I love you and adore you. I want to make you happy, and spend the rest of my days with you. Will you marry me?"

She hadn't seen it coming, she thought, genuinely stunned by the proposal. She stared at Giorgio, trying to take it all in. The sound of the music retreated until she could hear only her own heartbeat.

Happiness swelled, becoming joy, and she knew that she would never again experience a moment so perfect.

"Yes," she said, fighting tears. "Oh, yes, Giorgio. I'll marry you." Around them, everyone began to cheer and applaud.

He stood and slid a large diamond solitaire onto her finger, then cupped her face and kissed her. The feel of his warm lips on hers was magical. She felt like a princess. She felt thirty years younger.

"I love you," he whispered into her ear.

"I love you, too."

Around them, the clapping continued. Her children gathered around, hugging her and Giorgio.

"Did you know?" she asked Rhys.

Rhys grinned. "He asked for my permission. It was very honorable of him and I'm happy for you both, Mom."

"I didn't know," Mackenzie said, kissing her cheek. "Barbara, congratulations. You're going to be a beautiful bride. I know Giorgio will make you so happy."

Four and Lori rushed in to hug her.

"No one told us," Four said with a laugh. "What a wonderful surprise."

"I'm happy for you," Lori added, sounding slightly less than thrilled.

Barbara supposed the living arrangements would be a problem. Lori had never moved out of the large family home at the center of the compound. It was one thing to have Giorgio staying there when he visited, but another to have him a permanent resident. A problem she would deal with tomorrow, she told her-self, determined to enjoy every moment of the very perfect evening.

The music resumed and Giorgio drew her to the dance floor. She laughed when she heard the opening notes of "Lady in Red," then glanced down at her red cocktail dress.

"So that's why you asked me to wear this," she said, gazing up at him.

"It was all part of the plan."

She leaned her head against his shoulder. "I was surprised."

"I'm glad. Rhys knew, of course, and Stephanie."

"They kept the secret."

"Barbara?"

She looked at him.

"I don't want you to worry about anything," he said, his gaze filled with affection. "I'll be happy to sign a prenuptial agreement. I want no part of Bel Après."

"You will?"

She hadn't even thought of a prenup. She would have, probably before midnight, which would have kept her up the rest of the night. "Thank you for that. I'll sign whatever you want, as well."

Giorgio had plenty of money from the aerospace manufacturing firm he'd run in upstate New York.

"We're a very modern couple," he teased.

She raised herself on tiptoe and whispered in his ear, "Yes, and later, we're going to have lots of modern sex."

He chuckled. "How is it modern? I think of our lovemaking style as more traditional."

She grinned. "We keep the lights on."

"That we do."

They danced for another three songs before going to get something to drink. Several of the female guests stopped her to admire her ring. Barbara hadn't had much of a chance to study it herself. She would guess the diamond was at least three carats. A little large and flashy, but she was confident she could carry it off.

Stephanie met them by the bar.

"That was amazing," she said with a happy sigh. "I'm so thrilled for you both."

"You did a very nice job," Barbara told her, doing her best to keep the surprise out of her voice. "The moment was perfect."

Stephanie hugged her. "Next, the wedding. Let me know if you want my help planning that, Mom. It's one of my skill sets."

A wedding? Barbara hadn't thought that far ahead. Obviously she and Giorgio would have some kind of ceremony. At their age, it made sense to make it small—family and a few close friends.

She immediately recalled her first wedding. She and James had been young and there hadn't been any money to waste on something as frivolous as a wedding. They'd been married in a small church and the reception had been in the old farmhouse where they'd lived. It hadn't been the wedding of anyone's dreams.

She looked at the ring glinting on her left hand, then at the crowd enjoying themselves. She was the matriarch of Bel Après, and the owner of a successful business. Money was no object.

"Giorgio, what do you want for a wedding?"

He drew her hand to his mouth and kissed her

knuckles. "I want whatever makes you happy, my love."

He was such a good man.

Barbara considered her options. Having the wedding at Bel Après made the most sense. There were spaces for large events. Even though the winery wasn't gauche enough to pimp itself out as a destination anything, they did host parties for major customers or special occasions. Still, a wedding required planning.

Barbara looked at her oldest daughter. Stephanie managed the retail store and tasting room. She could, in a pinch, manage the wine club, as well, and she planned whatever parties were held on the property, including a handful of weddings. While Stephanie didn't have anything that could be considered talent, she was organized, and honestly, how hard could it be to plan a wedding?

"All right," Barbara said. "Stephanie, you can plan my wedding. I want a real one," she added. "Traditional. Nothing ridiculously modern. I'll accept fun and elegant and a little over-the-top, but that's all."

Stephanie grinned. "We can make that happen. We can even talk about a lot over-the-top."

Barbara held in a sigh. "We'll talk about it later. Right now I want to dance with my fiancé."

She turned to Giorgio and held out her hand. He pulled her close, then led her to the dance floor. So much happiness, she thought, leaning against him. The night was perfect, and the rest of her life was going to be just as wonderful.

Two hours and what Stephanie would guess was half a bottle of wine later, she was still processing what had happened. She was happy—of course she was happy. Giorgio was a wonderful man who adored her mother. There was also the happy side effect of Barbara being just a little easier to deal with when he was around, and who didn't want that?

She'd known about the engagement. She'd been the keeper of the ring and the decider of the timing. She was excited to be helping her mom plan a wedding. It was all good. Great, even. But—and it was a big but—she couldn't quite seem to wrap her mind around what she was feeling.

It wasn't just happy, she thought. It was something else. Something that made her uncomfortable and sad and maybe a few other things she couldn't or didn't want to name.

She stood by the bar, working on yet another glass of wine, when the truth hit her, like a sucker punch to the gut. All her air rushed out as she blinked back unexpected tears.

She wanted a different life. Her kids were great and she loved her family, but she wanted more. She wanted a job she loved—she wanted to be excited about how she spent her day, instead of just going through the motions. She wanted to be proud of herself and strong and brave, and that meant she really had to get off her ass and do something. Wishing was a waste of time. She'd spent the past five years talking about leaving Bel Après and going to work somewhere else and she'd done nothing to make that happen.

"Hey, babe."

The low words were accompanied by a finger sliding from her bare shoulder to her wrist. Stephanie turned and saw Kyle smiling at her.

"Stellar party, as per usual," he added with a wink.

"You're still here," she said, struggling to resurface from her confusing thoughts.

"Sure. I thought maybe we could spend a couple of hours together."

His tone was suggestive. As if to emphasize the point, he put his hand on the small of her back and then slid it down to cup her butt.

"No. Just no."

She spoke without thinking, taking a step away and staring at him, fighting the oddest sensation of having no idea who he was. Yes, they'd been married, but they'd divorced over a decade ago. What was she doing, having sex with him a couple of times a year, whenever it happened to fit into his schedule? She didn't want that, or him.

Why had she agreed to their sad arrangement? Ignoring the gross thought that she had no idea how many other women he slept with on a regular basis, didn't she deserve better? Didn't she deserve to be happy, with her own robust life? Instead she'd settled on ex-husband crumbs tossed her way. Kyle was a distraction, and one she'd allowed to go on for too long.

"You don't have to say it like that," he grumbled, sounding defensive. "Just tell me you're not interested."

"I'm not interested." Her voice was firm. "We talked about this before, Kyle. I said I was done and I meant it. Stop trying to get me into bed. I won't do that anymore. We're divorced. We should act like it."

With that, she walked away, looking for a safe group to join, then smiling when she spotted her kids talking to Lori.

"Having a good time?" she asked as she slipped between Avery and Carson.

"We are." Her daughter laughed. "Mom, I can't believe you didn't even hint about the proposal. It was so romantic. Even if they are, you know, old."

"Ancient," Stephanie teased. She turned to Carson. "What did you think about what happened?"

Her fourteen-year-old surprised her by grinning. "It was cool, Mom. Romantic, like girls want. Plus, it takes some, ah, courage to ask that in front of everyone. What if she'd said no? He would have been humiliated for life."

"Love gives you courage," she told him.

Avery sighed. "Great. Now she's going to make you watch that old movie she loves so much. What's it called?"

"Say Anything," Stephanie and Lori said together.

Avery groaned. "That's the one."

"I am kind of feeling it's time," Stephanie admitted.

"Do it quick," her daughter said. "Before Carson goes off to baseball camp. I don't want to get stuck being the only one who has to see it."

"You loved it."

"You wish."

Carson yawned. "It's late, Mom. I'm going to bed." He hugged her.

Her baby was four inches taller than her already and he still had a lot of growing to do. Of course, she was short, but still.

Avery hugged her, as well. "See you in the morning, Mom."

"Night."

She watched as they made their way across the patio

and went into their house, then she smiled at her sister. "Having a good time?"

"I was until the engagement." Lori's tone was sharp.

"I thought you liked Giorgio."

"I do, but now everything is going to change."

"I don't think he'll mind you living in the house, if that's what you're worried about. Besides, Mom would never make you move out."

Lori's expression tightened. "Oh, please. We both know she'd throw me out in a heartbeat if it served her purposes, or if Mackenzie asked her to." She exhaled sharply. "It's not that. Did you see how in love they are? I knew they were happy, but the look on her face when he proposed... I want that."

"To get married?" Stephanie tried to keep the surprise out of her voice.

"Of course. Everyone wants to belong. Some of us know when we should keep what we have rather than throw it away."

"Are you talking about my divorce?"

"You had something with Kyle. Maybe you should have stuck with what you had."

"A cheater who was never home?"

"It was a marriage."

"We were both miserable. Besides—" Stephanie pressed her lips together. She didn't need to defend her position to anyone. "It's better now," she said. "With us apart. But if you're interested in dating, I hope you meet someone."

"Nothing good ever happens to me."

With that, she turned and walked away. Stephanie watched her go, wondering how she and Lori and Four could be sisters when they were all so different. She supposed it was just one more thing that proved God had sense of humor.

She walked over to an empty chair and sat down. While the rest of the family were allowed to leave any time after ten, she was stuck for the duration. The party was her responsibility and she had to make sure everything was cleaned up and put away. She would be up until at least two in the morning.

On the bright side, she was apparently done with her ex. It had taken ten years and a cosmic slap in the face, but at least it had happened. First thing tomorrow, she would start looking for a job that excited her. She'd finally escaped from the trap of casual sex with her ex. Now it was time to escape from the family business and strike out on her own.

four

Mackenzie carefully studied the wine in the glass before taking another sip. This time she let the liquid sit on her tongue a bit longer before swirling it in her mouth and then spitting it into the coffee mug she'd brought with her.

Barrel tasting was essential so she could keep track of the progress of the wine, but getting drunk while doing so was a rookie mistake. She'd learned early that spitting came with the job. She picked up her clipboard and made a few notes. Later she would transfer the notes to a computer file. Old-school, for sure, but it was how she preferred to work.

This corner of the barrel room held her personal wines—blends she'd created because she'd had an idea and had wanted to see how it played out. The first three times that had happened, Barbara had flatout refused and then had told Mackenzie to stop asking. Frustrated, Mackenzie had told Barbara that if the wines didn't do well, she would cover the losses with her salary. But if they sold the way Mackenzie expected, she would get a cut of the profits for as long as the wines were made.

Barbara had agreed, drawing up a contract they'd both signed. Two years later the first of the Highland wines had been released. Highland Thistle—named in tribute to Mackenzie's Scottish ancestry—had sold out in two weeks. She'd used a more French style of blending the cab and merlot grapes, giving Thistle a softer finish that was appealing to a younger crowd.

The following year Highland Heather, a nearly botanical chardonnay, had sold out before the release. Last year, Highland Myrtle, a Syrah, had done the same. At that point, Barbara had stopped telling Mackenzie no on pretty much anything wine related. Still, the three wines provided a steady flow of money every quarter. The proceeds were currently just sitting in an investment account, but someday she would do something with them.

She reviewed her notes, then tucked the clipboard under her arm and headed for the offices on the second floor.

Bel Après had grown significantly over the past sixteen years. They'd always had enough capacity to produce more wine, but previous winemakers had sold off hundreds of tons of grapes rather than risk creating a new wine that failed. When Mackenzie had come on board, she and Barbara had come up with a strategic plan using the best of what Bel Après produced.

As she took the stairs to the second floor, she glanced at the awards lining the wall. Bel Après had started winning awards with Mackenzie's very first vintage, and Barbara had been giddy with the success. She'd wanted to enter every competition, but Mackenzie had insisted they be more selective. Better to place in a few prestigious competitions and get noticed rather than win awards no one had heard of.

Bel Après had been written up in journals and magazines, driving sales. Every year they'd expanded production. Ten years ago, they'd tripled the size of the barrel room.

She reached the top of the stairs and paused to look at the pictures mounted there. They showed Bel Après as it had been a generation ago, when Barbara had been a young bride. From there, all the way down the long hallway, photographs marked the growth of the winery and the family.

She smiled at a photograph of Rhys with his three sisters. He looked to be about ten or eleven with the girls ranging from nine to maybe five. The girls were all smiling and mugging for the camera, but Rhys looked serious, as if he already knew how much responsibility he had waiting for him.

He'd grown into a good man, she thought. He worked hard, was a fair employer and came home every night. Rhys was her rock—his steadiness freed her to send all her energy into the wines.

Mackenzie's parents had died when she'd been young, and her grandfather had raised her. He'd been a winemaker up in the Spokane area of the state, and she'd grown up understanding what it was to wrestle magic from the soil.

He'd gotten sick when she was fifteen—a cancer that could be slowed but not cured. Sheer will had kept him alive until she'd graduated from high school. He'd died that summer. Mackenzie still remembered the first day she'd moved into the residence hall, meeting her new roommate. Stephanie had been friendly and upbeat and exactly what Mackenzie had needed.

That first Christmas, Stephanie had brought her home. Mackenzie had been overwhelmed by Bel Après, dazzled by Barbara and swept away by Rhys.

He'd been so steady, she thought, smiling at the memory. Kind and strong, but with a sly sense of humor that made her laugh. Her second night there he'd knocked on her door at two in the morning, telling her to get dressed. He'd taken her outside, where unexpected snow fell from the sky. There, in the cold, dusted by new snow, he'd kissed her. It had been a perfect moment. She might not have fallen in love with him then, but she'd certainly cracked open her heart to the possibility.

She was still smiling at the thought when she walked down the hall, through the open door and into Barbara's large office. The corner space had huge windows that overlooked the property. The other two walls were covered with maps of the various vineyards owned by the family.

The Barcellona family was a dynasty. If Mackenzie and Rhys had had children, her blood would have blended with theirs, adding to the whole in some way. But they hadn't, so when she was gone, there would be no legacy. No piece of her to be found anywhere.

Except in the vineyards, she reminded herself. She had made her mark there. The wines of Bel Après owed what they were to her.

"Tell me good news," Barbara said, motioning to one of the chairs pulled up in front of her desk.

Mackenzie took a seat. "Rhys has been checking the Seven Hills drip system. The weather's getting hotter and I want to make sure there's enough water to protect the vines. I've spent yesterday and today barrel tasting. I'll get you my notes by tomorrow."

"We have that very expensive software system for your tablet," Barbara told her with a gentle laugh.

"Yes, and maybe one day I'll want to use it."

"You can be stubborn, Mackenzie Dienes."

"I get that from you."

The teasing between them was familiar—they both often mentioned sharing traits, despite the lack of blood relationship. Even looking at the two, a stranger would assume they were related.

Both were about five six, with dark red hair. They had strong, lean builds and wore an air of confidence. Mackenzie's eyes were green, while Barbara's were brown, but otherwise, they could easily pass for mother and daughter.

Stephanie, Lori and Four all took after their father in looks, as did Rhys. They had dark hair and brown eyes. Rhys was tall, but the sisters were on the shorter side, and curvy, with Lori the closest to plus-size.

Mackenzie flipped through her notes. "The '18 reserve cab is coming along nicely. It's already lush, with plenty of forward fruit. It's going to be dense, and it will cellar at least fifteen years. It's going to be big. We'll want to put some aside for competitions and at allocations for wine club. I'll want at least ten percent of the bottles for the library. This wine is going to score high and get snapped up quickly. We can sell the remainder in five years for at least double the original price."

Barbara leaned back in her oversize chair and smiled. "You said it was a great year."

"It *was*. We had perfect conditions and a harvest

to match. I want to hold it an extra three months before we sell it."

"What? No! You can't. The reserve is already scheduled to be bottled and we've told our wine club members when to expect it. There are events that—" Barbara pressed her lips together. "Mackenzie, you're being overly cautious."

"Three more months. I promise, it will be worth the wait."

"It had better be," Barbara grumbled. "Do you know the costs of keeping that many barrels in storage?"

"As a matter of fact, I do." Down to the penny. She might not run the business side of the winery, but she knew all the numbers.

She heard familiar footsteps in the hallway and smiled. Seconds later, Rhys walked in. He crossed to her, bent down and kissed her lightly on the mouth, before greeting his mother.

As he took his seat next to Mackenzie, he said, "You were right about the Seven Hills irrigation. Several of the drip lines had been chewed through. How do you know when stuff like that happens?"

"I just get a feeling."

Bel Après had acreage all over southeastern Washington State and into Oregon, from Red Mountain to the Walla Walla Valley and south to Seven Hills. The different areas had distinct characteristics that influenced the grapes. Mackenzie liked working with the various topographical challenges each vineyard offered.

Everyone was hot for Red Mountain, and she thought the vineyards there were special, as well, but she could make her magic just about anywhere. She supposed her ability to go with the flow, so to speak, was because she didn't own any of it. She was married to Rhys, but as for her work at Bel Après, she was simply an employee. She got a paycheck twice a month, along with quarterly royalties from her Highland wines, but at the end of the day, she worked for Barbara.

Her house was part of the Barcellona family compound, her truck was winery property. She supposed if she were to suddenly pack up and leave, she could fit everything that was actually hers into a handful of moving boxes and be gone in a few hours.

An unexpectedly sad thought. Not that she was going anywhere. This was home. Rhys was her husband, Stephanie was her best friend and Barbara was pretty much the closest thing to a mother she'd ever had.

She was a Barcellona, she reminded herself. In spirit if not in name. She was a part of the fabric of the family. If sometimes she thought about how nice it would be to buy a few acres just to play with, well, that wasn't going to happen.

There were more footsteps on the stairs. Stephanie and Four joined them. Stephanie sat next to Mackenzie and immediately started talking.

"Carson leaves tomorrow. I don't think I can let him go."

Mackenzie grabbed her friend's hand and smiled. "You do this every summer. He's been going to baseball camp since he was eleven. Yes, you'll miss him, but it's for the greater good. Let him go. It's what he wants."

"You're being rational. I find that offensive."

Mackenzie laughed. "No, you don't."

Stephanie's mouth turned up at the corners. "Okay, I don't, but why is this so hard? I thought it would get easier. But every summer it's just as painful to know he's leaving."

"You love him and you like having him around."

"I know. I suppose part of it is that he's gone the whole summer. When he gets back, we're two weeks from school starting. Why does camp have to be so long?"

Barbara turned toward them. "Dear God, Stephanie, let it go. We're all aware that you have trouble setting your children free. Catherine, say something about the cycle of life or the universe having angels to take care of teenage boys."

Four smiled. "You'll have more time with Avery. Maybe plan a girls' weekend in Portland or something."

Stephanie brightened. "You're right. That would be fun. Thank you."

"Order restored," Barbara said dryly. "Hallelujah."

She waved her hand as she spoke, her new engagement ring catching the light. Mackenzie leaned forward and touched her hand.

"I didn't get to see your ring up close, at the party. It's lovely."

Barbara splayed her fingers. "I'm still getting used to it, but yes, it is fabulous. Giorgio chose well."

"In his choice of bride as well as his choice of jewelry," Rhys said with a grin.

Stephanie glared at him. "Suck-up."

Barbara sighed. "Children, please."

"Have you decided on any wedding particulars?" Mackenzie asked.

"Something with the family over the holidays," Barbara told her. "I'm not sure. I was thinking small, but now I'm leaning toward ostentatious."

"You should," Mackenzie told her. "You're so very much in love. Everyone can see it."

Barbara's expression softened. "What a lovely thing to say. Thank you."

Lori walked in with five folders in her hand. Mackenzie didn't bother waiting for Barbara's pointed look. She rose and excused herself.

"I'll be home right after," Rhys said, taking the folder from his sister and opening it.

She nodded and waited to see if he would look up from the family's monthly financial report, but he didn't.

"Close the door behind you, Mackenzie," Barbara called.

She did as requested, then retraced her steps to the first floor. As she stepped outside, she calculated how many of those meetings had taken place since she and Rhys had gotten married.

And it was just family. Mackenzie had never attended a single meeting, nor had Jaguar, Four's husband. Nor Kyle, when he and Stephanie had been married.

She selected a golf cart and drove past the tasting room and onto the private road that led to the compound. Vineyards stretched out for as far as the eye could see. The sight of clusters of hard green fruit filled her with anticipation. In a few short months, the grapes would turn color and ripen, and then they would be harvested. An intoxicating scent would linger over the area, sweet with promise of what was to be.

As she approached the compound of four houses in a loose circle, she paused to collect the mail, then drove toward the house she shared with Rhys. In the distance, she saw Jaguar outside playing with his kids.

Overhead the sky was a perfect blue. The temperature had hit ninety, but it would cool off at night. She hit a button on her key chain, and a golf-cart-size garage door rose slowly, allowing her to zip inside.

The house was still and cool. After taking a glass from a cupboard, she filled it with water and ice, then opened the refrigerator to check what was for dinner.

A baking dish held chicken with sun-dried tomatoes and artichoke hearts. Next to that was a salad. On the counter she found a three-by-five card with heating instructions and a peach pie.

The four families shared the services of a professional chef. Chef Betsy came in five days a week. Dinners were left daily, along with the next day's lunch.

Mackenzie turned over the card and saw the next day she would be eating a shaved roast beef and arugula wrap with asiago cheese and a horseradish dressing for lunch. She put the card on the counter and took her water with her as she headed upstairs.

Like many of those who worked outside, she showered at the end of the day. As she tossed her clothes into the hamper and pinned up her hair to avoid the spray, she told herself she was really lucky. She had a pretty amazing life. A husband, a beautiful house, family and friends, a job she loved. Even someone else to do most of the cooking. She was truly blessed, in every way possible. As for those times when she found herself wondering if maybe there was something else out there—well, she should just suck it up and get over herself. Nothing could be better than what she had.

five

_____

Stephanie opened the closet by the front door and pulled the rolled decorative flag out of the corner. As she opened the front door, she gave the pole a little shake to unfurl the flag, then stepped onto the porch and slid the pole into place. A light breeze caught the fabric, causing the print of the giant cookie to ripple slightly.

In addition to the six dozen cookies she'd baked for Carson to take with him, she'd made four dozen more for the family. A few years ago, Mackenzie had started the tradition of putting out a flag whenever she baked cookies. Avery and Carson had gone running to grab a few and bring them home. Now that Zeus, Galaxy and Eternity were big enough to roam the compound, they watched for the cookie flag, as well.

Stephanie went back inside and carried two disposable containers up to her son's room.

Carson's large suitcase was ready to go. His carry-on backpack stood open on the desk. Her son was stretched out on his bed, his gaze locked on his tablet.

"I made you cookies for the trip," she said. "And the first few days of camp."

"Thanks, Mom."

When he didn't raise his gaze, she sighed heavily. "Look at me, Carson."

He did as she requested. She waved the two containers. "These are your cookies. The ones in the red container are peanut butter. You're fourteen, Carson, so I'm trusting you to be responsible with them."

The corners of his lips trembled as if he were trying not to smile. "With cookies, Mom? I think I'm up to the challenge."

"Peanut butter cookies. Just the thought of you carrying them with you makes me break out in a sweat. Remember that some kids are allergic. It's a real thing. Do not go passing them around without talking to everyone first. Peanut butter cookies can trigger nut allergies."

His dark eyes crinkled as he grinned. "Didn't you put walnuts into the chocolate chip cookies?"

"What? Crap. What was I thinking?"

He dropped his tablet onto the bed, stood and wrapped his arms around her. "Mom, don't sweat it. No one I know is allergic to nuts."

"What about at camp? Forget it. You're not taking these with you. No kid is dying on my watch—not because I made cookies."

He took the containers from her hands and dropped them into his backpack. "We'll be fine. I'll make sure everyone I bunk with is okay with nuts. There's four of us in a suite, Mom. The cookies won't last the night."

She knew he could be trusted to be responsible. "Okay, just be careful. Maybe I'll text your counselor."

He winced. "Don't set me up to be that freaky little kid who can't be away from his mommy."

"That's so judgmental."

"You know I'm telling the truth." He zipped up his backpack, then slung it over his shoulder and grabbed his suitcase. "It'll be fine. Have a little faith."

"I should go with you to the airport," she said.

"Mom, stop. I'm driving to Seattle with Grandma and Giorgio. Dad's meeting me there and getting me to my gate. I'm fourteen years old. I'll be fine."

She wanted to protest that he was still her baby, only she knew he wouldn't appreciate that. So instead of telling him he had to stay little forever, she followed him downstairs and found Rhys sitting on a stool by the island. Four and her three kids were there, as well, all eating cookies. Because in this family everyone came by to say goodbye. Mackenzie had stopped by that morning, as had Jaguar, and Avery had seen her brother before she'd gone off to work.

"Excited?" Rhys asked his nephew.

Carson grinned. "Can't wait."

They hugged. Four was next, whispering something in his ear. Carson chuckled but didn't respond. He hugged and kissed his cousins before heading out front. Stephanie went with him.

Right on time her mom and Giorgio pulled in front of her house. Giorgio popped the trunk of the late-model Mercedes and helped Carson with his luggage. Stephanie hugged her youngest.

"Text me the second you get to California," she said. "From the airport and then again when you arrive at camp. If you don't text me, I'll call your counselor and pretend that I'm crying and then you *will* be the freaky little kid who can't be away from his mommy."

Carson sighed. "Mom, you don't have to do that. I'll text you, I swear."

"Threaten to fly down and stay with him," her mother offered from the passenger seat in the car. "Remember when I had to do that with you?"

Stephanie did her best not to shudder at the memory. She'd been a bit chatty in high school and was constantly in trouble for talking to her friends. When the usual punishments—detention and being grounded—hadn't worked, her mother had told her that whatever was happening at school must be so very interesting, what with Stephanie unable to stop talking about it. So Barbara would come with her to every class, unless she could learn to be quiet.

Stephanie hadn't spoken for nearly four days.

"Text me or I'll come stay with you," she told her son. "Look into my eyes and see how much I mean that."

"You're scary sometimes," he told her as he kissed her cheek. "Love you, Mom."

"Love you, too."

She waved at the car until it was out of sight, then walked back into the house to find only Four still in her kitchen.

"They took cookies and ran," Four said cheerfully, pointing at the empty plate. "Sorry if you didn't get any."

Stephanie pulled a second, overflowing plate from the cupboard and placed it between them. She poured them each a cup of coffee from the pot, added cream, then settled next to her sister and picked up a chocolate chip cookie.

"You don't have to stay with me," she said conversationally.

"I'm just here to make sure you're okay."

"I'm fine."

"You're actually not fine. You're sad and worried." Four sipped her coffee. "I don't know how you do it. I couldn't let any of my kids go away for the summer."

"Zeus is only eight. He's too young to go away overnight. But later, if he wants to, you'll let him."

Four shook her head. "Never."

Stephanie smiled. "You will because it will be the best thing for him and you're that kind of mom."

"Don't try to sweet-talk me with rational thought. It doesn't work on me."

"Yes, it does."

"You're very contrary today."

"No, just pensive. I know they're supposed to grow up and have their own lives, but sometimes it's hard. Still, as you've often reminded me, there is a season for everything." She paused, thinking about all that had happened in the past few days. "I'm ready for a new chapter in my life."

Four looked at her speculatively. "What does that mean?"

Even though she'd seen her mother drive away not five minutes before, Stephanie still looked over her shoulder to make sure they were alone.

"I need to get a new job."

Four nibbled her cookie without speaking.

"What?" Stephanie demanded. "You have to say something. You always have an opinion."

"You've made this announcement before," her sister said gently. "I'm not sure you want to leave."

Ugh—there was an assessment she didn't want to hear. "I can't stay. Mom treats me like I'm an idiot. She's always double-checking my work and dismissing any ideas I have about how to make things better. I'm thirty-eight years old. It's time for me to strike out on my own, don't you think?"

"If it's what you want."

Stephanie supposed her sister's inability to believe in her was her own fault. She was the one who had been whining about leaving Bel Après for the past five years and to date she'd done exactly nothing. Zip. Zero. Nada.

"I'm pathetic," she said, pulling her phone from her jeans front pocket. "Or I was, but not anymore."

She scrolled through her emails, stopping when she found the one she was looking for.

"Here." She held out her phone to Four.

Her sister read the note. "You have an interview next week."

"I know. Marington Cheese. It's a small company, but they're determined to grow, and I'd like to be a part of that."

Four glanced back at the email. "Really? Cheese?"

Stephanie tried not to wince. "They make it and sell it. They're artisans. I know it's not wine, but going into that business feels like cheating or something." She took back the phone. "I haven't told Mackenzie."

Four's eyebrows rose. "That's almost more surprising than the interview itself."

"Yes, well, I'll tell her after the fact." Her shoulders rounded as she hunched forward. "It's just she's so damned brilliant at what she does. I think about that and I feel like a failure."

"Everyone is gifted in their own way."

"I'm not. I'm ordinary. Worse, I've settled. She has her wine, you're an amazing artist. If I don't have a special talent, at least I can be brave and get off my butt and do something."

"Then, yay cheese."

Stephanie laughed. "Thanks. I'm doing a lot of research on the industry and coming up with a few marketing plans. It's time I actually used my degree, you know?"

"You'll be brilliant."

"I'd accept getting a decent job offer."

Four tucked her long hair behind her ears. "You should start dating."

"Absolutely not. The last thing I need is a man in my life. I'd be forced to compare that relationship to the one Mom has with Giorgio. I don't need another place to feel that I'm lacking."

"It was a beautiful proposal," Four said. "I wish it was going to work out for them."

Stephanie nearly slid off the stool. "What do you mean? Of course it's going to work out. Why wouldn't it? They're so in love."

"She won't let go. The more she should, the harder she clings to whatever ridiculous idea she has. Giorgio is all about letting go. He loves her, but I don't think he understands who she is. Not really."

"That's really deep."

"I'm feeling a connection to Mother Earth today. It's powerful."

Stephanie reached for her coffee. "Want to give

me some lotto numbers? There's got to be a Power-ball somewhere."

Four patted her arm. "A, it doesn't work like that and you know it, and B, you don't need the money. Let someone else win. You'll find your joy and happiness in less material ways."

"I think anyone could find joy in fifty million dollars."

She owned her house outright and she had some savings, but she needed to work to pay the bills. Fifty million dollars would—

She held up her hand. "I take it back. I'm going to work to find my place in the world, not wish for it to be given to me. Someone else needs to win that money."

"Personal growth. I'm so proud." Four rose and hugged her. "I'm going to go meditate. I want to take advantage of my connection to Mother Earth today."

"Love you," Stephanie called as Four crossed to the door. "Say hi to Mother Earth from me."

"You could tell her yourself."

"She only likes you."

Four was still laughing when she shut the door behind her.

As far as Barbara was concerned, the Four Seasons Hotel in downtown Seattle was just about perfect. She loved the location, the views, the understated luxury, the staff. She always stayed at the hotel when she came over for business or shopping, but these days the hotel seemed even more wonderful than usual. A fact that had nothing to do with the hotel itself and everything to do with the man who shared her room.

Giorgio, handsome in a hotel robe, pointed to the

bottle of champagne resting in the ice bucket. "More, my love?"

She waved her half-empty glass. "In a minute. I'm still trying to catch my breath."

They'd checked in two days ago, after dropping Carson off at the airport. In that time, they'd been to museums, seen a show at the 5th Avenue Theatre and tried new restaurants. But their afternoon trip to Nordstrom had derailed when Giorgio had suggested they order in rather than shop.

After making love, they'd had champagne and small bites sent up to the room. Decadent, she thought with a smile. It was barely one in the afternoon and she'd already had champagne and a man in her bed. Let the millennials have their avocado toast—she would take sex with Giorgio instead, any day.

"What makes you so happy?" Giorgio asked.

She tucked her feet under her, adjusting her silk robe around her legs. "You."

"Good. That's what I want to do."

She studied the lines in his face. She could see the man he'd been when he was younger. He would have been difficult to resist, she thought. Not just because he was attractive, but also because he was strong and caring.

"Tell me about Beth Ann," she said, thinking about how lucky his late wife had been to have so many years with him.

"What do you want to know?"

"Did you have a big wedding?"

He smiled. "We each came from a large Italian family. Yes, it was a big wedding. Three hundred people. Grandparents, aunts, uncles, cousins, friends.

The church was overflowing. Our mothers and aunts cooked for days."

"That sounds nice." She sipped her champagne. "James and I had a small wedding. I didn't have any family and we didn't have any money. Do you mind if we have a big wedding?"

His eyes crinkled as he smiled at her. "Your happiness is my happiness, my love. I will be there regardless. I've talked to my children and they are excited to fly in here."

"Thank you for asking them."

"Of course. You remember we'll be flying to New York in a few weeks for Rosemary's birthday."

"I do. I'm looking forward to it."

She'd met his children a few times on their quick visits back east. His two sons were running the family business and his daughter was a pediatrician. Unlike her, he got to be proud of *all* his offspring.

"I'm thinking late fall or maybe over the holidays," she said. "Everyone is too busy around harvest and I don't want to wait until the new year."

"I agree. The sooner I claim you as mine, the better."

She laughed. "I think you do plenty of claiming, Giorgio. Sometimes twice in a day."

He grinned at her. "You know what I mean. I want to spend time with you, Barbara. Just the two of us." He waved his hand toward the walls of the suite. "I appreciate that we get away for a few days, but that's not enough."

She held in a sigh. "You mean work."

"I mean the lack of work. You said you'd start cutting back."

She had said that, she reminded herself. She was supposed to be handing off her responsibilities so she and Giorgio could travel. But who exactly could she trust to run the company? Rhys was busy managing the vineyards, Stephanie had an average skill set, at best. Lori would jump at the opportunity but had the imagination of a flea, and Catherine wasn't worth discussing.

"I should talk to Rhys about hiring someone to take over his job," she said, thinking out loud. "Then he could step in for me."

"You haven't talked to him about that yet?" Giorgio sounded more hurt than angry.

"I've meant to."

He set down his champagne glass. "Barbara, do you want us to spend more time together?"

"Of course. We've talked about traveling together. I look forward to that."

He took her hand in his. "Then I'll make you a deal. You plan the wedding of your dreams and I'll do the same with the honeymoon."

All of which sounded perfectly fine, she thought warily, but wasn't the same thing at all.

"What did you have in mind?" she asked, trying not to sound cautious.

He slid closer. "I've been thinking about a cruise."

"I've never been on a cruise."

"You'll love it. I'll find a wonderful itinerary. I was thinking of Australia and the South Pacific. Maybe we can sail from Los Angeles."

He lowered his head and began to kiss along her neck.

"From Los Angeles," she said, trying to ignore the tingles and heat he evoked. "That's a long cruise."

"Two months."

"What?" she asked with a yelp. "You want us to be gone for two months?"

He straightened and smiled. "No, three months. After that we'll fly to Italy and rent a villa, then explore."

Three months! Was he insane?

"I can't be gone that long," she began. "Bel Après needs me."

He took her champagne glass from her and set it on the coffee table. "You have good people, my love. Give them room to succeed."

Which sounded like something Catherine would say, she thought, fighting a flash of annoyance.

"Three months is ridiculous," she told him.

He untied her robe. When he put his hands on her breasts, she was much less interested in the argument.

"We need to talk about this," she said, but without much conviction.

"We will," he promised as his mouth settled on hers.

She really should insist they talk now, she told herself, then decided it could wait. It seemed that lately sex was always the answer, and why would she want to change that?

six

According to Stephanie's research, the Marington family had been making cheese in eastern Washington for about a hundred years. The milk used to make the cheese came from local cows and nearly half of it was certified organic. They had a good reputation for quality and taste, and from what she could tell, they were looking to expand their brand beyond the local markets and specialty stores. The fourth-generation Maringtons, fraternal twins Jack and Jill—Stephanie had confirmed the unfortunate names—were using social media to make that happen, and they were looking for someone to help with that.

To that end Stephanie had spent the past week studying the company and researching the market. She had three solid campaign ideas and a lot of numbers on cheese consumption, market entry and partnerships. Her plan was to dazzle and get the job offer of her dreams. The fact that the thought of telling her mother she was leaving Bel Après made her slightly sick to her stomach was something she was going to have to ignore. She needed more than she had, and the only way to make that happen was to be proactive. She was hopeful and nervous, but mostly hopeful.

After parking in front of the low, one-story building, she gave herself a twenty-second pep talk, grabbed her handbag and briefcase, and walked inside.

There was no receptionist. Just an open space with a couple of chairs and a hallway leading to several offices. She couldn't see or hear anyone, which made her wonder if she'd gotten the date or time wrong. She called out, "Hello?"

"Hey, Stephanie?" A tall, slim man walked out of one of the offices. He smiled when he saw her. "Right on time. I'm Jack."

They shook hands.

Jack had blond hair and blue eyes. His features weren't unattractive, but there was something very bland about his appearance.

"Good to meet you," he said. "Come on back and let's talk."

She followed him into a cluttered office. Papers were stacked everywhere, including on the only visitor's chair. She waited while he cleared that, trying not to flinch as she inhaled the smell of what could only be called bad cheese.

"There you go." He took the seat on the other side of the desk, glanced at his computer screen, frowned, then turned his attention to her.

"You work at Bel Après," he said. "That's wine. I'm not much of a wine drinker myself, but I know enough to put together a pairing. We send out suggestions of what wines to drink with our cheeses. Our customers like that sort of thing." He stared at her intently, his pale blue eyes watering slightly. "Wine is easy, just so you know. Cheese is hard. I hope you understand that."

She had no idea what to say to that comment, so she settled on a faint smile and nod.

"We're looking to grow the company," he said. "Find different markets, have a bigger online presence. Our cousin Bing has been doing our website. He's a great kid. Computers are his thing, but he doesn't always take care of everything, you know."

"Kid?" Stephanie asked faintly. "As in, he's young?"

"Fourteen. He took over the website when he was eleven. He prefers robotics, but family is family, right?"

Stephanie was saved from having to respond to that by the sound of footsteps in the hall. Seconds later a woman walked into the office. A woman who looked exactly like Jack. Same features, same coloring, same size, same blue shirt and khaki pants. They were identical—except for the whole man-woman thing.

"I'm Jill," the woman said, moving papers off the credenza and sitting there. "You're here about the marketing job, aren't you?"

"Yes."

Jill looked at her brother, her expression peevish. "I've told you, I can handle it."

Jack shook his head. "We've been over this. We need someone with training."

"Oh, please. So she has a college degree. Big whoop. I can do the job in my sleep."

"And yet you don't."

"I'm going to tell Dad what you're up to."

Jack offered Stephanie a tight smile. "You've

worked in a family company, so you understand the push-pull dynamics, I'm sure."

Jill turned to Stephanie. "Are you married?"

"I…what?"

"Married. A lot of women try to work here because they want to marry Jack. That's not going to happen. He's not going to be interested in you. He doesn't need you in his life. He has me."

Okay, so now the creep factor was a bigger deterrent than the cheese smell. Whatever hope she'd had crashed to the ground and crawled away. If the interview was going this badly, there was no chance the job was going to work out.

"Jill, come on. She's not here to marry me. She wants a job." He looked at Stephanie. "Why do you want to leave Bel Après?"

"I wanted to challenge myself with something new. Your expansion plans are exciting, and I was thinking I could help with that."

At least she *had* been thinking that. Now she was much less sure.

Jill stood up. "You're not right for the job. I don't care what Jack says. You can't have it."

Jack glared at her. "This is my interview, not yours. You don't get to say."

"I get as much say as you get. We're equal partners. Besides, you know what Mom and Dad are going to think. They don't like outsiders. I don't know why you even brought her in for the job." Jill looked at Stephanie. "You're not going to get it."

"Okay, then." Stephanie rose and smiled at both of them. "Thank you so much for your time. Good luck with the expansion."

With that, she walked out the way she'd come. Once in her car, she breathed in non-cheese-smelling air and told herself at least there was a bright side. She'd wasted—she glanced at her watch—only eight minutes of her life, not counting the research she'd done and, hey, the drive over. But better to know now rather than quit and take the job only to discover she couldn't make it work.

Which all sounded great but didn't shake her sense of disappointment. She hadn't even had a practice interview. Walla Walla wasn't a big town, so there weren't a lot of marketing jobs available, especially with her excluding the wine industry. So she was back to where she'd started—working for her mother and wishing for something more.

Mackenzie poured single malt Scotch into two glasses and carried them into Rhys's study. He stood behind his desk, sorting through the mail. She'd already looked at it herself, and there was nothing to concern her. A utility bill that he would pay and some flyers for local real estate for sale. The Walla Walla area was growing and the housing market had heated up.

When she set the glass on his desk, he smiled at her. "Thanks."

They moved to the sofa and sat at opposite ends.

"The drip system is fixed," he told her. "You'll want to drive out in the next few days and look it all over."

She smiled. "Because I don't trust your work?"

"Because you like to be sure."

She did and she *would* check. Her need to oversee all aspects of the vineyards had nothing to do with his ability and everything to do with her slightly obsessive nature.

"I heard one of the big grocery store chains applied for a permit," he said. "They're building down by that new development."

"That will make the people who live there happy. I was just thinking how the area is growing."

"It is."

They looked at each other, then away. Silence descended, making her uncomfortable. She and Rhys had always ended their days together, talking about what was going on in the vineyard and in town. But lately, conversation seemed harder to come by and she wasn't sure why. They were married, they loved each other. Surely there was something to talk about that wasn't work.

"Your mom texted," she said to fill the empty space. "She and Giorgio are staying an extra day in Seattle."

"Good for them."

She nodded. "They seem really happy and in love."

"They do."

She glanced at her husband and was surprised to find him looking at her with unexpected intensity.

"What?" she asked.

"Nothing. Just thinking about my mom. Who would have guessed she would meet someone so many years after my dad died?"

"You're not upset, are you?"

"No. I'm glad she won't be alone. Giorgio takes good care of her. It's just…" He looked away and the silence returned.

She set down the glass and wondered when everything had changed for them. They had been happy once.

"Do you think we—"

"Are you ever—"

They both stopped talking.

"You first," Rhys said.

She drew in a breath, wanting to ask the question and yet terrified of his answer. "Was it ever like that with us? The way they are with each other?"

He didn't meet her gaze. "I don't know. Maybe."

There was no maybe, she thought. If it had been like that, wouldn't they both remember? Would it be helping them now? A past filled with that much love and passion would smooth over the rough spots.

"I know you're not happy," he said quietly.

"Neither are you."

There was a finality to those words, she thought sadly. Or maybe just hopelessness.

He glanced at her, then away. "I still love you, Mackenzie."

"I love you, too."

Which should have been enough, she thought, suddenly overwhelmed with a sense of sadness so profound, she had trouble breathing. But it wasn't enough, because the love they were talking about wasn't passionate or even romantic. Not anymore. They were friends, not lovers. Companions rather than a romantic couple, and while marriages ebbed and flowed, theirs seemed to be draining away on a daily basis.

Rhys stood. She thought he was going to walk out of the room but instead he moved in front of her and pulled her to her feet. His arms came around her and he kissed her.

The action was so unexpected, she didn't know how

to react. The pressure of his mouth was insistent and she instinctively parted her lips.

He plunged his tongue into her mouth, stroking and seeking. At the same time, he moved his hands up and down her back before cupping her butt and pulling her against him. She was shocked to realize he had an erection.

She had no idea what to think or feel or how to act. Nothing he was doing was the least bit arousing but it was clear he wanted to have sex, and it had been literally years and they were married and saying no felt mean and punitive, somehow, even though that wouldn't have been how she meant it.

She ignored the awkwardness and the need to withdraw, instead putting her hands on his shoulders and kissing him back, leaning into him, rubbing her belly against his arousal, wishing she felt something. Anything. But she didn't. There was only a sense of duty and not wanting to hurt Rhys because, honest to God, the man hadn't done anything wrong.

He raised his head and stared at her. His eyes were dilated, his breathing heavy. She knew what he wanted. Nothing extraordinary—just sex with his wife. It had been so long since they'd been intimate. Guilt at that fact made her smile at him and hold out her hand. He took it and led her upstairs.

He led her into his bedroom. They went to opposite sides of the bed and quickly undressed. Mackenzie tried to remember the last time they'd done this. Had it been four years? Five? She wasn't sure which had come first—the separate bedrooms or the not having sex. Not that it much mattered.

They slid into bed. Rhys pulled her close and kissed

her. As his tongue tangled with hers, he cupped her breast and began teasing her nipple. After a minute or so, she felt the first flicker of interest low in her belly. A whisper of desire and the thought that maybe this really was a good idea. She relaxed into the sensation, willing it to grow. Maybe sex would help them find their way back to each other.

"Are you ready?" he asked eagerly, shifting her onto her back and moving between her legs. Before she could answer, he was pushing inside.

She wasn't close to ready. The first two thrusts were painful, but then her body adjusted. She moved in time with his movements and tried to get into what he was doing, but there wasn't time. As he moved faster inside of her, obviously getting closer, she thought briefly about faking an orgasm, but before she could decide or get started on the process, he groaned and was still.

For nearly a minute, his rapid breathing was the only sound in the room.

He withdrew and looked at her. "You didn't come."

"It's okay."

"Let me get cleaned up and I can do something."

He moved to his side and took a box of tissues out of the drawer. He passed her a couple, then took a few for himself. After pulling on his underwear, he returned to the bed and faced her.

"Mackenzie, I want to make you come." He gave her a wry smile. "I was a little rushed before because it's been a long time."

He sounded so earnest. Because Rhys always took care of her. She thought about what it would take to get her over the edge and knew she didn't want to go there. What was the point? Whatever interest she'd had was gone, leaving only a sense of sadness and a ridiculous urge to cry.

"It *has* been a while, but I'm okay."

His smile faded. "You don't want me to?"

She shook her head.

He stared at her. Just when she was about to ask what he was thinking, she saw tears in *his* eyes.

"It's over, isn't it?" he asked quietly. "Our marriage. We're done."

It was as if he'd hit her in the stomach. She couldn't breathe and she fought the instinctive need to curl into a protective ball and cover her head. Her body went cold and she thought she might throw up. Even as she told herself to run, she knew she couldn't possibly stand without crumbling to the ground.

"I'm sorry," he said quickly. "God, I'm sorry. I thought that's what you were thinking. Mackenzie, I'm sorry. I take it back. I swear, I take it back."

He couldn't, she thought, stunned by what he'd said. There was no taking it back. Horror joined shock as the truth crashed into her. He'd breathed life into the very thing they'd both avoided for a long time and now it was alive and they had to deal with it. *She* had to deal with it. With what they no longer had and how the speaking, the acknowledging, would change everything.

She wanted to reach into the past and pull the words away, crumbling them in her hands so they no longer existed or had power over her, but it was too late.

When she was reasonably sure she wouldn't shatter, she sat up, careful to pull the sheet with her. The tightness in her chest eased enough for her to catch her breath, as she tried to make sense of what he'd said.

Rhys thought their marriage was over. He thought

they were done. And if he thought that, then they were, because it took two people to be in a marriage. It took two people to—

"You're right," she whispered, staring at him. The shock faded enough for her to feel the sadness of the moment and maybe a little of the inevitability. It was done. They were done.

She sat with the truth, wondering how to get through this moment and the next and all the moments that would follow. Who was she if not married to Rhys? Being with him informed her life, the rhythm of her days. Without that, what did she have? He had been a part of her for her entire adult life. If that was gone, how would the hole he left ever fill in?

His tears returned. Without thinking, she reached for him. He did the same and they hung on to each other. She breathed in his familiar scent, felt the heat of his body and knew this was very likely the last time they would be naked together. Not in a sexual way, although that was true, too, but in a bared-to-the-soul kind of way. As soon as they let go, everything would change because there was no going back.

She didn't know how long they clung to each other or who leaned back first, but eventually they untangled and they were simply two people, staring at each other.

"I'm sorry," he repeated.

"Stop saying that. You don't have to be. You're right—it *is* over. I've known it somewhere inside, I just never articulated it, even to myself."

"I don't want to hurt you."

"You didn't."

"I did. I meant what I said before. I love you, Mackenzie."

She looked into his eyes. "But it's not enough any-more, is it? Our love is different. It's not what your mother has with Giorgio."

His mouth twisted. "You saw that, too?"

"How in love they are? Yes, and while I was happy for them, being around them made me feel sad."

He nodded. "The contrast. It made everything clear for me." He hesitated. "We don't have to do anything right away. We can take our time figuring it out. You know that a divorce won't change your position at Bel Après." He gave her a faint smile. "If my mother has to choose between the two of us, she's going to pick you. We both know that."

Divorce? Her position at Bel Après?

Reality gave her the second blow of the evening and she was no more prepared this time. If their marriage was over, of course they would be getting a divorce. That was what people did. And if she and Rhys weren't married, then she would have to move out and…and…

"Don't," he said quickly. "Nothing has to change."

"Everything has to change," she told him, feeling her chest tighten. "Everything."

He took her hand in his. "It doesn't. We don't have to decide anything tonight. Let's pretend we didn't talk about it."

"We can't." She looked at their hands, the famil-iar way they were clasped, then carefully pulled free. "You want a divorce."

He hesitated before nodding slowly.

She braced herself for the logical question. No, not the question. The answer.

"Is there someone else?"

Rhys drew back, his eyes wide. "Did I cheat? God, no. I wouldn't do that. I've never done that."

She believed him because of who he was. "But you wanted to."

"Haven't you?" He motioned to the space between them. "We haven't had sex in years. We're roommates, not a married couple. Yes, I've wanted to meet someone and fall in love. Hell, at this point, I would be happy just to have regular sex with pretty much anyone."

The words rained down like shards of glass, slicing her heart with wounds so deep, they would never heal.

"I'm sorry," she whispered. "I didn't know you were that unhappy."

"It's not your fault. We did this together. We're both to blame. Somehow everything we had got lost."

She nodded because her throat hurt too much for her to speak. Not just her throat—every part of her. She was shaking and sick and broken. Desperately broken.

"I can't talk about this anymore," she whispered. "I can't. Maybe tomorrow, if that's okay."

"Not tomorrow," he told her. "Take a few days, a few weeks. Like I said, nothing has to change, Mackenzie."

"You're wrong. Nothing can stay the same. We can't unsee this. What we've said... There's no going back. I just need some time to figure out what moving forward is going to look like."

He nodded. "What can I do to help?"

She shook her head and got out of bed. For the first time in sixteen years, she was uncomfortable being naked in front of him. She quickly pulled on her clothes, feeling the seeping dampness between her thighs—proof of the sex.

This had been their last time, she thought grimly,

as she put on her bra. They would never do it again. Pain and regret clutched at her, making her wish she'd let him bring her to orgasm. Not because she wanted the release but because it would have been something good they would have shared. It would have connected them, at least for a moment.

Afterward he would have smiled at her the way he always did—that totally male "I'm the man" smile. A combination of pride and happiness that came with knowing he'd pleased his partner. She wanted to see that smile just once more and now she wouldn't.

After pulling on her shirt and fastening her jeans, she picked up her socks. "I'm going to go to my room."

"Don't you want dinner?"

"I'm not hungry." She held up a hand. "I'm all right. I just need some time alone."

"Okay. I'll be here if you need me."

They looked at each other. Tears filled Rhys's eyes again. Her own burned.

She wanted to throw herself at him, to have him hold her and tell her everything was going to be fine. Only she couldn't. Not anymore. And if he said the words, he would be lying. So instead, she hurried out into the hallway and made her way to her own bedroom. Once inside, she carefully closed the door behind her, then collapsed onto the floor and gave in to the pain. Cries turned to sobs, shaking her entire body as, deep in her chest, her shattered heart broke into a thousand pieces.

seven

Stephanie pulled the small glass jar of ginger-infused simple syrup from the refrigerator. She and Mackenzie went all out when it came to their monthly Girls' Nights. Drinks, snacks and plenty of honest talk. Tonight she would be confessing the interview debacle and letting her best friend's sympathy and caring help heal the lingering disappointment. Mackenzie would tell her she wasn't trapped and right now she needed to hear that.

"So you're going out but I can't?"

Stephanie looked up as her daughter walked into the kitchen. Avery had always been a pretty child, but in the past couple of years, she'd turned into a real beauty. She had dark hair and big brown eyes. Apparently the Barcellona chubby-female curse had skipped a generation because Avery was thinner than either of her aunts.

Not that she would say any of that. Avery had been nothing but annoying all week.

"You know the rules," she said instead. "No boy-girl parties unless I talk to the parents and confirm there will be supervision."

"That's not fair."

"It is to me."

Avery flipped her long hair over her shoulder and glared. "You're a terrible mother."

"You used to be a wonderful kid. I really miss your My Little Pony stage. You were so sweet and we had so much fun together." She smiled. "Disappointment is multigenerational. That should give you comfort."

"Not enough. I want to go to the party. Alexander said it's going to be the best party of the summer."

Alexander was Avery's current boyfriend. They'd lasted past two months, so it was serious. Something else Stephanie got to worry about.

"No party unless I talk to the parents. Give me their number or resign yourself to staying home." She picked up the small tote with the drink supplies. "I'll be back by eleven."

"Whatever."

Avery flounced out of the room. Stephanie sighed, knowing it wasn't the last time she would have to say no to a party. It was going to be a very long, difficult summer. She could only hope that her daughter would be distracted by her new job working on the retail side of the Bel Après gift shop.

She carried her small tote through the house and out the front door. From there it was only a few steps to Mackenzie's house, where they had their evenings. The kid-free zone made it easy, and while Rhys was usually home, he pretty much stayed in his office.

She let herself in the unlocked door and called, "It's me."

"In the kitchen."

Stephanie walked through the large two-story foyer and into the spacious kitchen. It was the mirror image of her own. Her house, Mackenzie's and Four's were variations of the same floor plan. Four's had an extra bedroom and a big workspace over the garage while Mackenzie and Rhys had fewer bedrooms but two offices.

Mackenzie stood at the refrigerator, pulling out a prepared cheese plate their chef had left for them. Betsy always put together delicious snacks for their evenings, including appetizers that could be heated in the oven and then served.

"Hi," Stephanie said, dropping her tote and holding out her arms. "I need a hug."

Mackenzie smiled, then obliged, holding her tight. "Bad day?"

"Just some snipping from Avery. She's such a teenager."

"She'll outgrow it."

"I hope so. We don't actually fight, but there's sure plenty of bickering." She stepped back. "You're lucky. Your grapes don't talk back."

"I know, but they can get mold, which is hard to deal with. Carson and Avery seem mold-free."

"I'll try to keep that in mind the next time she makes me want to scream."

Stephanie put the simple syrup on the island. Mackenzie already had out rum and ginger ale, along with glasses and plates.

"We have cheddar crab puffs in the oven," Mackenzie said. "They need another ten minutes."

"I'll mix the drinks while we wait."

She squeezed lime quarters into a martini shaker, then added mint and blueberries. After muddling the mixture, she added rum and some simple syrup. Mackenzie had already put ice into two glasses. Stephanie shook the martini shaker, then poured the strained mixture into the glasses and topped it with a bit of ginger ale.

"You want me to talk to her?" Mackenzie asked. "Four and I could take Avery to lunch and find out if there's anything specific bothering her or if this is just usual teenage stuff."

Stephanie handed her a glass. "I'd love that. Thank you. Right now I'm the last person she'll confide in. And while you're at it, try to find out if she and Alexander are having sex. She swears they're not, but would she really tell me?"

"I'll do my best," Mackenzie told her. "But I can't promise she'll say anything."

"I know, but I appreciate any help. You're so good with her."

Mackenzie was good with all the kids, Stephanie thought, still surprised she and Rhys had never decided to have any of their own. Early on in their relationship there had been talk, but nothing had ever happened. She wondered briefly if her friend ever regretted that, but she wasn't sure how to ask. Before she could figure out a way, the timer dinged.

"Crab puffs," Mackenzie said, grabbing a hot pad and opening the oven.

It took only a few minutes to carry their food to the family room. They settled in familiar seats on the large sectional sofa with their snacks on the glass table in front of them. Sunlight spilled in from the big floor-to-ceiling windows.

Stephanie raised her glass. "Happy Thursday. My life sucks."

Something flickered in Mackenzie's eyes. "That's not true. Your life is great."

"I wish. Ignoring the ongoing Avery issue, I had a job interview a couple of days ago."

"What? You didn't tell me. Where? What happened? Did you get the job? Are you leaving?"

Stephanie held up her hand. "Nothing happened. I don't have a job, I'm not leaving. In fact, I'm probably never leaving because I can't seem to motivate myself, and when I finally do try to do something else, it all goes to shit."

She paused and looked at her glass. "Wow, I have attitude and I haven't even tasted my drink. I apologize in advance if I get bitchy with the alcohol." She took a sip of the cocktail and sighed. "And I didn't tell you about the interview because I was embarrassed."

"Why would you say that?"

"It was with cheese."

Mackenzie smiled. "You had an interview with cheese?"

"No, with Marington Cheese. A brother and sister are running it, sort of. Jack and Jill. They're fraternal twins who look and dress alike and are way too codependent."

She told Mackenzie about the very brief interview. Mackenzie winced when she explained about the "You can't marry him because he has me" comment.

"That's scary. You wouldn't have been happy there."

"That's what I tell myself, but it's not like there are

a lot of options in Walla Walla. Tri-Cities is bigger but that would mean an hour commute each way. Am I totally spoiled by saying I don't want to drive that far?"

"Yes, but it's understandable. Plus in winter, you'd be fighting the snow." Mackenzie put down her drink. "You know what I'm going to say, right?"

"Ack. Yes. Look at the wine industry."

"It's king. You could easily find a job if you were willing to work with what you know."

"It's not the knowledge thing, it's the Bel Après thing. I would feel like I was betraying my mother." She leaned back against the sofa and groaned. "I can't believe I just said that. Like she cares. I doubt she would even notice I was gone. I'm being stupid. Just say it. You think I'm an idiot."

She waited for a funny response, but Mackenzie only stared at her intently.

"What?" Stephanie asked. "What's wrong?"

"Nothing. I love you so much. I want you to know that. You're a wonderful friend and I'm grateful you're in my life. I don't want that to change."

"It's not going to. Me getting a job somewhere else, assuming I ever get off my ass and make that happen, won't change anything. I'll be right here." She studied her sister-in-law. "Are you okay? Did something happen?"

"I'm fine. It's just, you know, things change. Look at Avery. And you had an interview. That's huge. I'm so proud of you."

"Thanks. I just need to figure out what to do. It's weird, but I feel like Giorgio's proposal shifted my worldview or something. Does that make sense?"

Mackenzie stared at her drink. "I know exactly

what you mean. There was something so powerful in that moment—it put all our lives in perspective."

"And not in a good way," Stephanie grumbled. "I have a meeting with my mother on Saturday. We're going to talk about her wedding. There are no words to describe my lack of joy at the thought of getting through the wedding planning with her. I have no idea why I said I would help."

"Because she's your mom and you love her."

"Maybe, but I don't like her very much."

Mackenzie grinned. "No one does, sweetie. Don't worry about it. You'll do great and the wedding will be beautiful."

"I should get you to plan it," Stephanie said. "She'd agree to everything and adore it because it came from you."

She expected Mackenzie to laugh, but instead her friend's humor faded and her face paled.

"What?" Stephanie asked, sitting up straight. "There's something."

"Sorry. My period. I'm cramping."

"You sure?"

Mackenzie looked at her. "I could show you proof but it would be gross."

"You're right. Okay, finish your drink and I'll make us a second round. We'll drink to the thrill of being women and try to figure out what God was thinking when he invented menstruation."

Barbara ran her hands across the front of the binder Stephanie had handed her. The picture of the happy bride and groom on a beach at sunset should have been far too obvious for her taste, but instead of being annoyed by the photograph, she found herself happy and excited.

"This notebook will help keep all the information about the wedding in one place," Stephanie told her. "I have the same thing on my tablet. Whenever we make a decision, we'll update both."

They were in Barbara's dining room. Stephanie had arrived with three overflowing tote bags filled with magazines, folders and what looked like several table linen samples. Barbara would never admit it out loud, but she was impressed. She knew her daughter had handled at least a dozen weddings at Bel Après over the past few years. She couldn't remember any disasters, and the Solstice Party had gone well. Maybe she should assume the best about Stephanie and relax about the wedding. If worse came to worst, she could step in to run things herself.

But for now, she would play at being the bride and enjoy being taken care of. She appreciated that Stephanie understood the importance of the meeting. Despite the fact that it was a Saturday morning, Stephanie had dressed in an office-appropriate floral-print dress. She had on makeup and her long hair was pulled back in a low ponytail.

She was the prettiest of her three girls, Barbara thought. Catherine could be a beauty, if she wasn't so damned odd all the time. Her taste was appalling. Half the time she wore overalls with some ripped-up T-shirt. As if she and her family couldn't afford normal clothing. And she didn't want to get herself started on how those children of Catherine's dressed. When she was younger, Galaxy had spent an entire summer wearing a ridiculous bumblebee costume and Catherine had let her.

As for Lori, well, she was an ongoing problem. She certainly dressed professionally enough at work, but she always looked so frumpy. Maybe it was because she was fat. That girl put on five or ten pounds a year. In another decade, she was going to be as big as a house. Barbara held in a sigh. Where had she gone wrong?

She shook off the question and focused on what Stephanie was saying.

"The flow of most weddings is fairly traditional," her daughter explained. "A ceremony, followed by a reception. The wedding can be family only, with a larger reception to follow, or you can invite everyone to both. The reception dinner can be a sit-down with servers or buffet-style. We can have a DJ or a live band. It's all available."

Barbara almost felt light-headed by the possibilities. "No buffet," she said firmly. "That I know for sure. Otherwise, I just don't know. What do you think?"

Stephanie dug in one of the totes and pulled out several very thick bridal magazines. "Start with these. Look at the dresses, of course, but read the articles. They'll talk about everything from the right kind of makeup to how to have a themed wedding."

Barbara glared at her. "Have you lost your mind? Why would I want to do that?"

Stephanie grinned. "You wouldn't. My point is it's been a long time since we had a wedding in this family. When Mackenzie and Rhys got married, they wanted something simple. Only friends and a few family members."

"I remember," Barbara said, remembering the small but elegant event. She and Mackenzie had planned it all together, from the menu to the music. Mackenzie had even recycled Barbara's old wedding dress into something more stylish. "It was beautiful."

"But small and low-key," Stephanie pointed out. "You're going to want to make more of a statement."

Her daughter's perception surprised her. "You're right—I am. Not gaudy, of course, but with maybe two or three hundred people." She drew her lips together. "Nothing rushed, like your wedding."

Stephanie startled her by glancing at her watch and chuckling. "Ten minutes, Mom. Impressive. I thought it would take you at least twenty to bring up the fact that Kyle and I got married because I was pregnant. It's nice that we can still surprise each other."

"Are you being smart with me?"

"Would I do that?" She was still smiling as she pushed the magazines across the table. "These will help you get into the wedding swing of things. Once we know when, where, and how many guests, we can start narrowing down options."

Barbara nodded. "I want the wedding and reception here," she said. "Of course if it's over the holidays, it has to be indoors and I'm not sure we have a big enough space for that. Yes, you're correct. Those are the three most important decisions."

She paused for a moment, then added, "Don't talk to your sisters about this. I don't want either of them influencing you. Lori has the taste of a kangaroo and we all know that anything Catherine suggests would drive me mad."

"Don't worry. You're the bride, so you decide."

Barbara eyed her. "Are you seeing anyone? If you're not, you might want to get on that. You'll want a date for the wedding."

Stephanie laughed. "So that's the reason I should start seeing someone?"

"It's as good a reason as any. Plus, it's nice to have a man in one's life. I'd forgotten." Giorgio made her feel so many wonderful things, and not just in bed. Although she wouldn't discuss any of that with her daughter. "Let me know if you get involved with someone and it seems serious. I'll have him investigated."

"I can't decide if you're kidding or not."

"I'm not kidding. Why would I kid? If you get involved with someone and there's a chance the relationship might go somewhere, we will need to know about his background. Who is he? Who are his parents and siblings? What about his past? Is he a criminal? Did he do drugs?"

"You're assuming I couldn't figure that out for myself. Why would I date a drug-dealing criminal?"

Barbara waved away the question. "This isn't about you, darling. It's about being safe. I had Giorgio investigated when I realized we were going to be seeing each other when we came back to the States. It's a sensible thing to do." She smiled. "Giorgio understands how things are. He's already offered to sign a prenup. I didn't have to ask."

"How romantic."

Barbara narrowed her gaze. "Despite what you think, it's very romantic. Giorgio loves me and wants to take care of me. Not just in bed, but in every way, including protecting the family and the winery. I would think you would appreciate that. The land and the children are what matter."

"In that order," Stephanie said dryly.

"Children leave. The land is forever. But speaking of children, is Avery still seeing that boy?"

"Alexander?"

"Is he the blond one? Is he the least bit intelligent? You've talked to her about birth control, haven't you? We don't need another unplanned pregnancy in the family."

"Wow, Mom. When do you slow down enough to catch your breath?"

Barbara heard the hint of annoyance in her daughter's tone.

"I know you don't appreciate me butting in," Barbara said sharply. "But I'm saying all this for your own good, and for Avery's. You've always been a decent mother. This isn't the time to relax and simply let things happen. You have to stay firm and guide her."

"Because that worked so well for us?"

Barbara stared at her daughter, not sure if the comment was meant sincerely. She looked at the wedding magazines and the linen samples and knew they still had the rest of the meeting to get through. Perhaps she should back off and make her case another time.

"You turned out very well," she said, trying to sound gracious. "I'm sure Avery will do the same."

"Interesting." Stephanie hesitated, as if not sure she was willing to pass on the fight. Then she nodded and pulled a large piece of paper out of her tote bag and unfolded it. After smoothing it on the table between them, she pointed to the floor plan of the tasting area, the retail space and all the private rooms.

"Having a wedding between harvest and late spring means it has to be indoors. We have the private event room, which is big enough for a reception of up to a hundred people." She pointed to the room on the drawing. Small circles represented tables.

"You said two to three hundred people, which makes more sense to me. This is the wedding of Barbara Barcellona—people will be fighting for an invitation."

Barbara hoped that was true.

Stephanie continued. "So I had a crazy idea. If we use the event room for the ceremony, we can easily fit in three hundred guests. Then we'd hold the reception in the tasting and retail space."

She put down another large sheet of paper, showing the floor plan of that area and where the tables would go.

"We can move out all the inventory and the shelves, and empty most of the wine. I think it will take three days to get everything ready and three more days to put it all back. Assuming the wedding is on Saturday and no one works on Sunday, we're talking about having the tasting room closed for just over a week." She smiled. "It's up to you, but knowing how much Bel Après means to you, I wanted to find a way to give you the wedding of your dreams right here."

Barbara touched her daughter's hand. "It's lovely. A wonderful idea. Yes, let's do that. Then I can have my holiday wedding."

Maybe the Saturday before Christmas, when the tasting room was decorated to look like a winter wonderland. She and Giorgio could then have a beautiful tropical honeymoon for a couple of weeks. Three at the most.

She thought briefly of his claim to want to have her to himself for three entire months. How ridiculous. There was no way she could be gone that long—she had responsibilities and a life. But three weeks would be perfect. Maybe they could go to that place with the little huts on the water. She would like that.

"Great," Stephanie said. "I'll start working on specific dates and pulling together some ideas. You'll want to start thinking about your dress." She tapped the magazines. "You'll get a lot of ideas in these."

Barbara eyed the magazines and enjoyed her sense of anticipation. "I'll start looking at them tonight."

"I look forward to hearing what you ultimately decide." Stephanie scanned her tablet. "Do you want bridesmaids?"

Barbara tilted her head. "I never thought about that. I could have my four girls." Her mouth tightened. "But only if I get to pick what everyone wears."

Stephanie would look good in anything, she thought. As would Mackenzie. "Avery is old enough to be a bridesmaid, but Galaxy and Eternity are too young. No, just the adults in the ceremony. When does Avery start applying for college? Is it this fall?"

"She's only a junior. She applies next year."

"What is she thinking? I know WSU is the closest and most obvious, but it might be good for her to go out of state. Get some fresh ideas. UC Davis has an excellent wine program."

"She hasn't said she wants to go into the family business, Mom. Let her come to that on her own."

"Don't be ridiculous. It has to be Avery. Carson

isn't going to have anything but baseball in his head. If not her, then who? Do you really expect me to turn Bel Après over to Catherine's wild children?"

"One of them might have the passion for it, Mom."

Passion my ass, Barbara thought grimly. The way those children were being educated, she wasn't sure any of them even knew how to read. There was no way they would be prepared to run Bel Après.

"Back to the wedding," Stephanie said, waving a picture of a large four-tiered cake. "There are so many options with cakes these days. Traditional, of course, but also cupcakes."

Barbara looked at her. "You can't distract me with cake. I'm not five."

"But I can try." She put down a picture of a wedding cake made up of cupcakes, which was much nicer than Barbara would have thought. "These could be super cute."

Barbara raised her eyebrows. "Does anything in my life inspire the phrase 'super cute'?"

"No, but it could become a thing."

Barbara surprised herself by laughing. "Fine. We can talk about cupcakes as much as you want, but I'll be ordering a traditional cake."

eight

Monday morning Stephanie walked through the retail area that shared space with the tasting room. It was early—barely after eight. The tasting room didn't open until ten and the staff didn't arrive until nine. For the next hour the lack of customers and employees meant she could work in peace and get a clear idea of what had sold over the weekend.

Summer was busy at the winery. Tourists flocked to the area, standing four and five deep at the tasting bar and snapping up the glasses, tea towels and other kitchen and barware they offered. Printed inventory sheets gave her an up-to-the-minute accounting of sales. The more expensive glassware moved briskly, as did the wine openers, foil cutters and stoppers. But the real winners in terms of volume were the tea towels.

They regularly stocked six different designs, with a rotating seasonal stock. All the towels had an excellent markup, so much so that even on sale they were profitable. Barbara hated the tea towels, but she couldn't argue with the money they brought in. Sometimes Stephanie chose an especially whimsical design—just to annoy her mother. More often than not, it sold better than any of the more traditional designs. This summer she'd gone with a floral and ladybug theme, and based on the numbers, they were kicking some serious retail butt.

The tasting room at Bel Après had been remodeled four years ago. They'd increased the square footage, doubled the length of the tasting bar and added more retail items. Stephanie had wanted to include a small café in the remodel. Nothing fancy—just delicious food that could be taken off the premises or enjoyed on a few tables she'd wanted to put outside, in the shade.

She'd put together a business plan, including costs and sales projections. She'd even come up with a sample menu that included picnic baskets filled with things like ham and figs, gourmet sandwiches, and grilled corn with flavored butters and salads.

A lot of the larger wineries in the area offered lunches to go and she knew they were successful. But Barbara had simply shaken her head and muttered something about Stephanie's delusions of grandeur before moving on to the next item on the agenda.

Stephanie supposed that was when she'd stopped trying to grow her end of the business. Her mother was in charge and all Barbara cared about was the wine. So Stephanie found pleasure in small things, like ladybug tea towels that her mother found annoying. Not her proudest moment, but sometimes it was all she had left. Occasionally she opened the idea files on her computer and researched things like how to expand into the Chinese market. She'd put together an entire package on enticing Chinese tourists to visit the area, with Bel Après as the highlight of the trip. She knew it was a waste of time—her mother would never consider it. But there were days when Stephanie wanted to do more than go through the motions.

Leaving was the obvious solution, she told herself. She thought about what Mackenzie had said—that in this part of the state wine was king. She did know the industry, but could she work for a competitor? That would be a fight to end all fights. She supposed the very sad but realistic bottom line was that she wasn't willing to take on her mother. Which left her completely trapped. And if that wasn't grim enough, she knew she had only herself to blame.

With that depressing thought on her mind, she retreated to the break room, where she'd made coffee when she'd first come in. She poured a cup and walked to the window that overlooked the shaded grassy area dotted with a handful of picnic tables the employees used on their breaks. She imagined the grass replaced with pavers, some kind of pergola providing additional coverings, an outdoor wine bar and nicer tables and chairs.

"Not this week," she murmured to herself. "Or ever."

"Stephanie?"

The sound of Mackenzie's voice broke through her self-pity party.

"In the break room. There's coffee."

Her sister-in-law walked in and tried to smile. Stephanie took one look at her and knew something was wrong. Mackenzie's normally bright eyes were red—as if she hadn't been sleeping or, worse, she'd been crying. Her skin was pale and there was a slump to her shoulders that wasn't anything Stephanie had seen before.

"What?" Stephanie demanded. "Something's happened. Tell me."

Instead of brushing off the concern, Mackenzie motioned to one of the tables. "We should sit down."

Stephanie's stomach dropped and her body went stiff. There *was* something and it was bad. She knew it. Her mind searched for possibilities. Mackenzie didn't have any family, so there wasn't an unexpected death. Was it medical? Had Mackenzie had a doctor's appointment with bad news? No, it was early on a Monday morning—she couldn't have gotten news today and if there'd been something last week, she would have mentioned it sooner. They'd seen each other like five times during the weekend.

When they were seated across from each other, Mackenzie cleared her throat. Tears filled her eyes before she blinked them away.

"You're scaring me," Stephanie said, reaching for her hand. "Just say it."

"It's not awful," Mackenzie said quickly. "I mean it is, but it's not lethal. No one knows and I don't want anyone to know. Not yet. I'm still processing."

Stephanie stared at her, waiting, her sense of dread growing.

"Rhys and I are getting a divorce."

The words took a second to sink in. Stephanie heard them but couldn't understand what they meant.

"You're not," she said. "You can't be. You're fine."

Mackenzie's mouth twisted. "I wish that were true. Things haven't been right between us for a while.

We've drifted apart, and somewhere along the way, we lost our marriage."

"No." Stephanie pulled back her hand. "No, you didn't. You're fine. I've seen you together and it's like it always was. You were dancing at the party."

This wasn't happening. She didn't want it to be happening. "You can't get a divorce. That will change everything. We're sisters. You live here. You've always lived here. You can't change it."

Even as she spoke, she knew she was getting it all wrong. This wasn't about her—this was about Mackenzie—but no matter what she told herself, she couldn't get past how the news rocked her world.

"We're a family. We have traditions. We have Girls' Night and we work together. I see you all the time. What about family dinners and my kids? Are you just going to walk away from that?" Another thought occurred to her—one that was more shattering. "Are you leaving? Are you leaving Bel Après?"

"I don't know. I haven't thought that far ahead. This just came up a couple of days ago and I've been trying to deal with it. I wish you could understand that this is horrible for me. I'm devastated. Rhys and your family and Bel Après are all I know."

Stephanie stood. "Then make it stop. Get counseling. Fix it. Don't get a divorce. You'll change everything and it will be terrible. How could you do this to me?"

Mackenzie stared at her, wide-eyed. Anger replaced the sadness. "This isn't about you, Stephanie. I just told you my marriage is over and all you can talk about is how *you* feel? What about me? Rhys is the only man I've ever loved and we're splitting up. I might lose my home and my job, and you want to talk about Girls' Night?"

Mackenzie stood. "You're my best friend. How could you be so selfish? I thought I could count on you. I thought you cared about me. I've been wrong about everything."

The words were a slap. Shame overrode the shock, bringing Stephanie back to reality, but before she could say anything, Mackenzie was gone, leaving only the realization that nothing would ever be the same again.

Mackenzie couldn't decide if she felt more sick or more drained. She'd thought she was handling the situation well, dealing and trying to figure out the next step, but all that had gone to crap when she'd tried to talk to Stephanie. Her friend, her *best* friend, hadn't been there for her, leaving her feeling desperate, alone and afraid.

Despite the hot morning and sunny skies, she was cold. Every part of her still hurt and she couldn't quiet her swirling mind. Under other circumstances, she would have assumed she was coming down with something, but she knew her symptoms had nothing to do with a summer virus and everything to do with the painful realization that the solid ground she'd always counted on was about to become quicksand.

She fingered the lush green leaves of the grapevines. The canopy would soak up the sun and turn that light into nutrients to feed the clusters of grapes. It also protected them from the powerful rays. This she understood. This made sense to her. Everything else was a terrifying morass of confusion.

Her marriage was over. The bald truth had seeped

inside of her the night she'd huddled on the floor in her bedroom, lost, sad and alone. There was no going back, no changing what had been said. Rhys had told her she could take her time but they both knew the outcome was inevitable. And if she wasn't married to Rhys, then who was she and where did she belong?

She walked toward her truck, trying to breathe deeply so maybe her chest would stop hurting, only to pause with her hand on the door.

Not her truck. The company truck she drove. She didn't own a truck or a car or a house or a stick of furniture. She supposed she owned her clothes and her jewelry, such as it was. A few knickknacks and some artwork she'd bought. She had her salary, her savings and the royalties from the wine deal she'd made with Barbara.

There was the postnuptial agreement, she reminded herself, signed three years after she'd married Rhys. She'd been heartbroken to learn that no matter how hard or long she worked or how successful she was, Barbara wasn't interested in giving her even the tiniest piece of Bel Après.

Barbara had claimed it was the terms of her late husband's will—that only blood relatives could be a part of Bel Après, but Mackenzie suspected much of what went on was Barbara's decision.

Rhys had found her crying and been desperate to chase the sadness from her eyes. He'd explained that a postnuptial agreement was like a prenup, but signed after the wedding. While he couldn't give her a vineyard, he offered her the value of half the house, along with a portion of his trust fund. Later they'd amended the postnup to exclude her wine royalties from any community property claim. The combined assets were worth a chunk of money, but she would give it all back to him if only things could stay as they had been.

But that wasn't an option. She might not know anything about getting a divorce or what it would mean or what happened next, but she was certain that her marriage was over. Nearly as unsettling was the fact that Rhys was further along in the process than she was. While she was barely able to breathe, he was ready to be done with them. With her.

She fought against the tears burning in her eyes. She'd spent too many days giving in to the pain and she was done with that. From now on, she was going to be strong—that was her promise to herself. She was going to make plans and get on with her life—even if she no longer knew what that meant. Even if she was alone, with no husband and no best friend. She could count only on herself from now on.

She drove back toward the compound, taking in the beauty of the landscape. Vineyards stretched out on either side of the road. The distant mountains were dark against the blue sky. There were things she could count on, she told herself. The changing seasons, for one. Harvest, the frenetic few weeks that followed. The anticipation of what the new vintage would bring and how she would craft it into a perfect wine.

She parked by the main building and started for the production building, remembering how different it was now from what it had been sixteen years ago, when she'd first started working here. Bel Après was bigger, more successful, and she'd been a part of that.

Barbara had hired her as an apprentice winemaker right out of college. She'd also been engaged to Rhys, so taking the job had been the obvious thing to do. Two years later, she'd been promoted to head winemaker.

Her whole life was here, she thought, pausing at the foot of the stairs leading up to the offices. She didn't know what life was like without Bel Après and the family. Probably more significant, she didn't know who *she* was without them.

She took the stairs two at a time. Rhys's office was at the end, across from hers. Because they worked together. In a normal day, she saw him dozens of times—from breakfast until they said good-night. They made decisions together, they discussed every aspect of the business. They were a team...or at least they had been.

She stepped into his office. He didn't see her at first—he was too intent on whatever he was studying on his computer. Everything about him was familiar. The shape of his nose, the strong line of his jaw. He was a handsome man who looked like what he was—a decent guy who took his responsibilities seriously.

She remembered when Stephanie had first invited her home for the holidays. They'd both been freshmen at Washington State University. She and Stephanie had been roommates and friends from the first day they'd met. Mackenzie hadn't been sure about the wisdom of thrusting herself on her friend's family, but the alternative had been staying on campus by herself—a grim prospect considering the university all but shut down for Christmas. But with no family of her own and no place to go, she'd been grateful to have an alternative.

They'd made the drive to Walla Walla, going slowly over the snowy, mountainous roads. When they'd arrived, everyone had rushed out to greet them. There had been too many faces and names, but everyone had made her feel welcome. Rhys, the only man in a household of women, had made her heart beat faster with his kind smile.

Over that first holiday, she'd gotten to know everyone. Barbara had shown her around the property, taking her through the processing areas and into the barrel room. Lori and Four had been like younger sisters—friendly and eager to hang out with their older sister and her friend, and Rhys had invited Mackenzie out to dinner in town where they'd talked and laughed for hours.

They'd made love on Christmas Eve, in front of the family's large tree. By the time she and Stephanie had headed back to college, she'd already been more than half in love with him.

Rhys looked up and smiled at her. "Hi."

"Hi, yourself."

She closed the door behind her so they could have privacy, then took a seat across from him.

"I was remembering that first Christmas," she told him.

"That was a good time."

"It was. I don't think I had much of a choice about falling in love with you and Bel Après. I was alone in the world and you offered me everything I'd ever wanted."

"Mackenzie," he began, then stopped.

"What?" she asked softly. "It can't be unsaid. More important, you're right. Our marriage is finished. It has been for a long time. I didn't want to admit it, but that doesn't change the truth."

He looked both pained and relieved. "What do you want to do?"

"I don't know. I'd like us to stay friends."

"We have to. You're my best friend and I don't want to lose that."

"Me, either. I just know nothing is going to be the same." She thought about her horrible conversation with Stephanie but knew talking about that would be a distraction from what mattered. "I'm still trying to figure it all out. I like my job here and—" She stared at Rhys. "Why did you get scrunchy face just now?"

"I don't ever get scrunchy face, as you call it."

"You were thinking something."

He looked at her, his expression intense. "Don't you think you deserve more than just a job? You're the most talented winemaker I've ever met. Shouldn't you have something of your own? Don't you want to stand on a hill and look all around you and say, 'This is mine'?"

While the words didn't hurt as much as his recent statement that their marriage was over, they were still dangerous to her well-being, poking at an open wound she didn't allow herself to acknowledge.

Rhys leaned toward her. "Whatever you decide, my mom will keep you on for as long as you want."

"I know. She won't care if we get a divorce." She paused. "I don't mean that in a bad way."

"I know what you meant. Is that what you want? A divorce?"

She wanted to say that she didn't—she'd liked being married to him. Only she wasn't sure they actually had a marriage, not anymore. Besides, she knew it was what he wanted. He was ready to move on to something beyond what they had.

"It's the next step," she said instead. "I'm just not sure of the logistics."

"You'll have money," he said eagerly. "Lots of it. I've been running the numbers, and based on the value of the house and the amount from my trust, you should have close to two million dollars. That's enough for you to do anything."

As he spoke, he pulled a folder from a locked drawer in his desk and opened it.

"It's all here," he told her. "And that amount doesn't take into consideration the money from the wine royalties and whatever part of your salary you've saved."

She told herself he was being kind, trying to reassure her, but she couldn't help thinking this was more proof he was ready to be done with her. As for the money, it wasn't anything she could wrap her mind around.

"You think I should leave," she said faintly. "You want me to go."

"I'm not pushing you out. It's just you're gifted. You should have something of your own. You don't want to work for my mom for the rest of your life. How would that even happen? You'd get a place somewhere else, drive to Bel Après, then drive home at the end of the day? That's not going to make you happy."

She knew he was trying to help, but his words only made her feel worse. The bleak picture of her life had her fighting tears.

Was that what was next? A sad little apartment and working for Barbara? Rhys got to keep their house and his family and everything else, while she lost everything?

Apparently her pain didn't show, because he kept on talking.

"There's no rush." He passed her the folder. "We'll move forward when you're ready and not before. Until then, we'll live together in the house." He smiled at her. "You can stay there forever, as far as I'm concerned. I like living with you."

Which sounded nice but wasn't true. He wanted her to leave. Maybe not today, but soon.

She had to clear her throat before she could speak. "I appreciate that, but I think there needs to be an end date." She forced a smile. "Eventually I would cramp your style. You don't want to have to explain why your ex-wife is in the living room when you bring home a date."

He chuckled. "That would be awkward, but I can always go to her place."

She tried to keep her expression from tightening. He spoke so easily, she thought, as if he'd already worked everything out. Which he had. What was it he'd said? He wanted to have sex with anyone who would have him? None of this should be a surprise.

"I need to think," she told him. "Just a few more days. If we could keep this quiet a little longer."

"As long as you'd like. Did you tell Stephanie?"

She tried not to think about their conversation. "Yes, and she was upset."

She was deliberately vague, not wanting to go into what had actually been said. She didn't think she could get through the telling without losing what little control she had. Better to let him think Stephanie had been sad but supportive.

She got up and waved the folder. "Thanks for this. I'll look it over."

"You'll want to run it past your lawyer."

She stared at him blankly. She didn't have a lawyer. Then she got it. He meant a divorce lawyer.

"Sure," she whispered. "I'll get right on that."

And she would. Just as soon as she found a way to collect the pieces of her shattered life and start breathing again.

nine

Stephanie alternated between self-pity and guilt for the better part of four days before realizing she had to talk to someone. She decided to confront the one person she could yell at in total safety.

She waited until she knew Mackenzie would be in an evening meeting with Barbara, then walked into her brother's house and called his name.

"In my office," he replied.

She made her way to the large bookshelf-lined room. He was sitting at his desk, laptop open. It was well after seven, but sunlight still spilled into the room, warming the hardwood floors.

"Hey, Steph, what's up?"

She stared at her older brother for a second, before putting her hands on her hips. "A divorce?" she asked, her voice a shriek. "You want a divorce? I know it has to be you. Mackenzie would never ask for one. Why are you doing this? We're a family and you're ripping us apart. Get some counseling and get over yourself."

She paused to draw breath, then realized she had

nothing else to say, so she sank into the one of the chairs and braced herself for the pushback.

But instead of yelling, he only shook his head and said, "I'm sorry."

"That's it?"

"It's all I've got."

"Did you cheat? You can't keep your dick in your pants?" She fought against sudden tears. "Mackenzie's amazing and beautiful and smart and why don't you want to be married to her anymore?"

He stood and circled the desk. After pulling her to her feet, he held her close.

"I'm sorry," he repeated. "I didn't want to do this."

"Then don't."

"I have to."

He led her to the sofa and waited until she sat down.

"There's no one else," he told her. "I didn't cheat. What I did was let it go on too long. We're great as friends, but we're lousy in a marriage. We're roommates and we work together and nothing more. I can't live like that. I won't. I want more."

"So this is about you being selfish?"

"Dammit, Steph, I'm not the bad guy."

"Could have fooled me. What do you want that she's not giving you?"

"Love. Sex."

"Oh, please. Sex? Really? That's the reason? What, she won't put on a French maid costume for you? Grow up."

He sat on the sofa and faced her. After swearing softly, he said, "Mackenzie and I haven't had sex in five years. We sleep in separate rooms, in separate wings of the house. We only ever talk about business.

Call me all the names you want, I don't care. I want more than that. I'm tired of being lonely and horny and trapped in a relationship that isn't working for either of us."

Stephanie felt all the mad whoosh out of her. She stared at Rhys, unable to understand what he was saying. "You haven't had sex in five years?"

"Yeah. You know what really sucks? We did it last week. First time in forever, and that's when we knew it was over. Hell of a goodbye."

"But I thought you were happy. You were always together."

But not touching, she thought suddenly. They never touched. They didn't hold hands or hug. There was no secret communication or laughs or shared jokes. Not that she could remember. How could she not have seen that?

"I didn't know," she breathed. "She never said. You never hinted."

His mouth twisted. "A man doesn't like to admit he's not having sex with his wife. Besides, what was I going to say? We all like and respect Mackenzie. What happened is both our faults. It's over and you have to deal with that. It's not about you or the family, it's about us."

Even as she was unable to grasp it all, she knew he was telling the truth—about all of it. How could she not have seen through the facade? She and Mackenzie talked about everything—why had her friend kept this from her? Shame? Guilt?

"I'm sorry," she whispered. "About all of it." Oh, God, she'd been a horrible friend. She hadn't been supportive at all.

"I yelled at her," she admitted. "I said she was ruining my life."

"Not surprising."

"Hey, you're supposed to be sympathetic."

"You need to be there for her," he said. "I've got the whole family. I'm keeping my life, but not Mackenzie. She's not going to have anything. We're all she has, and she's about to lose that. You need to be her friend. You and Four. Lori's going to side with Mom, and depending on how this all plays out, you know how ugly things could get. If Mom turns on her, her life will be hell."

Stephanie nodded even as she began to cry. "Everything is going to change. I hate that. But I don't want you to be unhappy and I feel awful about Mackenzie."

He slid close and wrapped his arm around her. "I know. Me, too."

"This sucks. And there's no good solution."

"Tell me about it."

Mackenzie sat on the ground, a small amount of dry soil clutched in her hand. About fourteen thousand years ago, the Missoula floods, caused by melting glaciers, deposited a smorgasbord of nutrients all across eastern Washington. To the east were the wheat fields, but here, by the Columbia River, were the vineyards.

In 1977 Gary Figgins established Leonetti Cellar as Walla Walla's first commercial winery. In 1981 *Wine & Spirits* magazine named the first Leonetti cabernet sauvignon—the 1978 vintage—as the best in the nation. By 2012, six wineries from the Walla Walla area were on the list of Top 100 Wineries of the World. Bel Après was one of them.

In the past, knowing the history had always helped, but not today, she thought, letting the soil slip through her fingers. Today she was sick and confused and lost, and no amount of history was going to make that right. Everything was moving faster and faster and she didn't know how to make it stop.

The worst was the fear, the uncertainty. She was getting a divorce, she no longer had a best friend, she might lose her job, she might quit her job. She wanted nothing more than to go home, but even that wasn't a sure thing. The house wasn't hers, it never had been. It was part of the Barcellona family trust and she wasn't a member.

She covered her face with her hands and braced for tears, but she was all cried out. There was nothing left inside but a sense of foreboding. She felt like a speck of dust being blown around by cosmic winds, and that thought terrified her.

She knew that the worry and stress weren't helping. She had to figure out a way to get control. She had to decide on a first step, then the next one and the next one. She was thirty-eight years old, she was healthy and she was good at her job. That was a start. She needed to get off her ass and come up with a plan.

She'd spent the last two evenings reading articles online with subjects ranging from her rights in a divorce in Washington State, to how long it would take—a mere ninety days, assuming neither of them contested the settlement—to dealing with the emotional aftermath. She felt vaguely more knowledgeable but no more settled. Adding to her stress level was the question of her work. Did she stay? Did she leave? And if she left, where was she going to go and what was she going to do when she got there? Work for another winery? Buy a winery?

That last thought had been keeping her up nights. She'd tried to dismiss the possibility, but like the idea of the divorce itself, once thought, it couldn't be unthought.

Could she, would she, should she? Her own winery. There were so many things she wanted to do that Barbara had never agreed to. Styles she'd wanted to try, new trends in blending. At the same time, she'd wanted to play with going more old-school with some of the wines.

She rose to her knees and plucked a grape from the bunch closest to her. It was still hard and sour—more than two months from being ready. But the promise was there.

This she knew, she told herself. This was who she was and this was going to save her. She couldn't count on Rhys or Stephanie or anyone but herself. She wasn't a part of Bel Après—not really. So what did she want? What was her legacy? Was she willing to just work for someone for the rest of her life, or did she want more?

Rhys had told her the postnup would give her about two million dollars. That was enough to buy a small winery. Or be a down payment on a larger one. It was options and a safety net and very possibly the start of a dream. She could accept what was happening and do something positive or she could whine and complain and make herself sick with worry. The choice was hers.

"I don't want to live like this anymore," she whispered, coming to her feet. "I won't live like this. I want love and passion and something that matters to me."

She looked around. Vineyards stretched out to the

horizon, the even rows a testament to the meticulous care they received. This was her passion, she thought. It always had been. This was who she was. She might lose everything else, but she wasn't going to lose that. She refused to.

Dropping the grape to the ground, she started back for the truck. Before sliding behind the wheel, she stopped to trace the Bel Après logo on the side. She was still dealing with a ton of crap, but right now the weight of it was just a little bit less than it had been.

When she reached the highway, she headed for Walla Walla. The sun was high in the sky and the afternoon was hot. A good day to grow grapes, she thought. She turned toward town, then made a quick right turn when she spotted a sign for a used car lot.

A first step, she told herself. That was all she had to accomplish today. One small step. Tomorrow, she would make another. That was the only way she was going to get through.

She climbed out of the truck and looked around. An old man walked over, smiling as he approached.

"Afternoon," he called. "You looking for a new ride?"

She sucked in a breath, then smiled back. "I am. Either an SUV or a pickup. I want low miles and four-wheel drive."

Two hours later she was the proud owner of a late-model Jeep. After parking her work truck in its place by the offices, she took a golf cart to her house only to realize she wasn't sure who could give her a ride back to the car lot to pick up her Jeep. She and Stephanie weren't exactly speaking and Rhys was working. She didn't have any friends outside of the Barcellona family—something she was going to have to deal with, just not now.

She considered her options for a second before crossing the courtyard to Four's house. As she circled to the rear, she passed wind chimes and a miniature stone circle. The back steps were covered in hand-painted tiles. Mackenzie knocked once, then let herself inside.

"Four, it's me," she called.

"In the kitchen."

She walked through the mudroom and found her sister-in-law collecting flour and sugar. Several empty muffin pans stood on the counter, along with bowls overflowing with fresh blueberries.

Four smiled. "The first of the season. It will be a few more days until they're at peak ripeness, but these ones are good for baking. I'll bring by muffins later."

"Thank you." Mackenzie glanced around the kitchen. "I need a favor. Are you already into this, or can you take a break for about an hour?"

"I haven't started yet, so I'm available. What's up?"

Four wore a pretty summer dress. The pale flowy fabric was covered in rainbows and unicorns. She'd pulled her long hair back in a ponytail and had on dangling earrings shaped like green beans.

She was the youngest of the siblings, the most artistic and the one who made Barbara insane. Mackenzie had always liked her, and she admired Four's willingness to be exactly who she was, consequences be damned. While Stephanie was her best friend, Mackenzie and Four were also close. Mackenzie was godmother to her three children. She showed up for school plays and birthday parties. On the first day of school, she walked the kids to the bus stop.

What if all that was lost? What if she wasn't around for Galaxy to show her a new hair ribbon or to see Zeus's latest frog find? What if there were no more art projects or nights spent lying on a blanket to look at stars?

Four's breath caught, then she rushed forward and pulled Mackenzie into a bruising hug.

"Breathe," her sister-in-law told her. "Breathe deeply. Pull in the essence of the universe and exhale the broken pieces."

Mackenzie managed to laugh. "I appreciate the hug if not the advice. What are you talking about?"

"Whatever's bothering you. Tell me what happened."

"Rhys and I are getting a divorce."

She braced herself for judgment or anger or for Four to step away. Instead her friend just held on, offering comfort and warmth.

"I'm sorry," Four said at last.

"Me, too."

Four stepped back and sighed. "I'm not surprised, but I'm sorry."

"Why aren't you surprised?"

"Neither of you has been happy for a long time. There's no connection between you. You don't fight because that would require a level of passion you don't have anymore."

Mackenzie stared at her. "You didn't want to share any of these insights with me a year ago?"

"Would you have listened?"

"I don't know. Maybe."

Four smiled. "You make your choices in your own time. We all do." Her smile faded. "You're not just leaving him, though, are you? I'm going to miss you so much."

Mackenzie fought tears. "I don't want to leave, but I don't know if I have a choice."

"You don't. Bel Après isn't right for you. My mother has spent the last eighteen years using your talent while trying to control your spirit. That was never going to work. You deserve so much more." Four reached for her hands. "Know that whatever happens, I'm your sister and I love you. I'll always be there for you and I know you'll always be there for me and my family. I trust you completely."

The words were comforting and welcome. For these few minutes, Mackenzie felt nurtured and loved. If a part of her wished Stephanie had responded the same way, well, she was going to have to get over that.

"Thank you," Mackenzie said, drawing in a full breath for the first time in days.

"You're welcome. Now how can I help?"

Mackenzie laughed. "At the risk of sounding like one of your kids, I need a ride."

Stephanie wondered if she felt as bad as she looked. She hadn't showered in two days, she'd barely left her bedroom. Now as she sat in her kitchen, sipping coffee just after seven in the morning, she tried to tell herself she had to get over herself and do the right thing. Only she didn't seem to want to listen.

Her phone buzzed. She glanced down and saw a text from Carson.

Hey, Mom. Checking in. Things are great. I pitched a perfect 6 innings yesterday. Love you.

Despite everything, she managed a smile. At least she'd done one thing right. Carson was a good kid. Avery probably was, too, and she would notice just as soon as her daughter let go of some of the attitude, but as for the rest of it…she was a hideous human being.

She'd realized that at about two in the morning, had cried, stomped around her bedroom, then cried some more. But no amount of self-loathing was going to change what she'd done and now she was stuck having to fix it.

Only she was just weak enough to want to pass over that part—the apology—and go back to how things were with Mackenzie. Except she couldn't. There was a big, fat problem in the way, and that problem was her and what she'd said.

She forced herself to her feet and went upstairs. One shower and a change of clothes later, she was feeling half-human. She came out of her bedroom and saw Avery in the hall. Her daughter looked at her.

"Mom, what's wrong?"

"Nothing."

"You've been crying."

"I know, but it's not anything you did." She tried to temper the words with a smile. Avery didn't look convinced.

"Do you want me to do something?"

The unexpected offer gave her a brief respite from the voice in her head chanting endlessly that she was slime.

"Get better grades and tell me I'm your best friend?"

Avery grinned. "Anything else?"

"I'm okay. Just some stuff. I'll figure it out."

Avery surprised her by moving close and giving her a quick hug. "If you need me, I'll be around all day."

"That's sweet. Thank you."

Avery nodded and went downstairs. Stephanie pulled her phone out of her pocket and sent a quick text before she could talk herself out of it.

You home?

Yes.

I'll be right over.

She waited but there was no response to that. She would guess that Mackenzie wasn't sure what to say—especially after how Stephanie had gone off on her the last time they'd spoken.

"It's going to be different this time," she promised aloud before following her daughter to the first floor.

"I'm going to talk to Mackenzie," she called, heading for the front door. "Then I'll see you at work."

"Okay."

Once outside, Stephanie inhaled the already warm air. It was going to be a scorcher—temperatures well into the nineties. Mackenzie and her crew would be prowling the vineyards, looking for signs of stress. Some heat was good for the grapes, but too much, too early could be a problem.

She walked the short distance between the houses, trying to figure out what she was going to say about the divorce. Rhys's confession had completely changed her perspective and made her sad. Two people she loved most in the world had been in pain and she hadn't known.

She walked up the three stairs to the front door and let herself in.

"It's me," she called.

"In the kitchen."

She walked in that direction, stopping when she saw Mackenzie.

Her friend looked as bad as Stephanie felt. Pale and thin, with shadows under her eyes. They stared at each other, then Stephanie rushed toward her. Mackenzie did the same and they met in the doorway, arms wrapped hard around each other as they hung on tight.

"I'm sorry," Stephanie said, tears filling her eyes. "I'm sorry. I was terrible. I said awful things and I made you feel bad. I wasn't there when you needed me. I don't know how that happened. All I could think of was myself and how the divorce would affect me, which is wrong and makes me feel like a worm. I won't do it again. I swear. I love you so much. I want to be there for you. Please, please believe me."

Mackenzie continued to hold her. They clung to each other for a couple of minutes before stepping back and smiling. They were both wiping away tears.

"We're a mess," Mackenzie said. "We need tissues and coffee."

"Any liquor?"

"It's seven thirty in the morning."

"Not in Vienna."

Mackenzie laughed. "You are right about that. How about some toast, instead?"

"I'll eat toast."

They sat at the island, each on a corner, their knees bumping. Stephanie squeezed Mackenzie's hand.

"I really am sorry. I was so wrong. I reacted without thinking and I hurt you."

"It's okay."

"It's not. I'm going to do better."

"I appreciate the apology." She reached for a tissue and blew her nose. "It's been a hard few days."

"I'll bet. What's going on? Are you and Rhys talking about anything? Are you fighting?"

"No fighting. Some talking." She got up and poured them each coffee, then put bread into the toaster. "I'm trying to adjust to what's happening. I'm not surprised but it feels really fast, if that makes sense."

"It does." Stephanie hesitated. "Is the divorce a sure thing?"

Mackenzie nodded. "Rhys is more than ready and I'm getting there. I thought about asking him to go into counseling, but there isn't anything for us to save. Not really. We haven't been truly married in a long time."

Stephanie thought about her brother's confession that they no longer slept in the same room or had sex, then wasn't sure if she should mention that.

"So what are you going to do?" she asked instead.

"Get a divorce lawyer. Figure out my life." She faked a smile. "You know—the easy stuff."

"Are you going to keep working at Bel Après?"

Mackenzie hesitated and Stephanie felt her stomach knot.

"You're not."

"I don't know," Mackenzie told her. "I haven't decided. I'm pretty sure Barbara would keep me on, regardless of the divorce, but then what? That's what I've been thinking about. Do I get an apartment in town, or even a condo, and drive here every day to do the job I've been doing? Do I want to be an employee here for the rest of my life? Before I felt like I was part of the family, but without that, what do I have?"

A legitimate question, Stephanie thought, trying not to be bitter. The fact that she'd never bothered to get her own life in order wasn't anyone's fault but hers. Even if having Mackenzie leave made her feel trapped, again, not her friend's problem.

"Would you go to work somewhere else or start your own thing?" She sat up straighter. "You have money. From the postnup. It's probably a lot of money. Could you buy a winery? That would be great." She got up and collected butter and jam from the refrigerator.

"Maybe."

The toast popped and Mackenzie put the slices on a plate, then placed it in front of Stephanie.

"What does maybe mean?"

Mackenzie resumed her seat and picked up her coffee. "I don't know what to do. I don't like change. I want things to be how they've always been."

"Don't you ever think about having your own label, making all the decisions without my mother breathing down your neck?"

Mackenzie's mouth turned up. "I have fantasized about that."

"Well, sure. So make it happen."

"There's a lot more to running a winery than just growing grapes. I don't know the business end of things. Maybe it would be better to go work for someone."

"You'd hate that. It's the same as you have now. I'm

encouraging you to think about buying something. You'd do great." Stephanie was proud of herself for meaning the words.

"Thanks. Your support means a lot. I've hated us fighting."

Stephanie nodded. "Me, too. I'm sorry. I won't be stupid again." She paused. "Okay, I'll probably be stupid, but I'll do it in a supportive way. You matter to me. I love you and I don't want to lose our friendship."

"I love you, too. And I want to stay friends, no matter what." She paused.

"You're thinking of my mom," Stephanie said as she finished buttering her toast.

"She's not going to be happy."

"It's not her life. She doesn't get a say."

Mackenzie nodded. "I wish things had been different. Rhys deserved better than he had."

"Didn't you?"

"Yes, but it's easier to worry about him. We both let go of what was important and we lost it." She set down her coffee. "Thinking about the future is terrifying. It's this void and I don't know what's going to happen. Since college, Bel Après has been my home. I don't know how to be anywhere else."

"Come live with me," Stephanie told her. "I have an extra bedroom on the first floor. There's a bathroom and everything. You'll have me and the kids and you can stay as long as you like."

Mackenzie's eyes filled with tears. "Thank you. That means a lot. I may take you up on that."

"You should. We'll have fun together and it will annoy my mother. A true win-win."

Mackenzie chuckled. "One day you're going to have to figure out how to get along with her."

"Oh, why start now?"

Mackenzie took a slice of toast. "I bought a Jeep. It's black and kind of cool looking. In high school, I drove my grandfather's car and then I married Rhys and I always had a company truck, so this is the first car I've owned."

"Congratulations. Good for you."

"I know. I had to get insurance and everything."

"Look at you, with the adulting."

Mackenzie smiled. "One step down, four thousand ninety-seven to go."

ten

Mackenzie drove east, past the small airport, then turned into a quiet industrial area. At the end of a dead-end road was a Mexican restaurant that had been at the same location for at least twenty-five years. The food was cheap and plentiful, making the place a favorite of high school kids, but it was far enough out of the way that no one she knew should be there at two o'clock on a Thursday. No one except the man she was meeting.

Nader English ran the biggest winery in the state of Washington. His production was measured in millions of gallons per year and the finished product had a worldwide distribution. She'd known him for years, and nearly every time they ran into each other at an industry event, he offered her a job. The offer was accompanied by a chuckle and a comment that Barbara would skin him alive if Mackenzie accepted, but it was always made. Now she wanted to know if it was real, or just cheap talk.

She parked next to the only other vehicle in the

parking lot—a late-model full-size F-150 with the winery logo on the side. At least she hadn't had her Jeep long enough for people to associate it with her, she thought, turning off the engine and wiping her suddenly sweaty hands on her jeans.

This was a mistake, she thought, her stomach twisting. She didn't want to go to work for Nader or anyone. She wanted to stay right where she was. She loved Bel Après. Only staying might not be an option, not just because of the divorce, but also because the hope of having more—something she could build herself—had taken root deep inside. Maybe she was wishing for the moon, but right now she needed a little wishing in her life.

"In the meantime, there's no harm in having the conversation," she whispered to herself as she slid out of the Jeep.

She walked inside. Battered tables and chairs filled the space. There was a counter at one end and a broken jukebox at the other. Nader, a sunburned man in his late fifties, had already claimed a table by the window. He had a beer in one hand and a chip in the other.

"Mackenzie," he called, waving her over. "What can I get you to drink?"

She sat down and tried to ignore the continued writhing in her stomach. "Nothing for me."

He frowned. "We're not having lunch?"

"I wanted to talk but you go ahead."

"Damned straight, I will," he said with a grin. "I've been looking forward to eating here since you called. At home, Jody's practically gone vegan." He shuddered. "I'm here for carnitas tacos with extra cheese. You sure you don't want anything?"

Their server, an attractive dark-haired woman, appeared.

"Mackenzie," she said with a smile. "So nice to see you."

"Hello, Orla. Could I have a Sprite, please?"

"Of course." Orla looked at Nader. "I heard what you want. How about a couple of chicken taquitos on the side?"

Nader grinned. "You're my kind of woman. I'll take 'em."

Mackenzie and Nader talked about what was going on in the area until her drink was delivered, then he leaned back in his chair and crossed his arms over his big belly.

"You called this meeting."

And here it was. She drew in a breath. "I'm thinking of making some changes in my career. I love Bel Après and everything I do there, but I'll never be more than an employee and I'm considering other options."

"Holy shit," he said, then gave her a wry smile. "Excuse my French. Are you serious? You'd leave Bel Après and come to work for me?"

"Maybe. I don't know. I'm at the exploring stage. You're always offering me a job and I didn't know if that was real or not."

"It's real. It's twenty times real." He glanced around and returned his attention to her before lowering his voice. "Mackenzie, I'd hire you in a hot second. Just tell me what you want. Your own label? Done. Complete control? You got it. I'll give you a percentage. Ten percent of the net. Hell, twenty. We could do great things together. We have vineyards all over. You could pick and choose the best grapes from Washington and

Oregon and make something great. Just tell me what it would take. Your own offices, of course. You pick the staff. I can get you a travel budget, a house, a pony. Anything."

His words overwhelmed her, making it hard for her to catch her breath.

"Probably not a pony," she managed.

"How about Mackenzie Dienes Presents on the label?"

She looked at him. "That would be nice."

He reached for a chip. "So why are you doing this? You really gonna leave Bel Après? You've been there for years. What, twelve? Fifteen?"

"Sixteen," she said. "Since I graduated from college and Rhys and I got married."

"Uh-huh. That's a hell of a long time. So what does Rhys think about all this? You making a change."

She avoided his gaze. "He's very supportive."

He studied her for a long time. "Mackenzie, what's going on?"

"Nothing," she hedged. "Like I said, I'm considering options."

"You're getting a divorce."

"What? No. How did you know?" She pressed her lips together. "I mean we are, but that's not the reason I want to leave Bel Après. I mean it's not the only reason I'm thinking about..." Why was she so bad at this? It was just a conversation. "I'm doing this all wrong."

Orla walked up balancing three plates. She set the tacos and taquitos in front of Nader and put a cheese quesadilla in front of her.

"You look hungry," Orla told her. "I can tell you

haven't been eating. You need food in your stomach, Mackenzie."

The act of kindness nearly made her cry. "Thank you," she whispered, inhaling the scent of cheese and tortilla and feeling her mouth water. "I am a little hungry."

"Good." Orla patted her shoulder, then left.

Nader picked up a taco. "When did this all happen?"

"In the last few weeks. It's not dramatic or anything. Rhys and I are friends and always will be. But it's made me think about other things. Like what to do about my career."

She picked up a slice of quesadilla and took a bite. The delicious combination of cheese and mild chilies reminded her she hadn't eaten in days. Suddenly she was starving.

While she gulped the first slice, Nader ate a couple of tacos, then wiped his hands on a paper napkin.

"I'm going to give you some advice," he said, picking up his beer. "Good advice, so you should listen. You helped me out a couple of years back when I was in a bad way."

She nodded, remembering how his crew of pickers had gotten waylaid by a bad bout of food poisoning in Oregon. He'd had acres of Syrah ready to be harvested and no way to do it with a limited team. Mackenzie had wanted to wait a couple of extra days on her own Syrah, so she'd sent her crew over to work for him. Barbara hadn't been pleased, but Mackenzie had felt taking care of a friend was more important than her mother-in-law's ire.

"I'm listening," she told him.

He leaned toward her. "Jesus H. You-know-what.

You can't be telling everyone that you're thinking of leaving Bel Après. Word will get back to Barbara before you want her to know and then you're going to be in big trouble."

"How do you know I haven't told her already?"

"Because I didn't see a mushroom cloud anywhere. She's not going to take it well."

Something Mackenzie knew to be true. "Maybe I won't leave."

"You've already made up your mind, kid. Now you're just looking for what's next. While I would give up two of my kids to have it be with me, we both know that's not gonna happen. You don't want to work for someone. You want your own thing. Man, if I had a few million dollars, I'd go into business with you pronto." He grinned. "But the good Lord blessed me only with a pretty face."

She smiled. "That's sweet, but I really haven't decided what I want to do."

"Maybe you can lie to yourself, but you can't lie to me." He lowered his voice. "Here's the advice. No talking to people the way you did to me. You get an NDA first. A nondisclosure agreement. You protect yourself. Find a lawyer. Find two lawyers. One for the divorce and one for the business. Make people earn your trust. Once you leave, you're not going to be under the protection of the Barcellona family. It's a big, bad world out there, kid. You've got to take care of yourself."

He was making sense, she thought. "Thank you. You're being very sweet to me."

"I know. I'm a saint." He sighed, then pointed at her food. "Eat up. I'm buying, so you might as well take advantage of me. Who knows—you might fall

and hit your head, then wake up and think you want
to come work for me."

She laughed. "I promise if I don't do my own thing,
I will give your offer very serious consideration."

"You do that."

Mackenzie spent the rest of the afternoon driving
around the area. She stopped in at a couple of small
wineries and tasted their wines, walked through an
open house for a condo by the golf course, and spent an
hour walking around a park, trying to get her thoughts
together. It was close to seven before she drove home.

She pulled into the garage, going slowly to make
sure she didn't ding the Jeep. Parking something this
big, rather than one of the golf carts, was still new
to her. While she was used to driving trucks for the
winery, parking those was more of a matter of pulling
off a dirt road than maneuvering in a confined area.

As she climbed out, she saw two carts by the back
door, which meant Rhys was home. She hurried inside.

"It's me," she called.

"In the kitchen."

She found him standing by the microwave, the scent
of a heating frozen dinner filling the air.

"What are you doing?" she asked.

"Making dinner."

"Why didn't you take what the chef left us?"

He grimaced. "I didn't want to bother cooking anything."

"You are such a guy." She picked up the package
and glanced at the picture of some kind of pasta. "You
hate these dinners. I only buy them for myself."

"I know but I was hungry."

She walked to the refrigerator and checked on the meal that had been left earlier that day. There were two pork chops, twice-baked potatoes and salad.

"Give me five minutes and I'll have dinner on the table," she said as she walked to the sink and washed her hands.

"You don't have to cook for me," Rhys said.

"I'm cooking for both of us. And brace yourself, I have things I want to talk about."

Twenty minutes later, they were seated across from each other. Despite having had a quesadilla only a few hours before, she was hungry—probably because she hadn't been eating much lately.

Rhys had set the table in the dining room, as he always did. He'd also put a folder and a pad of paper next to his place setting.

She picked up her water glass and pointed to the folder. "So you have things to discuss, as well?"

"This is more related to your topic."

"But you don't know what I'm going to say."

He smiled. "I have an idea our conversation is work related. It's not as if we're going to be planning a trip to Europe."

Which was true, of course, but hearing him say it made her sad. Some because they'd never planned a trip anywhere and some because he was such a good guy and she was going to miss him.

How many more dinners would they share? How many more times around this table? How many more nights would she sleep in this house? There was no way to know and no point in speculating, she told herself. She was moving forward. Perhaps reluctantly, but as long as she got where she needed to go, did the motivation matter?

She passed him the salad. "I'm ready to get started with the divorce. I've done a little research, and if we agree on a settlement, then we just have to fill out some paperwork and wait ninety days."

His dark gaze was steady. "You need to get a lawyer."

"I will."

"I'm not going to be an asshole, Mackenzie, but you have to protect yourself."

"I will," she repeated before taking a bite of her salad. Nader had told her the same thing. She was going to get a few names and start doing phone interviews to find someone to help with the divorce.

He opened the folder. "I've scheduled a valuation of the house. We'll have that by the end of next week. Your share of my trust is a flat amount, so there's no work there. It is what it is."

He flipped to another page. "We've banked most of our salaries. Neither of us spends a lot of money on living expenses. We get paid about the same, so I suggest we simply split the accounts in half. Your wine royalties are in a separate account, so that's easy. Those are yours."

She nodded, trying not to think how, in the end, she would have a boatload of money and no family. Not exactly a fair exchange.

He passed her a piece of paper. She saw the totals of various accounts added up and divided by two. When that number was combined with her royalties…

"It's the two million dollars you mentioned before,"

she said, raising her head and staring at him. "Is that number right?"

"It should be. I've checked everything."

"I'm not sure what to say."

The amount shouldn't be a surprise, but seeing it in writing made it real. Two million dollars. She couldn't begin to grasp what that meant.

She stood and collected their empty salad plates, then went into the kitchen. After pulling the pork chops and potatoes out of the oven, she plated them and carried their entrée into the dining room.

"You'll have options," he said when she was seated. "Put the money away, buy a winery. You can do anything."

Which should have sounded amazing, but instead left her feeling lost and unsettled.

"I spoke to Nader today."

Rhys cut into his pork chop. "Did his head explode at the thought of you working for him?"

"He was excited by the idea but didn't think it was going to happen. He gave me a lot of good advice."

"Do you want to get a job there?"

"I don't know." She'd never seriously thought about having her own winery. Oh, sure, there had been times when she'd wished she could do things differently, but that wasn't the same as having her own place. But over the last few days, she'd started accepting the concept as more of a possibility rather than a far-fetched dream.

"I've never run a business," she admitted. "I manage my crews and I'm responsible for the wine, but that's not the same as handling the finances, marketing and everything else. I've only done the parts I like."

"So take on a business partner." He waved his

fork. "You're the best winemaker in the state—anyone would be happy to go into business with you. The other person can provide the business expertise and you make the wine. Oh, and find someone with money—that way you can buy something good-sized and you won't need a loan."

Was it her imagination or was he pushing, ever so gently? She put down her fork and tested her theory with a teasing, "Plus if I go into business with someone else, you don't have to feel guilty anymore."

She expected (or hoped) for some denial. Instead Rhys looked away and shrugged.

"I'd feel better if you weren't going through everything alone."

And just like that, her appetite fled.

"I'm not. We're still friends and I have Stephanie."

"You two made up?"

"You knew we were fighting?"

He nodded. "She felt bad for what had happened and came over to yell at me for not keeping my dick in my pants." He grinned. "My sister has a way with words."

"I hope you told her the divorce wasn't your fault. We're both to blame."

"I did, but she wasn't listening. Back to the partnership, Mackenzie. It's something you need to consider."

"Right, because I have so many people like that on my contact list. How would I even find someone?" She remembered Nader's advice. "I can't just ask around."

"You know one person with all those qualifications. Bruno."

Mackenzie picked up her wineglass. Rhys was right. Bruno had money and plenty of business experience.

He'd even mentioned wanting to buy into a winery, but that was a long way from wanting her as a business partner.

"Talk to him," Rhys said. "If nothing else, get his take on things. He knows a lot of people and he knows what's happening in the industry. He could be a good resource."

And a way out for Rhys, she thought, trying not to feel bitter. "I'd need him to sign an NDA."

Rhys looked at her. "Someone's been doing her homework. You're right, you would want that."

"I can't take credit for the idea. Nader told me about it. He was very protective."

"Don't sound so surprised. You're well liked and respected."

"Thank you," she murmured. "Everything is happening so fast. I'm having trouble keeping up."

"Technically nothing has happened," he pointed out. "We're just talking."

"It's more than that. We're getting a divorce. That's real. And once that happens, I need to move on with the rest of my life."

"I'll say it again. You can stay at Bel Après for as long as you want. My mom won't care about our marriage."

She drew in a breath, bracing herself to speak the truth that she'd been avoiding. "I can't continue working here. Not just because of the divorce, but for a lot of other reasons. I need to do something else."

"Buy a winery?"

"I don't know. Maybe." Because going to work for someone else was just more of the same, and wasn't she tired of that?

Maybe Rhys *was* pushing her, but that didn't mean his advice wasn't sound. Especially about Bruno. She'd always respected him, and what she knew about him, she liked. If nothing else, she knew he would give her honest advice.

"You're right about talking to Bruno. I'll get that set up right away."

He smiled at her. "You're going to do great."

"I could fall on my butt."

"It's never going to happen. You're too good and you work too hard."

She hoped he was right about that. Since graduating college, she'd only ever had one job for one company and that was a family business. Did she even know what the real world was like?

Not that it mattered, she told herself, because she was about to find out.

eleven

Barbara reviewed the stack of checks in front of her. Lori handled the day-to-day bills, but every quarter, Barbara insisted on a review of all payments. There were also larger checks that she signed herself, such as the property tax payment and the royalty checks to Mackenzie.

"You're sure these are right?" she asked automatically, not bothering to look at Lori seated on the opposite side of the desk.

"Yes."

The review complete, Barbara signed the checks. She lingered over the one to Mackenzie, telling herself not to feel bitter about the money. For every dollar her daughter-in-law made, Bel Après made four, so that was a win. Still, she shouldn't have taken the bet, she thought, feeling mildly resentful.

"Knock!"

She looked up and saw Catherine standing in the doorway to her large office. As always, the sight of her youngest made her tense. Just the outfit alone—a hideous, shapeless dress with giant printed flowers—was enough to make her wince.

Catherine had so much promise. She was smart and creative. If she'd shown the slightest bit of interest, Barbara would have been thrilled to teach her about the business. She suspected that of all her children, Catherine was the one with the gift for winemaking. But like Stephanie, Catherine hadn't wanted anything to do with Bel Après. Instead she played with paints and clay, claiming art was her destiny.

"I wanted to let you two know I left baskets of blueberries in your kitchen."

Barbara took off her reading glasses. "There's a perfectly good farmer's market not three miles from the house. Why do you waste your time on that ridiculous garden?"

Catherine smiled. "Mom, given how much you love the vineyards, I would think you would be pleased that I want to grow something."

"The vineyards serve a purpose."

"So does my garden. It's important for my children to understand where things come from. There's magic in planting a seed and watching it become a carrot or a blueberry. Mother Earth is a great blessing to us, and we should respect that."

For the millionth time, Barbara wondered where she'd gone wrong with her youngest. She'd never been dropped on her head, so there wasn't an injury to blame.

Jaguar was far more grounded—he worked for a farm-equipment repair company. If it was big and had an engine, he could fix it. Barbara could respect his abilities and his work ethic. She might question his taste in women, but he was basically a good man. Honest and steady. But Catherine was another matter.

"I'll make some muffins," Lori said. "We can freeze them."

"How delightful," Barbara murmured. "Was there anything else?"

"That's all I have, Barbara. Enjoy the berries."

With that, Catherine left. Barbara shook her head. That girl. But aside from her youngest, she had to admit everything else was going very well, especially with Bel Après.

"Your father would be proud of what we've accomplished," she said aloud.

Lori looked slightly startled, then nodded. "He would. The winery has grown so much. You've done a great job, Mom."

"Thank you. I believe you're right. Now, what's next?"

One quick trip to Seattle and a five-thousand-dollar retainer later, Mackenzie had a divorce lawyer. Ramona Spencer had walked her through the process and agreed that if she and Rhys could come to terms on the settlement, it would be easier for everyone. But, her lawyer had warned her, people got weird about money, so she shouldn't get her hopes up that there wasn't going to be a hiccup somewhere. The postnup agreement would help, but divorces could be tricky.

Mackenzie had tried to explain that Rhys was a really great guy and that they'd already talked everything through, but Ramona's pitying look had stopped her midsentence. She'd returned home with a stack of paperwork to fill out and a list of online articles about how the divorce would proceed. She'd left Ramona's contact info with Rhys so he could share his lawyer's information with her and they could get the divorce started.

If she thought about the divorce as if it were a project, she was fine. It was only when she allowed herself to realize that it was actually the death of her marriage that she had a difficult time. Adding to the stress was the fact that Barbara didn't know and Mackenzie didn't want to tell her. While she thought of Barbara as a surrogate mother, she wasn't sure their relationship was up to the strain of a divorce—especially if Mackenzie decided to also leave Bel Après.

And it was a big if. Her head told her staying wasn't an option, but her heart wasn't ready to walk away from her home, her family and her life. But staying meant surrendering to a paycheck every two weeks and nothing else. If she had the ability to make her dream come true, shouldn't she go for it?

Fortunately for her scattered mind, it was midsummer and there was less for her to do at work. She continued to monitor the vineyards. She'd completed a barrel tasting a couple of days ago and had reported her results to Barbara. Facing her mother-in-law wasn't easy, but Mackenzie had tried to act as normal as possible and Barbara hadn't seemed to sense anything was wrong.

Mackenzie drove to the house and went into her small office. After booting up her laptop, she created a file for the divorce, then downloaded the files her lawyer had sent her. After scanning them, she saved them, then opened a separate folder—this one on Bruno.

She'd started researching him after Rhys had mentioned him as a possible business partner. At this point she knew about as much as she could for $49.95. He was single, wealthy and successful. There weren't any bankruptcies, liens or pending lawsuits. He'd never been arrested. He owned several properties—some houses, some commercial. His private jet was leased.

On paper he seemed like someone she would be comfortable doing business with. But real life was different. Messier. Or maybe her hesitation was more about being scared.

She looked from the screen to her phone and back, then swore softly as she picked up her phone and searched her contact list, before pushing the button to call the number. He answered on the second ring.

"Hello?"

"Hi, Bruno. It's Mackenzie."

He was silent for a second. "How nice to hear from you. Surprising but nice."

She heard the smile in his voice and smiled in return. "Yes, I know. I don't usually call." Actually she never had before. She cleared her throat. "I was wondering if maybe the next time you're in town we could talk. Away from the winery. And if you could not say anything to anyone, well, that would be great."

She closed her eyes and thought that she should have really thought the conversation through before getting in touch with him.

"It's not bad," she added quickly. "It's a, um, business thing." She paused, not sure if she should mention an NDA or not. How exactly did people work that into the conversation? And speaking of an NDA, where on earth was she going to get one? Could she just find one online?

"I'm here right now," he said. "I can meet you in an hour."

"Oh. That's great. Thank you. I'm not sure where would be a good place. I don't want to be seen with you." She groaned. "Sorry. That came out wrong. It's not just you. I don't want us to be seen together." *Crap!* "I'm saying this all wrong."

He chuckled. "Now I'm intrigued. Let's meet at my hotel. We'll have privacy in my room. And before you start to freak out, I have a suite. We'll be in the living room. I'm not trying to lure you anywhere."

"I'm not worried about that," she told him. She so wasn't the "lure" type. "Where are you staying?"

She expected him to mention the Marcus Whitman Hotel or one of the upscale B and Bs, but instead he said, "I'm at the Marriott Courtyard."

"Really?"

"You sound surprised. I like the hotel. Summer is busy and sometimes it's hard to get a room, so I rent one for July and August. They take good care of me here." He gave her the room number.

"A man of surprises. I will see you at the Marriot Courtyard in an hour."

"Looking forward to it."

He hung up. Mackenzie did the same, then wondered what she'd gotten herself into. Maybe she was taking on too much. Once the divorce was final, she could think about making other changes. Like in a year or two. If she left now, she would miss harvest. She loved harvest. Without her, what would happen to all her grapes? They needed her.

She rested her arms on the desk and her head on

her arms and told herself to either grow a pair or accept she was stuck at Bel Après forever.

As soon as the thought formed, she straightened. *Stuck*, she thought in surprise. Was that how she felt? And if it was, then doing something about it was the only option.

Feeling like a third-rate actress in a high school production of a mystery play, Mackenzie drove to the hotel and parked. Nerves battled with fear and apprehension. She had no idea what she was doing and yet here she was—doing it. Whatever "it" was.

Talking, she told herself as she walked inside and headed for the elevators. They were going to be talking. She would ask for information and hopefully he would give it to her. Then she would know more than she had before.

After exiting on the top floor, she followed the room numbers to his, then knocked.

"Mackenzie," he said, as he opened the door.

"Hi."

He stepped back to let her in.

She had a brief impression of a sitting area, a small table and chairs, and a closed door leading to what she would guess was the bedroom.

This was so weird, she thought as she sat at the table. Bruno settled across from her, his expression curious, his posture relaxed. It was only then that she realized he was in suit pants and a dress shirt, while she had on jeans and a T-shirt. No doubt there was mud on her boots, and she wasn't sure she'd combed her hair even once since getting up that morning. Maybe she should start paying more attention to her wardrobe, she thought glumly. Dressing up for meetings. Only she hadn't known there was going to be a meeting and Bruno had met her dozens of times. She knew she was very—

"Mackenzie?"

She jerked her attention back to the room. "Sorry. I'm a little scattered."

He nodded politely.

She considered how to start, then remembered that she was supposed to have an NDA for him to sign. She really was going to have to get one of those.

"Can I have your word that what we're about to talk about remains confidential?"

One eyebrow rose. "Of course."

"Like NDA confidential?"

"You have my word, Mackenzie. Nothing you tell me will leave this room."

"Thank you." She hesitated. "I'm leaving Bel Après."

She spoke without thinking, then realized what she'd said. Her plan had been to tell him about the divorce, but apparently that was not what was most on her mind.

"You look shocked," he said mildly. "Did you just surprise yourself?"

"I did. What I meant to say was that Rhys and I are getting a divorce and that I was thinking about leaving, but maybe it's more than that." She pressed a hand to her chest and tried to relax. "Assuming I do leave, I don't know what to do with my career. I keep coming back to having my own place. I have all these ideas."

She paused. "Everyone has ideas, of course, but I think mine are pretty grounded. I know how to make good wine. I have some money, so buying a place is an option, only I don't want to do all the business stuff."

She met his steady gaze. "Bel Après is all I know, so the whole thing is scary, but it's exciting, too. You're the most successful person I know, so I thought maybe you could give me some advice." She stopped there, not sure how to mention the potential partnership thing. Asking him about that seemed presumptuous on her part.

"What do you want in a winery?" he asked.

"I haven't really thought about it."

"That's not true. You've been thinking about it your whole life. Tell me."

She closed her eyes and tried to imagine the perfect place. "Lots of land. More land than I would need at the beginning. Good vines. Healthy and strong. I want something established, but not so defined that there isn't room to play, you know? I have techniques I want to try. Wine can be trendy. At the same time, classic is wonderful and I wouldn't want to lose that. I want to make something great."

"So you're smart to think about buying an established vineyard. Building one from the ground up would take years and millions of dollars."

"I only have two million." Only. She tried not to laugh at the ridiculousness of the statement.

"Where have you looked?"

"I haven't. I don't know where to start and I haven't told Barbara anything, so there's that. Rhys knows. He's the one who said I should talk to you."

"Would you consider taking on a partner?"

Oh, so that was how it was done. He made it look easy. "I would. I'd want someone who would handle the business end of things, including marketing. I want to be left alone to do what I do."

"Would you consider going into business with me?"

She felt her eyes widen. "You'd want to do that with me?"

He smiled. "Mackenzie, you're the most talented winemaker I've ever met. You're smart, you're intuitive and you work hard. You create magic. Yes, I'd very much like to go into business with you."

"That would be great. Sure. How would it happen?"

"First I'd want you to really think about it. This is a big deal. Everything would be different. We'd be fifty-fifty partners. You'd put in your two million and your talent, and I'd front the other money. I'm thinking about six million."

She held in a gasp. Eight million dollars in total? For that, couldn't they buy a small state?

"That would allow us to purchase something we could work with," he continued. "Something in the area, because you know the land here."

"Who would run the business?"

"I would."

"But you don't live here."

"I'm looking to settle somewhere," he told her. "If we did this, I'd stay here, in town."

"But we're so small."

The smile returned. "I'd adjust. Tell me what you're thinking. I'm not asking for a commitment, just if you can see yourself saying maybe."

"I'm very maybe."

"Good. Then I know a winery that might be coming up for sale. A winery that would meet all our criteria."

Did they have criteria? "Okay, which one?"

"Painted Moon."

She nearly came out of her seat. "Herman is going to sell Painted Moon?" She supposed it shouldn't be a surprise—he was in his eighties and his kids had never wanted anything to do with the business, but still.

"It's amazing land," she said. "Not just the acres on Red Mountain but the rest of it. Although the Red Mountain land is perfect. At the base, so it has centuries of runoff. All those nutrients. His cabs are incredible. I was sorry when he reduced wine production and started selling the grapes instead. I wonder what his library is like. It could be tens of thousands of bottles. He always cellared well. I'd want to know what's contracted from the harvest. We'd want to keep as many tons as possible because I can work with almost anything and—"

She realized she was doing all the talking. "Too enthusiastic?"

He laughed. "No. You're the perfect amount of enthused. He has wine in barrels, by the way. We'll have to sell that."

"Is it any good?"

"You'll have to tell me."

"He hasn't really been selling any retail and I don't think he has a wine club," she said. "It could be difficult to get distribution on finished wine." They would need to sell it regardless, she thought. Depending on the size of the barrels, they were talking thousands of gallons, which translated into hundreds of thousands of dollars.

"I already have that figured out," Bruno told her. "Give me a high-quality blend and I have a waiting customer."

"Who?"

"It's more a *where*. I know a distributor in China. They want great wine that's exclusive."

"Then I can make it great. We might have to buy from other wineries, but with the right blending, I can do it. Herman knows how to make wine."

Bruno nodded. "Want me to make a call and set up an appointment for us to talk to Herman?"

Her head was spinning, but she liked the sensation. "Yes, please."

"I'll also have my attorney draw up a preliminary agreement for you to consider. You're going to need to have your lawyer look at it. Run it by Rhys, as well."

Another lawyer? "I don't suppose it's something my divorce lawyer could handle."

"No. You need someone who understands contracts."

She nodded. "Why did Rhys give me your name as a potential partner?"

"I've talked to him about buying something. I wanted his advice." He rose. "We need to keep this quiet, Mackenzie. Rhys can know but no one else."

"I agree. I won't say anything. Not even to Stephanie."

He held out his hand. "Then we're moving forward with this?"

She, stood, shook his hand and smiled. "Is this like a gentleman's agreement?"

"It is."

She laughed. "Painted Moon. I can't tell you how excited I am. Let me know when we can go talk to Herman. I can't wait to taste what he has in the barrels and tour the vineyards."

"I'll get in touch with him today, then call you."

"Thanks."

She stepped out into the hallway and forced herself to walk normally to the elevator when what she wanted to do was dance and skip and spin. Painted Moon! There were so many possibilities. She knew the vineyards Herman owned and the quality of the grapes. There was so much potential, so much she could make happen. Between now and when she heard from Bruno, she was going to keep positive thoughts and try not to smile too much. Bruno was right—no one could know what they were considering. But she knew—and for now that was plenty.

twelve

Stephanie pulled into the parking lot of the restaurant. Even as she turned off her car engine, she thought about simply going home instead. She wasn't up for dinner out, but Kyle had caught her at a weak moment, and his claim that he was interested in dinner and not sex had reassured her. Not that she was worried about giving in to him. She was still dealing with the aftermath of her bad reaction to Mackenzie telling her about the divorce. While she'd made up with her sister-in-law, she was shocked about her behavior, and doing the wild thing was not on her radar.

She got out of the car. She'd put on makeup, she might as well have a nice meal. Maybe hanging out with Kyle would take her mind off things. He was easy company, she reminded herself.

She gave her name to the hostess and was shown back to a corner table. Kyle smiled and rose as she approached.

"Hey, beautiful."

The silly greeting made her smile in return. "Hardly,"

she said, leaning in and kissing his cheek. "Although you look good."

He did, as always. Well-groomed, classically handsome with blond hair and blue eyes. There was a reason he was successful on TV and it wasn't just his love of sports. Women adored him—they always had. Sadly for their marriage, he'd adored them right back.

"Just so we're clear," she said, "I meant what I said on the phone. There will be no seducing."

He pressed a hand to his chest. "You wound me. I said just dinner and I meant it."

She eyed him suspiciously. "Really? Because Seattle is about a six-hour drive."

"I was in Pullman," he told her. "I had an interview with one of the football coaches."

"So I'm a convenient stop on your way home." The news was reassuring.

She looked around the trendy bistro. "I haven't been here in forever. The food is really good, as is the wine list. Sadly I drove, so only a glass for me."

"We'll get a bottle. If you have too much to drink, you can text Avery to come get you. Your car will be safe in the parking lot."

"What about you?"

"I'm staying at a hotel nearby. Avery and I are having brunch in the morning."

"You are? She never said anything to me." Great. First she'd been a horrible friend and now she and her daughter weren't communicating at all.

"Stop," he said gently. "Whatever you're thinking, it's wrong. I texted her ten minutes ago and set up brunch. I waited until I knew I had a room in town."

"Oh. That's better."

He gave her best smile. "Why do you always go to the bad place?"

"You can't know that's what I was thinking."

He raised his eyebrows but didn't speak. She sighed.

"Fine. I was thinking she and I never communicate anymore, except when we fight. Did she tell you I'm keeping her from the love of her life?"

"She mentioned you were being difficult about all the summer parties she's been invited to."

"I'm worried about her sleeping with Alexander. She's too young and he's going to break her heart."

"You're a good mom."

"I wish."

Their server appeared and took their drink orders. Stephanie decided to take Kyle up on his suggestion about Avery picking her up and ordered a cocktail. He did the same.

When they were alone again, she said, "Carson's having a good time at baseball camp. His ERA is fantastic."

"Down a full point from last year. And his hitting is getting better."

"He gets his athletic ability from you," she admitted.

"I want to take credit, but I think our son is just a quirk of nature. No one on my side is as gifted as he is."

She smiled. "Maybe he'll get a multimillion-dollar contract and buy us each a house."

"We both already have a house."

"I wouldn't mind one a little farther from my mother."

"You could move back to Seattle."

She wrinkled her nose. "And do what? My skill set is very limited."

"Is that what you've been upset about?"

She stared at him. "How do you know I've been upset?"

"Avery told me there was something going on."

"I'm amazed she noticed. So that's why you wanted to have dinner? You're checking up on me?" She wasn't sure how she felt about that.

"Not checking up. I'm concerned. You're my kids' mother and we've always been friends." He leaned toward her. "Tell me what's going on, Steph. I want to help."

She debated whether or not she could trust him. "You have to keep it to yourself."

He made an X over his heart. "Scout's honor. Tell me."

She explained about Mackenzie and Rhys. "I was so shocked," she admitted. "I didn't handle it well, at all. I yelled at her for changing everything, because I didn't want my life upset." She covered her face with her hands. "I was a terrible friend and I'm so embarrassed and ashamed of how I behaved. I should have been supportive and I wasn't."

"You're being too hard on yourself."

"Oh, please. I completely let her down."

"Did you go back and apologize?"

"Yes."

"Then you're fine. You made a mistake and you corrected it. Of course it was a shock. Rhys and Mackenzie have been together since you were in college. Having them split up screws with the family dynamic."

Their server appeared with their drinks. He had a

whiskey and soda while she'd chosen a margarita on the rocks.

"I'm still beating myself up about all of it," she told him.

"Is that your way of distracting yourself from what's actually happening? You have to be sad about the divorce."

She glared at him. "Where do you get off being so insightful? Stop it right now."

He grinned. "I can't help it, Steph. Sometimes I'm impressive. Admit it."

"Sometimes," she grumbled, then sighed. "Am I using guilt to protect myself from what's really going on with them? Maybe. I don't know. It makes me sad. Plus I had no idea they were unhappy."

"You're kidding. How could you not know? They never acted like a couple. They didn't talk to each other or touch or even sit together at meals."

"Why didn't I see it?"

"You were too close. I came in every now and then so it was easier to figure out the pattern. I'm not saying they hate each other, but they weren't a couple."

"So you're not surprised about the divorce?"

He shook his head. "Not really. She should go out on her own." He sipped his drink. "Which leaves you screwed. You're trying to get up the courage to find another job and suddenly Mackenzie snaps up the only chance to leave."

All of which sounded sensible in her head, but ridiculous when he said it.

"There's not just one chance to get away," she said defensively. "It's not like the last seat on a plane. I could still leave if I wanted."

He raised his eyebrows. "You're saying it but I doubt you believe it."

She deflated. "I don't. As soon as she told me, I felt like my only chance to escape had been stolen from me. I'm so weak."

"You're not weak, you just don't know what you want. You have a sweet deal. You live in a great house that you own, your kids are happy, you have family nearby. Sure, a part of you wants more—a job you like that challenges you—but there's a price for that. Why rock the boat?"

She took a gulp of her margarita. "You're saying I'm spineless."

"I'm saying you're comfortable. That makes it hard to do the work that change requires."

He was telling the truth but she sure didn't like what it said about her.

"I need to be a better person," she grumbled.

"You need to decide what you really want."

"I went on an interview. Sort of." She told him about the meeting with the twins. By the end of the story, he was laughing.

"So are they having sex?"

"Yuck, they're brother and sister, so don't even think that. And why do you have to go right to the sex question?"

"I'm a guy. It's what we do."

"Well, stop it. Sex isn't the answer to everything. Look at us. We're doing much better now that we've stopped having sex."

"Speak for yourself."

She ignored the comment. No way she was stepping back into that mess. Sleeping with Kyle was nothing but a distraction. Sort of like her semi-great life. She was just comfortable enough to not be motivated to find something better.

"I need goals," she said firmly. "And a plan to achieve them."

He leaned close and smiled at her. "How about we start with a second round of drinks? Then we'll conquer the world."

She raised her glass. "I'm in."

Mackenzie felt like she was four and it was the night before Christmas. She was excited and happy and filled with anticipation and possibilities. In her head she knew there were about a thousand steps to be taken between where she and Bruno were and buying Painted Moon, but just thinking about what could happen made her so happy.

Over the next couple of days, she did her job at Bel Après, but all her downtime was spent thinking about what she would want to do differently if given the chance. She had so many ideas, so many things she wanted to try and change and expand.

Rather than talk to Rhys, she contacted her divorce lawyer for a recommendation for a business lawyer who could help with the partnership agreement. A two-hour phone call and yet another check for five thousand dollars later, she officially had her second lawyer on retainer. Along with the contract and the receipt for the check, the lawyer had sent her a list of articles to read on starting a partnership, including a couple on pitfalls and mistakes the novice could make. He'd included an NDA that she could print out as needed and get people to sign.

As she'd promised Bruno, she didn't say anything to anyone—not Rhys or Stephanie, although it was difficult to keep quiet. At times she thought she would burst from the gloriousness of the secret.

She drove back from inspecting the vineyards in Oregon. Midday, midweek meant the traffic wasn't bad and she got to her office in time for a late lunch. The chef had left quinoa salads with a peanut dressing, which sounded delicious. Mackenzie was starving—she'd skipped breakfast to get an early start on her day.

As she poured the small container of dressing over the vegetables, grains and chickpeas, she wondered if Rhys had slipped away for a fast-food lunch. He refused to eat quinoa on principle. Something about being a guy and standing in solidarity against grain oppression.

She was still smiling about that when he walked into the upstairs break room, a large envelope in his hand.

"I was just thinking about you," she said with a laugh and waved her salad. "Did you eat yours?"

Instead of grinning back at her, he half turned away. "I went out for lunch."

"Rhys? What's wrong?"

He tensed, then faced her again, his expression serious. "Nothing. Did you look at the Seven Hills vineyards?"

"Yes. The irrigation is working fine and I'm loving how the grapes are ripening. We're going to have a good year."

He made a motion toward the hallway with his hand. A man she didn't know walked in. "Mackenzie Dienes?"

She looked from the stranger to Rhys and back. "Yes."

"I didn't know how to do this," Rhys told her. "I didn't know the right time or—"

The other man took the envelope Rhys held and offered it to her. She instinctively took it.

"You've been served," the man said and walked out.

Mackenzie stared at Rhys. "I don't understand."

He hunched a little. "I know. It's the divorce papers."

She nearly dropped the envelope as the meaning of his words sunk in. Divorce papers? Yes, she'd seen a lawyer, and this was where they were headed, but she hadn't thought, hadn't expected…

All the happiness of the previous days evaporated, taking her upbeat mood with it. Her body seemed to deflate, as if she were getting smaller and smaller and would, in a very short time, disappear.

Slowly, carefully, she put the large envelope on the counter and fought against the need to scrub her hands until every trace of the paper had been erased.

"Mackenzie?"

"It's okay," she said, not looking at him and hoping she sounded less upset than she was. "We talked about this. It's the next step, right?" She faked a smile as she finally turned to him. "I'll look these over, then get a copy to Ramona to review."

His gaze searched her face. "Are you all right?"

"Perfectly fine. Don't worry." She drew in a breath and went for perky. "At some point we're going to have to come up with a plan on who we're telling and when. I guess that's on me, with Barbara and all. I'm thinking we could mention the divorce first and leave the other stuff until I know what I'm doing. Just not today. If it could not be today, that would be great. We have the family dinner tomorrow, but we can pretend for that, can't we? Unless you're going to bring someone, in which case—"

He put his hands on her upper arms. "Mackenzie, stop talking."

"All right."

"I'm sorry," he told her. "I thought you were ready."

"I am," she lied.

"I hope that's true. I'm not trying to rush you."

The words were just right, but his actions belied the truth of them. Or maybe he really wasn't rushing, but instead was going at his speed, which was a lot closer to "get this over *now*" than hers was.

"We don't have to say anything to my family until you're ready. We'll be fine at the dinner, just like our living arrangements are working out for us."

He was right about that. They were still in the same house, living the lives they'd had before. How sad was it that getting a divorce had changed so little? And if that was true, why did she feel so awful inside?

"Thank you." She stepped back and forced herself to pick up the envelope. "Thanks for getting me these."

He watched her cautiously. "There's a tentative settlement agreement in there. It's what we talked about. I want to be fair."

"I appreciate that. I'll talk to Ramona."

He hesitated a second, then opened the break room door and left. Mackenzie glanced from the envelope to her salad. She picked up the latter and dropped it into the trash. On the way to her office, she swung by the bathroom and threw up the meager contents of her stomach. After rinsing out her mouth, she leaned against the cool tiles and told herself she wasn't going to cry. She couldn't—not without everyone wondering what was wrong. So from now until she could go home, she would have to pretend that everything was going to be all right. Even if she knew it wasn't.

Mackenzie stood in her closet, not sure what to wear to dinner. Every few weeks, Barbara called for a family dinner. Attendance was mandatory. Normally Mackenzie looked forward to the get-togethers as a chance to catch up with everyone and hang out with the people she loved most in the world. But not tonight—not when she and Rhys were working their way through a divorce and she was considering leaving Bel Après. Pretending normalcy under those circumstances was going to require a level of acting ability she was fairly sure she didn't possess.

Still, not going wasn't an option, so she studied the dresses hanging in her closet and hoped one of them would provide a little courage.

She settled on a simple sheath with a square neckline. The dark green fabric brought out the red in her hair. She stepped into a pair of nude pumps and returned to the bathroom, where she checked that her minimal makeup was all right, then walked downstairs.

Rhys, already showered and changed into dress pants and a long-sleeved shirt, was at his computer. He was typing and smiling. She was about to ask what he was doing when he looked up and saw her. His smile faded and his gaze darted away from her to the screen and back. If she had to pick an emotion from the look on his face, she would say he was feeling guilty. Why on earth—

Her stomach clenched as she realized he was doing something online with a woman who wasn't her. Probably just sending an email, but still.

"You look nice," he said. "We're not expected for another twenty minutes."

"I know. I thought I'd go see Stephanie first. I'll meet you there?"

"Sure." He glanced at the screen, then back at her. "Anything else?"

She thought about asking who he was online with but didn't. Whatever was happening wasn't her business. And if knowing he'd already moved on still shocked her, then that was her problem.

She walked the short distance to Stephanie's house and let herself inside.

"It's me," she called.

"In my office," her sister-in-law yelled back.

Mackenzie walked down the short hallway and stepped into Stephanie's home office.

Stephanie had decorated her space with pale walls and brightly colored paintings. Open shelving displayed awards and certificates her children had earned, along with various art projects. A few drawings were framed—the primitive stick figures nestled up against professionally painted scenes.

Stephanie glanced up and smiled. "Hey, you. How's it going? I've stopped by to see you a few times, but you're never home these days."

"Sorry. I've been busy with different stuff." Mackenzie closed the door behind her and settled in a chair. "Rhys served me with divorce papers."

Stephanie's eyes filled with sympathy. "Are you okay with that or do I need to march over there and slap him really hard?"

"I'm okay. Sort of." She thought about the shock when he'd handed her the envelope. "I didn't know a person was actually served with the paperwork. I wasn't expecting it."

Stephanie closed her laptop. "You need to get mad at him. Anger gives you purpose."

"Four would tell you that's the wrong thing to say."

"Four lives in a world where woodland creatures help her dress every morning." Stephanie held up a hand. "That came out more bitchy than I mean, but you get my point. Divorce sucks, even if you both want it. I was crushed to end things with Kyle, and he'd been cheating on me for years. You commit yourself to someone when you get married and you assume it's going to last forever. Finding out that's not true isn't easy to deal with. There's a sense of failure, of loss. I was terrified, and I had a place to run to. You're going to be striking out on your own. It's got to be confusing and hard to think about and I'm sure you feel lost. Then my stupid brother serves you with papers. Want me to beat him up?"

Mackenzie managed a smile. "Thank you, but no."

"I could do it, mostly because he would never hit me back. You okay?"

"Sometimes. Other times, like you said, I feel lost." She sighed. "I've been thinking about all the last times. Is this the last family dinner? The last time I'll put out the cookie flag, the last time I'll visit you here?" She blinked against burning in her eyes.

"You'll visit me here lots of times. We're going to

stay friends. If you try pulling back, I'll stalk you until you give in. We're friends. Forever friends. Don't you believe that?"

"I do, but I'm worried your mom will put you in a difficult situation. I don't want you to have to choose."

"She's a pain, but she's not totally unreasonable." Stephanie paused. "Well, she is, but not all the time. You and I are going to grow old together."

Mackenzie nodded. "I want that, but sometimes it's hard to see past what's happening right now. I'm losing everything I've felt anchored to. It's hard to just drift around."

"I'll be your anchor." Stephanie frowned. "Why does that sound like the title of a song?"

"I don't know. Maybe it is. Probably from the eighties. They had some great song titles back then."

"You were barely born in the eighties. How would you know?"

Mackenzie smiled. "I know things."

Stephanie laughed. "You're so weird." She glanced at the clock on the wall. "Okay, we need to leave now or we'll be late, and you know how my mom gets if someone is late."

They both rose and walked out together. When they reached the front door, Mackenzie paused. "Isn't Avery coming with us?"

"She went over before you got here. She likes hanging out with her grandmother, if you can believe it." Stephanie shuddered, then laughed.

Mackenzie didn't know what to say to that. She and Barbara had always gotten along, as well. Maybe because they weren't blood relatives. Mackenzie had been so grateful to have a mother figure in her life that

she'd been able to overlook the other woman's, um, id-
iosyncrasies. They also had the winery in common.
Each of them could talk about Bel Après for hours and
still have more to say.

They crossed the courtyard together and went
up the front stairs of the largest house. As Stephanie knocked once, then pushed open the door, Mackenzie couldn't help thinking again about the "lasts."
Was this the last time she would walk through the big
wooden door? The last time she would greet everyone
with smiles and hugs? Had she already lived through
the last Christmas, the last Easter, the last Summer
Solstice Party?

Sadness gripped her, making it hard to breathe.
Change was hard, but this was much more difficult
than she'd thought it would be. Her fears weren't about
the various holidays so much as wondering when she
would experience the last time she could say this was
her family. Because this was the only family she had
in the world, and when she and Rhys were divorced,
she would be completely on her own. And then who
would she be?

thirteen

Stephanie spent a couple of days watching Avery without seeming to watch her. Not an easy trick, considering Avery was a sixteen-year-old and, by nature, suspicious of her mother. But at the family dinner, Avery had overheard her asking Mackenzie if she was doing all right and had wanted to know what was wrong. Stephanie wondered if she'd done the right thing in telling the girl. Was Avery mature enough to handle the information?

Things seemed to go fine until Sunday morning when Stephanie knocked on her daughter's bedroom door. Whatever else was going on in their lives, she always made a big breakfast with whatever the kids wanted.

"Avery, sweetie, I'm going to make breakfast. What do you want? Pancakes and bacon? An omelet?"

"Nothing. Go away."

Normally the rude response would have made Stephanie bristle, but there was something in her daughter's tone that made her open the door and step inside.

Summer sunlight spilled into the room, illuminating the unmade bed and clothes tossed everywhere. But what actually caught her attention was the sight of her daughter curled up on the floor, in a far corner of the room.

Stephanie rushed to her, sinking down to her knees and reaching for her.

"What happened? Are you sick? Did someone hurt you?"

Avery pushed her away and sat up on her own. "I'm fine. Leave me alone." Tears poured down her cheeks as she spoke. Her eyes were red, her face pale. "I don't want to talk about it. Go away."

Stephanie ignored all that and pulled her daughter close. Avery resisted for a second, then sagged against her. Tears turned into sobs, shaking her body with their intensity.

Stephanie hung on, rubbing her back, waiting out the storm. She was fairly sure her daughter wasn't sick, which left heartache or something much worse. Rape crossed her mind, but she pushed the thought aside. She would wait to find out what was wrong before she freaked out.

After a few minutes, Avery straightened. "Alexander slept with Bettina. He said he had to because I wouldn't sleep with him so I can't be upset because it's my fault. That made me mad so I broke up with him. Then he got mad at me and said I'm a stupid, immature little girl and he's done wasting his time with me."

Instead of screaming and then getting in her car to

go beat up the boy in question, Stephanie forced herself to stay where she was.

"I'm sorry," she murmured. "Boys can be real jerks. You did the right thing. I'm so proud of you, sweetie. I know it hurts so much. I know you feel sick inside and you're questioning everything you said and did, but you are so strong."

Avery nodded, then grabbed a box of tissues from the desk. "I had to be, you know? I wasn't going to let him treat me the way you let Daddy treat you."

The statement was made so casually, in such a normal tone, that Stephanie didn't get it at first.

"What are you talking about?"

Avery wiped her face. "Dad's cheating. I've known, Mom, for a while now. About all the stuff he did."

She blew her nose. "I talked to him about it. He told me he'd been wrong and that I should never let a guy do to me what he did to you. That he made mistakes, but you suffered for them."

Stephanie was so incredibly grateful she was sitting on the floor—otherwise she would have collapsed in a heap. Shock and shame and horror swept through her.

"I never knew why you and Dad split up, but when I found out about the cheating, it made sense. I didn't tell Carson. He doesn't want to know about stuff like that." Avery's eyes filled with tears. "When Alexander told me what he did, I felt so awful. Like he'd betrayed everything we'd had, even as he tried to make it my fault. I knew then it was over, that I had to be strong. I wasn't going to do what you did and stick around."

The words were earnest and guileless, Stephanie thought, fighting the need to run as far and as fast as she could manage. Avery wasn't trying to hurt her—

she was explaining the situation from her point of view. Just like Stephanie didn't want to be like Barbara, Avery didn't want to be like her. It was the circle of life when it came to mothers and daughters.

But that didn't stop her from feeling as if her daughter had ripped out her heart with her bare hands and then torn it up into tiny pieces.

Avery surprised her by leaning against her. "I just wish it didn't hurt so much to be strong."

"You did the right thing. When it gets really bad, keep telling yourself that. I'm proud of you and you should be proud of yourself."

"Thanks."

"Want some pancakes and bacon?"

"Okay."

Stephanie forced a smile, then got to her feet. She had to hang on to the wall to make it back to the kitchen, and when she was there, she looked down at the floor, expecting to see a pool of her own blood. There was only the hardwood and a few crumbs. Nothing that indicated she'd been emotionally flayed open by the casual comments of her teenage daughter.

Guilt trailed Mackenzie her entire drive to Painted Moon. Ever since Bruno's call two days before, she'd been torn between wild excitement at the possibilities and fear and worry about making such a big change. The "should she or shouldn't she" question had filled her waking hours, but the moment she drove through the big open gates, the feeling was replaced with one of anticipation.

The winery had been established for two generations. Not the first vineyard in the valley, but close.

She drove by a couple of acres of vineyard that had been planted for show on her way up to what had been the tasting room. That big building was closed now. Herman had stopped bottling wine a few years back. Now he sold grapes and directly from the barrel.

She'd met the old guy dozens of times at various events. He was knowledgeable and always friendly, but she'd sensed his heart hadn't been in the business for a while.

As she parked next to a new Mercedes she would guess belonged to Bruno, she tried to slow her breathing. Whatever the outcome, just asking the questions would be good for her. She was open to moving on. While buying Painted Moon would be an incredible opportunity, she shouldn't get her hopes up. A whole lot could go wrong.

All of which was true, but didn't stop the fluttering in her chest as she got out of her Jeep. In the distance was the old farmhouse, set up on a rise that would overlook much of the property. The morning was warm, the sun bright.

She found Bruno and Herman talking. She shook hands with both.

Herman, a small man with gray hair and weathered skin, grinned at her. "Your business partner there already had me sign an NDA. I like that you're protecting yourself. If we do this, Barbara is going to want to set us all on fire, so you want to cover your backside, for sure."

The combination of visuals had her struggling to keep up, although his point about Barbara was a good one.

"We're still just exploring," she said. "Thank you for signing the NDA."

"Did I have a choice?" he asked with a chuckle. "All right, let's get started." He started walking at a brisk pace. "My children have no interest in the wine business. They want me to sell, and to be honest, I'm getting old enough that I see their point. Painted Moon is producing about eighty-five thousand gallons a year." He winked at Mackenzie. "More than Bel Après, missy."

That many gallons? She'd had no idea. "You're right, it is." It was substantially less than the bigger, well-known wineries, such as Ste. Michelle, which produced over two million gallons a year, but it was plenty for her to work with.

He led them into the barrel room. The heavy barrels stretched out in rows, vertically and horizontally.

"Most of this is sold," he said. "There are about twenty thousand gallons I meant to do something with, but haven't yet." His humor faded. "I don't taste as well as I used to." He pointed at her. "You could make something happen here. You have the gift."

"Thank you."

They walked over to one of the barrels. Herman collected glasses and a pitcher, then they tasted a few different wines. Mackenzie swirled the liquid in her mouth before spitting it out. There was potential here, she thought. She could do something with this.

"I have contracts for about half of this year's crop," Herman told them. "But only for this year. I've been thinking of selling for a while now and didn't want to tie up my assets."

They tasted more wine. She wasn't happy with the whites, but all the reds had real potential.

"I had the business valued a couple of years ago," Herman said as they moved down the rows. "A couple of guys came from Seattle and walked around with clipboards. I'm in the nine-five range."

"Nine million, five hundred thousand," Mackenzie said, trying not to faint.

"Yup."

She looked at Bruno, who seemed unconcerned.

They spent the better part of the day looking at the facilities and a couple of the vineyards. By four, Mackenzie was exhausted and her head hurt from all she'd tried to absorb. She and Bruno thanked Herman, then they drove back to his hotel and went up to his room.

"What did you think?" he asked after getting them each a bottle of water and sitting across from her at the table.

"It was a lot to take in," she said. "The land is incredible. I'd want to see the rest of it and I'm guessing you'd need to look at his books and stuff. Nine-five seems like a lot."

"It is. I think we'd settle closer to eight. What did you think about the wines?"

"The white is crap. Honestly it was so bad, I'd want to dump it."

Bruno winced. "Seriously?"

She smiled. "Yes, I'd want to, but I'm sure we could sell it to someone to bottle and distribute. The reds are great. They have plenty of fruit and tannin. They could be blended a lot of different ways. They're money in the barrel."

She leaned back in her chair. "How do you even start with something like that? We'd have to check all the deeds, look at the contracts, look at any liabilities. We have to confirm the water rights, because without them, we have nothing. All the equipment needs to be evaluated. The buildings themselves have to be inspected. What about liens and lawsuits and I don't know what else?"

Bruno smiled. "You've been doing your homework."

"It's all I can think about, when I'm not feeling guilty for considering leaving Bel Après."

"Is it still just a consideration?"

She thought about the divorce papers.

"No, it's not just a consideration," she said, reality hitting her in the gut. "But it makes me sad."

"You still want to move forward with this?"

"Is it possible?"

"Us buying a business together? Sure. I'm good with what we talked about. You put in your two million, I take care of the rest. We'll write up an agreement such that if we sell, I get a bigger cut of that. Until then, it's fifty-fifty. I run the business side and you run the winery. Painted Moon will be your vision." He finished his bottle of water. "You can have the house, if you want. It's not really my style. I'm thinking of buying a condo on the golf course."

"I'm interested," she said, "but it's a lot to take in. Plus I won't have my money until the divorce is final. That's three months from the day we file. What if we need the cash before then?"

"We'll work out a bridge loan."

"With a bank?"

His dark eyes glinted with amusement. "We'll keep it in the family."

Oh, sure, because he had an extra two million lying around. "How rich are you?" she asked before she could stop herself. "Sorry. Pretend I didn't ask that."

"There's something of a family fortune and I've done well on my own."

Must be nice, she thought. "So what happens now?"

"If you want to move forward, I'll draw up the partnership agreement with the terms we've agreed upon. You get your lawyer to look it over. Once that's signed, I'll get a team going on appraising Painted Moon. I'll have my finance people look over the books and you'll head the team that will be responsible for the vineyards and the winery. Once we know what we're talking about, we'll make an offer."

"Just like that?"

"Is there a reason to wait?"

"You're making it really easy," she said.

"I'm getting what I want. I have plenty of money, Mackenzie. What I don't have is your talent. You're the best and I want to work with you. Whatever I can do to make your decision easier is on my get-done list. Are you ready to move forward?"

He held out his hand. She thought about all that had happened in the past few weeks. Her life had changed in every way possible. If she wanted to keep her job at Bel Après, she could, but she wouldn't be part of the family anymore. Not after the divorce. Bruno was offering her the moon. She smiled. A painted moon, but a moon all the same.

"I'm in," she said, shaking his hand. "Let's do this."

Three days later, Mackenzie was drowning in paperwork. Her potential business partner hadn't wasted any time getting the process started. She already had a partnership agreement, a preliminary sales offer for

Herman and the first of what she would guess were going to be dozens of survey reports.

She'd emailed a copy of the partnership and purchase agreements to her business lawyer but was determined to review them herself. To that end, she had a stack of sticky notes and a legal pad next to her so she could figure out her questions as she went. To switch things up, she also had the divorce settlement to go through—oh, and in her spare time, a winery to run.

It was a lot to deal with, but also exciting. Lately she'd been waking up at four and reading for a couple of hours before starting her day job. After work, she rushed through dinner to spend several more hours in her office. At Bruno's suggestion, she'd purchased a small lockbox in which to keep all the paperwork—no doubt the smart thing to do, but it made her feel guilty every time she put all the various files away.

About seven, Rhys knocked on her half-open door. "Hi. I haven't seen you much in the past week or so. I thought I'd check in and find out how things are going."

He looked good, she thought with a twinge of sadness. Tall and strong. Steady. Rhys had always been steady. She didn't miss him romantically, but she regretted what had been lost.

She opened her desk drawer and pulled out a single sheet of paper. She slid a pen close and said, "Unless you want to talk weather and the divorce, you'll have to sign this first."

Her soon-to-be ex-husband stepped forward and scanned the NDA, then started to laugh. "Seriously?"

Her natural instinct was to tell him no, of course he didn't have to sign it. She trusted him—if he said he wouldn't tell anyone, he wouldn't. But her lawyer and Bruno had been very clear. Without an NDA, no one found out anything.

He grinned as he signed, then took the seat opposite her. "Someone's been giving you good advice."

"I hope so. Lawyers are expensive."

"But necessary. So what's going on?"

She drew in a breath. She and Rhys might be splitting up, but she respected his opinion. "We're looking at Painted Moon."

His eyebrows rose and he gave a low whistle. "Herman's property. That's a beauty. Great land. Quality, established vines. Make sure you confirm the water rights. No water, no business."

She smiled. "That's what I thought."

"Are you going to make an offer?"

"We're considering it." She held several papers. "My partnership agreement with Bruno. The lawyer's looking it over right now."

Rhys's humor faded. "I'd offer to read it, but that isn't my place anymore, is it?"

They looked at each other, then both turned away. She spoke first.

"Speaking of the divorce, I've gone over the settlement agreement and it seems okay. I'm waiting for a final approval from Ramona, but I don't anticipate any problems."

He shifted in his seat. "Once we file, it's ninety days until everything is final."

"Assuming we don't contest it."

He looked at her. "That would be like fighting. We never fight."

"I know." That was part of the problem. They hadn't

had the energy to fight about anything. And without that energy, there wasn't any passion or drive.

Their marriage had been like the conversation they were currently having. At this point in a breakup, other couples would be casting blame and throwing accusations like knives. Not them. They were sensible and rational. Logical. They were both moving on and soon everything they'd had would be a memory.

Somehow that realization was the worst thing of all. Shouldn't sixteen years together have left a few visible scars?

"We need to tell my mom about the divorce, Mackenzie," he said. "You can keep the rest of it from her for as long as you'd like, but letting her know about us splitting up should happen soon."

"I agree."

"I can do it."

He was giving her an easy out—because he was the kind of man who did that sort of thing.

"I'll tell her," she said slowly. "I have a meeting with her tomorrow. I'll give her the news then, both about the divorce and about me leaving."

Rhys winced. "So soon? What if it doesn't work out with Painted Moon?"

"Then Bruno and I will buy something else. I can't stay here anymore. I'm hoping to take you up on your offer to live in the house for a month or so, just to give me time to settle everything, but then I need to be gone."

Saying the words made them real, she thought. So far there had been only bits and pieces of reality. Or maybe that wasn't true. Maybe it had become real the second Rhys had looked at her and asked if their marriage was over.

"Do you want me to come with you?"

"I'll be all right. It should be me, Rhys. You know that."

He nodded slowly. "I'll be around if you need me."

"Or protection?" she asked, mostly joking.

"You can always hide behind me."

A sweet offer, but not one she could take advantage of, she told herself. At least not anymore.

fourteen

Mackenzie tried to tell herself she wasn't nervous about her meeting with Barbara, only she knew she was lying. How could she not be? She'd been a part of Bel Après since college—basically her entire adult life. She didn't know anything else. Was she wrong to want more?

Trying to ignore the question, she prowled the barrel room, hoping to distract herself but unable to do anything but check the large clock on the wall and see if it was close enough to eight thirty for her to go into the main building and see Barbara in her office.

"I'm doing the right thing," she whispered to herself. "She'll understand."

Barbara, while occasionally difficult, had always been warm and affectionate toward Mackenzie. She remembered her first time on the property—when Barbara had invited her on a tour of the winery. They'd driven to the closest vineyards and Barbara had talked about her hopes and dreams for the business. They'd walked the barrel room and discussed the differences between a good wine and a great one. They had talked for so long that Rhys had finally come looking for them.

Over the next couple of years, Barbara had become like a second mother. She was the one Mackenzie turned to for advice. She'd been the one to give Mackenzie away when she'd married Rhys, joking that she was happy to perform the duty because she was getting Mackenzie right back. At social events, Barbara introduced her as her daughter of the heart—a title that had both embarrassed and warmed Mackenzie.

Now she looked around at the familiar room and wondered if she was making a mistake. Should she stay here instead of leaving? But she already knew the answer, and the truth was, she'd already decided what she wanted. As for Barbara and their closeness, perhaps that, too, had faded with time. Gone were the long walks in the vineyards and the late-afternoon talks that spilled into the evening. These days she saw her mother-in-law during their weekly meetings, at family dinners and in passing.

She walked to the office building, took the stairs two at a time and entered Barbara's office.

Her mother-in-law, dressed perfectly in a deep blue suit and pearls, smiled at her.

"You're right on time, as always." Barbara motioned to a chair. "I feel as if I haven't seen you in ages."

The warm tone and welcoming words made Mackenzie swallow hard. She closed the door and took a seat.

"I've been busy," she said. "There's a lot going on." She paused, not sure how to begin.

Barbara leaned toward her. "Oh, dear. Something's

wrong. I can see it in your eyes. Tell me what it is. We don't have a pest problem anywhere, do we? I know the new fencing has made a difference with the deer. I hope it's not a bear getting into the grapes. Bears can do so much damage."

"It's not about the winery," Mackenzie told her, twisting her fingers together, trying to ignore the sense of foreboding. "It's about Rhys and me. We're getting a divorce."

Barbara's concerned expression didn't change. "Are you? I'm sorry to hear that. I thought you were happy together."

"We're not and we haven't been for a while. It's a mutual decision. It's sad for both of us."

"Of course it is." Barbara leaned back in her chair. "You must be disappointed. Do you want me to talk to Rhys for you?"

"What? No. We're actually getting along." She managed a slight smile. "We're being very sensible as we uncouple."

Barbara nodded but otherwise didn't seem to react. Was she not surprised or did the marriage not matter? Mackenzie wasn't sure which.

Barbara sighed. "However well you're getting along, the situation must be painful. I'm sorry, my dear. Let me know if I can help in any way. And to be clear, nothing between us changes. Your job isn't in jeopardy at all. I hope you know that already, but I want to say it anyway. You're a significant part of Bel Après. I'll miss having you as my daughter-in-law, but you'll always have a place here." She smiled. "We'd be lost without you."

"Thank you for saying that." Mackenzie's stomach

flipped over and her chest got tight. "The thing is, I wanted to talk about that, too."

Barbara's body stiffened as her expression tightened. "I don't know what that means. Talk about what?"

"My future."

"Which is here, where you belong. I won't hear otherwise. You need to be here, Mackenzie. You and I are Bel Après. You're the winemaker. Together we create magic." She gave a high-pitched laugh. "Thinking of being anywhere else is madness."

"I can't stay," she murmured, wishing she could run and knowing she had to face whatever happened.

"Of course you can." Barbara's voice sharpened. "You must. This is your home. A divorce doesn't change that. Are you concerned about the house? We can have another one built. You can't walk away from this. We're part of your family, your history. Without us, what would you have?"

Her gaze narrowed. "Are you going to work for someone else? You can't. I forbid it."

"How can you forbid it? You don't own me." Irritation replaced worry.

"You have a noncompete contract with the winery."

"I don't have a contract with you at all. I never signed one."

Barbara rose to her feet. "You're wrong. Everyone signs one. I would have made sure of it. Don't you dare think about working for anyone else. If you try, I'll ruin you."

If the words were intended to intimidate, they weren't working. The madder Barbara got, the more determined Mackenzie felt.

"It doesn't have to be like this," she said, careful to keep her voice calm and reasonable. "I don't want to fight with you."

"Too late for that. You're leaving? Is that your point? Well, you can forget that. You're fired! Do you hear me? You're fired. I should never have trusted you. Never. I bought into that poor orphan-girl routine and the whole time you were planning to betray me."

Mackenzie stared at her, unable to believe what was happening. She'd always known the conversation was going to be difficult, but she hadn't expected anything like this. The ridiculous accusations bombarded her from all sides, making her want to find a way to protect herself.

"Barbara, please," she began.

Her mother-in-law cut her off. "Don't try changing your mind now. We're done."

"Barbara, I've been a part of this family for sixteen years. Surely we can talk about this." There had to be some middle ground where they could remember how much they meant to each other.

"Get out!"

Mackenzie realized there was no point in trying to reason with her. Maybe later they could have a real conversation. She walked out the door and down the hall, not sure what to do now.

She felt hollow and cold, and a little bit unsteady. She'd been fired. Should she empty her desk? Just leave? She had the thought that she should have let Rhys come with her. Even if he'd just waited in his office, she would have known he was close by.

Only he wasn't her husband anymore, she reminded herself, suddenly fighting tears.

"Bitch."

She turned and saw Lori glaring at her.

"I heard everything," Lori continued. "I'm glad she fired you."

The cold loathing in the other woman's voice was as shocking as a slap. Mackenzie took a step back.

"Lori, why are you acting like this? You *know* me."

"Better than you think. You're horrible and I hate you."

Mackenzie felt her stomach lurch and worried she was going to throw up. She ran downstairs and took a golf cart back to the house. When she was inside, she did something she'd never done in all the years she'd lived there—she locked the doors.

She texted Stephanie and Rhys to warn them what had happened. Stephanie didn't answer but Rhys texted he was on his way home.

Ten minutes later, she heard knocking at the back door. She ran through the kitchen and opened it, then threw herself into his arms. He held her tight.

"I'm sorry," he murmured, kissing the top of her head. "I knew it was going to be bad, but I didn't expect her to fire you."

"Me, either."

He urged her to sit at the kitchen table, then tell him what had happened.

"It was awful," Mackenzie said, wiping away tears. "She fired me and told me to get out. Just like that. I didn't know what to do. So much for being the daughter of the heart."

"She was in shock. She'll come around."

"You really believe that?"

He hesitated. "Maybe."

Despite everything, she managed to smile. "You are so lying."

"Just a little. I am sorry."

"I know. Me, too."

She told him what had happened with Lori.

"That almost shocks me more," he admitted. "I'll go talk to her."

"Don't. It's done now. I guess she and I weren't friends. I can handle it. If Stephanie turns on me, I'll have a big problem, but I can deal with Lori not being a fan."

Rhys took her hands. "How can I help?"

"Listening is big. Thank you. And it would be nice if you got my personal stuff from my desk at the office." She tried to smile. "At least I have more time to work on buying Painted Moon. Oh, and I need to find a place to live."

"No. You're staying here, just like we agreed."

"Rhys, no. It will make trouble with your mom."

He grinned. "All the more reason to stay. Look, you and Bruno are paying cash for the winery, so you can close in a couple of months. Stay here until then."

"I'll think about it."

Before she could say anything else, Stephanie raced into the kitchen.

"I just saw your text. Mom fired you? How could she?" she demanded, hurrying over to Mackenzie and hugging her. "Are you okay? How can I help? It's early to start drinking, but I'm all in if you want to go that route."

Mackenzie felt a little of her fear fading. "All I need to know is that we're still friends."

"Always." Stephanie sat next to her and grabbed her

hand. "Best friends. Come on, I'm not going to let my mother get between us. Who do you think I am? Lori?"

Mackenzie found herself laughing and crying. "Never that."

"I'm here," Stephanie told her. She waved at Rhys. "Go back to work, big brother. I've got this."

He nodded and stood. "Text if you need anything."

"I will."

When he had left, Stephanie leaned in. "So I'm thinking we find a witch and make a voodoo doll of my mom."

"I don't think witches do that sort of thing."

"Whatever. Come on. We'll go online and search for mystical revenge. That should bring up some really fun websites."

Mackenzie hugged her. "You're the best."

Barbara sat at her desk, trying to catch her breath. She felt as if the room had started spinning, and she couldn't make it stop. Fury welled up inside of her, making her want to throw something, but under that was a growing sense of betrayal and panic.

Mackenzie was leaving! How was that possible? They were a team, they'd always been a team. The two of them and the wine and everything they'd done together. Mackenzie was Bel Après. Without her, there was nothing.

The bitch had betrayed them all and, yes, that had to be dealt with, but first, what was she going to do now? If Mackenzie left—

"She can't," Barbara said aloud. "I won't let her. I'll take her to court. I'll have her arrested. I'll do something!"

She reached for her phone only to realize her hands were shaking. Two attempts later, she managed to pick it up and place the call.

Giorgio picked up on the second ring.

"I was just thinking about you, my love," he said, his voice full of affection. "But that's how I spend most of my time, so I doubt the news is a surprise."

At the sound of his voice, she started to cry. The action shocked her nearly as much as the news about Mackenzie—she never cried. Not once in twenty-six years. The last time she'd cried had been at James's funeral. Standing there as they'd lowered his coffin into the ground, she'd vowed to be strong, and she had been—until this.

"What is it?" he asked, his voice thick with concern. "What happened?"

"I need you. Can you come to my office?"

"I'll be there in fifteen minutes. Whatever it is, we'll take care of it together."

She nodded, even though he couldn't see her, and hung up. She was still shaking, and her heart was pounding so hard in her chest she thought she might throw up.

She had to focus, she told herself. Start thinking about what this all meant and how to make the situation workable. She had to figure out what she—

"Mom?"

She looked up and saw Lori standing in the doorway. The sight of her middle daughter with her too-tight suit and hangdog expression annoyed her more than usual.

"What?" she asked, her voice tense.

"I heard what happened with Mackenzie," Lori began.

"Of course you did. God forbid I have one second of privacy in this damn place. Fine. You heard. Now keep the information to yourself. No one needs to know until I decide what to do next."

"Maybe I can help."

"How, exactly? How could you possibly replace Mackenzie? She's a master winemaker. Your little foray into that side of the business was a disaster and cost me thousands of dollars. You have the taste buds of paint. So if not that, what other brilliant ideas do you have?"

Lori's lower lip began to tremble—a telltale sign that she was about to cry. Barbara deliberately turned away from her and opened her lower desk drawer. Behind a box of envelopes was a small bottle of tequila she kept for emergencies.

She unscrewed the top and took a long swallow. The liquor burned the entire way down her throat. When she set the bottle on her desk, she saw her daughter had left. Thank God. She couldn't take one more thing.

She sat there, sipping tequila, staring at the wall until Giorgio walked in.

"What happened?" he asked, holding open his arms.

She rose and ran into his embrace, letting his warmth and strength give her a false sense of security.

"It's Mackenzie," she said. "She's betrayed me. She's a horrible, lying, awful person and I never saw it until today."

The tears returned. Giorgio held her tight, murmuring soothingly until she had a little more control, then he led her over to the sofa in the corner.

"Tell me everything," he said.

She told him about the divorce and how she'd assured Mackenzie that it wouldn't affect her position at Bel Après. He listened attentively, holding her hands in his.

"It's just such a slap in the face," she concluded. "What is she going to do? Work somewhere else?" She stared at him. "What if she steals our secrets? What if she steals our customers? She's going to try to destroy us and I don't know why. We've been her family, her life. To act like this tells me there's something fundamentally wrong with her. Do you think I could get her committed somewhere?"

Giorgio smiled. "I love how you try to see the humor in such a difficult situation."

Barbara didn't bother pointing out that she hadn't been kidding. Getting Mackenzie into a mental institution was probably a little far-fetched, but it would certainly suit her purposes.

"I'm sorry about their divorce," he said. "It's always tragic when love is lost. Did you know they were unhappy?"

Why in God's name was he asking about that? She didn't care about their feelings or their marriage. Bel Après was at stake! But she understood that Giorgio was much kinder than she was, and while she might find that tedious at times, it was one of the reasons she'd fallen in love with him.

"Neither of them ever said anything," she told him. "She said it's a mutual decision and very amicable, so the winery is slightly more pressing. We don't have a winemaker. I always meant to get around to hiring a backup, but with Mackenzie here, it didn't seem necessary. None of the children can do it. I've stepped in before, but we were much smaller then. With how many gallons we bottle each year, I don't think I'm qualified. I need a plan."

"You need to talk to Mackenzie. Why is she leaving?"

"I don't know. She's a bitch. Isn't that a good enough reason?"

He squeezed her fingers. "My love, she's like a daughter to you. You've worked together so closely. But maybe her decision to leave is about being unhappy. You and yours are the only family she has. She wouldn't give that up easily, so there must be something else. Has she ever said anything to you about what she wanted from her life that she doesn't have?"

Barbara quickly tried to suppress the memories, but they were too strong. She recalled years ago when Mackenzie had asked if she would ever have a part of Bel Après. Barbara had explained about the will and how only blood relatives could inherit. Mackenzie had been desperate to somehow buy in or work hard so she could be one of the owners, but Barbara had told her that would never happen.

"What are you thinking?"

She pressed her lips together. "Oh, she talked about wanting to have a share of the winery. It couldn't possibly happen, and I told her to never ask again. It's not my fault," she added, knowing she sounded defensive. "James's will is very clear."

"There must be ways around that."

Possibly, but why would she want to look for them? Instead of saying that, she murmured, "I'm not sure it would help."

"Mackenzie's alone in the world. It makes sense she wants to feel connected to something as wonderful as Bel Après. Perhaps a tiny percentage of—"

"No."

"But my sweet—"

"Giorgio, no. She can't have any ownership in the winery. That's just how it is."

"But you love her."

"Not anymore."

He drew back. "You don't mean that. She's the daughter of your heart."

"She's a lying bitch who wants to leave us."

He studied her for a few seconds. "You're still upset. I'm sorry—I shouldn't have pushed you. Forgive me?"

"Of course. You're not the problem, you're never the problem. It's Bel Après. Everything could be ruined."

"Then focus all your incredible talents on finding a new winemaker. I would imagine there are dozens who would jump at the chance to work for such a prestigious label." He leaned close and kissed her. "How can I help?"

"Just being here makes me feel better."

"Good." He pulled her into his embrace. "Sweet, sweet Barbara. We'll get through this together."

She nodded, because it was the kind thing to do, but knew in her heart that there was no "we" when it came to this problem. There was only her and finding a solution to a horrible situation.

Damn Mackenzie, she thought grimly. Damn her straight to hell.

fifteen

Stephanie was not happy to be summoned to her mother's house, especially not on the day Mackenzie had told Barbara she was leaving. But the text had been specific enough that she couldn't figure out a way to get out of going.

Be at my house at 7 p.m. I will accept no excuses.

Stephanie stared at her phone, hoping for a reprieve, but sadly the screen stayed dark. In fifteen minutes she was going to have to walk the too-short distance between their homes and deal with whatever crap her mother wanted to send her way.

She debated getting drunk before heading over. A coward's way to deal, but she could live with that. Only there wasn't enough time, and in the name of self-preservation, she should probably keep her wits about herself—as much as she could, under the circumstances.

"Mom?"

She looked up from her place at the kitchen island

and saw Avery standing in the doorway. Her daughter was still a little pale and there were shadows under her eyes, but she seemed to be on the road to recovery. Oh, to be young again, and bounce back quickly, she thought. Stephanie, on the other hand, kept flashing back to the conversation from a few days ago when her daughter had matter-of-factly mentioned she knew about Kyle's cheating and was doing her best not to be the fool her mother had been. Humbling, humiliating, but wise on Avery's part.

"Madison invited me over to her place," she said. "I'll be back by eleven."

Stephanie forced a smile. "I'm glad you're getting out."

"I heard from Alexander. He's sorry and wants me to meet him tomorrow."

"What are you going to do?" she asked, careful to keep her tone and expression neutral.

"I told him we were done and that I was blocking him on my phone."

Stephanie relaxed. "You're amazing. I'm so proud of you, sweetie."

Avery nodded without much enthusiasm. "I know it's the right thing to do, but it still hurts."

Stephanie risked rejection and wrath by hugging her daughter. "I know it's hard to believe now, but eventually you're going to feel better. Then you're going to find a great guy who treats you the way you deserve to be treated."

Avery returned the hug before stepping back. "Am I? You never have. You don't date or anything. Your whole life is here. You work for Bel Après, your best friend is your sister-in-law. Don't you ever want a bigger life?"

Stephanie did her best not to flinch. "I have a good job and I spend my days with the people I love best."

The words came automatically. It was only after she spoke that she remembered she hated her job and working for her mother, and that not saying that to her daughter was ignoring the truth and a chance to share an important life lesson.

"If you say so," Avery murmured before walking to the back door. "See you later."

"Wait!" Stephanie called, but it was too late. Her daughter was gone and she was left alone with her half-truths and regrets.

Ugh. Not the best frame of mind to go deal with her mother, she thought as she walked across the courtyard and into her mother's house.

Of the four homes clustered together, Barbara's was the most traditional. A two-story foyer opened into a formal living room. The dining room had a long table that could seat twenty when all the leaves were put in. High ceilings were decorated with elegant molding, and expensive rugs covered hardwood floors.

Stephanie walked into the family room at the rear of the house. Large sofas formed a U shape in front of a huge stone fireplace. There was no television— that was upstairs, in the media room. One did not visit Barbara Barcellona to be distracted by a cartoon or a football game.

She saw her mother and Lori already seated on one of the sofas.

"Hey, Mom," Stephanie said as she approached.

"You're here. Good." Her mother waved a crystal highball glass. "What would you like to drink?"

Stephanie eyed the liquid already in her mother's glass and had a bad feeling it was tequila. Wine was Barbara's usual drink, but when life got tough, she opted for the serious liquor and things generally went downhill from there.

Stephanie saw Lori had a glass of white wine in front of her. "I'll have what Lori's having."

She retreated to the kitchen and found an open bottle of chardonnay in the refrigerator. She poured herself a glass. She chugged half of it, then refilled it before putting the bottle back. She'd just settled across from her mother when Four walked in.

"Tell me you didn't start without me," Four said cheerfully. "I hate to miss anything."

Stephanie held in a groan. She'd texted Four earlier to warn her that Mackenzie had told Barbara she was leaving and had then been fired, so she couldn't say her sister didn't know she was stepping into a minefield. But that was Four's way—she often sailed unafraid into troubled waters.

"I can't believe you don't know what happened today," her mother snapped. "Stop acting so ridiculously happy and get yourself a drink."

"No thanks." Four sat next to Stephanie and tucked her feet under her. "I take it from your tone that you're upset about Mackenzie."

Barbara glared at her. "Why did I ever think you had a brain?"

"I must have a brain. I'm alive and fully functional. My nervous system and brain seem intact."

Stephanie couldn't decide if Four was the bravest person she knew or the dumbest.

"Besides," Four continued with a winning smile, "it's not a surprise that Mackenzie would want to leave. This was never her dream. She has to find where she'll be happy."

"She should be happy here," Barbara said, her tone a low growl. "I gave her everything and she betrayed us."

"She did," Lori echoed.

"Not everything," Stephanie said before she could stop herself. "She wanted to be a part of the winery and you wouldn't let that happen."

Her mother turned her cold, angry gaze on her. "You do realize how ridiculous you sound."

"Actually, I'm making sense. Everyone deserves to feel they belong to something. She wanted to be more than an employee. You made sure that wouldn't happen and now she's leaving. Do you think that makes any of us happy? She's my best friend, Mom. I see her all the time. We're in and out of each other's houses. We work in the same building and now all that is going to change. She was good for Bel Après and she was good for our family."

Four reached across the cushions and took Stephanie's hand in hers.

Barbara finished her tequila. After holding the glass out to Lori for a refill, she slid to the edge of the sofa, her gaze intense.

"You take that back."

"Take what back? It's the truth. She was devoted to you and the wines, she's a wonderful friend, and she loves us all."

"Not enough to stay."

"I go back to my original premise. What is she supposed to stay for? A paycheck? She can get that anywhere."

Lori got up and poured more tequila and handed the glass to her mother.

"She's a terrible person," Lori said. "I hate her. I always knew she was going to be trouble."

Stephanie rolled her eyes. "That is so much crap. You've always resented that Mom liked her best. There's a difference."

"Did not."

Four squeezed Stephanie's fingers, as if reminding her what was important.

"Barbara, what did you want to tell us?" Four asked.

Their mother swallowed a good portion of her drink. "She has to be punished."

"Flogged?" Stephanie asked, her tone snippy. "Are you going to take out a contract on her? You're being ridiculous, Mom. You made this happen and now you're having to deal with the consequences. She's going to leave and I don't blame her."

Her mother leaned back in the sofa. "You're very free with your opinion tonight."

Probably because she was trying to make up for not telling Avery the truth, Stephanie thought, still disappointed by her earlier behavior. Plus, she hadn't been supportive when Mackenzie had first told her about the divorce.

"I'm telling the truth."

"You're being disloyal. I would be careful about that if I were you." Her mother glanced at all three of them. "As of today, none of you will have any contact with

Mackenzie. You're not to speak to her or text with her. As far as you're concerned, she's dead to all of us."

"Gladly," Lori said quickly.

"I don't think so," Four told her.

"Not happening," Stephanie added. "She's my best friend, Mom. That's not changing. I love her and I want her in my life. I want her in my kids' lives. Whatever she needs, I'm going to help her get."

Her mother stared at her, her expression stern. "You say the words so easily, but know this. There will come a time when you have to choose. Trust me when I tell you that you don't want to cross me, Stephanie."

Despite the shiver that rippled down her spine, Stephanie remained defiant. "Or what? I'll be punished, too? We're all adults, Mom. You can't ground us. Besides, you're wrong about how you're handling this."

Four leaned toward their mother. "We're a family, Barbara. No matter how angry you are, that doesn't change."

"And you two need to remember your places in my world. I can make things uncomfortable."

Stephanie stood. "I've had enough. I know you're upset, and yes, it's awful that she's leaving, but it's also your fault. You did this to yourself and to us. We're all going to suffer because of you. I don't care about your threats. I care about losing someone who matters to me. While Mackenzie and I will always be friends, everything is going to change. So threaten me all you want, but know that it's going to take me a long time to forgive you for this. For how you're acting. You're giving mothers everywhere a really bad name."

With that, she walked out of the house. Her defiance lasted until she was into her own place. Once there, she closed the door, then leaned against it, trying to ignore the trembling that started in her hands and worked its way down to her legs.

Unlike Four, she'd never gone out of her way to stand up to her mother. Mostly she simply ignored what Barbara said and went her own way. But not tonight. Tonight she'd overtly rebelled, and while she wasn't sorry, she couldn't help wondering if, one day very soon, she would be.

Mackenzie walked into the restaurant and moved toward the hostess station, but before she got there, she spotted Stephanie and Four already at a table and turned in their direction.

She was dealing with so many emotions—feeling both hopeful and adrift at the same time. She was still upset about her encounter with Barbara, sad about her divorce and scared about her future. Everything was different now, including the fact that she had to meet her sisters-in-law at a restaurant instead of just having lunch in one of their kitchens.

Mackenzie paused a few feet from the table, wondering what other changes there would be in her life. A few short weeks ago, she'd known exactly how each day was going to go. Her work and her days had been defined by the seasons. Now she wasn't sure about anything.

Stephanie looked up and saw her. Her immediate smile drew Mackenzie forward. Four followed her gaze and her mouth turned up in a huge grin. Their obvious pleasure at seeing her eased a tension she'd refused to acknowledge until that second.

Mackenzie walked into the three-way hug and hung

on. "I was so scared you'd be mad at me for what happened with your mom," she admitted.

"Never," Stephanie promised.

"You've done nothing to make me mad," Four pointed out. "Besides, I'm not sure how you could upset my energy that much. I do my best to go with the flow. To observe rather than embrace negative emotions."

The very "Fourness" of that comment made Mackenzie laugh. She squeezed them both one last time, then released her sisters-in-law.

"Thanks for suggesting lunch," she said, taking her seat.

Stephanie sat across from her with Four between them.

"In a restaurant," Stephanie said with a laugh. "It feels very clandestine. Like we're in a spy novel and discussing an insurgency."

"With Mackenzie as our own insurgent."

Mackenzie shook her head. "That implies more strength and planning than I'm capable of at the moment. Right now I'm just getting by as best I can."

Stephanie and Four exchanged a look.

"At the risk of adding to your stress level, we wanted to talk to you about a few things." Stephanie sighed. "One thing."

Mackenzie tried not to let her apprehension show. "Barbara?"

"That's it," Four said cheerfully. "She totally went off on you last night. We're forbidden from having contact with you." Her smile turned impish. "Which is when I texted Stephanie and suggested we have lunch with you today."

"I should have thought of it myself," Stephanie said.

Mackenzie hated to think about what she'd done to the family. "I'm sorry," she began.

Stephanie shook her head. "No. You're not and you shouldn't be. This is my mom's doing, not yours. The work stuff. You and Rhys are responsible for your marriage."

"It was inevitable," Four added. "The change. You couldn't have stayed where you were forever. It wasn't right for you."

Mackenzie wondered if that was true. Until Rhys had mentioned getting a divorce, she'd been fairly content. Yes, there had been problems and disappointments, but she wasn't sure she would have ever thought to leave on her own.

"We don't expect you to do anything with the information about our mom," Stephanie said. "But we thought you should know she's gone a little cray-cray. Watch your back."

"I will."

"We're both going to let you know if we hear anything of real concern," Four told her. She smiled. "And that's all the grim news. How are things otherwise?"

"And how are you doing?" Stephanie asked.

"I'm trying to figure it all out. So much has changed so fast that it's hard to get my head around it all. I'm still recovering from my encounter with Barbara."

"She does love to leave a scar," Stephanie said.

The server appeared and took their drink orders. When she was gone, Four turned to Mackenzie.

"Barbara's just as lost and confused. I suspect she's not totally sure if you're really leaving or if you're playing her to get more money. She's also hoping she can figure out a way to make the winery work without you. She's angry, hurt and scared, not to mention furious that she doesn't have a backup plan. Every other winery has an assistant winemaker, an assistant to the assistant and so on. You and Barbara have always been so intertwined that you two never wanted to add a third person to the mix. You each resisted taking the sensible next step and now she's paying the price."

Mackenzie stared at her. "You are the most amazing person. Everyone assumes you're just a crystal-loving tree hugger, but you are emotionally deep."

"I observe," Four said modestly.

"I think she's secretly psychic," Stephanie teased.

They bantered for a few seconds, their familiar teasing helping Mackenzie feel as if there was a chance that one day things could be normal again. A new normal for her, but she was open to that. Just being around her friends was comforting. What Four would describe as grounding.

The server returned with their drinks. They ordered lunch. When they were alone again, Stephanie said, "How are you doing? Really? Are you sleeping? Eating right?"

Mackenzie smiled. "I'm taking care of myself. I'm not drinking and I'm also not sleeping that well, but I'm using the extra awake time to work on my business plan."

Which reminded her. She pulled out two pieces of paper from her handbag and handed them to her sisters-in-law. "If you want details, I'm afraid you're going to have to sign these."

Stephanie and Four glanced at each other, then at the NDA. Four finished reading first. She reached for Mackenzie's hand.

"I'm proud of you for taking care of yourself and for taking your future seriously. You have a true heart, you always have. That's what draws people to you."

Stephanie scrawled her name on the page, then handed the pen to her sister. "You're right. This is starting to feel like a spy novel. I like it."

"I'm going into business with Bruno," Mackenzie said, tucking the signed papers back into her bag. "We're looking at buying Painted Moon."

Both sisters stared at her with identical expressions of delight and shock. Stephanie recovered first.

"It's perfect. Big, and the land is excellent. Now that I think about it, I'm not too surprised Herman wants to sell. I'm so glad you'll be staying in the valley. I've been terrified that you'd leave me."

"Does Barbara know?" Four asked.

"No. I'm not telling her until we have an accepted offer. Or maybe not until we close."

"Keep it quiet as long as you can," Stephanie advised. "She'll only make trouble if she can."

"That was my thought," Mackenzie said.

"Where are you going to live?" Four asked. "I know Rhys will tell you to stay in the house for as long as you want, but eventually you'll have to go somewhere."

"If we buy Painted Moon, I'll move into the farmhouse there. If that doesn't work—"

"I have room," Stephanie said, interrupting.

"Us, too," Four added. "The kids would love having you around."

Their generosity made Mackenzie's throat a little tight.

"Thank you," she managed. "Let's see how this works out."

"Since Barbara fired you, you're eligible for unemployment," Four pointed out.

Mackenzie managed a chuckle. "I never thought about that. You're right."

She still hadn't processed her lack of a job. Currently she was telling herself that she was just taking a few days off. Her work with Bruno kept her plenty busy, so her hours weren't empty. But after working at Bel Après so long, it was going to be hard to let go.

"Enough," she said, holding up her hand. "How are you two doing? How's Carson enjoying camp?"

"He loves it. He texts me every day, mostly, I think because he knows if he doesn't, I'll fly down and humiliate him by hugging and kissing him in front of his friends. But I still miss him. Avery's dealing with her breakup with Alexander." She turned to Four.

"We're all fine," Four said. "I'm thinking of doing a mural in the dining room. I told the kids they could help."

The normalcy of the conversation comforted Mackenzie. This was what she'd been missing, she told herself. Hanging out with her friends in a fun, supportive environment. No drama, nothing but talking and laughing and being together.

She thought about how she'd felt after her grandfather had died. She remembered how alone and terrified she'd been.

This wasn't that. She was older, with more life experience, and she had family. Maybe not Barbara or Lori, but these two would stand by her. Of that she was sure.

Emotionally healed by her long lunch with friends, Mackenzie drove back home. She wanted to go through the house and decide if there was anything she wanted to take with her when she inevitably had to leave. There wouldn't be a lot—maybe a few mementos from her life, the odd piece of art. As she and Barbara had decorated the house together, she wasn't comfortable taking much with her. Too many memories, she thought.

She drove onto the property and turned toward her house, passing a sheriff's car on the way. The law enforcement vehicle was so unexpected, she didn't react at first, then slowed to stare at the car turning onto the main road. Someone from the sheriff's office had been here? But why?

She parked in the garage, next to Rhys's SUV, then hurried inside. She found him standing in the kitchen. In the half second before he saw her, she studied the sharp lines in his brow. Lines that hadn't been there the last time she'd seen him. If she had to pick a word to describe his mood, she would say he was furious about something.

"Rhys? What's going on? Why are you home in the middle of the day and why did I see a sheriff's car leaving the property?"

He turned toward her. The fake smile made her chest tighten.

"Everything is fine," he said, his voice falsely hardy. "Nothing to worry about."

"These aren't the droids you're looking for?" she asked, quoting the original *Star Wars* movie line they often used on each other. "I think they probably are. What happened?"

He sighed heavily. "You couldn't have been five minutes later?"

"Rhys, please. If you're trying not to tell me something, it must be about your mother. She's already fired me. I'm not sure it can get worse than that."

The twist of his mouth told her she was wrong.

"My mother called the sheriff's office to have you evicted." His voice was flat.

"What? But we're married and this is my house." Except it wasn't, she thought bitterly. Only Rhys's name was on the deed—because he was family and she wasn't. "Can she do that?"

"No. That's what I told the sheriff. It's my house, and until the divorce is final, you're my wife and you can damn well live here as long as I let you."

"Thank you." Mackenzie still couldn't take in what had happened. Barbara wanted her gone that much? Mackenzie had known the other woman would be upset, but to try to evict her?

Rhys drew in a breath. "How can you think about moving on with everything if she's distracting you like this?" He crossed to her and pulled her close. "I'm sorry."

"I'm okay," she lied, trying to take comfort in his words and embrace and not question how much of his concern was about her getting out of his life.

"You're stronger than I would be under the circumstances." He released her. "I really am sorry about what my mother did."

But he wasn't sorry about the divorce, she thought sadly. He was ready to move on. She was, too, but she knew he was further along the path.

"I'm fine," she said, telling herself that with a little luck and time it would be true.

sixteen

Barbara tapped her fingers on her desk. The phone call from her contact at the sheriff's office had been disappointing. Apparently there were laws against evicting someone from their home, even when they deserved it. The best she'd been able to get was a visit by a deputy. She needed Mackenzie punished and broken so she would come crawling back. Perhaps not logical, but it was the truth.

She turned her attention back to her computer screen, but before she could start to make sense of the report, Rhys stalked into her office. He stood over her, glaring, as if he was trying to intimidate her.

"What the hell were you thinking?" he demanded.

She raised her eyebrows and pointed to the chair. "If you want to have a conversation, please do me the courtesy of speaking in a civil tone and refrain from swearing."

"You tried to have Mackenzie evicted."

"*Tried* being the operative word. I knew it wasn't going to work, but I had to do something. It's not as if you're helping, and this is all your fault." She pointed to the chair again.

As expected, he sat down. "How is it my fault?"

"You obviously didn't make her happy in the marriage and now we all have to pay the price for that. Why didn't you tell me there were problems in your relationship?" Actually the more important question was why he hadn't fixed them in the first place, but asking that would get her nowhere.

"My marriage isn't your business."

"If only that were true, but when your wife works in the family firm, it's all our business. Did you cheat?"

Rhys sighed. "I'm not discussing that with you."

She wasn't sure if that meant yes or no. Rhys didn't strike her as the kind of man who would do that sort of thing. He was a good man—honest and hardworking. He was also handsome and wealthy, which would make him irresistible to most women. So he would have had opportunity.

"So you're not going to fight for her?"

"Mom, this isn't your business. Mackenzie and I are getting a divorce. End of story."

"Perhaps for you, but not for me. Your divorce affects Bel Après and that means it affects us all."

She pressed her fingers to her temple, knowing that later she would have a headache.

Everything had been going along so well, she thought bitterly. The wines were excellent. Mackenzie was doing such good work and now it could all be lost.

"Why didn't you two have children? That would have kept you together."

"Now you want her pregnant? You were always

happy Mackenzie didn't have any kids to distract her from her work."

"I never said that."

Rhys looked at her without speaking.

She waved the comment away. "Fine, I might have said it once or twice, but I didn't mean it. Had I known you needed children to stay married, I would have encouraged it."

"I'm sorry to have missed that."

She ignored his sarcasm. "We have to fix this."

"No, we don't. Mackenzie and I are splitting up. That's on us. What happens with the winery is on you, Mom. You're the one who lost your temper and fired her."

"She told me she was leaving Bel Après. What was I supposed to do?"

"Ask her why she wanted to go. Maybe show a little compassion and understanding."

His idiocy shouldn't have surprised her and yet it did. "Perhaps have given her a parting gift? You do realize we don't have a backup winemaker. We'll be left with nothing. We could be ruined."

Rhys shook his head. "You'll find a solution, Mom. You always do. My point was you could have worked it out with Mackenzie. All she wanted was to feel like she belonged and was a part of things."

Barbara thought about her conversation with Giorgio. Rhys sounded exactly like him. Was there a conspiracy?

"The terms of the will are very clear. You know I can't violate them. Besides, what more does she want? I gave her everything. Free rein in all the winemaking." She felt her temper flaring and consciously suppressed it. "Someone's going to hire her. I wish I could stop that."

Rhys glanced away without saying anything. Barbara stared at him.

"What do you know that I don't?" she demanded.

He looked at her. "Mackenzie and I have a post-nuptial agreement."

The edges of the room blurred a little as she struggled to comprehend what he was saying. A postnuptial agreement meant Mackenzie was going to get money from him.

"Why am I just hearing about this now?"

He looked away again. "It was between the two of us."

Anger rushed through her. "When did this happen?"

"Back when you told her she would never have a piece of the winery. She was devastated."

"So you gave her money?" she asked. "Dear God, you're an idiot. How much?"

He squared his shoulders. "Half the value of the house, some of my trust fund. I signed off on the royalties from her wines. In total, about two million."

"Dollars? You gave that bitch two million dollars?" She half rose, then collapsed back in her chair. No. It wasn't possible. With that kind of money, Mackenzie could buy something. Worse, she could use it as a down payment on a real winery and compete with Bel Après.

"It was right at the time," he said. "We were still happy together and I hated to see her so upset. She felt betrayed and dismissed by you."

Barbara ignored the rest of what he'd said and focused on what was important. "Right at the time? You're regretting the agreement?"

"Some. Maybe. It's unbreakable. I already asked my attorney. I'm going to live up to my part of the agreement. The point is, she's getting the money."

Maybe he wasn't as stupid as she'd feared, she thought, still enraged by what that kind of money would mean to Mackenzie.

"Ask your attorney again. There has to be a way to keep her from getting her hands on that much. It's ridiculous. What were you thinking?"

He stared at her for a long time. "I was thinking that I loved my wife. It's where we are. She's getting the money, Mom. You're going to have to deal."

"Oh, right. You create the problem and then leave me to fix it. How typical." She was back to wanting to slap him. "Why can't you comprehend what's happening? We're only a couple of months away from harvest. And then what? Who is going to take the grapes and make them into wonderful Bel Après wines? We all work hard, and yet without Mackenzie, what is there? Grapes. You have to make her stay."

"She offered to stay through harvest, Mom. You fired her."

"I didn't have a choice."

"You always have a choice." He stood. "No more evictions, no more anything like that. It's done. She's leaving. Let the rest of it go."

"I will not," she snapped. "Keeping her happy was up to you and you failed."

He walked out of her office. When she was alone, she stood and paced to the window, staring out at the view that usually delighted her.

Mackenzie had to stay, she thought grimly. That was all that mattered. Bel Après needed her, something her own son didn't seem to understand. Ironically Mackenzie would know what she meant. For Mackenzie, the winery had always come first. With her gone…

"I won't think about that," she said aloud. Except she couldn't think of anything else. Once people knew, they would—

She swore under her breath, then hurried back to her desk. She wrote a quick email to all her children, telling them to keep quiet about Mackenzie's threat to leave. No one else could know—not until Barbara had figured out a way to solve the problem. One way or another, she was going to get Mackenzie to see she couldn't leave.

Friday morning Mackenzie met Rhys in the kitchen while he was eating breakfast at the kitchen table by the window.

"Morning," he said.

"Morning. I need your help. I want to clean out my desk at the office and, well, I don't want to go there alone."

She half expected him to tease her about being a coward, but instead he nodded.

"Sure. I'll go with you. We can get it done before I head out to check the Seven Hills vines."

She poured herself a cup of coffee and sat across from him. "Is everything all right? I'm worried about the canopy on the south side. The weather has been so hot for the past couple of days and—"

She pressed her lips together. "Sorry. I forgot I was fired."

"I'll check the canopy for you." He gave her a slight smile. "I do know how to do my job."

"You're the best. I know that. It's just I'm a natural-born worrier."

"You're a great winemaker. It's how you're wired." He sipped his coffee. "If she'd offered you a piece of it, would you have stayed?"

She considered the question. "Yes. I never wanted to leave. This is all I know. You're my family and this is my life's work. But everything is different now. Bruno and I are business partners and we're moving forward with the purchase of Painted Moon." She smiled. "We have an office in town."

"No more working out of a hotel?" he asked, his voice teasing.

She smiled. "It was getting a little weird. The office is better. We have more space. I'm excited about the opportunity but sad that everything has changed." She paused. "I miss you," she admitted. "I miss us."

"The old us or the us we came to be?"

"Both. Mostly the old us. We were good together."

He nodded. "Just never that special."

Was that how he saw their relationship? She'd thought it was very special. Obviously she'd been wrong about that, too.

"Let me know when you want to go to the office," she said.

"We can go now," he told her, carrying his dishes over to the sink.

She'd already put a couple of tote bags by her purse. She collected them and followed him out to the garage. They each took a golf cart and drove the short distance to the office building, then climbed the stairs.

Mackenzie hurried into her office and glanced around. The only items she wanted were the personal ones. Rhys made himself comfortable in the visitor's chair while she collected photographs and put them in the first tote bag. There were a couple of knickknacks Rhys had given her, along with a few pictures Stephanie's and Four's kids had made for her.

She'd just sat behind her desk to check the drawers when Lori appeared in the doorway.

"You can't be here. Mom fired you."

Rhys turned to his sister. "Leave it alone."

"She's been fired. What if she steals proprietary information?" She turned to Mackenzie. "I'm going through your bags before you leave."

"No, you're not," Rhys told her. "She's getting what's hers and that's all. Jeez, Lori, give it a rest."

Mackenzie pulled open each of the drawers. She had some protein bars, hand lotion, a few Band-Aids, a charger for her phone. None of it significant, but all of it hers. She put everything into the second tote bag and tried not to think about how little she was taking. Shouldn't she have more to show for sixteen years of work?

But there wasn't anything else, she reminded herself. The rest of it belonged to the company. At least she had the memories. Those were hers to keep for as long as she liked. She thought about the late nights poring over reports, the times she'd stood at the window and watched a summer storm roll in as she eyed the sky and wondered about hail. Hail could ruin a crop in seconds. Here that rarely happened, but she still worried.

She stood and grabbed a couple of jackets she'd left on the coatrack in the corner. "This is everything," she said.

Rhys rose. "I'll walk you out."

"That won't be necessary."

They both turned and saw Barbara standing behind Lori. Mackenzie hoped she didn't flinch as she stared at the other woman. Their eyes met.

"Go back to work, Lori," Barbara said, her voice surprisingly pleasant. "You, too, Rhys. I want to have a word with Mackenzie." She smiled slightly. "I promise there will be no bloodshed."

Rhys glanced at Mackenzie. "You okay?"

She nodded.

He leaned close. "I'll stay in my office until you two are finished."

"It's okay. You need to get to Seven Hills."

He hesitated. "Are you sure?"

"I'm fine." She lowered her voice. "I'm pretty sure I could take her if I had to."

"Unless Lori joins in. Then it's two against one."

"Stop worrying. You need to check on the vines."

He nodded and left. Mackenzie followed him out of what had been her office and went into Barbara's.

"Close the door, would you please?"

Mackenzie did as she was asked. She left her totes by the door and took the visitor's chair.

Barbara sat with her hands folded on top of her desk. She looked as she always did—perfectly groomed, wearing a suit. There were no dark circles, no hint of worry. Mackenzie didn't know if the other woman was that unconcerned about what was happening or if she was just that good at makeup.

"We seem to have found ourselves in a pickle," Barbara said with a smile. "Maybe it's time to talk about getting ourselves out of it."

"I don't know what that means," Mackenzie admitted, wanting to believe they could work out some kind of compromise, but not willing to trust her soon-to-be-former mother-in-law.

"I want things to be right between us, Mackenzie. We've always been so close. I was just thinking about how long it took us to find the right sofas for your living room."

Despite everything, Mackenzie smiled. "I was thinking about the decorating, too. We did a good job."

"That's because we're a good team."

"We are. Barbara, you're so important to me. You've been like a second mother to me. I don't want us to fight."

"Good. I don't want that, either. So let's see if we can fix the problem. I'll double your salary. How does that sound?"

Mackenzie didn't know what to say. She'd been talking about their emotional connection while Barbara had obviously meant her job at Bel Après.

"So I'm not fired?"

"That depends on you, my dear. Do you want to not be fired?"

She thought about what she was doing with Bruno. The partnership and how generous he was being with everything. She thought about waking up every morning knowing she owned the land, the vines and everything in it. Or at least half of it.

"Would I own any part of Bel Après?"

"No, but you'd be very valued. Your work has always been the biggest part of your life. Why should that change?" Barbara leaned back in her chair. "I wish you wouldn't get in a snit about ownership. It comes with a lot of responsibility. Wouldn't you rather spend your time making beautiful wines?"

"And then what? Put money in my 401(k) every month and get a gold watch when I'm ready to retire?"

"No one gets a gold watch these days. Mackenzie, there's no need to be difficult."

"So I should just shut up and do my job."

Barbara's pleasant expression faded. "Expecting more is unreasonable. You're divorcing Rhys. You won't be one of us anymore. I'm willing to give you more money. You already have control of the wines. Do you think you can do better somewhere else? On your own?"

Barbara raised her eyebrows. "I know about the postnuptial agreement. Rhys mentioned how much he regrets it. What if he fights you for the money? What if you end up with nothing?"

Mackenzie told herself not to react. Barbara was trying to hurt her, to frighten her, and while she was doing a damned good job, there was no reason to let her know it was working.

"I'll be fine," Mackenzie said as confidently as she could. "I know what I'm doing."

Barbara laughed. "Do you really? Do you actually think you can run a winery on your own? You can't manage the costs, the marketing and keep it all going. You *are* good at what you do, but that is all you can do. If you try to do more, you're going to fail."

"Thanks for the pep talk."

Barbara's expression darkened. "I'm telling you the truth. That isn't always kind, but that doesn't mean what I'm saying isn't true."

Mackenzie told herself to ignore the sting of the words. She would deal with the pain of them later.

"While we're talking truths," she said, "let me give you a few of my own. I would have stayed for very little. I don't want more money. I want to belong. But you've never been willing to let that happen. You hold on so tight and I can't figure out what you're afraid of losing. I suppose it doesn't matter, because when you squeeze something that hard, you destroy it." She gave her a bitter smile. "I was going to offer to help with harvest, but I can see you're not interested in that." She rose. "I can't be bought. Not for what you're offering."

"You ungrateful bitch." Barbara stood. "I should never have trusted you. Well, don't try getting a job in this town. I'm going to warn everyone about you. I'm going to tell them how you betrayed me, betrayed all of us."

"Go ahead. Say what you'd like." Mackenzie walked to the door and picked up her bags. "One last truth. You can't say anything to hurt my career. Want to know why? Everyone likes me better than they like you, and they won't believe a word you say."

With that she walked out of Barbara's office for what she was sure was the last time. She made her way downstairs and into the golf cart. Minutes later she was at the house. It was only when she was inside that she gave in to tears. She sank onto the kitchen floor and cried until she was empty. The entire time she half expected Rhys to come in and check on her, knowing when he did, he would hold her and tell her everything was going to be all right. That of course he wanted her to have the money because he cared about her. Only he never did and, in the end, she was left completely on her own.

seventeen

Saturday morning, Stephanie drove into the parking garage behind Bellevue Square. The multistory shopping center was an upscale, busy place with lots of stores and restaurants, and was only a sky bridge away from not one but two movie theaters.

She'd brought Avery and her BFF, Madison, over the night before. The three of them had stayed in a cute Airbnb close by and would head back to Walla Walla on Sunday afternoon. In the meantime there would be plenty of shopping and hanging out. The teens had a list of three movies they wanted to see. Stephanie planned to do a little wardrobe update for herself, and maybe buy some things for Carson. Not that he cared about clothes, but she had a feeling he would need a few things when he got home from baseball camp.

Once she'd parked, she turned to her daughter.

"Are you two going to be all right on your own?" she asked, careful to keep her voice teasing rather than concerned. In the past week or so, she and Avery were getting along better and she didn't want to upset their tenuous détente.

"We'll be fine, Mom." Avery waved her phone. "We have movie tickets to the 2:10 showing. We're going to eat lunch at The Cheesecake Factory and meet you at five at the Starbucks on the second level."

Madison leaned forward from her place in the back seat. "The rest of the time, we're going to be shopping," she said in a singsong voice.

The previous evening they'd had dinner at the Mexican place and had walked around, but there hadn't been time to do much more than stare at store windows.

"You two have fun," Stephanie said as she got out of the car.

"What are you going to do?" Avery asked.

"A little shopping. I'm meeting your dad for lunch." The real reason for the trip, although she hadn't shared that with her daughter when she'd suggested the outing.

They headed into the mall together, then split up by Nordstrom. While the girls went off in search of trendy boutiques, Stephanie browsed her favorite store.

Even as she tried on a few dresses and looked for a pair of new jeans, she was aware of the time. She was meeting Kyle at noon and didn't want to be late.

He'd been surprised when she'd told him she was coming over the pass to the Seattle side of the state for the weekend, but had quickly agreed to lunch. What she hadn't shared was the topic she wanted to discuss.

A little before noon, she stowed her purchases in her car, then walked through the mall and across the sky bridge to the restaurant. Kyle was already waiting by the host station, and he smiled when he saw her.

"How does it feel to be back in the big city?" he asked with a grin.

"I'm a simple country girl, trying not to get lost among you sophisticated people."

He laughed, then turned to the host and gave his name.

They were shown to a table by the window. They were over thirty stories up and the views were fantastic, but Stephanie was more concerned about their conversation than the view of the Sound and Mount Rainier. She fiddled with her menu, picking it up, then putting it down until Kyle took it from her.

"Talk," he said firmly. "You obviously have something on your mind. Let's get it out and then we can enjoy lunch."

She wasn't happy that he could read her so easily, but while that was interesting, it wasn't relevant to the moment.

"Avery and her boyfriend broke up a few weeks ago," she said, forcing herself to look at him. "She dumped him after he cheated on her, then said it was her fault, claiming he had to do it because she wouldn't have sex with him."

A muscle in Kyle's jaw tightened. "Alexander did that? She told me they weren't seeing each other anymore but didn't tell me why. That little bastard."

"Yes, it's awful, but not the point. I told Avery I was proud of her for being so strong." She squeezed her fingers into her palms, telling herself she wasn't going to cry.

"She said she had to end things because she wasn't

going to be like me. She wasn't going to be weak and stay with a guy who cheated on her." She sharpened her gaze. "You told our sixteen-year-old daughter that you cheated on me and you didn't tell me she knew. You let me be blindsided, which is bad enough, but worse, you dropped the information on her without giving her any support, or letting me tell my side of things."

He flinched. "I'm sorry. I should have let you know what happened. She and I talked and I thought she was fine."

"When did this happen and why didn't you say something to me?"

"Over the holidays last year, when she and Carson were staying with me. A guy I know at the station came by to talk about what was going on in his marriage. He'd cheated and his wife found out and he didn't know what to do. It was late and I thought both kids were asleep."

Their server approached, but Kyle waved him away.

"I said that I'd been in his position and I'd handled it badly. That I'd been a fool and I'd lost something important to me because of that. I told him to own up to his mistake and make it right."

"Something you never did," she snapped.

"You're right. I didn't and I regret that more than you can know."

"Which sounds lovely and yay you, but why didn't you tell me? I should have known that Avery had been told."

"I know. I'm sorry." His mouth twisted. "When my friend left, Avery confronted me. She was mad and crying and she wanted to go home. I talked to her for a couple of hours. I told her I was wrong and a fool. I said you'd given me several chances to shape up and I'd been too immature to recognize what I was going to lose. By the time we were done, she said she was fine and I believed her."

He looked at her. "I didn't tell you because it's not behavior I'm proud of. I was ashamed and embarrassed. I really am sorry, Stephanie."

"Me, too."

"I should have said something."

"Yes, you should have. Is there anything else I don't know about my children?"

"No. That's the only secret I've kept from you. I know you're upset and I apologize for being responsible for that. I mean it, Steph."

She wanted to throw something heavy at his head but knew that wouldn't accomplish anything. "You were really stupid," she told him.

"I was."

"I'm getting the most expensive thing on the menu."

"I would encourage that. And we'll get a fancy bottle of champagne, if you'd like."

"It has to be over two hundred dollars."

"I'm sure they have that here. Are we okay?"

"I'm still upset. You pissed me off. We're their parents, Kyle. We have to be on the same team or it's not going to work."

"I know. You're right. I won't do it again."

She motioned to the server who was hovering outside of earshot, then pointed at her ex. "He's going to order a nice bottle of champagne."

Kyle quickly glanced through the wine list. "Dom Pérignon all right?"

"I guess," she said with a mock sigh.

When they were alone again, Kyle looked at her. "How are things with your mom?"

"A nightmare. She's ordered us all to not speak to Mackenzie."

"You doing all right?"

"No, but I'll figure it out. There's so much change. It's hard to take it all in."

"Did Carson text you about his no-hitter yesterday?"

She smiled. "He actually called me and gave me an inning-by-inning recap of the game."

"Our kids are pretty special."

"You're a good dad." She paused. "Most of the time."

He chuckled. "You're a better mom."

"That is true." She smiled.

He leaned toward her. "Friends?"

"Yes. I forgive you."

Instead of smiling, he nodded slowly. "You always were good that way, Steph. I should have appreciated it while I had it."

Mackenzie spent the next week or so burying herself in paperwork, which was not her favorite. Bruno had rented them an office in town. They each had a desk and there was a large filing cabinet with an impressive lock. Every document was carefully put away before they left and the cabinet locked. Just in case. She didn't think Barbara would send someone to break in and look at the paperwork, but why take the risk?

She'd already walked all the vineyards at Painted Moon. Most were in good shape. Parts of the irrigation system would have to be replaced in the next couple of years, but other than that, she was pleased with what she saw.

She still wasn't sure what to do about the wine in the barrels. Once they completed the purchase, she would have to take a few weeks to taste everything and then start making notes and, from there, decisions. It would be time-consuming but it was the only way to get high-quality wines. She had to find a few really good barrels to serve as the base, then pick directions.

"You're looking fierce," Bruno said.

She looked up and smiled. "I'm thinking about the blending. It's going to be a massive project. Until I know what's in every barrel, I can't start making decisions. Some of it will depend on what we want to do with the wine. We could just sell it as is and start over fresh."

There was a market for barrels of wine, and Painted Moon wines would bring decent prices.

"Wouldn't we make more if we got to the point of bottling it?" he asked. "I'm still working my contacts in China. They would like an exclusive vintage. We could move a few hundred cases there."

"I'm not comfortable making that decision," she said. "I don't know enough about the cost-benefit ratio."

"That's why you have a business partner."

Something she was still having trouble grasping. She and Bruno had come to terms and signed the paperwork. Barbara had taken care of any hesitation she might have had. Based on their last conversation, there was no going back to Bel Après. Not that she'd planned to. She couldn't keep doing what she'd always done. Not anymore.

She liked Bruno's calm nature. Whatever was happening, he listened, got all the facts and was reasonable in his decision making. There was no drama. Although the man still wore a tailored suit every day, she thought with a smile. He looked good in a suit, but still.

"What's so funny?" he asked.

"Are you going to wear a suit when we own Painted Moon?"

"What would you prefer?"

She rested her elbow on the desk and leaned her head on her hand. "Wineries aren't corporate America and you'll be going out into the vineyards with me, so it might be more practical to be a little more casual."

"Jeans?"

"Do you own any?"

"I do."

"Are they custom-made?"

He chuckled. "No. They're store-bought."

"Did you go to a mall yourself or did you send someone?"

He hesitated just long enough for her to start laughing. "You have staff that shops for you?"

"I might have sent an assistant out to buy some things for me."

"That still counts as staff. This is a small town, Bruno. I'm going to have to teach you to shop. We'll start at Walmart. You'll be impressed."

"I've been in a Walmart before."

She raised her eyebrows and waited. He laughed.

"Okay, maybe not, but I own shares."

"Are we going to have to hire you an assistant here?"

"I'm thinking an office manager is a better use of our funds." He glanced down at his desk, then back at her. "We have confirmation of the water rights."

"Do we? That's huge."

Water rights meant they were allowed to get their water directly from the source and weren't dependent on any municipalities. In times of drought, the winery would have priority over limited supply. Just as important, she would be able to control the amount going to her vines. Depending on the time of year, the amount of sun and the temperature, water meant the difference between success and everything dying.

"We're moving closer," she said. "I'm nearly finished with my five-year projection."

"Don't worry about formatting. Just get the information down. We can clean it up later."

He'd wanted her to develop a year-by-year projection of yields and the subsequent wines she would produce. They needed a master plan and targets along the way. She'd done similar work at Bel Après, but nothing this detailed. For every projection, Bruno estimated the profitability of each decision they made. Not every decision had to be made based on the bottom line, but some did.

"How's it going with Barbara?" he asked.

The question surprised her. For the most part she and Bruno didn't discuss anything personal.

"Not great," she admitted.

Instead of responding, he waited, as if expecting her to say more.

"She's not making it easy."

"Did you expect her to?"

"No, but I didn't think it would be this bad." She

explained about the eviction. "Rhys says I can stay in the house for as long as I'd like, but that's only a temporary solution. Plus I'm right there on the property, so I need to avoid Barbara as much as possible." She gave him a faint smile. "I know what you're thinking."

"I doubt that."

"I shouldn't be surprised or even hurt. Of course Barbara isn't happy with me. I should have seen that coming."

"Do you think I'm judging you, Mackenzie? I'm not. In the past couple of months, you've made huge changes in your life. I'm impressed by your personal strength and character. You're exactly who I want to go into business with. We're going to be a very successful team."

His kind words made her eyes burn.

"Thank you," she said, then cleared her throat. "I like our partnership, too. You're very steady and you know a lot. I like the lack of drama."

"I'm not a screamer," he teased.

"Good to know." She smiled. "What does your family think of you settling here?"

"They're used to me being on the West Coast. My mother complains that it's all her fault." He smiled. "When my parents divorced, my mom moved to Napa for a couple of years. My sisters couldn't wait to leave, but I fell in love with the area. Eventually we returned to New York, but I came back as soon as I could." He raised a shoulder. "I went to UC Berkeley, much to the chagrin of both my parents."

"Your dad was in New York, too?"

"Yes, he was a hedge fund manager. He was killed on 9/11 when the towers came down."

"What? No. Bruno, I'm sorry."

"It was a long time ago."

"It's still not easy," she said, thinking of her grandfather and how much she missed him, even now.

"It's not," he agreed. "My sisters and I inherited a fair amount from him. I also had a trust fund from my paternal grandparents. I learned how to take care of money and to grow it. Eventually that got boring, so I decided to pursue my interests."

"Including wine?"

"Including that. My mother remarried and she's happy with her new husband. I see her and my sisters every couple of years."

She wanted to ask why he hadn't remarried. He was a good-looking guy who was easy to be around. The kid thing might bother some women, but not others. Did he not want to try to meet someone? Didn't he mind being alone?

Not that she would ask. It wasn't really her business, nor did she want him asking the same questions of her. She couldn't imagine going out with anyone ever. As for falling in love—she didn't see that happening, either. She was good at her job and she planned for that to be her focus for the next few years. She just wished she could figure out a way not to feel so alone all the time. While the future was exciting, the price was high—the only family she'd ever known.

She knew she and Stephanie and Four would remain friends, but it wasn't going to be the same. She wasn't just losing proximity—she was losing all the little moments that made up the rhythm of her days. The quick hugs, the impromptu hanging out, the everyday things she had, until now, taken for granted.

Bruno glanced at his watch. "We should head over to meet the inspector at the house." Bruno had insisted on having a home inspection on Herman's old place, not that it mattered what kind of shape it was in. They would buy the property regardless. But it would affect the price a little bit and Bruno wanted Mackenzie to know what kind of situation she was getting into.

The hundred-plus-year-old house had been remodeled a few times. The main floor consisted of a living room, dining room, half bath and kitchen. Upstairs were two full baths and three bedrooms. There was a big porch out front and an even larger deck out back. The house sat on a rise, overlooking the property.

"I still feel guilty about you giving me the house," she said.

"I told you, I don't want to live there. It's not my style. Besides, you'll like being close to the grapes."

She smiled. "That is my happy place. If you're sure."

"I am."

"Thank you. It's a little big for what I need."

"You'll want the space when your friends and family come to visit."

"I'm not going to have family after the divorce," she said, hoping she didn't sound pathetic. "But my friends will come over and that will be fun."

He looked at her. "Mackenzie, you have a lot of family. If you don't think that, you're underestimating yourself and them."

eighteen

Barbara found solace in the barrel room. There was something about the space that was soothing on those days when everyone seemed to be on a mission to annoy her. Lately, that was every minute of every day.

She rested her palm on a new French oak barrel and breathed in the glorious scent. The tag stapled to the barrel detailed what was inside—the vineyard, date and other notes. She recognized Mackenzie's handwriting. It was on every tag, on every barrel.

In the beginning, she and Mackenzie had tasted from each varietal, each vineyard every single year. Always together, walking through the barrel room, analyzing, discussing, keeping detailed notes. Later, when Mackenzie began blending, they did that together, as well, Mackenzie tasting everything and Barbara writing down her thoughts. Eventually, though, that had changed. Barbara had stopped going into the vineyards and Mackenzie had started managing the wine on her own. For the past few years, they'd had their defined areas of expertise—Mackenzie handled

the winemaking, leaving the business end of things
to Barbara.

When had everything changed, she wondered, still
furious and at the same time incredibly sad. When had
everything gotten out of hand? When had her trusted
employee—someone she'd invited into her family—
decided to stab her in the back?

She walked through the barrel room to where the
wine was bottled. The equipment was silent now, but
when it was ready, it would move the empty bottles
along, applying labels and filling them, then pushing
in the new corks and sealing the foil. The noise was
incredible, the motors rumbling, the bottles clinking.
And in the end…magic.

And it was all lost, she thought grimly. Destroyed
by an ungrateful bitch who had decided to go out on
her own. Barbara grimaced, again chastising herself
for not taking care to have replacements waiting. There
should have been two or three assistants ready to step
in, but there weren't.

She was going to have to fix that. Hire someone, but
as soon as she started asking around, word would get
out about what had happened. She'd been so careful
to keep it all quiet—some because it was good business practice and some out of shame.

"Damn her," she muttered, then pressed her lips together when she heard footsteps in the hallway.

Her level of irritation rose until she saw Giorgio
walk into the bottling room. Instantly her breathing
slowed and her anger faded as she rushed toward him.

"What are you doing here?" she asked. "Did I know
you were coming?"

He smiled and drew her against him. "I've been

thinking about you, my love. I can't think of anything else." He pulled back just enough to stare into her eyes. "How are you feeling?"

"Sad," she admitted. "Betrayed. Angry."

"Of course. You have lost a piece of your heart." He kissed her forehead. "I don't understand why Mackenzie is being so stubborn. You've offered her everything she wants, including a piece of the business. I was sure that would be enough to convince her to stay."

Barbara ignored the sliver of guilt that stabbed her. Giorgio had done his best to convince her that she should give Mackenzie a small share of Bel Après. Barbara had promised to "think about it." Obviously he'd assumed he'd changed her mind, which he hadn't. She would never give a single spoonful of soil to anyone who wasn't family, especially not her soon-to-be-former daughter-in-law.

"She's ungrateful," Barbara said, avoiding the truth.

"I'm surprised." He kissed her lips. "And disappointed. Perhaps I should go talk to her."

"I don't think that's a good idea," she said quickly, knowing she had to keep them apart. If Giorgio spoke with Mackenzie, he would find out Barbara hadn't offered her anything but more pay.

His dark gaze met hers. "Are you sure? I'm very good at negotiating."

She faked a smile. "Let's give her time."

"As always, you are right, my love. A few weeks away from all this will have her rethinking her stubbornness. I'm usually a good judge of character, but I was wrong about her. I thought she was reasonable."

"I don't think she ever was. We just didn't see it. At

least not until now. She left without a word, without hinting." Real tears formed in her eyes.

He wrapped his arms around her, stroking her back. "You deserve better. Whatever happens with Mackenzie, we'll fix this."

She tried not to stiffen at his words. There was no "us" fixing the problem, she thought. She loved Giorgio more than she'd ever loved anyone in her life, but even he wasn't getting involved with Bel Après. That was for family only.

But then his mouth was on hers, and talking about the winery seemed less important. Later she would remind him about the prenup he'd signed and how she wanted him in her life, her heart and her bed, but not in Bel Après.

Mackenzie stared at the alert on her phone. The simple message, one she saw every single month, shouldn't have upset her. It was a gentle reminder, a way of saving herself difficulties. It wasn't supposed to make her stomach clench or her heart beat faster or her skin go cold. But it did.

Put on a pad. That was it. Four simple words. Put on a pad.

Depending on the time of year, much of her work was outdoors where she didn't have easy access to a bathroom. Getting her period when she was out walking a fence line wasn't convenient. So at six fifteen in the morning, once a month, her phone alerted her to put on a pad so that if her period started that day, she was ready.

She'd seen the alert last month, had followed the instructions but had never gotten her period. That happened from time to time, when she was stressed. But she'd never gone two months in a row without her period. And the alert had first appeared three days ago. She was three days late.

No. She was one month and three days late, a fact that wouldn't have concerned her if she and Rhys hadn't had sex about six weeks ago. Unprotected sex.

She closed her eyes and told herself it wasn't possible. It was just one time. No one got pregnant after just one time, did they?

She covered her face with her hands and told herself to breathe. There had to be another explanation. There was no way she was pregnant. She couldn't be. She was in the process of getting a divorce. She'd just signed a partnership agreement with Bruno, and they were buying a winery. Having a baby right now would be a big, fat mess.

She wasn't pregnant, she told herself. She was stressed. Her hormones were out of whack. Plus, she was thirty-eight. Maybe it was early menopause.

Unable to continue to worry without actually knowing, she left the office. At least Bruno was out of town for a couple of days. She didn't have to face him while she sweated this unexpected crisis.

She drove to the Walmart and bought three different pregnancy kits, using the self-checkout so she didn't have to talk to anyone. The whole way back to the office, she told herself she was fine. She wasn't pregnant—she wasn't. It was impossible.

Three bottles of water and a bunch of peeing later, the truth stared up at her. The information, while delivered in different forms, depending on the kit, was very clear. She was going to have a baby.

Mackenzie sat in her chair and tried to decide what to do now. Obviously she had to call her doctor and make an appointment, but that was the easy part. What about telling Rhys? And Bruno? What about the fact that being pregnant changed everything in her life?

A baby. She had no idea how she felt about that. The concept didn't make any sense. Children? Now? When they'd first been married, she and Rhys had assumed they were going to have children, but somehow it had never happened. Neither of them had pushed for it and eventually she'd decided she was okay with that. She had her nieces and nephews and they were enough. Plus, she had her work and she'd always secretly thought kids would take away from that.

Now it was even worse. A child would tie her to Rhys forever. A child meant they would be in each other's lives, despite the divorce. Worse, she didn't know how he was going to react to the news. While he'd been easy to deal with on the divorce front, he'd made it obvious he was ready to be done with her. A kid would get in the way of that. A kid would—

"Shit. Barbara's going to be my kid's grandmother."

She leaned back in her chair, not sure if she should laugh, cry or simply crawl under the desk and wish it all away. She was pregnant with her almost ex-husband's baby. She had to tell him and her new business partner, then she was going to have to decide how much this changed anything. Could she start a new business and be pregnant? What about after the baby was born? What about—

Mackenzie rose to her feet. "This is Barbara's grandchild," she said aloud. "It's a blood relation."

She let the irony of the moment wash over her. "He or she is going to inherit a part of Bel Après."

And then she started to laugh.

"I don't know," Barbara said, with a sigh. "A DJ seems so tacky."

"We can have a live band," Stephanie murmured, trying to hang on to her patience as they entered hour two of wedding planning that afternoon. "It's up to you. However, they take up a lot more floor space and you don't have as much control over what they play or how they sound. It's your call, Mom."

Stephanie hadn't been sure her mother would want her to handle the event after their most recent encounter, but Barbara had sent her an email suggesting a date and time for them to "move things forward" regarding the wedding, so here she was, sitting in her mother's dining room, notebook in hand.

They'd agreed on the Saturday before Christmas as the date for the event and her mother had decided on the tasting room as the venue.

"Can I hear the bands play? Live?" Barbara asked.

"Live is more of a problem. We'll have to find out where they're going to be, then get permission to attend the event. It's going to take time. I know it seems like we have weeks and weeks, but bands book up early and the holidays are a popular party time."

Her mother glared at her. "Are you being deliberately difficult?"

"How am I being difficult? I'm doing my best to make sure you get exactly what you want. We can arrange to go listen to two or three bands if that's important to you, but I'm simply letting you know that by the time you decide, they will probably be booked, if they're not already."

"Surely they could change their plans."

"You mean blow off their other client for you?" Barbara frowned. "That's very crude."

"But accurate."

They stared at each other. Barbara surprised her by looking away first.

"Fine. Get me the website links for samples and I'll make a decision in the next few days." She tapped the menus Stephanie had suggested. "These are awful. How would you even serve soup three ways? It's ridiculous."

Stephanie drew in a deep, slow breath, telling herself that she was proud of her menu suggestions, and if her mother didn't like them, she was a big old doo-doo head.

"The caterer uses small mugs that hold about four ounces each. Obviously they're not filled to the top, so each serving is between two and three ounces. The presentation is elegant, and the trio makes guests think they're being treated to something special without it being expensive."

Her mother pressed her lips together. "Well, I suppose that isn't a terrible idea."

"Gee, thanks."

Her mother's head snapped up. "Is that sarcasm? Don't try to sell me on one of your harebrained ideas. Just stick to what's traditional and we'll be fine."

"Harebrained ideas? What are you talking about?"

Her mother waved her hand. "You're forever coming up with ridiculous plans for the retail space. The café is a classic example. Why would we bother? Just do your job and don't try to be special."

Stephanie put down her pad of paper and stared at her mother. "Is that really how you see me?" she asked quietly. "When I took over the retail space, sales were stagnant. Now they're up over twenty percent every year."

"Of course they are. The wines are selling better and better. People come to taste them and buy whatever is in there." Her mother raised her eyebrows. "You didn't think you were making it happen, did you?" She smiled. "Oh, Stephanie. Really? It's not you. It has nothing to do with you."

The sentiment shouldn't have been a surprise or an emotional slap and yet it was both those things.

Barbara sighed heavily. "So now what? You're going to pout? I don't understand why you don't comprehend what's important. We are a winery. Everything else is simply there to support that. Why can't you learn that?"

"Just the wine, not the people?"

Her mother stared, her irritation obvious. "Oh, please, can we get emotional, because you know how I love that. Fine. Make me the bad guy in all this. After your divorce, was I too supportive? Poor you. Your evil mother had a house built for you and created a job for you. How do you stand the pain?" She patted the stack of magazines on the dining room table. "If you're done being ridiculous, can we please talk about the flowers?"

Stephanie felt as if she were observing herself from a distance. Her body was in the room, but the rest of her wasn't. She could see herself sitting there, hurt and sadness visible in her eyes.

She looked small, she thought in surprise. She looked small and weak and a little bit like a person who had never been brave. Perhaps because she hadn't been. Not once.

She'd left her husband, but instead of going out on her own, she'd run back to her mother, where, yes, a house had been built and a job arranged. Ten years later, she hadn't done anything to improve her skills, and her efforts to find a different job had been lackluster at best.

She complained plenty but did nothing. What kind of example was that for her children, and what did it say about how she respected—or didn't respect—herself?

"You're right, Mom," she said, looking at her mother. "It's not about me at all, is it? The work I do doesn't matter. The retail is just there to make the wine customers happy. The wine is what's important. You don't need me."

"Darling, I don't need any of my children. Don't take it personally."

If Stephanie had to guess, she would assume that her mother meant the words kindly. At least in her own way of being kind, which wasn't anyone else's definition of it.

She began collecting her notes. "I can't do this right now. I'm sorry. We'll have to reschedule."

"No, we won't. I want to get through this today. Don't you dare leave."

"Or what? I'm thirty-eight years old, Mom. What are you going to do? Tell me I can't go to a party?"

"Don't push me. I have too much going on right now to deal with one of your tantrums. Sit down and plan the damn wedding."

Stephanie could see the crossroads in front of her. She could stay where she'd been for too long, working a job she didn't like, feeling trapped and helpless. Or she could get off her butt and demand a little something of herself. She could, just this once, be brave.

"I quit."

She hadn't meant to say the words, but as soon as she did, she felt stronger, happier and empowered. Also frightened, but somehow that was okay.

"I quit," she repeated.

Her mother stared at her. "What are you talking about? You can't quit."

"I can. I just did." She picked up her papers and schedule. "Mom, if you want me to plan the wedding, I'm happy to help. Just not today. As for working for Bel Après, I'm done. It's only the retail section that doesn't really matter, so you shouldn't miss me at all."

"You sit back down right now. If you walk out of this house, you'll regret it. You don't want to cross me."

Stephanie shoved her things into her tote bag and started out of the house. Her mother was still screaming when she closed the door behind her.

Once outside, she was surprised that it was still sunny, still warm and beautiful. There weren't any dark clouds, no threatening storm. The world went on.

"I quit," she whispered to herself, proud and terrified in equal measures. She knew she'd done the right thing. Her method might not have been the most mature, but the results were excellent. Or they would be once she figured out what on earth she was going to do next.

nineteen

Barbara's very bad week improved slightly as she read the list of potential winemakers Rhys had brought her. While none of them were Mackenzie, they all had possibility.

At least something was going right, she thought grimly, refusing to waste even a second of her workday thinking about her daughter's defection. What did she care if Stephanie didn't work for her anymore? A monkey could be trained to do her job.

Which might be true, but didn't take away the odd sense of loss she'd been feeling for the past few days. A ridiculous emptiness she couldn't explain and didn't like at all.

She glanced at Rhys over her reading glasses. "This is good," she said, waving the names of people he'd suggested they approach about a job at Bel Après. "You've been thorough."

"Just doing my job. We're going to find someone, Mom."

"Make sure they sign something saying they can't

talk about what's happening here. I don't want word getting out."

"An NDA," he said with a smile. "Nondisclosure agreement."

There was something in his look, she thought. Some inside joke she didn't get, not that she cared.

"I'm still angry about the money you're giving Mackenzie."

"I'm not happy about it, either, but it's done. You have to let it go."

"Do I?" She tossed the papers onto her desk. "Her leaving is going to ruin us."

"It's not. Depending on the wine, we have anywhere from two to four years in the cellar. That buys us time. Most consumers don't know who the winemaker is for any given label. We'll get someone good and we'll get a backup person. We're going to get through this."

"You're thinking it's my fault we don't have someone to step into Mackenzie's job."

"You're the one who resisted adding the extra staff. She brought it up several times, Mom, and so did I."

He was right, which annoyed her. "I didn't think that tramp you married would do this to us."

"Mom." His tone warned her. "Don't bad-mouth her. She wasn't a tramp."

"You don't know that. She could have had lovers all over the valley."

"Stop it."

"You're getting a divorce. Why do you care if I say something bad about her?"

"Because it's not right. We're still friends."

How like him to disappoint her with that, as well.

Friends. "Reasonable people dislike each other when they get a divorce."

"I've heard that." He nodded at the papers on her desk. "Once you approve the names, I'll get in touch with them individually. Set up a casual meeting without telling them why. I know most of them, so hearing from me won't raise any alarms."

"That makes sense."

She would rather do it herself, but she wasn't a casual-meeting kind of person, and while she knew most of the people on the list, they would be shocked if she called and suggested they get together to talk. Except for Lori, all her children were much more outgoing than she had ever been. Not that it—

Her office door burst open. Lori stared wide-eyed. "There's been an accident in the warehouse."

As one, they headed out the door and down the stairs. In the main building they raced toward the cellaring rooms. The smell of wine reached them long before they saw the disaster.

Barbara glanced around and saw that a pallet of cases of wine had somehow fallen. Hundreds of bottles lay smashed. Glass and ripped cardboard were everywhere and red wine pooled on the floor.

One of the warehouse guys stepped forward, his eyes wide, his hands twisting together. "I'm sorry. I was making a turn and one side of the pallet snapped and they went falling."

Barbara saw the broken pallet and knew he was probably telling the truth. Space was tight in here, so the pallets were moved high above the tops of the shelves, something Rhys had told her was a mistake. "How much?" she asked.

"About a hundred and fifty cases."

Rhys picked up a broken bottle, showing her the label. "Not our most expensive, but pricey enough. Twelve bottles a case, at maybe forty dollars a bottle."

"We have insurance," Lori said quickly. "This will be covered."

Financially they would be, Barbara thought, feeling hollow and depressed at the sight. But the wine was gone forever.

She was aware of them all monitoring her, as if waiting for her to explode, despite the fact that it was an obvious accident. She watched the wine make its way toward the drain in the center of the warehouse. As the liquid swirled away, she knew that was how she felt. As if everything she'd worked for was slowly being sucked out of her.

"Handle it," she told Rhys and started back to her office. The symbolism, while not the least bit subtle, was painfully accurate. She could feel herself losing control and she had no idea how to get it back.

The land on Red Mountain was the most expensive in the state—for wine, that was. Mackenzie was sure a few blocks in downtown Seattle would go for a lot more—but on the agriculture front, this was Park Avenue, the Left Bank in Paris and the best part of pick-your-city pricey.

There were reasons. The soil, the sun, the wind, all of which combined to create perfect growing conditions for the fruity, full-bodied red wines the state was known for.

Once the deal went through for them to buy Painted Moon, this land would be hers, or at least half hers, which was plenty. She should be excited and giddy and overflowing with ideas. Her head was spinning but not from possibilities. All she could think about was the fact that she was pregnant.

She wanted to ask how it had happened, but she already knew the answer to that. A single night, a single event, had changed everything.

She glanced at Bruno, who was walking beside her. He'd traded in a suit and a white button-down dress shirt for jeans and a dark green polo shirt. He looked good. Tall, with broad shoulders. He was fit and had that air of easy confidence. Maybe he was one of those people who was comfortable anywhere. She wasn't like that. This was the one place where she felt at home, only she didn't today. She felt awkward and uncomfortable and scared and confused.

"What's wrong?" he asked, turning to look at her. "There's something on your mind. Usually when we walk a vineyard, you're studying every plant, hovering over them, practically communing with them."

His tone was light, but she saw the concern in his eyes. She had to tell him the truth—she knew that. What she didn't know was how he would react. Was the dream she'd barely allowed herself to believe could happen going to come to an end before it had begun?

"I'm pregnant."

She had to give him credit, he barely reacted. One eyebrow rose slightly, but that was it.

"Rhys?" he asked.

She nodded.

"Goodbye sex is very powerful," he said, watching her carefully.

"It was more like we haven't had sex in years and

is this really the death of our marriage." She looked away. "I only found out yesterday. I still have to see my doctor and figure out what I'm going to do."

"You're keeping the baby."

Not a question, but she nodded anyway. "I have to. I want to," she amended. "It's just shocking. Did I spit?"

He tilted his head. "Just now?"

She managed a slight smile. "No. When we were tasting Herman's barrels. Did I spit? That's what I remember, but now I have to worry about the baby. You're not supposed to drink alcohol while you're pregnant and I'm a winemaker. How is that going to work?"

"You spit every time," he told her. "It was very elegant."

"I hope I did." She fingered a grape leaf. "I haven't told anyone yet. I barely believe it myself. I have to let Rhys know. I don't think he'll be happy."

Something else she was worried about. They'd never had kids. If they'd wanted to, they could have gotten pregnant a thousand times over. But they never had. Until now.

"Does the pregnancy change anything about the divorce?"

A reasonable question, she thought. "No. Neither of us is going to change our mind." She looked at Bruno. "Does it change things with you?"

"Do you want it to?"

"That's not answering the question."

"I still want to go into business with you."

"But I'm pregnant. I'm excited about what we can do here, and I want to move forward with the deal. Having said that, a kid is going to change things and

I don't know how. I don't see myself becoming a stay-at-home parent, but I could get weird with hormones. And I don't know how much I'll be able to do the last couple of months of the pregnancy." She waved her hand. "I'm guessing at all this. I don't know the first thing about being pregnant or having a baby."

He smiled. "I'm not worried that you'll suddenly want to spend your day knitting. I see you more as the strapping on the baby and heading into the fields type."

"I like that image a lot."

Thinking about carrying her baby with her as she worked made her feel good.

"We have a partnership agreement," he said. "I don't want to change that. You're the best, Mackenzie. You'll always be the best. Besides, I like kids."

His voice was a little wistful. She remembered him telling her he couldn't have children. Would her being pregnant be difficult for him?

Even as she thought the question, she shook it off. She was hardly the first pregnant woman he'd been around.

"You can bring the baby to work with you," he added. "We'll find someone to help with day care and move forward with our plan."

"Thank you. That's what I want, too." She hesitated. "I was afraid you'd back out of the deal."

He smiled. "It's going to take a whole lot more than a pregnancy to get rid of me."

Four's family room perfectly reflected the personality of the owners. The hardwood floors had been whitewashed. Sliding doors allowed sunlight to pour into the space, illuminating the floor-to-ceiling mural.

The forest scene had a castle in the distance, trolls under bridges, sprites, unicorns, a very wild-looking bear and three children proudly marching together under a banner of what Four claimed was the family crest. Stephanie was less sure the small picture of a dragon holding a hamburger was historically accurate, but she wasn't in a position to say either way.

She curled up in the corner of a large sectional that faced the backyard. The square coffee table had been painted to represent a bouquet of summer flowers. The petals clustered together, while the legs were the green stems. In the corner, by the fireplace, a climbing wall was anchored to the wall and the ceiling. Brightly colored mats were scattered underneath, to protect the kids in case of a fall.

Painted baskets were filled with books and colored markers and building blocks and stickers. A nearly life-size rocking horse—Jaguar's fifth anniversary present to his wife—took the place of a table and chairs in the eat-in kitchen. Four's family ate in the dining room. Or outside. Or in the attic on nights when there was a thunderstorm.

The house smelled of flowers and herbs with an unexpected undernote of clean. The fabrics were things like organic cotton and bamboo. Splashes of color surprised from around every corner and the sound of a playful stream could be heard over the house's built-in sound system.

With the kids at summer camp and Jaguar at work, Four and Stephanie were alone in the house. Stephanie had shown up with no warning and immediately burst into tears. Her sister had settled her on the sofa, then retreated to the kitchen, where she quickly made chocolate martinis—heavy on both the chocolate and the vodka.

Stephanie took the finished drink and sniffed. "It's nine thirty in the morning," she said before taking a sip. "Not that this isn't delicious."

"Something happened," Four told her. "It felt more like an alcohol event. But if you'd like to go sit in the sauna and sweat out your pain, we can do that."

When the house was built, Jaguar and Four had insisted on a meditation space on one side. The quiet room led to an honest-to-God sauna, along with a Jacuzzi. Every December, during the winter solstice, Stephanie and her kids joined Four and her family, along with Mackenzie, for a meditation, followed by them all squeezing into the sauna.

After that they feasted on hamburgers, hot dogs and potato salad, as a reminder that summer was coming.

Stephanie smiled. "I think the martini will work just fine."

Four sat cross-legged on the chaise of the sofa, her long hair pulled back in a braid. She had on shorts and a T-shirt and, just for today, looked pretty much like any other stay-at-home mom her age.

"You took a while to come see me," her sister said.

Stephanie raised her eyebrows. "What are you talking about?"

"Whatever happened took place—" Four closed her eyes "—three days ago. I felt the disturbance, but I didn't know what it was."

Stephanie took a big sip of her drink. "Now you're scaring me."

"Why? My oneness with the universe should be a comfort. We all need to be connected with something larger than ourselves. That way we're reminded how we all fit together and should be working for the greater good."

Stephanie wanted to ask if Four had spoken to their mother but knew she didn't have to. If Four had heard about what had happened, she would have said so. Four said what was on her mind. She didn't believe in playing emotional games—it blocked her mental flow.

Stephanie set down her drink. "That's really good, by the way."

"I use dark chocolate syrup. It has a little bite to it."

"I quit my job."

Four's expression didn't change. "Go on."

"We were planning the wedding. I'd come up with several ideas I thought would make Mom happy. Somehow we ended up talking about my work at the winery and how I thought I made a difference. She called my ideas harebrained and said any increase in sales was about the wine and not anything I've done." Stephanie picked up her glass. "I'm saying this all wrong."

"You're saying it exactly right."

"I got mad, but I was hurt. It was like an out-of-body experience. I saw myself, sitting there. I looked small and then I decided I was done. So I quit."

Four smiled. "I'm really proud of you. Congratulations. You're free."

"Yeah? I mostly feel a little sick to my stomach. Avery took it fine when I told her." She raised a shoulder. "We went through a rough patch a few weeks ago, but things are good between us now. She actually told me that Grandma doesn't appreciate anyone who isn't Mackenzie and not to take her insults personally. Oh, and she wants to know if she can come work for me when I get settled somewhere."

"That has to make you feel good."

"It does." She and Avery had also talked a little more about Kyle's cheating and why Stephanie had stayed. Hopefully there would be no more surprises from Kyle and things could stay calm on the kid front.

Stephanie leaned forward. "I've been trying to figure out what to do now. There are financial considerations. I own the house, but I have to put food on the table and pay the bills. Not that I want to stay home. I like having a job. I like feeling as if I'm helping and I enjoy the challenge. But this is Walla Walla. Where am I going to find a decent job?"

Four tilted her head, her long braid hanging down and brushing against the sofa. "Really? That's the question?"

"You're going to say I should work for a winery, aren't you? There are dozens, maybe hundreds, in the area, and I know the business. Which sounds great, but I don't know if I can do it. Ignoring the guilt of working for what our mother would call 'the enemy.'" She made air quotes. "What if Mom is right? What if I didn't improve sales? What if I'm just a cog in a wheel?"

"What if you're not? What if you're creative and re-sourceful and you're finally able to be your best self? What if this is a new beginning and you can find the contentment that has always eluded you?"

"You're putting a lot of pressure on one little job."

"I'm asking the question."

"It's a scary question."

Four smiled. "All the good ones are." She finished

her drink. "You can do this. You want to do this. Use your experience and your ideas to create something that will make you proud."

Stephanie nodded slowly. The pep talk was exactly why she'd come to see her baby sister.

"You are wise beyond your years."

"I think I was a shaman in a previous life."

Stephanie grinned. "I have no doubt about that."

twenty

Barbara sat in her usual seat at the table, with Giorgio at the opposite end. He was deep in conversation with Jaguar, perhaps discussing the farm equipment her son-in-law repaired. All her grandchildren were there, except for Carson, who was still at baseball camp. Avery, such a beauty with her long hair and big eyes, talked to Lori. Catherine and Stephanie were whispering and glancing in her direction.

Stephanie's appearance at the dinner surprised her. She had thought her daughter would boycott the event. But instead, she'd arrived on time, greeted everyone and acted as though nothing was wrong. Barbara couldn't decide if she was genuinely fine with what had happened, or if she was simply too stupid to recognize the danger she was in.

There was no going back, she thought grimly. Stephanie had betrayed her and she had to be punished. Should her daughter come crawling back for her job, Barbara was going to tell her no. To be honest, she quite looked forward to saying the words and reminding Stephanie that there was a price for her behavior. But so far, that hadn't happened.

Everyone was acting so normally, she wasn't sure if anyone even knew about Stephanie's little fit. Avery hadn't said anything, nor had Catherine. Perhaps Stephanie was keeping it a secret so she could simply ease back into what she'd done before. Or so she thought.

Barbara had no idea what she was going to do about the wedding. Stephanie couldn't plan it now and Lori was truly less than useless. Catherine would offer, but there was no way Barbara would let her youngest plan the purchase of a hamster, let alone a wedding. Just thinking about how hideous it would be made her shudder.

Regret tasted bitter on her tongue. It wasn't just the pieces of her family that had been lost, she thought grimly. Her enthusiasm at the thought of planning her big day had faded. Now a big wedding seemed like a chore—one more thing she had to get done. So what was she to do? Cancel the wedding? She and Giorgio could elope, she thought. Surely there had to be somewhere elegant they could go. She couldn't stand a tacky little plastic place where she waited in line with the other pathetic wedding couples.

Shaking off the image, she glanced around the table. The dinner was nearly finished, and while she should be happy to have her family around her, she wasn't. Despite the rearrangement of the chairs and place settings, in her mind there was still an empty seat and an equally large hole in her heart.

She missed her. There, she'd thought it, admitted it, if only to herself. She missed Mackenzie. Missed her helping with the meal. Mackenzie had always been the first to join her in the kitchen, eager to do whatever job Barbara assigned her. Mackenzie was the one who helped her pick out the linens and made sure the table was set the way Barbara liked it.

When the meal was served, Mackenzie sat close to her. They talked wines and who was doing what in the valley. She enjoyed her time with the family and laughed often and now Barbara would never share that laugh with her again.

She caught sight of Rhys glancing at his watch.

"That's the third time you've checked your watch in the past half hour," she said. "Do you have somewhere you have to be?"

Rhys looked at her before nodding. "I'm meeting someone this evening."

Barbara tried to take in the words. "You have a date with a woman?"

The table went silent as everyone glanced between them.

Rhys smiled at her. "Yes, Mom. With a woman."

Not Mackenzie, she thought, feeling pain on her daughter-in-law's behalf.

"It seems a little soon," she snapped.

Giorgio watched her, as if prepared to rush to her side to comfort her, something she usually enjoyed. Just not today, she thought. Today she was sad and there was no solace to be found. A melodramatic thought, but still an accurate one.

"Jaguar and I have been looking at a new school for the kids," Catherine said in an obvious attempt to change the subject. "They'll be using a lot of new teaching techniques that are more nurturing than traditional teaching methods."

"Let me guess," Barbara said dryly. "No curriculum, no tests. In fact the children decide what they want to learn."

"You shouldn't dismiss something just because it's new," Catherine told her. "The old ways aren't always best."

"Explain that to my grandchildren when they discover how helpful reading and math would have been to get a decent job."

"Children need to be allowed to be themselves."

"So they can grow up and leave you without a second thought?" she asked, tossing her napkin onto her half-eaten lasagna. "Excuse me, I have a headache."

She walked out of the dining room and into the kitchen. Once there, she didn't know where to go. Damn her! This was all Mackenzie's fault. The pain of missing her, how everything was different.

Familiar hands settled on her shoulders. She turned and let Giorgio pull her close.

"I miss her," she whispered into his shoulder. "I miss her so much. I hate her and I miss her."

"You love her," he corrected, stroking her hair. "It's a natural thing to be sad. To love her and want things back how they were."

She nodded. "You saw Rhys. He's already moved on. He doesn't care about their marriage. And Catherine with her ridiculous ideas. Where did I go wrong with my children?"

"They are beautiful children. You did a wonderful job."

She stepped back and looked at him. "Why do you always see the best in me?"

"I see what's real."

She wanted that to be true but knew it wasn't. He had an idealized vision of her that in no way matched reality. If he knew about the anger in her heart, how she wanted revenge and Mackenzie punished... But he didn't. He saw only what he wanted to see, which was probably for the best. Of course it meant that he never really saw her for who she was.

He pulled her close again. "We will be married soon and that will help. You won't have to be alone, as you have been all these years."

Alone? She wasn't alone. She had Bel Après, but he wouldn't understand that. Giorgio had created a business, but she'd been part of a legacy. There was a difference. Still, he loved her deeply and he tried. She really couldn't ask for more.

Mackenzie finished dressing. After picking up her purse, she walked the short distance to her doctor's office. Dr. Brighton was in her forties, with short hair and a confident air. She smiled when Mackenzie took a seat.

"I have some questions," Mackenzie said. "I'm a winemaker. It's my job to taste wine. I know alcohol is bad for the baby, so what do I do?" She tried to keep the panic out of her voice as she spoke. Telling her doctor about all the barrels waiting at Painted Moon wasn't going to help.

Dr. Brighton shook her head. "I know plenty of winemakers and they all spit rather than swallow when barrel tasting. I assume you do the same?"

Mackenzie nodded. "I can't get drunk first thing in the morning. It makes for a bad day."

"Then keep up the practice. Be more vigilant about it. The first three weeks after conception the fetus doesn't absorb alcohol. The first two trimesters are the most sensitive time. No drinking for pleasure. When you're going to be tasting, make sure you're completely hydrated so your body doesn't want to suck in the moisture. Keep the sessions short. Rinse out your mouth with water between sips. Spread out your tastings over days rather than hours. You don't have to give up your job, you just have to be careful."

"That makes sense." She could follow all those rules. She'd been doing a lot of reading online, and while there weren't a lot of articles about being a winemaker while pregnant, she'd been able to pick up a few tips. "And sampling at harvest is safe, right? They're just grapes at that point."

"Exactly. Sample away. Now, about the rest of your pregnancy." Dr. Brighton looked at her chart. "You're healthy. Your last bloodwork was excellent. Still, you're thirty-eight and this is a first pregnancy, so I'll want to watch you a little more closely until we see how things shake out. Do you have a personal support system?"

"I have friends."

"The baby's father?"

Mackenzie hesitated. "My husband. We're getting a divorce."

"How does he feel about the baby?"

"I haven't told him yet. I'm doing that tomorrow. I wanted to see you first."

"Pregnancy is a perfectly natural thing for a woman to experience, but that doesn't mean it's easy. Every system in your body will be affected. You'll be tired more, you'll have mood swings. At times your body is going to feel like an alien teenage creature, doing things out of spite." She smiled. "You need to eat right, get plenty of sleep and make sure the people around you are taking care of you. How does that sound?"

"Daunting, but doable."

At least she hoped it would be. Mackenzie knew she could count on Stephanie, for sure, and Four. She didn't know about Rhys—she hoped he would be happy and there for her, but with the divorce and all, she couldn't be sure. She also had Bruno. Something in her gut said he would be someone she could depend on. As for the rest of her world, she had no idea.

Dr. Brighton passed her several brochures. "Some reading material to get you started. You'll have to make some changes in your diet. Healthy eating is key. Lots of protein, fruits and vegetables. There's a list of foods to avoid."

Mackenzie took all the offered papers, thanked the doctor, then went and sat in her Jeep. Except for her head spinning, she didn't feel any differently than she had a week ago. So far she wasn't extra tired or experiencing morning sickness. But she would have to make changes to her routine. She was also going to have to start letting people know she was pregnant. She had a feeling she knew what Stephanie and Four were going to say. Barbara was going to have a fit, but the one reaction she couldn't anticipate was that of the man who no longer wanted to be married to her.

Stephanie had gone all out for her lunch date with Mackenzie. Sliced chicken breast, bacon and extra avocado. Easy on the mayo. A big bag of barbecue potato chips for them to share and, not one, not two, but four dark nut-filled brownies. In an effort to keep the calorie count down, she'd passed on the soda and had instead bought them each a bottle of water. Her meal in hand, she walked past several stores, a couple of tasting rooms, then turned at the corner and entered the small office building where Mackenzie and Bruno now worked.

She'd texted the previous evening, asking if they could hang out for lunch. With Bruno out of town, Mackenzie had suggested their office and Stephanie had offered to bring lunch. There was much to discuss.

Stephanie followed the suite numbers to the correct door, then knocked. Mackenzie let her in, smiling broadly as she pulled her close.

"I've missed you," Mackenzie said, taking the big lunch bag from her and setting it on a desk, then hugging her again. "It's been forever. I don't get home until late and I'm gone early and, wow, you look great."

Stephanie relaxed into the familiar embrace, thinking this was exactly what she needed in her life. More Mackenzie time.

As she drew back, she wrinkled her nose. "We've both been bad friends. We're letting circumstances get in the way of us hanging out. We're going to have to work harder to stay connected."

Mackenzie nodded. "I totally agree. Let's start texting every day. Just quick check-in texts, so we're in touch. And we'll have to plan more times to get together. It's not going to happen organically anymore. I really love you and I've missed you."

"I love you, too."

They smiled at each other. Stephanie felt a little of

her worry fade away. She closed the door behind her, then took in the plain office. There were two desks that faced each other, a small round conference table, a couple of filing cabinets, some shelving and a door that led to what Stephanie would guess was a restroom.

"I would have thought this would be more fancy," she teased.

Mackenzie laughed. "We're saving the money for the winery. Actually this place works great. It's quiet and it's on the side of town closest to Painted Moon."

Stephanie watched as her friend set out the lunch. Mackenzie looked good. Maybe a little thinner, but she seemed fairly rested and there was a bounce to her actions that hadn't been there before.

"You're happy to be in business with Bruno?" she asked, taking a seat at the conference table.

"I am. He's great. Very knowledgeable and under-standing. He's also calm. There's no screaming, no accusations."

"So the opposite of my mother."

Mackenzie grinned. "Yeah, there is that. I'll admit, I like it."

She passed Stephanie a sandwich and gave her one of the waters, then sat down. Stephanie opened the bag of chips and placed it between them.

"I keep thinking about your working there," Mackenzie added. "I feel guilty. I know she's making your life miserable, punishing you for what I did."

Stephanie opened her water. "Yeah, well, that's less of a problem. I quit my job."

Mackenzie paused with a sandwich partway to her mouth. Her eyes widened as she returned the food to the wrapper.

"You what?"

"Quit." Stephanie explained about helping Barbara with the wedding and how things had spiraled out of control.

"I felt ridiculous," she admitted. "She basically said my hard work didn't matter." She shook her head. "No. That's not right. I didn't matter. It was humiliating but ultimately freeing. Why was I torturing myself?"

"You quit?"

Stephanie laughed. "You have to stop saying that. Yes, it's done."

"I feel awful. It's all my fault."

"See, you always assume you have power that you don't have. I made the decision on my own."

"She wouldn't have been so difficult if I'd stayed."

"You're right and then I would have been stuck there another ten years, hating what I was doing and wishing I could be strong enough to leave. I finally did it. Maybe not in the most mature, thoughtful way possible, but it's done and I say yay me."

Mackenzie held up her water. "Yay you! If you're happy, I'm happy. What are you going to do about a job? Do you have to work?"

"If we're going to keep eating, then yes. Right now I'm considering my options. Four, like you, told me I have to get over the whole guilt thing about working for another winery. I've been putting together some ideas for marketing and retail. Once I do that, I'll set up some appointments."

Which sounded way more together than it was, but she was moving forward. She'd found several old campaigns she'd done for the retail space and had added those to her portfolio. After a couple of years of just phoning it in, she felt good being creative again.

"You sure you're all right?" Mackenzie asked.

"I have my dark moments, but I ignore them and do the work. I'm giving myself a few weeks to get a plan finalized. By then Carson will be home from camp and both kids will be ready to go back to school."

"You don't want to apply during harvest," Mackenzie told her. "Even though the marketing people and retail staff aren't part of it, there's still an air of frantic energy. They might not be able to give you the attention you need."

Stephanie knew that was true, but she wasn't waiting until mid-to-late October to start looking for a job.

"I'll make it work," she said. "So how's the sale coming?"

"Good. Fast." Mackenzie pressed a hand to her chest. "Some days I can barely catch my breath. I'm so grateful Bruno's handling all that. I just have to deal with the wines and plan for harvest."

"You love harvest."

"I do. It's the promise of what the wine is going to be. I just…" She drew in a breath. "I'm going to say something and you're going to react, but I need you to promise you won't say anything to anyone before I talk to Rhys. Really promise. I just have to figure—"

Stephanie threw a chip at her. "Stop stalling. Tell me!"

Stephanie half expected her friend to say she'd met someone or maybe kissed hunky Bruno, but instead Mackenzie looked at her and said, "I'm pregnant."

Stephanie heard the words clearly, but at first she

had no idea what they meant. "Pregnant as in—" She stood up. "Holy crap! You're pregnant!"

She danced around the table and pulled Mackenzie to her feet, then hugged her. "You're having a baby? When did this happen? You had sex with someone? Who? When?"

There had to be a guy, because according to Rhys, he and Mackenzie hadn't done the deed in forever. So why hadn't she mentioned whoever it was she was sleeping with?

"It's Rhys," Mackenzie said with a shrug when they both settled back in their chairs.

"But I thought, I mean, you're getting a divorce. Are you still sleeping together?"

"We weren't. We're not now. It was a onetime thing." Mackenzie poked at her sandwich. "Actually that was the night we realized we were done. It was so sad."

Stephanie suddenly remembered Rhys telling her the same thing.

"As for birth control," Mackenzie continued, "I used to have an IUD, but I got it taken out."

"You did. A couple of summers ago. You were bleeding a lot. You never got it put back?"

Mackenzie shook her head. "No. We weren't exactly, you know, close. There didn't seem to be any reason, then I didn't think about it." She looked at Stephanie. "Just as an FYI, one time is all it takes."

"You're going to have a baby."

"I know. I'm scared and nervous and kind of excited, too. Not that I know what I'm doing."

That was a lot to take in, Stephanie thought. "Wow. Go you. Oh, wait. What about Bruno?"

"He knows and he says he's fine with it." She smiled. "He told me I'm going to be the kind of mom who straps on the baby and heads out into the fields."

"He's not wrong." Stephanie reached for her sandwich. "My head is spinning."

"Mine, too."

"Whatever you need, I'm here. I can go with you to appointments and be your labor coach. Four will want to help, especially with setting up the baby's room. You're not alone." She grinned. "I still have that spare room if you want to come live with me."

"Thanks, but I'm holding out for the farmhouse at Painted Moon."

"That will be a quieter option." Stephanie took a bite of her sandwich. "Pregnant. That's huge. Have you seen the doctor? There are things you can't eat and—" She stared at her friend. "You can't drink! You drink for a living."

"It's going to be a challenge." Mackenzie explained what the doctor had said.

"I've never liked the spitting," Stephanie admitted. "I get why it has to be done, but it's gross."

"You get used to it. I'm going to have to taste barrels and I'll be drinking tons of water before I do that. It's scary. I don't want to hurt the baby, but I still have a job."

An unexpected complication, Stephanie thought. "Let me know when you tell Rhys so I can be on the lookout for any behavior changes." She stared at her. "My mom. She's going to find out eventually. Oh, no! You're having Rhys's baby, so he or she will be part of the inheritance." Stephanie started to laugh.

"I've thought about that, too. She's going to freak and possibly firebomb my car."

"I think the firebomb is unlikely but she's going to lose it. I'm petty enough to be excited about that. Who says God doesn't have a sense of humor?"

Mackenzie held up her water. "Not me."

Stephanie bumped her bottle with her own. "Here's to beautiful babies and new jobs. May we always surprise each other in good ways."

"To my best friend."

"And to mine."

twenty-one

Barbara had no qualms about walking into her son's house in the middle of the day. If they wanted to keep people out, they should lock the doors. But of course they didn't. Everyone was forever running back and forth between the homes, putting up cookie flags and playing ridiculous games with the children.

Or at least they had been, she thought as she paused in the foyer. Lately there had been less of that. Probably because Mackenzie was never here anymore.

But there had been a time, she thought. When Mackenzie had arranged multigenerational hide-and-seek, or when she and Rhys had built a firepit and they'd stayed up past midnight to watch a meteor shower. Everyone had brought blankets and pillows and they'd all sprawled out together.

When had evenings like that stopped happening, Barbara wondered as she wandered through the downstairs of the house. When had Mackenzie and Rhys pulled back, retreating to their house rather than joining in? She supposed the change had been gradual enough that no one had noticed—not even them, she would guess.

She ignored Rhys's office, instead stepping into her daughter-in-law's. The colors were brighter, the desk smaller. There were photographs on the wall. A few of the wedding, some of the sisters, one of Mackenzie and Barbara, their arms wrapped around each other.

Barbara lingered over that one. Ten years ago, maybe twelve. They'd just finished harvest. They were dirty and exhausted, but happy. They'd both known it was going to be their best year yet and it had been.

She sat in front of the desk and began opening drawers. She wasn't looking for anything in particular. She shuffled through office supplies and an old bottle of aspirin. There was a half roll of mints and some hair ties. Nothing else—nothing significant.

She returned to the hallway and ran her hands along a table she and Mackenzie had bought on one of their shopping trips to Seattle. They'd also picked out the dining room set together, and the dishes.

She went upstairs and turned toward the master. The bedroom set was one that Barbara and James had inherited from his grandparents. A beautiful antique that she'd had refinished for the newlyweds. She wondered when the young couple had stopped being happy.

In the bathroom she found no trace of her son, nor did he have anything in the closet. There were only Mackenzie's clothes, neatly sorted. The shirts and jeans she wore for work were folded on a shelf. Her cocktail dresses were at one end, with more casual dresses next to them.

Barbara returned to the bedroom where she opened dresser drawers, not sure what she was looking for, then turned her attention to the jewelry box on the dresser.

In the top drawer sat the diamond stud earrings Mackenzie wore when she got dressed up. She wasn't really a jewelry type of person, so she had only a few things. Gold hoops, a pair of ridiculous hippo earrings that Catherine had made for her. In the bottom drawer of the jewelry box, sitting alone, was her wedding set.

Barbara picked up the rings and put them in the palm of her hand. Rhys had asked her advice about the rings. He'd wanted to pick out something that Mackenzie would like.

"Simple but elegant," she'd advised him. "A round solitaire and a plain, platinum band."

He hadn't been sure, but in the end he'd listened, and Mackenzie had been thrilled with his choices. She rarely wore the engagement ring, but she used to wear the wedding band. When had she stopped?

Barbara put them back and closed the drawer, then looked around the room. She still had no idea what she was looking for, but it wasn't here. Not anymore. Everything she'd hoped for Rhys and Mackenzie had been lost or possibly destroyed. The broken pieces could never be made whole. There was nothing to do but pretend it didn't matter and keep moving forward.

She walked out of the bedroom, down the stairs and into the sunlight, blinking in the brightness of the early afternoon. Then she drove to the office and returned to her desk. At least there she controlled her world and those in it.

Mackenzie hesitated just inside the kitchen. She'd texted Rhys and asked him to meet her late Saturday afternoon, after work and before heading out for the evening.

She'd gone over what she was going to say a thousand times in her head but still found herself unsure of how much to get into when it came to things like custody and a joint-parenting plan. There was a fluttering in the pit of her stomach that had nothing to do with her pregnancy and everything to do with nerves.

She told herself she would be fine. This was Rhys. She knew him, loved him, had married him. He wasn't going to be mad or blame her. He might not be thrilled, but he was a rational human being. He would listen, deal and together they would come up with a plan.

They still lived in the same house, ate the food left by the family chef. He took her calls, answered her texts. In truth, very little about their lives together had changed. A reality that made her sad down to her bones.

When had that happened? When had they started living separate lives and why hadn't she noticed it happening? She supposed the changes had been small until they added up to something that mattered. Something that had ultimately broken their marriage.

"Why are you lurking?"

The teasing question came from behind her. She turned and saw Rhys walking toward her. She faked a smile.

"I was lost in thought."

"I don't know. It looked like a lurk to me." He crossed his arms and leaned against the island. "How are you? I haven't seen you in days. Bruno keeping you busy?"

"We're both scrambling to keep up with events," she said, sitting at the table and motioning for Rhys to join her. "Things are going very smoothly, which is both good and a little scary. I'm daunted by the paperwork."

"Herman's a motivated seller. He wants you to have Painted Moon because he knows you'll always care about it."

Rhys picked up a bottle of red wine and waved it toward her, as if offering a glass. She shook her head no. He sat across from her.

"So what's up? I know you don't want my advice on the business."

She managed a smile. "I already know what you think."

"It's a great opportunity for you. A chance to do your own thing. That would never happen here."

"I'm sorry about the trouble with your mom."

He shrugged. "You know how she gets. Eventually she'll move on to hating someone else."

Barbara hated her? Mackenzie tried not to react to the casual words, even though they cut down to her heart.

"Interesting about Stephanie," he added, as if he didn't know she was struggling to act normal. "Quitting like that. I guess she and Mom really went at it. Everything's changing."

She fought against a flood of guilt, knowing she had culpability in that breakup, as well. If she and Rhys hadn't split up, she wouldn't have left Bel Après. If she hadn't left, Stephanie wouldn't have had to defend her. And so on and so on.

He looked at her. "You called this meeting. What's up?"

Part of her wanted to say "Nothing" and bolt, putting off the confession, but she wouldn't do that. Hiding only made things worse. She looked directly at him and said, "I'm pregnant."

He stared at her blankly. "You can't be. You have an IUD. You're not pregnant."

"I had it taken out two years ago. Rhys, you knew that. You drove me to the procedure."

"No." He stood and moved until the island was between them, shaking his head the entire time. "No. You're not. You can't be. Not now. A kid?" He swore.

"You're upset," she whispered, mostly because she couldn't think of what else to say.

"Upset? I'm upset?" His voice rose. "I don't think that comes close to describing what I am. Pregnant? That's the last thing either of us needs." He turned and hit the wall with his fist, then spun back to her. "All I wanted was a life. Is that too much to ask? I've spent the past five years living like a goddamned monk in this house. No sex, no connection of any kind. All we ever talked about was work. I wanted something more. Anything that wasn't this and now you're pregnant?"

She hadn't expected him to be happy, but she hadn't expected this kind of reaction. Each of his words was a punch in the gut until she was mentally hunched over, trying to protect herself.

"I'm going to want you to have a DNA test when the baby's born."

She half rose, then sank down in the chair. "You really are a bastard. I wouldn't have known."

"What do you expect me to say?" he demanded.

"That you believe me. You know I wasn't having sex with anyone else. How exactly would that happen? I was on Bel Après property every second of every day. Do you think I was meeting some guy out in the vineyards? That's romantic."

"I know. I'm sorry. I just…" He braced himself against the island. "I don't want any of this. I just want to get a divorce." He looked at her. "You never thought to get on some kind of birth control?"

"Why would I bother?" she snapped, digging for the anger that would give her strength. "As you keep saying, we weren't having sex. For the second time in five minutes, I point out that you *drove* me to the doctor when I got out my IUD. You knew exactly as much as I did. We both forgot. If you remember, you're the one who started the whole let's-have-sex thing. I wasn't trying to get pregnant on purpose."

He drew in a breath and held up both hands. "You're right. I'm sorry." He glanced around, as if searching for an escape, then he slowly walked back to the table and sat down.

She thought about the early days of their marriage, when they'd still been talking about having kids. If only this had happened ten years ago, or even seven, she thought sadly. They would be so happy—excited about their child and the future. Something else that had been lost.

"What are we going to do?" he asked, sounding defeated. "Do you want this?"

"I'm having the baby." She'd never thought otherwise. Yes, she was pro-choice, but she was a healthy woman with a good job and was perfectly capable of raising a child by herself.

"I wasn't asking you to have an abortion."

"No, but it would solve a lot of your problems."

"I'm not a jerk."

"You just play one on TV?"

He drew in a breath. "Let's start over. You're pregnant. Now what?"

"Now I have a kid and you have to decide what you want to do about it. Oh, and I get a DNA test because we need to make sure it's yours." She leaned back in the chair. "Don't worry. I'm not angling to stop the divorce. I'm telling you because it changes some things. Our simple property split isn't so simple anymore."

He rubbed his face with his hands. "I didn't even think about that. We have to do something legally, right?"

"It's called a parenting plan. I'll be the custodial parent, but you'll want to decide how much visitation you want. Or you can just sign away your rights."

She wasn't sure about the latter. Was it even legal? It happened all the time in movies and TV, but real life was often different.

He dropped his hands. "I'm not walking away from my kid. I don't know enough about this to have the conversation. Let me talk to my lawyer and get back to you. If we can come to some agreement, then we shouldn't have to hold up the divorce."

The all-important divorce, she thought bitterly. Because Rhys couldn't get away from her fast enough.

"Have your lawyer put together a proposal for a parenting plan and child support," she said, coming to her feet. "Once we agree on that, we can move forward with the divorce."

He stood and looked at her. "I'm not mad," he began. "I wasn't expecting a baby."

"Me, either, but here we are."

She searched for some trace of the guy she'd married, but he was nowhere to be found. Rhys might not be pounding his fist into the wall anymore, but he wasn't happy. Whatever fantasies she might have secretly held about them still being a team had just been flushed down the toilet.

After sixteen years of marriage, she was totally on her own. Single and pregnant. Hardly a new story, but certainly not one she'd expected to have to live through.

She went upstairs to her room and sat on the edge of the bed. Somehow she'd thought the conversation would take longer. It was funny what a couple could get through in fifteen minutes when they no longer cared about each other.

Stephanie hung on to Kyle's hand, not caring if she was digging her nails into his flesh. He was a tough sports guy—he could take it.

The last four hours had passed in a blur, starting with a call from Carson's coach saying her son had been in an accident. He and his friends had gone rock climbing at the sports center where they trained and Carson had fallen, breaking his arm and hitting his head on the mat.

"I'm going to throw up," she said, feeling her stomach writhing.

Kyle looked at her, his brows pulled together. "Do you mean that? Want me to find a bucket? I really don't think you should throw up on the seat. It's a crappy way to thank Bruno."

She stared at him, not quite able to understand what he was saying only to look around and remember that, yes, they were in a very well-appointed private jet.

As soon as Stephanie had gotten the call from the

coach, she'd called Mackenzie to see if Avery could stay with her overnight while Stephanie went to be with Carson. Stephanie's second call had been to Kyle, who'd immediately started looking to get them a flight to Sacramento. The problem was Walla Walla was hours by car from Seattle and there were only a couple of flights a day between the two cities.

Mackenzie had interrupted that call to say Bruno was offering his private jet. The pilots would stay in Sacramento as long as needed, then fly the three of them back.

Less than an hour after she'd gotten the initial call from the coach, Stephanie found herself being flown to Seattle's Boeing Field, where Kyle got on board. The second she saw him, she'd let go of her self-control and fallen into his arms, sobbing.

"I'm not going to throw up," she said, trying to slow her breathing. "I have to hold it together."

"He's fine."

"He hit his head and they're keeping him overnight in the hospital."

"For observation."

She shook her head. "It's overnight, Kyle. There could be something wrong with his brain."

"He's going to be fine."

"You don't know any more than I do," she snapped.

Instead of pushing back, he wrapped his arm around her. "I know that imagining the worst won't make this trip go any faster. Now try to relax and enjoy our luxurious surroundings. You're probably never going to fly in a private jet again."

"I'll enjoy it on the trip home," she muttered, silently urging the pilots to fly faster.

Less than an hour later, they touched down. Kyle plugged the hospital address into the rental car's GPS and drove them directly there.

When they walked into the Emergency Department, Stephanie did her best not to start by screaming that she needed to see her son. Kyle headed directly to the information desk.

It took only a few minutes for them to be directed to Carson's room. They found their fourteen-year-old sitting up in bed, pale, a little wide-eyed, with his left forearm in a cast.

"Hey, Mom," he said weakly, waving his arm, then wincing. "So I kind of fell off the rock wall."

She rushed to him and wrapped her arms around him, determined to never let go. Thoughts crowded her head, mostly that he was never leaving the house again, and that she'd been wrong to let him go to baseball camp.

"I'm fine," Carson insisted. "It's no big deal."

She stepped back to allow Kyle to hug him, using the time to look for damage. Except for the broken arm and the pale skin, he seemed all right. Before she could start grilling him on other symptoms, a middle-aged woman in a white coat walked in.

"Hello," she said, holding out her hand. "I'm Dr. Leishman. You must be Carson's parents. The break was very clean and should heal quickly. We can't find any indication of head trauma or a concussion, but we're going to keep him overnight, just in case." She smiled.

"Can I go back to baseball camp?" Carson asked quickly. "We only have a week left. I won't be able to play, but I have to be there for my team."

Stephanie was about to tell him he was so coming home when she felt Kyle touch her shoulder. She glanced at him and saw he was slowly shaking his head.

"Let's see how you are in the morning," she said reluctantly.

"I'm fine now, Mom."

"And yet you're spending the night in the hospital."

Dr. Leishman looked between them. "Carson will be moved up to Pediatrics sometime in the next hour. We can have a cot brought in so one of you can spend the night with him. The doctor on duty will check in with you once he's settled."

"Thank you," Stephanie said, moving close to Carson and taking his hand. "Thank you for everything."

When the doctor left, Carson rolled his eyes. "It's not that bad, Mom. Look at me. Don't I sound normal? My head doesn't even hurt."

"Like you would tell me if it did."

He smiled. "I'm not that good at pretending I'm not in pain."

"Still, we'll talk about camp in the morning. First I want you to get a good night's sleep."

Once Carson was settled in his room in Pediatrics, Kyle pulled Stephanie out into the hallway.

"I'm going to go find a hotel. I'm sure there's one that's close. I know you need to stay here tonight, but you'll want to come over and use the shower in the morning. Once I'm checked in, I'll find out about takeout in the area, then come back for food orders. Carson isn't going to want hospital food for dinner."

"If they let him eat."

He smiled at her. "They're going to let him eat. Steph, I don't think there's anything wrong with his head. Let's assume the best until we have reason to think otherwise."

"Being that positive isn't in my nature."

"But you are feeling better about him."

She nodded slowly. "He seems completely normal and he's not in a lot of pain. He really doesn't fake that well. But he's still in the hospital. Doesn't that freak you out?"

"A little, but it's a short-term thing. You going to be okay by yourself?"

"Yes. Go find a hotel. While you're gone, I'll ask the nurse about what he can eat for dinner. Oh, and when you come back, can you bring my overnight bag? It's in the car."

"Sure." He leaned in and lightly brushed her mouth with his. "We'll get through this together."

"I know. You have many flaws, but you're a good dad."

"You're a good mom."

She managed a smile. "True, and I don't have any flaws."

He laughed. "If only that were true. See you soon."

She watched him walk to the elevator, then returned to her son's room. While she fussed over Carson and made sure he was comfortable, she thought about how grateful she was to have Kyle with her. There were times when he made her insane, but lately he'd been a really good guy. She knew he would take care of whatever needed doing. Funny how it had taken them ten years of being divorced to finally find a relationship that worked for them.

twenty-two

The farmhouse was at least a hundred years old, but it had obviously been loved. The outside paint was fresh, the big front porch sturdy. Mackenzie watched as Bruno walked toward the windows.

"Double pane," he said. "They've been replaced in the past five years. You won't have to worry about them."

"That's about the time Herman's wife got sick. She had cancer and only lasted a few months after diagnosis. I'm sure he had the windows replaced so she would be more comfortable in the house."

He opened the front door and motioned for her to go in first. There was a good-sized living room with a big fireplace on the left and a small guest bath off to the right. Stairs led to the second floor. She could see into the dining room and guessed the kitchen was to the right of that.

The ceilings were high, the floors refinished wood and probably the originals. The leaf-print wallpaper wasn't to her liking, but that was easily fixed.

It was a good house—solid and more than enough for her. She should be enthused, and she was trying to be. The problem was she couldn't shake her conversation with Rhys. While she hadn't expected him to dance for joy, she'd hoped for a slightly more positive reaction.

She forced her attention from that disastrous conversation to the house.

"It's nice," she said. "Are you sure you don't want to live here?"

Bruno looked at her. "We've discussed this. I'm in escrow for a large condo overlooking the golf course. That's much more my style. This is a perfect house for you and the baby."

"I guess." She wasn't sure what made a house perfect for a child. She supposed anywhere would work as long as it was safe, warm and filled with love.

They went into the kitchen. It was bigger than she'd been hoping, although fairly old-fashioned. The huge farm sink was a bit battered and the appliances had seen better days, but everything was clean and there were plenty of cabinets.

"You can gut this and have the kitchen of your dreams," he told her.

She laughed. "I don't usually dream about kitchens. I'm more into wine."

"Then get a designer to come up with a plan."

"Every penny I own is trapped until the divorce. The second that happens, it goes to you." She smiled. "I bring nothing to the table but my sparkling personality."

He chuckled. "You'll be making plenty within a

year or two. Plus, you're getting paid a salary and you have your royalties from your Bel Après wine."

She nodded instead of admitting she was fully expecting Barbara to find a way to weasel out of paying her that. Bruno would tell her to stand strong and hire a lawyer, which was probably good advice, but everything was happening so quickly—the divorce, buying the winery, finding out she was pregnant. She wasn't sure she could take on one more thing.

They went upstairs. There was a large master with an attached bath and walk-in closet. Lavender rose wallpaper covered the walls and there was a faint scent of an old-fashioned soap, but nothing Mackenzie couldn't live with.

She made notes on the pad she'd brought. She needed to get a bed ordered, a couple of nightstands and a dresser. Downstairs she would need a sofa and maybe a TV. Everything else could wait.

When she was done writing, she and Bruno went into the first of the two secondary bedrooms. They shared a bathroom. Bruno stood in the center of the one with the big bay window.

"This one for the baby," he said. "There's lots of light. When she gets older, you can get her a curved sofa to put there so she can curl up on it and read."

"She?"

He gave her a sheepish smile. "I'm hoping for a girl."

"Are you? Then you're further along than I am. I can barely grasp the fact that I'm pregnant. Except for vitamins and the ridiculous amount of vegetables I have to eat every day, very little has changed for me."

A girl? "You have a fifty-fifty chance of getting what you want," she added.

"I'd be happy with either. Did you talk to Rhys?"

She nodded, hoping she didn't look as uncomfortable as she felt. Apparently she failed because Bruno exhaled.

"That bad?" he asked.

"He wasn't happy. There was swearing and he tried to put his fist through the wall. He was unsuccessful and the wall is very proud of the win." She kept her tone light, hoping to make Bruno think she was doing better than she was.

"When he blamed you, did you remind him it takes two?"

"Yeah, and I also pointed out that he'd driven me to the appointment to get my IUD out, so pretending he didn't know it was gone wasn't going to—"

She slapped her hand over her mouth and groaned. After lowering her arm to her side, she said, "I'm so sorry. I shouldn't have said that. It's way too personal and not anything you wanted to know."

"I've seen you spit, Mackenzie. This is nothing."

"Still. I'm humiliated."

"Don't be. Relationships are messy when they're ending. Anything you want to talk about, I can handle."

She appreciated his kindness and desperately wanted to change the subject. "Be careful what you offer, mister. I've been doing a little reading on the whole pregnancy thing, and there are facts that would put you off eating for a week."

"I don't scare that easily."

They went into the other bedroom.

"This would be a good home office," he said.

"Why wouldn't I just come into my regular office? It's like a fifteen-minute walk away."

"Because you're going to have a newborn, then a toddler, then a kid who might get sick and need you."

Oh, right. "A home office it is." She added a desk and chair to her list.

They walked back downstairs. Mackenzie paused to breathe in the feel of the house.

"I'm going to be happy here," she said. "Thank you."

"It's not just me. We're a team."

She and Rhys had been a team once, she thought wistfully. Not anymore. She looked at Bruno and thought maybe they would last a little longer together. They knew what they were getting into and there were no messy emotions to complicate things.

"What are you going to do about dating?" she asked. "Walla Walla's a pretty small town. I guess you could meet someone in Seattle. You have a private jet, so it's not like the distance is going to be an issue."

He raised his eyebrows. "Are you speculating about my love life?"

"Yes. It's so interesting to think about, mostly because I need a good distraction right about now."

"I'm focused on buying Painted Moon."

"You're saying I should mind my own business."

"I'm saying I'm not in a position to fulfill your speculation needs."

They walked outside and Bruno locked the door behind them, then handed her the key.

"Legally you can't move in until we close, but Herman said you were welcome to measure for furniture or rugs or whatever."

She hesitated before taking the single key from him.

"This is going to be the first home I've ever owned," she admitted. "My grandfather rented a small place by his work, and after he passed away, I went to college and lived in the dorms, and then I moved in with Rhys after college." She looked at him. "How ridiculous is it that I'm thirty-eight years old and I've never lived alone?"

"It's not ridiculous at all."

His brown eyes were kind, she thought. She had the strangest urge to ask him to hold her. Just for a minute, until she was feeling strong again.

But she didn't. Bruno was her business partner and he expected her to be tough enough to handle her own life. Speaking of which...

"Guess what I'm going to do now," she said.

"I have no idea."

She sucked in a breath and squared her shoulders. "I'm going to tell Barbara I'm pregnant."

Bruno stared at her. "Are you sure you want to do that?"

"Not in the least. I was going to wait, but based on how Rhys reacted, I need to get the word out on my terms."

"Do you want me to come with you? I can wait outside her office, or even in the car. I'm not trying to put myself in the middle of something personal, but you shouldn't do this alone. That woman is volatile."

"You're sweet, but I can handle her."

At least she hoped she could.

Bruno didn't look convinced, but he nodded anyway. "Text me when you're done."

"I will."

She would also text Stephanie and Four to warn them to stay clear because their mom wasn't going to take the news well. A sad statement, but a true one.

She made her way to her Jeep. Bruno held open the door.

"I'm sorry," he said. "Having a baby should be joyous news and she's going to make it anything but."

"Thank you for getting that. I was thinking the same thing. Wish me luck."

"You don't need luck, Mackenzie. You never have."

Mackenzie tried to hang on to Bruno's empowering words as she drove onto the Bel Après property. She slept at the house every night, but heading to the business side of the property wasn't something she did anymore.

Ignoring all the feelings swelling inside of her, she went into the building and up the stairs to Barbara's office. No one tried to stop her and she was careful not to look into any other offices as she walked to the end.

Barbara sat at her desk, her reading glasses on her nose. She was dressed in a suit, as always, her dark hair perfect, her makeup tasteful. Her engagement ring sparkled in the overhead lights.

That ring, Mackenzie thought. Funny how everything had started with the proposal. Sharing in the romantic moment had shown her the empty parts of her own life. She'd been restless for years, but that moment had brought everything into sharp relief.

Her mother-in-law looked up and saw her. After removing her glasses, she leaned back in her chair.

"I can't imagine what we have to say to each other."

Mackenzie closed the door and walked toward the desk. For a second she thought about blurting out the news and then running, but she knew that was wrong. Whatever might be happening between them now, at one time Barbara had been like a mother to her. If nothing else, Mackenzie owed her the respect of sitting down.

When she was seated, she got right to the point. "I'm pregnant."

Barbara stared at her unblinking. "Is it Rhys's?"

The question shouldn't have been surprising, but it was. "Yes, otherwise why would I bother telling you?" She held up her hand. "Before you ask, I'll have it confirmed via DNA when the baby is born. Rhys knows it's his." At least she was pretty sure he knew it, as much as he might wish it wasn't.

Barbara's eyes darkened with suppressed emotion. "Men believe what we want them to believe and nothing else."

Mackenzie told herself not to be distracted. "I don't want to fight with you. I told you because I thought you'd want to know you're going to have another grandchild. I'm hoping my pregnancy doesn't get wrapped up in your anger about me leaving."

Barbara leaned toward her. "Is that what you hope? That's sweet. So you think I should be happy that you've tricked Rhys into getting you pregnant. I should have seen this coming."

The outrageous statement wasn't even a surprise. Mackenzie shook her head. "I don't know how you maintain that level of fight. It's exhausting. I didn't trick Rhys and I didn't plan on getting pregnant, not that you'll believe me. And in the end, what you believe doesn't matter. I am genuinely heartbroken about how this has gone between us. I loved you so much. I thought we would always be close."

"Then you shouldn't have walked away. You started this, Mackenzie. Not me, not Rhys, not anyone but you."

"You don't care about the child at all, do you?"

"No. You're nothing to me. You were always a means to an end."

Mackenzie knew Barbara wanted to hurt her and she was doing a good job of it. What she didn't know was if she was telling the truth.

"Ironically that will you've always thrown in my face is about to bite you in the butt," Mackenzie said, rising to her feet. "Because the DNA evidence that proves my baby is a member of the family will entitle her to inherit just as much as your other grandchildren."

She started for the door, then turned back. "I wanted to make it about us having a familial connection, about you being my baby's grandmother. You want to make it about money and land. It's not a fight I went looking for, but if that's what you want, bring it on, because I'm going to win."

With that, she walked out. She was halfway down the stairs when she heard something heavy slam into the wall, followed by a high-pitched scream.

When she reached her car, she texted Stephanie and Four a quick Brace yourself. She knows. That done, she drove back to the offices she shared with Bruno. She had a stack of paperwork to read through. Escrow was very good at generating documents. Later, when she wasn't feeling quite so sick to her stomach, she would indulge in a big bowl of chocolate ice cream and day-dream about everything she was going to do at Painted Moon. As long as she kept moving forward, she would be fine. Which turned out to be an okay thing because she'd never much liked standing still.

Barbara waited until just after six, then drove to the compound. She parked behind her son's house and walked in through the always open back door. As she'd expected, she found Rhys sitting at his desk in his office.

He was focused on his computer and jumped when she said his name.

"You about gave me a heart attack," he said, press-ing a hand to his chest. "Don't you knock?"

"No, I don't." She walked over to the desk and clutched the back of the chair. "She told me about the baby."

Rhys leaned back in his chair. "She told me, as well."

"Is it yours?"

"Yes."

Barbara collapsed into a chair, the last of her hope fading away.

"You had to get her pregnant?"

"I don't like this, either, Mom. You think I want a kid now? I was finally going to be free of my mar-riage and start the life I wanted to have." He waved his hand at her. "It's done and I'm going to have to deal."

Her head shot up. "Not just you, Rhys. All of us.

This is a nightmare on many levels." She leaned toward him. "I want you to sue for custody."

"What?" He stared at her. "No."

"Why not? You're the father. Society is different now. Lots of men raise children on their own. You'd have help. We'd all be here for you. We'd hire a nanny for the day-to-day work."

"Forget it. I have no interest in being the custodial parent. You want the baby so much, you sue for custody."

"Believe me, I've thought about it." And she would talk to her lawyer, if she couldn't convince Rhys to do the right thing.

"I'm shocked at how little interest you're showing in your own child," she said, wanting to gauge how much she could guilt him into doing what she wanted.

"Like you're the most maternal woman on the planet. Forget it, Mom. You're not going to get me to fight Mackenzie for the baby. My lawyer's working on a visitation plan. I'll show up because it's the right thing to do, but don't expect me to do more than what I have to."

She should have known he was going to be difficult.

"That doesn't work for me," she snapped. "She can't be allowed to keep it. What if it really is yours? Is my grandchild going to be raised by that woman?"

"As she's the mother, yes. That's exactly what's going to happen."

She knew yelling at him wouldn't help, although she desperately wanted to vent her frustration. "I just need you to cooperate on this," she said between clenched teeth. "I want to talk to your lawyer."

He stood up and put his hands on the desk. "Listen to me carefully, Mom. You're not going to screw with my life. Mackenzie and I will work out the parenting plan. When the baby's born, we'll confirm that I'm the father with a DNA test, and that's all you need to know. I'm not interested in any crazy plans you might come up with. It's done. Leave it alone. In a few months, we'll talk about how you can make things right with Mackenzie so you can have time with your new grandchild."

"Make things right with her?" she shouted, coming to her feet. "Did you really say that? She doesn't deserve that child. I wish she'd miscarry. She's the one who wants to destroy us. She's the one who—"

"Barbara!"

She turned and saw Giorgio standing in Rhys's office. He was pale with shock.

This was bad timing, she thought in annoyance. No doubt he'd seen her golf cart behind Rhys's house.

"What are you saying?" he demanded. "Tell me you don't mean it. Mackenzie's pregnant? That's something to celebrate."

She loved Giorgio's kind heart, but right now it was nothing but a pain in her ass. Of course he wouldn't understand because to him family was everything. He didn't share her connection to the land. He'd blithely walked away from his business, something she could never do. He wasn't ruthless and he didn't want her to be that way, either.

Funny how he thought he loved her when he didn't know her at all. She, on the other hand, was very clear about his strengths and weaknesses.

"You're right," she said quickly, pretending to sway

on her feet before sinking back into the chair. "I'm
overwhelmed by everything that's happening."

Given how on edge she was, she had no difficulty
summoning a few tears. Giorgio was at her side in an
instant, taking her hand in his and kissing her cheek.

"I'll take you home," he told her. "You need to rest."

"I do. Thank you, my love."

She let him help her out of the room and through the
house. She had no idea what Rhys was thinking, but
at this moment, she didn't care. One crisis at a time.

twenty-three

Stephanie saved the file on her computer and told herself she was doing great, all things considered. Carson had been released from the hospital and she'd been brave enough to allow him to stay the last week of camp. He would be home in a couple of days, right in time for school to start. She and Avery had maintained their friendly status, with her daughter announcing she was done with boys, at least for her junior year of high school. She was going to focus on academics and after-school activities.

Stephanie had agreed the plan had merit while secretly thinking it wouldn't last through the first two weeks of the semester, but at least Avery wasn't pining for Alexander anymore.

On the work front, she had an interview lined up with a local winery right after harvest, which was the most exciting news of all. She was working hard to get her portfolio in order so she could be dazzling. In the meantime, she'd signed on to help at Painted Moon during harvest. The temp work would keep her bank account healthy enough that she could sleep most nights. Things were looking up.

She was about to start paying bills when her phone buzzed with a text.

U around

She shook her head before replying. What is it with you and abbreviations when you text? You're not 17. Write out the entire sentence. I know you can. And yes, I'm in my office. There are cookies in the kitchen.

She pushed Send and began to shut down her laptop. A few minutes later Rhys walked into her study and threw himself on the sofa.

"You didn't want cookies?" she asked.

"I'm not hungry."

Her big brother's normal good humor was nowhere to be seen and there was a decidedly downward turn to his mouth.

She wondered if he was regretting the divorce. While his marriage hadn't been perfect, from the outside it seemed that he and Mackenzie got along. Okay, sure, the sex thing was a problem, but they could fix that maybe with some counseling or watching porn or something. If he was—

"Mackenzie's pregnant," he announced.

"I know. She told me."

Stephanie had been thrilled for her and secretly proud of herself for reacting the way a best friend should.

He leaned back in the sofa and stared at the ceiling. "I don't want a kid."

"But you used to talk about having a family."

He looked at her. "Years ago, right after we were married, but not now. I'm finally free to live my life, and instead of enjoying myself, I'm going to be stuck with some baby." He exhaled. "She had to have her IUD taken out. I guess I drove her to the appointment, although I sure don't remember it. So she wasn't on anything. It was just one time."

"That is all it takes. One time."

He glared at her. "How does that help?"

"I didn't know you wanted help. I thought you were just grumbling."

"I just don't want to deal with a baby."

"Rhys, this is your child. It's a part of you, a part of the family."

"I don't care. I wish I could sign my rights away."

Stephanie nearly fell off her chair. "Do you mean that?"

"Maybe. I don't know. I mean, I suppose there are legal ways to abandon a child, but I'm not sure I'm capable of doing that. Or if I should, you know. What if I have regrets later? Mom wants me to sue for custody, which is not happening."

She wasn't even surprised that her mother was looking for ways to make Mackenzie's life difficult. "Our mother is a horrible woman."

"She's never boring—I'll give her that."

"What are you going to do?"

He shook his head. "I've got my lawyer working on a parenting plan. There's a minimum amount of visitation that's considered acceptable. I'm going to ask for that. Plus I'll have to pay child support, but that's based only on my salary, not the trust or anything. I almost don't care about the money. It's everything else."

Stephanie knew that neither of them had expected a pregnancy, but she was still surprised at Rhys's resistance to being a father.

"Don't go into this with the idea of being half-hearted," she said. "Don't let your child grow up knowing he or she isn't wanted. That's a devastating thing to do to an innocent kid. You're not happy, but you're not a bad person, Rhys. Don't start acting like one now."

"Don't judge me. Your life isn't being twisted all around."

"You're right. I'm also not the one who knocked up his wife, so there's that."

He frowned at her. "You're not being very supportive."

"You're not being very human, so hey, we're even."

"We have to find a way to break the contracts with Mackenzie," Barbara said as she walked into Lori's office. "The ones for the wine royalties," she added when her fat daughter stared at her in obvious confusion.

"You can't break them," Lori said. "You went over them yourself and made sure Mackenzie could never get out of them. Remember how impressed the lawyer was?"

Barbara wondered why everyone had to be so stupid all the time.

"I'm not senile. Of course I remember. That's not the point. There's always a way out and I want you to call him and have him find it. Mackenzie is going to need the money to live on and I don't want her to get it from me."

Lori, frumpy as always in her ill-fitting suit, hunched over in her chair. "Money isn't a problem for her. She's going into business with Bruno Provencio. He's funding their purchase of Painted Moon. Mackenzie will pay him her share with the money she's getting from the divorce."

Barbara glared at her. "Are you sure? How do you know that? Who told you?"

"Herman told his foreman who told Jaguar when he was working on a tractor and Jaguar mentioned it to me. Bruno's already in escrow with a condo by the golf course. He's selling his wine distribution company and some other assets so he can focus on Painted Moon."

Barbara curled her fingers into her palms until her nails dug into her skin. "Why didn't someone tell me this? Does Rhys know?"

"I think so. She still lives with him so I'm sure they talk."

Outrage joined the fury. Everyone had turned their backs on her. Everyone wanted to hurt her and take what she had, even her own children. First Mackenzie left, then Stephanie quit and now Mackenzie was getting everything she wanted with the purchase of Painted Moon.

"This can't be allowed to happen. I was hoping she would go to a bank for a loan. I'd have leverage there, but if she's partnering with Bruno, there's nothing I can do." She sank into the visitor's chair and pressed her fingertips to her temples. "And to think I invited him to the Summer Solstice Party."

She looked at Lori. "We should have Mackenzie declared mentally unfit. She's obviously not well. Who would I talk to about that?"

"I don't like her, either, but there's nothing wrong with her brain."

"Oh, you don't like her. Well, isn't that nice." Barbara stood. "She's ruining us," she shouted. "Ruining. Why am I the only one who sees that?"

She stalked back to her office and slammed the door. The fury inside of her burned so hot, she thought

she might set the building on fire. Something had to
be done and everywhere she turned she was met with
stonewalling and incompetence.

She paced the length of her office. Bruno. She knew
she couldn't fight him—he played at a level she could
only dream about. If he and Mackenzie went into business together, there was nothing to be done.

Tears burned, but she blinked them away. No, she
told herself fiercely. She would not be defeated. She
was Barbara Barcellona and she'd faced worse than
this. She'd survived the loss of her husband. She'd built
Bel Après into what it was today. She'd had four small
children and little help and she'd worked day and night
to make the winery a success.

She'd taught herself every aspect of the business.
She'd stood against disbelievers, mostly men, who
said she couldn't do it. She hadn't just survived, she'd
thrived, and she'd created an empire. By God, she was
not going to let some no-name interloper ruin her.

Signing the bridge loan paperwork with Bruno took
about fifteen minutes. The purchase documents to buy
Painted Moon were more complicated and required the
services of a notary, along with what felt like a couple of
hundred signatures, but by eleven on Wednesday morning, it was done. Mackenzie walked out of the escrow
office with Bruno, not sure how much the weird feeling
in her stomach had to do with her being pregnant and
how much of it was a combination of excitement, nerves
and a real sense of wishing the moment felt bigger.

"Maybe I should have brought balloons or something," she said as they stood together on the sidewalk.
"I thought there would be more."

Bruno, back in one of his expensive and well-tailored suits, smiled. "Normally I would suggest a fancy lunch with champagne, but under the circumstances, that doesn't feel appropriate."

She instinctively pressed a hand to her belly. "Yes, well, I would normally agree to the fancy lunch except I'm feeling a little queasy."

"Morning sickness?"

"I think it's more the fact that we bought a winery. How did it happen so fast? We made the offer six weeks ago."

"Having the cash helped."

She grinned. "Note to self—always go into business with a man with money."

"It makes life much easier." He led her toward the parking lot. "Are you going to pick up your things at Bel Après now? If so, I'll go with you to help you carry the boxes."

She tried not to roll her eyes. "I'm perfectly capable of lifting a few boxes. Seriously, Bruno, it's like five, maybe six. I'm only taking personal things. No box weighs over fifteen pounds. Besides, I took over most of my clothes yesterday, so there's very little left." She met his gaze. "Look at how determined I am. I'll be fine."

"All right. I'll accept that. I won't like it but I'll accept it. So you'll get settled today, and in the morning, we'll meet with the employees and talk about our plans for the winery."

"How many people do you think will want to stay on?"

"If we're lucky, eighty percent. If we're unlucky, about half will leave."

She winced. "We're only a week or so from harvest. I'd hate to go through that without a full team."

He looked at her, his brows raised. "We're going to use mechanical harvest for everything this year."

Something they'd talked about and she'd agreed to. Technological advances meant all the old concerns about mechanical harvesting—bruised fruit, too much MOG (material other than grapes) and damage to the vineyards—were no longer a problem. The winery already had contracts for machines that could pick over a hundred thousand tons, or the equivalent to nearly sixty-five thousand cases of wine in a couple of days. The machines were cheaper and more reliable than training hundreds of workers to pick grapes by hand. It was the logical solution. And yet...

"It makes me sad," she admitted. "I miss harvesting by hand."

"Next year, when you get the vineyards in shape, you can handpick the premium grapes." His tone gentled. "We have too many vineyards to harvest by hand. It would take too long and we'd lose acres of fruit."

"I know. You're right. I can't help it, I'm a traditionalist."

"And the best in the business." He unlocked his Mercedes. "I'll be at the house in a couple of hours to help you unpack."

She knew better than to tell him yet again that he didn't have to. She'd spent the weekend collecting her personal belongings and stacking the boxes by the back door. There weren't very many and she was sure she could be done in a single trip. She hadn't taken very much with her. The furniture she'd ordered for the house was being delivered that afternoon.

Mackenzie waved at Bruno and watched him drive away. She followed, trying to reconcile all the changes in her life in the past three months. She was on her way to a divorce, had bought a winery and was pregnant. While the divorce wasn't happy news, leaving her marriage was the right decision. She should be pleased with how things were going.

But as she drove toward Bel Après, tears spilled down her cheeks. No matter how promising the future, there were elements of her past she couldn't help missing. Living close to her sisters-in-law, hanging out with the family. She'd missed the first day of school. She always joined Four and Stephanie as they walked the kids to the bus stop. But this year she hadn't felt right joining in.

She still missed Barbara. Not the horrible woman who yelled at her, but the kind, loving woman who had shared her dream of what Bel Après could become. Although based on recent behavior, maybe that had all been a sham.

She was starting a new adventure and longing for the past, which made her feel foolish. But the sadness was real, and she supposed she simply had to work her way through it.

"Rethinking your choice of parent?" she asked, lightly touching her stomach. "I'll do my best to have my act together by the time you're born."

She turned onto the long private driveway leading to the house where she'd lived for most of her adult life, trying to grasp the fact that, as of today, she didn't live here anymore.

She got out of her Jeep and walked to the back door. The boxes were right where she'd left them. As she worked, she half expected Stephanie or Four to stop

by to tell her goodbye. Or even Rhys, who knew she
was leaving today. But no one came.

It took only a few minutes to get the boxes loaded.
When that was done, she went inside and walked
through the house one last time. Her closet was empty,
as was the dresser in her bedroom. She'd already packed
up her things from the bathroom. She went across the
house to Rhys's room and started to go inside, then
stopped just before the doorway. No, she thought, turning away. She couldn't go in there. Not anymore.

Downstairs she double-checked her office. She'd
left everything but the artwork her nieces and nephews
had made for her along with a few personal photos.
Funny how even without her things, the house looked
as it always had. She was starting to wonder if she'd
ever really belonged here at all.

She walked into the kitchen and stood by the island.
Aside from the low hum of the refrigerator, there was
only silence. It was as if she were alone in the world.
Her throat tightened and her chest hurt a little—symptoms of sadness she decided to ignore. This part of her
life was over—it was time to move on.

She pulled the house key from her jeans pocket
and carefully put it on the counter, then went outside
and started the Jeep. As she pulled out of the driveway, she had the thought that after sixteen years she
should have more to show for her marriage and being
a part of the Barcellona family. More than six boxes
and the memories. But she didn't, and maybe that was
the hardest truth of all.

twenty-four

By three that afternoon, the last of the furniture delivery trucks had left. Pushed for time, Mackenzie had chosen the least amount of furniture she could get away with. She had a leather sectional and a TV in the living room, a bed, a nightstand and a dresser in the master, and a desk and chair in what was going to be her office. She'd decided to make the room with the big bay window the baby's room, as Bruno had suggested. She would fill in things like a dining room table and side tables as she had time.

It was only when she walked into the kitchen that she realized she had no dishes, no pots and pans, and nowhere to sit and eat her meals. She also hadn't thought to buy towels or linens for the bed or pillows. Or food. Or toilet paper.

Not her finest hour. She returned to the living room where she sat on the sofa and told herself she would be fine. This was a huge day for her, and she wasn't going to let it be ruined by the fact that she'd forgotten the basics of living on her own.

If only she didn't feel so alone, she thought, trying not to be sad that she hadn't heard from Stephanie or Four all day. They knew she was moving out. She would have thought at least one of them would have been in touch.

"I'm fine," she told herself, not caring that she was lying. "I'll make a list and go to Walmart."

At least Herman had left her a washer and dryer. Once she had enough supplies to get by, she would spend at least an hour a week doing things like taking care of the house and buying supplies. Make that two hours a week—she was going to have to start cleaning and paying bills and doing laundry. As for her friends, well, they had lives. If she'd wanted company, she should have told them. Expecting them to read her mind wasn't rational.

She dug a notepad out of her backpack. The list of everything she thought she needed was nearly a page long when she heard a truck rumbling outside the house.

She crossed to the front window and saw Stephanie's car parking next to hers. Four's SUV stopped behind her and a big pickup pulling a trailer circled around behind the cars.

"What on earth?" She walked out onto the front porch and smiled at her friends. "Are you lost?"

Stephanie and Four ran up to hug her. Their warm embrace chased away her sadness and made her feel loved again. She shouldn't have questioned them—they were her family and always would be.

"We came by last week," Stephanie told her. "After you told me how little furniture you'd bought. Herman gave us a quick tour of the house. I knew you wouldn't take anything from Rhys, because that would be weird, and I know you've been too busy buying the winery to think about things like getting milk and bread, so we're going to help with that."

Four squeezed her arm. "I'm also here to do a quick cleanse of the house. I brought sage and salt. It won't take long to have this beautiful house brimming with positive energy."

"So this is why you didn't come say goodbye earlier," Mackenzie said, fighting stupid tears. "I thought you were too busy."

"Never," Stephanie told her. "We were planning a surprise instead."

"It's a really good surprise. Thank you."

The three women hugged, then broke apart as Jaguar approached.

"I hear you're moving out," he said with a grin.

"I am."

"We have some stuff we don't need, so we brought it here."

"I love castoffs."

Four put her hands on her hips. "Castoffs? I don't think so."

Mackenzie followed them to the trailer and saw it was filled with furniture. There was a dining room set with a long table and six chairs. The old art deco piece had been stripped and painted pale green with beautiful flowers across the top. The chair cushions were a dark green velvet. There was a matching buffet with the flower motif on the drawer fronts.

"No," Mackenzie breathed, looking at Four. "You could sell this for thousands. I love it so much. Let me pay you for it."

Four smiled at her. "Or you could let me show you how much I love *you* and accept the gift graciously."

Stephanie put her arm around Mackenzie. "Gracious is not her thing. She's too bossy." She looked at Mackenzie. "Wait until you see the baby stuff. You're going to cry so hard, you'll embarrass yourself."

"There's baby stuff?"

There was a beautiful crib and changing table, a dresser and, most amazing of all, a wooden rocking chair.

Stephanie ran her hands over it. "I love this chair. I rocked both my kids in it. I've had it in storage for, what, twelve years now. I think it needs a new home."

Mackenzie shook her head. "You can't give this to me."

"I can, but if it makes you feel better, if I ever get pregnant again, you can give it back."

"Deal."

They carried the furniture inside. Her friends had thought of everything. There were lamps, throw rugs, an entry table, bookcases and waste baskets. Once the trailer was empty, Jaguar drove off, leaving the women to unload the two vehicles.

By the time the bags and boxes were empty, Mackenzie had linens, dishes, flatware, pots and pans, and her refrigerator was full. Cleaning supplies sat under the sink, laundry detergent was up by the washer and hand soap had been distributed to all the bathrooms. Stephanie had even bought her a copy of *What to Expect When You're Expecting.* It was every Christmas and birthday rolled into one. Mackenzie had never felt so cherished in her life.

A little after six, they collapsed on the new sofa.

The scent of burning sage had faded, leaving behind the promise of something new and wonderful.

"This is amazing," Mackenzie said, fighting the tears Stephanie had promised she would shed. "You helped me make a home."

"You didn't need us for that," Four told her. "You bring home with you. We just took care of the details." She looked around. "You're going to be happy here. Of course without the resident chef, you're going to have to learn how to cook."

"And pay bills," Mackenzie admitted. "Rhys always did that. I was very fortunate in my previous life. But enough about me. How are the kids? Stephanie, when's your interview? Four, what's your latest art project? Tell me everything I've been missing."

Four motioned to Stephanie, who tucked her feet under her and smiled.

"I'm good. The kids like their classes. Carson will get his cast off in a few weeks. His coach is worried about Carson being recruited too early. It's a high-quality thing to worry about. Avery is still claiming she's not dating the entire school year, but we'll see how long that lasts, and I'm prepared for my interview, which will be right after harvest. So yay."

Four stretched. "We're doing well at our end of the compound. The kids are happy and Jaguar remains the love of my life. Barbara continues to be a problem, but now that you've moved, I'm hoping her negative energy will start to calm down."

She grabbed Mackenzie's hand. "Focus on being happy. You've made all the right decisions. You know your place in the universe. Believe in yourself."

Stephanie poked her in the ribs. "Stop with the spiritual sayings."

"I offer blessings."

"You need to spend more time on the internet. That will cure you from being so positive."

Four grinned. "I like being positive. It annoys people."

Mackenzie laughed. "I love you two so much."

"And we love you." Stephanie glanced at her watch. "Oh, look at the time. Any second now there's going to be a knock at the door."

She stood and pulled Four to her feet. Mackenzie rose, as well. "What are you talking about?"

The sisters grinned at each other, then at her.

"You're going to have a visitor," Four told her. "A very handsome man with impressive masculine energy is bringing over dinner."

Before she could ask what they were talking about, her doorbell rang. Stephanie reached it first and let in Bruno. He had a pizza box in one hand and a shopping bag in another.

"Am I early?" he asked.

"Right on time," Stephanie told him. She turned to Mackenzie. "We're heading home. I'll be by in a couple of days to hang out. Enjoy your new house."

They all hugged, then her friends left. Bruno had retreated to the kitchen, where he unpacked a container of salad, a small cake and a bottle of sparkling apple juice.

"Plates and glasses?" he asked.

Mackenzie nodded at the cabinets. "You planned this with them."

"I did. Once Stephanie told me what she and Four

were doing, I thought it would be nice to have a celebratory dinner together. Today was a big day." He glanced at her. "Unless you have something else going on?"

"I was going to fold the load of towels I have in the dryer and that's about it."

She helped him carry the food to the table. He poured them each a glass of the sparkling apple juice and took a seat across from her.

After running his hands along the table, he said, "Beautiful piece. Unusual."

"Four painted it."

"She's very talented." He raised his glass. "To our partnership, to Painted Moon and to your new home."

"Thank you."

They touched glasses. Mackenzie stared at her drink. "I miss wine."

"I'm sure you do, but it's for a greater good." He put a piece of pizza on her plate and took one for himself. "How are you feeling about the house?"

"I love it. With all the furniture, it's perfect for me. After dinner you'll have to come upstairs and see the baby furniture Stephanie and Four brought for me. I have Stephanie's old rocking chair and one of the cribs Four used." She pointed to the book lying on the counter. "Even reading material."

"So you're ready."

"Oh, I wouldn't go that far, but I feel slightly more prepared."

"Is the baby more real?"

"No, and I wish it was."

"You'll get there."

"If I don't, I'm in for a real shock when the labor pains start."

He chuckled. "But you're happier about the baby?"

"Yes. Despite everything, I'm excited about being a mom and having my own family."

"You and Rhys never wanted children?"

"I thought we did but we never made it happen. There are a lot of reasons. Timing, the business. I wonder if we subconsciously knew things weren't right between us."

"Barbara didn't pressure you?"

"I think she was afraid having a child would distract me from the business."

"That's a ridiculous fear. You can do more than one thing at a time."

"That's the plan." She took a bite of her pizza. "I'm really happy with the house and the winery."

"I'm glad. I have big plans for us. The contractor is getting started on the office remodel right away. It shouldn't take more than a few weeks. I'm less sure about the tasting room. Retail isn't my thing. I'm wondering if we should hire someone to help us plan that."

"It's probably a good idea. My taste is all in my mouth," she said with a laugh.

"Considering why I wanted you as my business partner, that's a good thing."

He'd changed into jeans and a shirt with the sleeves rolled up to his elbows. His hair was dark, his jaw strong. He was a good-looking man, she thought. Capable and smart, but kind. Not the type of man to be single.

"What are you thinking?" he asked.

"I'm speculating about your personal life again. You really weren't dating anyone back home?"

She asked the question as lightly as she could, trying not to be concerned about the answer.

"I'm moving here alone. I have been dating someone casually, but it's not going anywhere."

The unexpected admission produced a thousand questions. "You never said. Who is she? Where is she? What does she do? Does she know it's not going anywhere or is that your decision?" She pressed her lips together. "Sorry. I can't help being curious."

He laughed. "Her name is Gloria and she's a former model who is now a physical therapist who works with sick kids."

Mackenzie felt her eyes widen. "Please tell me you're kidding."

He picked up his glass. "It's all true."

"Great. So she's beautiful, altruistic and has a body five ways to Sunday. Why don't you want to go out with her anymore?"

"She doesn't make me laugh."

"Do you make her laugh?"

"Not often enough." His gaze met hers. "Sometimes laughter is important."

"Rhys and I didn't laugh that much, but I don't think of myself as funny. Stephanie has a good sense of humor. Better than me."

"You can be funny."

"Yes, but am I doing it on purpose?"

He chuckled.

"Gloria sounds very intimidating," she admitted. "Is she really beautiful?"

He hesitated just long enough to make her groan.

"Ugh. I'm so never dating. I won't be good at it. I wasn't good at it before. Rhys and I just kind of happened." She served herself salad. "Plus I'm going to have a baby. Don't guys hate dealing with other men's children?"

"Are you looking to get involved with someone?"

"Not really. I mean maybe, at some point. I don't know. It's hard to think about. I get buried in my work. I'm not a brilliant conversationalist. Not like Gloria." She emphasized the name.

"Maybe she isn't, either."

"Oh, please. She's perfect. I hate her and I don't care if that makes me shallow." She ate more pizza. "Stephanie's single, and as we've discussed, she's funny. And pretty. And smart."

"I'm not interested in Stephanie."

There was something in the tone of his voice, although she couldn't begin to name it.

"Considering my lack of experience, I probably shouldn't get involved in your dating life," she said.

"I think that's for the best."

"Don't tell Gloria what I said, please. She'll think I'm mean."

"I thought you hated her."

"I do, but I don't want her to know."

He smiled at her. "It will be our secret."

Eight days after taking ownership of Painted Moon, Mackenzie woke at 3:29 in the morning, exactly one minute before her alarm was due to go off. She got up and turned on the small lamp by her bed, then walked to the window and opened the curtain.

The sky was clear, the air still and cool. Sunrise was

more than two hours away, but by the time the first rays crept over the vineyard, she would be out there to greet it. Harvest would begin today.

She turned off her phone's alarm, dressed quickly, applied sunscreen and made her way downstairs. It took only a few minutes to mix up her smoothie and pack plenty of water. Normally she would go the whole day without eating, but being pregnant changed that. Stephanie would come find her and bring lunch, along with snacks and more water to keep her hydrated.

They would start in the southernmost vineyards. She'd been driving to them every day, checking the grapes visually, measuring the sugar, or Brix. They were ready.

She made sure she had a hat, sunglasses, a portable charger for her phone, her paperwork and her drinks, then headed for her Jeep. She was on the road by four, driving across the Columbia River to Oregon and Painted Moon's Seven Hills vineyards.

Anticipation fluttered in her stomach. All the hard work from early spring came down to this moment. Once the grapes were harvested, she would work with what she had, but until then, there was the promise of possibilities. The only dark cloud on her otherwise sunny day was that this harvest would be different. She didn't know the grapes or the vineyards—not the way she normally did. There would be no family dinner later to discuss how it had gone. Barbara wouldn't drive out to watch and give her a hug. She wouldn't see Rhys several rows away, pitching in where needed, waving at her when he caught her eye.

Change was hard, she reminded herself, and she'd been through a lot. Next year would be better. Next year the grapes would be hers and she would be more comfortable in her role. Next year she would have a baby.

That last thought shocked her more than any of the others. A baby. The pregnancy was still more intellectual exercise than reality, but in a year it would be a lot more than that.

"No distractions," she murmured to herself. "I'll deal with the baby when this part is done."

She pulled off the highway and onto the smaller road, then turned onto a dirt trail where she would park out of the way of the big equipment. Shortly after dawn the giant harvesters would rumble to life and start down the rows, picking fruit and sorting out the leaves and branches. Grapes would be carried across the row and dropped into waiting bins.

Once the first truck was full, Mackenzie would follow it back to the winery, where she would oversee the crushing process. She would monitor every delivery until sunset, and in the morning they would do it all again, with her staying with the harvested grapes and Bruno in charge of what happened in the vineyards.

She'd already set the order in which the various vineyards would be harvested but reserved the right to change her mind. Stephanie was spot-checking certain plants Mackenzie had marked, texting her the results of her testing. The Brix level would ultimately determine the order of harvest for the last three vineyards. When they were done, the big equipment would head off to another winery and start the work there.

Next year they would handpick some of the vineyards, she told herself. Next year she would have time to plan better, but for now, they were going high-tech.

She'd barely finished half her disgusting smoothie when Bruno pulled up behind her, his sleek sports car out of place in the rural setting.

"Be careful you don't break an axel," she said as she got out of the Jeep.

"My car is tougher than it looks."

"I doubt that." She looked up at the stars twinkling overhead. "It's going to be a perfect day."

"You ready?" he asked.

"Yes. Nervous, but ready."

"Good nervous or bad nervous?"

"It's always good nervous." She pointed at the large harvesters. "And there are the dreaded machines that will do the work."

"You're going to be impressed."

"I hope so." She shook her head. "I'm interested to see how this all goes."

He motioned to the quiet vineyards. "Any last-minute testing or words of wisdom?"

"I trust Herman to have done the best he could. Now we blend science and magic to produce wine."

His dark gaze met hers. "Regrets?"

There was a bigger question in that single word, she thought. Did she regret the changes in her life? Her pregnancy, her divorce, leaving Bel Après. Did she regret leaving her home, her routine, her future, to step out into the unknown? Was she afraid? Did she want to go back to how things had been?

She looked past him to the vineyards that stretched for as far as the eye could see. In the east was the first hint of light at the top of the mountains. This was hers, she thought contentedly. She and Bruno owned every acre, every grape, every leaf. There was no one to tell her she couldn't, she shouldn't or that she was wrong. The mistakes were all on her, as were the rewards.

"No regrets," she told him. "Not a single one."

Barbara woke to the feel of a heavy arm around her waist. Giorgio had spent the night and, as usual, kept her awake pulling her close as he slept. It was a characteristic she usually found charming, just not this morning. Her eyes were gritty, and she felt as if she was operating on two hours of rest. Even the sex hadn't been as spectacular as usual. She'd been unable to shut off her thoughts and had failed to orgasm, despite Giorgio's efforts.

As she walked to the shower, she felt her ever-present irritation at the world in general and Mackenzie in particular crank up at least two levels. They were in the middle of harvest and there was no one overseeing the operation. Not the way Mackenzie usually did. Rhys was doing his best, but that was hardly enough. She tried to tell herself they would get through it, but she wasn't sure that was true.

With coffee and a few minutes alone in her office, she would get her feelings under control. She'd been on edge for weeks, something else she could blame Mackenzie for. She really hated that bitch.

Giorgio joined her in the shower. Before she could protest, he'd moved behind her. He slid his slick, soapy hands over her body, finding all the spots she liked. She was about to tell him not to bother, but before she could speak, his fingers were between her legs and the interest that had been lacking the night before sprang to life.

He made her climax in less than a minute, then

dragged her laughing and dripping to the bed where he had his way with her again. When they were done, the sheets were drenched, conditioner was on everything and she just plain didn't care.

"You're so good for me," she said, lying on her side, staring into his eyes. "I've been horrible for the past couple of months and you've been there for me."

"I love you. Where else would I be?"

She kissed him, thinking that if she were him, she wouldn't have put up with her own behavior. Which was why she loved him—he was a better person than she was.

"You're a good man."

"Then come away with me. We're going to New York for my daughter's birthday. Let's add a week and fly to Bermuda first."

She sighed. "You know I can't be gone that long." At this point, she didn't think she could go to the birthday celebration, but she wasn't going to spoil the mood by saying that.

"Don't say no. I'll ask again in a week."

She touched his face. "How did I get so lucky?"

He smiled. "I'm the lucky one."

An hour later, Barbara made her way to her coffee. Her bad mood had vanished and she was no longer tired. Giorgio truly was magic.

She climbed the steps to her office, determined to get as much work done as possible in the next couple of days so that she could consider going to Bermuda with Giorgio. It was a silly idea, but if it made him happy, then it was worth considering.

But all her good intentions vanished the second

she saw her son sitting in front of her desk. He didn't look happy.

"What?" she asked, dropping her purse into the bottom desk drawer and taking her seat. "Why aren't you out harvesting grapes?"

Mackenzie would have been there. When it was time, nothing could tear her away. Once she'd cut herself so badly she couldn't stop the bleeding, but she'd still stayed out until sunset, then had gone to the emergency room for stitches.

"Soon. I wanted to talk to you first." Rhys stared at her desk rather than her. "I'm having trouble finding a local winemaker willing to work here."

"What does that even mean? How many have you talked to?"

He raised his gaze to hers. "All of them. I'm expanding the search to California. We should be able to find someone there."

"No one will consider Bel Après? That's ridiculous. We're an award-winning company. Is it the salary?"

"No."

"Then what is…" She stared at him as an uncomfortable thought occurred to her. "Are you saying they won't work for me?"

He glanced away. "No one said that."

Which wasn't an answer. "Because I demand excellence," she grumbled. "That's fair. I work my ass off and I'm the bad guy. Did Mackenzie get to them first?"

"This has nothing to do with Mackenzie."

She could see he was waiting for her to explode, but she didn't feel angry. Instead her face was hot and her stomach hurt. All the glory from that morning faded, leaving her hollow inside.

"Fine. Find someone in California. We don't need anyone from around here. Better to start fresh anyway. All right. Get back to work."

He looked startled but rose. "I'll get interviews scheduled."

"You do that."

When he left, she tried to take a few deep breaths, but her chest was too tight. Her eyes burned, as well. As if she were going to cry, which she wasn't. What did she care if she had a reputation? She'd faced worse as she'd grown the company. She was a woman and not from around here—proving herself had taken years.

She wasn't a bitch, but let them think she was. Let them be afraid. They were all idiots and she would prove them wrong in the end.

She started to rise to get herself coffee only to realize she was actually crying. Frustrated with herself and her silly hurt feelings, she sat back down and waited for the emotional outburst to pass.

She was better than all of them, she reminded herself. Smarter, more determined, more willing to do what others wouldn't. That was why she always won. Tears were useless. What she needed instead was a plan.

twenty-five

Once harvest ended, the real work began for Mackenzie. She oversaw the beginning of fermentation, checking on the progress daily. When she wasn't prowling around the tanks, she was at her computer, transferring her notes to the files she kept on all the varietals.

The sound of saws, nail guns and compressors made it hard to concentrate. After trying to ignore the commotion, Mackenzie and Bruno had agreed that working in the offices was going to be impossible until the construction was done. They'd rerouted the phone lines and had sent the office staff to the space they'd rented in town, and the two of them had set up their computers on her new dining room table.

Bruno had insisted on buying a piece of glass to cover the surface, so their equipment wouldn't damage Four's exquisite painting. There were file cabinets in the corner and printers on two of the chairs. They were crowded, but Mackenzie didn't mind. This was going to push her and Bruno toward being a team.

There were a thousand things to get done. The office remodel, which was underway. Once fermentation and clarifying were finished and the wine was aging in the barrels, she had to make decisions about the vineyards. Did she want to keep everything as it was? Make changes? Grafting took time, although the rootstock was strong and healthy.

She'd never been an owner before, so had never had to deal with all the details. Despite finishing with harvest, she was having trouble relaxing enough to sleep. They really had to start making decisions.

"We have to talk about what to do with the library wines," she said, glancing across the table, her mind spinning with all they had to consider. "Some can stay where they are, but some need to be sold in the next year or so. And the tasting room needs serious work. You're right about hiring someone to manage that, along with the retail space, assuming we have some. Which I think we should. I mean, why just sell wine when people will buy knickknacks and kitchen stuff? Plus there's a wine club. Do we want to start one? It's probably too soon, but we should be collecting names. And what about selling our wines in restaurants? We could offer private brands for a few years while we're getting on our feet. Either exclusive or we provide the wine and they label as their house wine, although that might be a price-point problem."

She paused for breath.

Bruno looked up from his computer. "No."

"What do you mean, no?"

"We don't have to make any of those decisions today. Get settled into the new software and think about the wines. Breathe. We'll deal with the rest of it over the next few months."

"But we just paid eight million dollars for a winery. We need money coming in."

"It will happen. Trust me."

"But it seems like a good time to panic. Shouldn't we do that together?"

He smiled. "No panic. It's going to be fine."

"You said something about China. What's happening with that? Are we—"

She noticed that he was looking past her, out the front window. She turned in her seat and saw a familiar car parking behind hers. The driver's door opened and Barbara stepped out.

"Ugh," she said, coming to her feet. "That can't be good."

"Maybe she wants to be friends again."

She sighed. "Really? What are the odds?"

"Slim. I'll step out to give you some privacy, but I'll stay close. Scream if you need help." He paused. "Maybe I should go get my shotgun."

Despite the apprehension tightening her chest, she smiled. "Do you own a shotgun?"

"No, but getting one is now on my to-do list."

He opened the front door as Barbara stepped up to knock.

"Barbara."

"Bruno."

He flashed a smile. "That was meaningful. Enjoy your visit." He glanced over his shoulder. "Leave the front door open."

Mackenzie nodded as she faced her soon-to-be-former mother-in-law.

"This is unexpected."

"I can imagine. May I come in?"

Mackenzie thought briefly about searching the other woman's bag for explosive devices. She stepped back but left the front door open as Barbara entered.

Barbara glanced at the computers on the dining room table.

"Can't afford an office?"

"We're in the middle of a remodel," Mackenzie told her. She waved to the sofa. "Have a seat."

Barbara shook her head. "I won't be here that long." She pulled a piece of paper from her purse, then passed it over.

The room went in and out of focus as Mackenzie absorbed the number on the check.

"Three million dollars?" She looked at Barbara, hoping she was doing a decent job of faking nonchalance. "I assume there's something you want in exchange?"

"Money must be tight," Barbara said. "Bruno's loaded, but you're not. I would guess every penny you're getting from your overly generous divorce settlement is tied up in the winery. This would help you sleep at night."

"I sleep just fine," she lied, handing back the check.

Barbara didn't take it. "You don't know what I want."

Because her soon-to-be-former mother-in-law wanted something. It was the only reason she would stop by.

Mackenzie looked at her, at the familiar features, at the cold expression that had once been so warm and welcoming. Had any of it been real? Had she been an actual person to Barbara? Had their relationship ever been more than a means to an end? Not that she would ask any of those questions—mostly because she didn't want to hear the answers.

Mackenzie held in a sigh. "Just go. We have nothing more to say to each other."

"Hear me out. What I want has nothing to do with you. There's nothing you have to give up. All I want is for you to sign away the baby's rights to Bel Après."

She knew she shouldn't be surprised, but the words still found her soft underbelly and dug in deep. "We're talking about your grandchild."

Barbara shrugged. "Sign away the baby's inheritance and the check is yours. It's a good deal. There are already five grandchildren. Yours makes six. The three million is a sure thing. Invest it and your child will be a multimillionaire. The winery divided seven ways is going to be worth less."

Mackenzie stared at the check. Barbara was right—until the settlement from her divorce, she wasn't just broke, she was broke with a two-million-dollar bridge loan. It would be easy to cash the check and have it all. Her kid would inherit Painted Moon—what did Bel Après matter?

Only her baby was family and that should matter. Her baby was going to have cousins and aunts and uncles. Her baby was going to belong—something Mackenzie had wanted her whole life, something she'd thought she had. Only she'd been wrong.

She carefully tore the check in half and handed the pieces to her mother-in-law.

Barbara's mouth tightened with anger. "You'll do anything to get back at me, won't you?"

Mackenzie sighed. "This isn't about you. It's about

belonging and connection. I never wanted the money.
I wanted to be a part of something."

"You will never be a part of Bel Après. Never!"

"Maybe not, but my child will be."

Barbara sat alone in her dining room, bridal magazines spread out all around her. It was the middle of
a workday, but she'd had an appointment with Stephanie to discuss the wedding and, ridiculously, she'd
come home to be there in case her daughter showed
up. Which she hadn't.

"Not a surprise," Barbara murmured, thinking that
her children always let her down. Of course if Stephanie had shown up, Barbara would have tossed her out
on her butt, but still. She should have been here. Apparently quitting her job also meant not working on
the wedding. Well, fine. Barbara could do it all herself.

She had a master list of what needed to be done.
The entire process was choosing and ordering—hardly
a mental challenge. She would take an hour or so, finalize her decisions and make a few phone calls. But
even as she picked up the first checklist, she wondered
what was the point of a big party. So she could show
off her happiness to her friends and family? Right now
she didn't feel the least bit happy.

The sense of being adrift wasn't like her. Whenever things got bad, she pulled herself together and
managed the problem. She was strong. She was used
to being the only one who did what had to be done.
Only this time, she couldn't summon the will.

She couldn't believe Mackenzie had turned down
the money. No, that wasn't true. Honestly, she'd expected no less. Mackenzie had always had courage and

strength and a moral compass. In some ways, Barbara thought grimly, Mackenzie was the most like her. She saw what had to be done and waded in through the muck and did it.

She heard her front door open and the sound of footsteps in the foyer. For a second, her spirits lightened as she imagined Stephanie had come to apologize. Barbara told herself she would be stern but forgiving, telling her daughter that she had to—

"Hello, Barbara."

Not Stephanie, she thought, holding a sigh. Instead her youngest stood in front of her. As always, Catherine's choice of clothing was questionable, at best. Her blouse—a pretty sea-green color—was acceptable but her cropped pants were covered in quilted fish the size of dinner plates. The fish were three-dimensional with fins that stuck out and waved as Catherine moved. Her shoes continued the fish motif. They were covered in sequins that created a fish-scale pattern.

The outfit was nearly outrageous enough to distract Barbara from her disappointment.

"Why are you here?"

Catherine smiled. "To help with the wedding. Stephanie and I talked about it, and we agreed given what has happened, you wouldn't want to work with her, so I volunteered to come in her place."

"You decided amongst yourselves but no one thought to check with me?" she asked. "How incredibly typical."

Catherine pulled out a chair and sat across from her. "Do you want Stephanie planning your wedding?"

Yes, of course she did. Stephanie might not be the most talented person, but she had offered and Barbara had expected her to see her commitment through. Her sense of being abandoned was nothing more than an extension of her daughter's broken promise.

"I don't need anyone's help," Barbara snapped. "Certainly not yours."

Instead of bristling, Catherine smiled. "Oh, Barbara, how difficult you always make things. Where's the fun in planning your wedding alone? Let me take care of some of the little things." She held up her hand. "I know we don't have the same taste in anything."

"You have no taste. You want to dazzle everyone with your originality and end up looking ridiculous."

Catherine's smile never wavered. "I promise to be completely conventional. As the bride, your decisions are the ones that matter. I'm here to help, nothing more."

Perhaps all that was true, but she wasn't the daughter Barbara wanted. At least Stephanie had managed several parties, so she knew what she was doing. But she'd left. Like Mackenzie.

That was the real loss, Barbara thought, and the source of her emptiness.

"I miss her, too," Catherine said quietly.

"I have no idea what you're talking about."

"You were thinking about Mackenzie. You had to be. You got so sad. She is a huge part of this family and we—"

"She's nothing to this family and nothing to me. We're better off without her. She can't be trusted, and when she fails, we'll celebrate."

Catherine shook her head. "I'll never understand why, if you loved her best, you treated her the way you did. She might not have been born into this family, but she was the heart of us. We're never going to be the same—you most of all."

Catherine's mouth straightened into a flat line. "It must be hard to be you, Barbara. To be so unrelenting in your harshness, to always assume the worst. Living like that would crush my soul."

Barbara glared at her. "Get out."

"You're right." Catherine rose. "What was I thinking? You can't accept a gift, even one given freely. An act of kindness must be like an attack. Which makes your relationship with Giorgio so confusing. Why do you let him in and no one else? Is it because he's a man? Or is it that you know, in the end, it's never going to last?"

"You will leave here immediately," Barbara shrieked, coming to her feet and pointing to the door. "Get out right now!"

"You're going to drive him away. I'm sorry about that because he really seemed to make you happy. I wish you could be different." Catherine smiled. "But I'm sure you say the same thing about me."

With that, she left, her fish pants flapping as she went. Barbara waited until the door closed before sinking into the chair and covering her face with her hands. Her daughter's words echoed in the room, mocking her.

"It's not me," she yelled back. "It's everyone else. It's always been everyone else."

She swept the lists and magazines to the floor, then picked up her coffee mug and threw it against the wall. Even as the dark liquid stained the paint, she got up and walked out.

She would go to the office, she told herself. Things

made sense there, and if that started to change, she would spend the rest of the day figuring out a way to make Mackenzie pay.

"I've had a lot of success with corporate events," Stephanie said, feeling her interview nerves calm down as she spoke. "Weddings are an excellent source of revenue, but my main focus has been the retail store in the tasting room."

Elias, the general manager for a local winery, flipped through her portfolio. She'd included samples of her promotional material, pictures of displays and menus from events she'd pulled together.

Everything she'd read about interviews and getting a job said to always go in fully prepared but not to appear too eager. She was doing her best to show her capable side, while keeping the urge to beg with "Oh, please, oh, please, hire me!" tucked away. Her financial situation wasn't dire, and if this didn't work out, she would find another "opportunity," but it would be so great if Elias thought she was exactly what he was looking for.

Elias closed the large folder and looked at her. He was in his midfifties, with graying hair and glasses.

"I know your mom," he said.

Stephanie smiled. "Everyone does."

He didn't smile back. "The few times she's mentioned you, she hasn't been complimentary."

Stephanie told herself not to react to that. She kept her expression neutral and hands relaxed.

"I figured she was just being herself. Barbara rarely has anything nice to say about anyone. Except Mackenzie, of course."

Stephanie nodded. There was no need to panic. She'd known there was a very good chance that her mother had trashed her over the years. People understood that and would dismiss her words. Right?

"But this makes me wonder," he said, tapping the folder before opening it. "Maybe she's not wrong."

Stephanie felt her eyes widen. "I don't understand."

He pulled out a flyer for an end-of-season sale seven years ago. He drew out a second one that looked almost identical.

"This is from last year. You used the same flyer. Now, I don't have a problem with recycling work, but you put both of them in the material you wanted to show me. I'm assuming you consider this your best work. So why two of the same? A simple mistake maybe. I don't know."

She felt her cheeks start to burn. How could she have missed that?

"The work from when you first started is fresh and energetic," he continued. "But later, there's nothing original. What's the deal?"

She wasn't sure if the question was rhetorical or if she was supposed to answer. Fortunately, he kept talking.

"Every job has parts that are boring. I get that. But you weren't even trying. Worse, you brought me proof of that. You have a great plan for selling library wines, but we're not Bel Après. We're a high-volume, low-cost winery. If it's in a bottle, it's getting sold. Our customers don't care about things like library wines. They want a seasonal bottle with Santa on the label."

He pushed the folder toward her. "You should know that, Stephanie. You spent all your prep time thinking about what you wanted to say but very little thinking about what I wanted to hear."

"I researched the winery," she whispered, an amazing feat, considering she was barely able to breathe. Humiliation burned through her body. "I know how much you had in sales and where you're placed in retail."

"Those are just numbers. You don't know us." He shrugged. "I think you could probably do a decent job, if you gave us your full attention. But here's the thing. I don't want a maybe. I want to be sure, and with you, I'm not." He glanced at the door. "But I appreciate you coming in."

It took her a second to realize she'd just been dismissed. She reached for her folder and fumbled with it a couple of times before finally grabbing it. She collected her purse and her briefcase and stood.

"Thank you for your time," she managed, then bolted. Walking as quickly as her three-inch black pumps would let her, she made her way to her SUV.

She pulled into the parking lot of the nearest fast-food place, carefully turned off the engine, then clutched the steering wheel as tears filled her eyes. Mortification didn't begin to describe how horrible she felt. She hadn't just screwed up an interview, she'd exposed her lack of experience and talent to someone who knew her and her family. Elias was a big deal in the area. He could tell everyone what had happened and that her mother was right about her. The entire industry would be laughing at her.

She brushed away tears, only to have more take their place.

She'd been so sure, she thought, but she'd screwed

up so badly. She'd done research on the presentation, she'd pulled the samples and laid them out on her desk. How hadn't she seen the duplicate? How had she not noticed that her work from the last couple of years was crappy? She'd thought she had talent but she was nothing. Nothing!

She managed to get the crying under control. She drove home and made her way to her bedroom. After stepping out of her shoes, she hurried to the bathroom and threw up the little she had in her stomach.

Lying there on the cold tile, she relived the interview while waiting for the nausea to pass. She saw herself walking in and proudly presenting Elias with her portfolio. She watched his expression tighten a little, probably because he was trying to conceal his shock at how bad she was. When he looked up, she saw the pity in his eyes.

She slowly got up, changed her clothes and went back downstairs, her portfolio tucked under her arm. In her study, she sat in her chair and wondered what she was going to do now.

If Elias spread the word, she would never find a job in Walla Walla. While she didn't think he was likely to do that, she couldn't be sure. Worse, she couldn't blame him. He'd been right about her not caring the last couple of years. Yes, her mother was a pain to work for, but so what? Compared to most people, she'd had it easy.

She fanned her samples out in front of her. The early work *was* exciting, she thought wistfully. Creative and eye-catching. After that, not so much, which was her own fault.

She wasn't surprised her mother had said awful

things about her—she could live with that. But that she'd proved them to be true was unbearable.

She looked at the pages of research she'd done on Elias's winery. Knowing how many bottles sold a year was one thing, but not understanding the true nature of his customers was unforgiveable.

She picked up her marketing plan for the library wines. So what if she'd done a great campaign—he couldn't use it because he didn't have library wines. She should have known that. And because she hadn't, she'd lost a chance at a great job. Worse, she'd figured out she wasn't someone even she would want to hire.

twenty-six

At lunch Mackenzie did what women across the country did on a regular basis—she ran errands. After putting gas in her Jeep, she headed for the grocery store, a shopping list in her back pocket. She was still trying to figure out a routine, which was harder than she'd anticipated. She'd been so spoiled at Bel Après, what with a chef, a housecleaning service and Rhys handling things like bills and putting gas in her car. Now it was all on her—daunting, but worth it.

Two weeks after moving into the house, she was finally sleeping better and settling in. She liked how homey the place felt. Bruno was right—she would eventually want to remodel the kitchen and the two upstairs bathrooms, but for now it was enough that she had a place to call home.

The hardest adjustment was living by herself. She never had. She'd gone from living with her grandfather to rooming with Stephanie in college to moving in with Rhys. On the bright side, whatever leftovers she put in the refrigerator were always waiting for her.

Sadly there was no one else to load the dishwasher when she was tired after a long day.

Last time she'd shopped, she'd wandered the aisles, forgetting half of what she needed. Last night she'd made a list, even planning out a few dinners. On Sunday she was going to get out her new Crock-Pot and find a couple of recipes that looked good. She would make batches and freeze single-size meals for herself.

She got a cart and headed into the store. She had to backtrack a couple of times but finished her shopping in under twenty minutes. After paying, she carried the bags to her Jeep and felt a strong sense of accomplishment. She would quickly unload everything at home, then return to work. With the grapes busy fermenting, she could get caught up on paperwork. Later, after drinking two full glasses of water, she would sample from two more barrels and add to her growing file of notes.

She stopped at a traffic light. As she waited for it to turn green, she noticed a café taking advantage of the unseasonable warm October weather by setting out tables and chairs on the sidewalk.

The familiar silhouette of one customer caught her attention. Her whole body tensed as she saw Rhys sitting across from a pretty blonde. They were leaning toward each other, laughing at something one of them had said.

Behind her, a horn honked. She returned her attention to the road and pulled into the intersection, on her way back to the house.

"I'm fine," she told herself, ignoring her rapidly beating heart and the sudden dryness in her mouth.

"We're getting a divorce. Of course he's seeing other people."

She wasn't surprised. She didn't mind. This was what happened. People moved on. She'd moved on. She was perfectly all right with what she'd seen.

Only she wasn't all right, mostly because she'd always been one step behind Rhys on the divorce. He'd brought it up first, he'd had her served, and while she wanted all that, too, she couldn't help thinking that maybe they could have mourned what they'd had a little longer. She didn't miss him so much as what she'd always thought of as "them."

She got back to the house and put away her groceries. Bruno was sitting at the dining room table, two computer screens in front of him. She squinted as she stared at what looked like a very complicated spreadsheet, grateful she wasn't responsible for the finances.

"We have barn cats," he said, studying the screens as she took her seat. "I've counted four of them."

"Most wineries have cats. They're close to feral and help keep down the rodent population."

"I'm arranging for someone to come trap them and get them in to the vet. They need checkups. If they haven't been already, they need to be vaccinated, spayed and neutered before they're returned to us." He glanced up. "We don't want—" He swore under his breath. "What's wrong?"

She knew she should eat something, but right now she wasn't very hungry.

"Nothing. Why do you ask? I'm great."

He stared at her. "No, you're not. Something happened. You're pale and you look shaken." He swore.

"Did Barbara come back? We can get a restraining order against her."

"I hardly think she's broken any laws and I doubt any judge would see her as a threat."

"She tried to buy your kid."

"No, she tried to buy my kid's inheritance. There's a difference." She managed a smile as she sat down. "I can handle her."

"Maybe. What happened?"

She had a feeling Bruno wasn't going to let it go and wished there was something dramatic she could share. Something that would justify her reaction. Unfortunately, all she had was the truth.

"I saw Rhys having lunch with a woman." She held up a hand. "I'm not upset. It's more the shock of it. They were laughing and having a good time. She's very pretty."

He watched her cautiously.

"Bruno, I'm really okay. It's just everything has happened so fast, and even though I didn't want to stay married, divorce is hard. He was a part of my life for a long time and now he's gone. I thought Barbara was my second mom and obviously she's not. I still have Stephanie and Four, but sometimes it feels like my emotional life is slipping away from me. The day before the Summer Solstice Party, I knew what the rest of my life was going to look like. After that, everything changed and I'm still catching up. Being pregnant doesn't help."

She put her hands flat on the table. "Stephanie mentioned me needing maternity clothes the other day. I can't wear my regular stuff much longer, but I never thought about that myself, and to be honest, I'm resisting the thought. Isn't that bad? I don't feel connected to the baby. What if that never happens? What if I'm a terrible mother?"

He smiled at her. "Maternity clothes have nothing to do with being a mom. Bad parents don't worry about being bad parents."

"Logic? Really? This hardly seems like the appropriate time."

He chuckled. "It's always time for logic. Let's take these one at a time. The divorce. Of course it's hard. You were with him, what, sixteen years? You loved him. You don't just turn that off."

"He did," she grumbled.

"This isn't about him, it's about you. It's going to take time. The same with how you feel about Barbara. You're mourning that relationship, as well. You loved her and believed she loved you, too. You've been betrayed. That's a tough thing to get over. As for the baby, you'll get there."

"You're so rational. I must look like an idiot to you. You're seeing me at my worst."

"If this is you at your worst, then I have nothing to worry about."

She rested her elbow on the table and leaned her head against her hand. "You're nice. I knew you'd be a brilliant businessman and great partner in the winery, but I didn't know about the nice part."

"I'm not nice, but I do understand feeling badly about something that's happened. We've all done things we regret."

"Tell me one."

He hesitated before leaning back in his chair. "I fell for a married woman."

Mackenzie felt her eyes widen. "For real? But you so don't seem the type."

"I'm not. I know better. Her name is Kristine. She lives on Blackberry Island." He gave her a faint smile. "We met because she was the caterer for my private jet."

She straightened and smiled. "So a Cinderella story."

"Not exactly. Her marriage was going through a rough patch and she had three boys she talked about all the time. I knew better but I began to imagine stepping into his place. Being a dad, being a husband. Not my finest hour."

She didn't know what to say. Bruno was always capable, sophisticated and urbane. The vulnerable man in front of her was someone she'd never seen before.

"Were you in love with her?"

"No. I didn't know her well enough for that. We flirted and she immediately retreated. She didn't want someone else, she wanted the man in her life to step up."

"Did he?"

"Eventually. Last I heard, they're together and very happy."

"I'm sorry you got hurt."

"I wasn't involved enough to be hurt. However, the situation showed me that I needed to make some changes. That's when I decided I wanted a new career challenge."

She smiled. "We've certainly given you that, haven't we?"

"Painted Moon is going to become a name to be reckoned with in the wine industry."

"I hope you're right."

"I'm rarely wrong in business. It's my personal life that sucks."

"I don't understand why that is. Have you seen yourself? You're very dateable."

One eyebrow rose as he looked at her. Mackenzie immediately felt flustered and didn't know what to do with her hands. She wanted to call back the statement, only it was true and they were friends, so why couldn't she say it?

She supposed the problem was she was afraid he would see it as an invitation rather than an observation and she didn't want Bruno thinking she was interested in him that way. Mostly because, well, um...

He saved her from her spinning thoughts by smiling slightly and saying, "In my free time?"

She grabbed the gracious lifeline he threw her way.

"Yes, well, there is that. I know I wouldn't have time to date, either. Although the real difference between us is you're some good-looking rich guy and I'm a single, pregnant mom-to-be. I suspect you're the more desirable addition to the dating pool."

His dark gaze met hers. "You're not ready to start dating."

"You're right, but eventually I'd like to, I don't know, fall in love. Sometimes I wonder if I ever really loved Rhys." She shook her head. "That came out wrong. I loved him. I still do. What was missing was the 'in love' part. I think ours was a love built on shared interests and expediency."

"You'll do better next time."

"I trust your business track record. I'm less confident about your ability to see into my future."

"I know you, Mackenzie. You don't fail the same way twice." He stood. "Come on."

She looked at him. "Where are we going?"

"Nowhere. Stand up. I'm going to hug you. After what happened today, you need a hug from a friend."

Despite a sudden flush of awkwardness, she did as he requested. She rose and stepped toward him. Strong arms came around her and drew her close. She hugged him back, letting herself lean against him and absorb his strength and warmth.

She'd thought he would let go immediately, but he held on for several seconds, letting her step back first. As she looked at him, she realized she felt less tense and more like she was going to be all right.

"Thanks. You give really good hugs."

He smiled and lightly brushed her cheek with his thumb. "A perk of the partnership."

"I don't remember reading that in the paperwork."

"Some things are simply understood."

As she took her seat and opened her email program, she found herself thinking Bruno really was a good man. And a great hugger. Both characteristics she was pleased to find in her new business partner.

Barbara sat across from her lawyer and tried to keep her impatience to herself. They'd worked through nearly all of the things on the list she'd sent. But so far Dan hadn't said a single word about Mackenzie.

"I can't decide if you're being deliberately difficult or if you have a plan," she said when he'd brought up an annual review of the trust that had been set up for the investment accounts. "I don't want to discuss the trust. I want to know if you've gone over the contracts I have with Mackenzie."

Dan, a middle-aged man with brown hair and a fondness for three-piece suits, pressed his lips together.

"I told you in my email that the contracts were solid, Barbara. You insisted on that. For as long as you're selling those wines, Mackenzie gets her cut."

"That's ridiculous."

"That's the law."

"It's a stupid law. There's nothing you can do?"

"I've been over them myself, and I had one of my partners review them, as well."

"Can I sue her?"

"For what?"

She waved her hand. "You're the lawyer, you tell me. Anything. Walking away from her job. Buying Painted Moon. Divorcing my son."

"None of those are actionable. You didn't have an employment agreement with her or a do-not-compete contract. She was an at-will employee and she wanted to leave. The divorce is between her and Rhys."

"Well, it shouldn't be. It affects us all." She wasn't surprised by his assessment, but she didn't like it. "We'll have to stop producing the wines. That way she won't get anything."

"Aren't they profitable for the company?"

"Yes." Very profitable. All Mackenzie's wines were sought after and sold out within weeks of their release.

"Wouldn't it make more sense to simply pay her what she's owed?"

"I'm not interested in sensible. I want her punished. She's pregnant."

Dan's neutral expression didn't change. "I didn't know. Is Rhys the father?"

"So he tells me."

Dan shocked her by smiling. "Then congratulations."

She glared at him. "Is that you being funny?"

"What? No. I thought… She's having your grand-child."

"I already have grandchildren. I don't need any more and certainly not hers. Can I sue for custody?"

"Of what?"

Were all lawyers as stupid as him? "Can I sue Mackenzie for custody of her baby?"

Dan drew back in his chair, and his features tight-ened. "I don't handle family law. I'd need to refer you to someone else. Having said that, I don't see any grounds to sue her for custody of her unborn baby. The courts favor the biological parents. Now, Rhys would have a case."

"He's not interested in having much to do with the child. I'm insisting on a DNA test, but the way things are going, the baby probably is his."

She picked up the cup of coffee she'd been given when she first sat down. "It's the inheritance. I don't care how many children she has, but if Rhys is the father, then her child is going to inherit a part of Bel Après. I want to stop that from happening." She looked at him. "That would be where you come in."

"Once she has the DNA test and proves Rhys is the father, there's nothing you can do. The will is very clear on who inherits."

"Are you sure? Can you even pretend to find a so-lution?" Frustration bubbled inside of her.

Dan shook his head. "I'm sorry. No."

She sensed his disapproval. No doubt he thought she was cruel and heartless. Not that she cared about that. Protecting Bel Après was all that mattered, and to that end, she would do anything.

twenty-seven

Stephanie had trouble shaking her sense of shame and failure. She went through the motions of her life, telling herself that in a few days she would snap out of it and come up with a new direction. Or at least a plan to get a job. But nearly two weeks after the humiliating interview with Elias, she felt no more capable of putting herself out there again than she had the day it had happened.

She did her best to act normal in front of the kids. Carson was all about his friends and sports, and didn't notice anything was wrong. He'd recently started thinking about playing baseball in college rather than going from high school to the minor league, which meant he suddenly cared about his grades. That was only good news to her.

She was less sure if she was convincing Avery that all was well. She'd caught her daughter watching her a couple of times, but maybe that was just ordinary teenage wondering about how incredibly dumb parents were and why did it have to be that way.

When Kyle called and suggested they have dinner together Friday night, she'd agreed because why not. He was a friendly face and she needed a distraction. He was heading east to Pullman for a WSU home game the next day.

She pulled herself together enough to shower and put on a little makeup, then lost interest when it came to finding something cute to wear. In the end, she pulled on leggings and a tunic top, and slipped her feet into ballet flats.

She was tired from not sleeping well and still getting flashbacks where she relived the horror of the interview. At some point she really was going to have to get her butt in gear and find a job. Her savings wouldn't last forever.

If only she could know if Elias was going to tell everyone what had happened. It wasn't as if she could call and ask if he planned to blab about what an idiot she was. But the thought of word spreading, of her mother finding out, haunted her.

Right on time, Kyle knocked on the door. Avery was babysitting for Four, and Carson was at a friend's house. Stephanie let him in while she grabbed her purse.

"Hi," she said, hoping she sounded more upbeat than she felt. "How was the drive?"

"Good." He leaned in and kissed her cheek. "It's raining in Seattle, but the skies cleared when I went over the pass." He frowned. "You okay?"

She started to say she was, then found herself blurting out, "No. I'm a mess." Tears filled her eyes. She tried to blink them away, but a couple escaped to slide down her cheeks.

Kyle surprised her by closing the front door, taking her purse from her and setting it on the entry table, then leading her into the living room.

"What's going on?" he asked when they were seated next to each other on the sofa. He angled toward her, his expression concerned.

"I'm such a disaster," she said, wiping her face. "I thought I was doing better, standing up to my mom and wanting to find a new job, but I've made so many mistakes. I've embarrassed myself and now I may not be able to find a job anywhere near here and then what?"

He frowned. "I have no idea what you're talking about. Start at the beginning."

She hesitated, not wanting to share the shame, but then reminded herself the man had seen her screaming in pain as she pushed out a baby, not to mention vomiting through the flu, so he could probably handle what she had to say.

"I had a job interview."

She told him how excited she'd been and how confident she'd felt about her answers and her material. Until Elias had started pointing out her failures.

"He was right about all of it," she admitted, fighting tears again. "I did a ton of research on the industry but none on his winery. I put so much effort into how to sell the library wines because Mackenzie was talking about the ones at Painted Moon. That's where I got the idea."

"So you had a good plan, but for the wrong business."

She nodded. "And the flyers. Why didn't I see how my work had gone downhill over the past few years? I'm mortified and I'm terrified Elias is going to tell everyone he knows that my mom was right about me and no one else will hire me and she'll get to *say* she was right."

Kyle pulled her close and held on to her. "He's not going to go around and talk about you like that."

"Maybe he will."

She felt him chuckle. "That's my little ray of sunshine."

"I'm so embarrassed. I don't know what to do now. I have to get a job, but I have no experience out of the wine industry and I'm afraid no one in the industry wants to hire me." She drew back and wiped away more tears. "I'm a failure."

He took her hand in his. "You're not. You had a setback. That's all. You'll learn from the experience and do better next time."

"Easy for you to say. You're a famous TV sportscaster. What do you know about failure?"

"I lost you."

"Oh, please. That was a decade ago and you barely noticed I was gone."

"That's not true. I screwed up, Stephanie, and I have a lot of regrets."

While the words were nice to hear, she wasn't sure she believed him. "Thank you for saying that."

He squeezed her fingers. "Go work for Mackenzie. She and Bruno must need help with the retail space and other stuff. You already have a plan for their library wines."

She pulled her hand free of his. "No. I'm not going to ask my best friend to give me a job." She shuddered. "I want to be hired because I'll be the right person, not out of pity."

"You're not giving yourself enough credit. You're good at what you do."

She appreciated the words, even if once again she doubted the truth of them. "You want to see the best in me. That's really nice, but the last couple of years at Bel Après, I was phoning it in. I can see that now. I was bored and frustrated and I didn't do my best."

"So you learn from that, too. You have a lot to offer. You're honest and smart and you raised great kids." He smiled. "You put up with me longer than you should have."

She managed to smile back. "I did, but that was because I was crazy in love with you. I didn't want to walk away."

She'd kept hoping he would change so that she could stay, but in the end, she'd done the right thing. She supposed that was something to be proud of. Of course she'd continued to have sex with her ex for the next decade, which was so incredibly dumb.

"I'm a slow learner," she said with a groan. "I've got to get better at figuring out the problem and solving it."

"I have a thought," he said. "Give us another chance."

She stared at him, not sure she'd heard him correctly. "What did you say?"

"Give us another chance." He reached for her hand again. "I miss you, Steph. I miss us. I was so wrong before. I threw away the most important thing in my life and I didn't realize it. But I do now. I have so many regrets. I'm asking for a second chance. I know I have to earn your trust, but I'm up for the challenge. I've never stopped loving you."

She couldn't seem to form actual thoughts. There

were a handful of words strung together, but they made no sense. In love with her? She couldn't grasp the concept.

"It's been ten years," she said, hoping she didn't look as confused as she felt.

"All that means is we've both had a chance to grow and change. I know I have." He gave her a rueful smile. "You were pretty perfect to begin with, so you had less of a journey. I mean it. I love you. I want us to try again."

He loved her? Since when? And how did she feel about what he was saying? Did she want to get back together with him? How would that work? Avery was a junior in high school. She wouldn't want to move and Carson had all his friends and—

Stephanie shook her head. No! This wasn't about her kids—this was about her and Kyle, and what she wanted.

"We could make it work," he continued. "I could move in here and commute to Seattle. You wouldn't have to worry about working unless you wanted to. I want to take care of you the way I should have before. I want to be everything you want me to be."

He sounded sincere, she thought, still having trouble grasping what was happening. He was offering her everything he thought she wanted. Everything she *had* wanted when she'd left him and run back home. They got along well, the sex had always been impressive and being around Kyle was fun. But was that enough? What about her hopes for her own future? Where would he fit in with those? Not that she had much of a future right now. Part of her was tempted—seriously tempted. After all, he was making it so very easy.

For a second time, she pulled her hand free of his as the truth smacked her in the face. It would be easy to say yes, to avoid all the problems in her life. Getting back with Kyle could solve them all. She wouldn't have to worry about money or what to do with her life.

But was that enough? Didn't she want—just once—to be brave? She'd been unhappy in her marriage for years before she'd gathered the courage to leave, and then all she'd done was run back to her mother. She'd taken even longer to try to find another job, and when the cheese place had been a disaster, she'd done nothing. She'd quit on impulse, which wasn't the least bit brave. And now she was facing the reality of a mediocre skill set and a bad reputation. Rather than get off her ass and deal, she'd been hiding and feeling sorry for herself. Worse, she was considering marrying Kyle because it was the easy solution.

"I'm a complete and total wuss," she said aloud.

"What?"

She looked at him. "I am. I've taken the easy way out my entire life. I wanted you, so I got pregnant to trap you. I left you and expected my mom to take care of me. I hated my job here, but I didn't do anything about it. I kept having sex with you so I wouldn't have to find someone I really wanted to be with. I've always taken the easy way out."

"You're being too hard on yourself."

"I'm not. Maybe for the first time in my life, I'm being honest." She sucked in a breath. "I don't love you, Kyle. I'm sorry, but I don't. I haven't for a long time. I think we're good as friends, but we can't get back together. It's been over between us for a long time. We both need to move toward the future, not retreat to the past."

He drew back, his mouth twisting. "You're not going to give us a chance?" His voice was laced with pain.

His obvious surprise, his emotional reaction, triggered guilt, but she ignored it.

"I care about you," she told him. "I always will. We're stuck with each other and I like that. But as friends. You need to find someone who can appreciate the man you've become."

He stood up and glared at her. "I could have gone national. I stayed with the Seattle station because I wanted to be close to you, and all this time, you didn't care what I did."

He was reacting out of anger, she told herself. Best if she didn't do the same. "I didn't know you'd had the chance to go national. Can you still? The kids would love visiting you in New York, and so would I."

As soon as the words came out, she knew they were wrong. He flinched.

"You don't even care if I'm around, do you?"

"Kyle, no! That's not what I meant. I want you to be happy. I want you to have whatever you want."

"Just not you."

There was nothing she could say to that. The awkward silence grew until he turned for the door. She went after him.

"I'm sorry," she said. "I don't want to hurt you."

He faced her. "We could have had it all, Steph."

He was right—they could have. But that chance had ended ten years ago. After all this time, there was no going back.

"I'm sorry," she repeated.

"Me, too."

He walked out into the evening. She watched him get into his car and drive away, then she closed the door and leaned against it.

She didn't feel good about what had happened, but at least she knew she'd done the right thing. For once, she hadn't taken the easy way out. Now the question was what was she going to do next.

Barbara drank wine because she loved it, but she drank tequila to get drunk. Sometimes she made a margarita and sometimes she drank it straight. On this particular afternoon, she was at least pretending, so had mixed it with fresh lime juice and Cointreau.

She sat in her family room, off the kitchen, staring out the window, wondering how her entire life had gone to shit so quickly. Everything was a disaster, and nothing made her feel better, not even gazing at her sparkly engagement ring. The idea of planning a wedding made her shudder—she hardly had time for what she had to do in a day, let alone plan a ridiculous celebration. What did her marriage matter—Bel Après had lost its winemaker and she didn't have a replacement. Even as she sat there, grapes were fermenting and then what? Who would decide what happened next, which were blended and in what ratios? You couldn't just ferment a bunch of grapes, pour the result into a bottle and expect to have something wonderful.

"No one in the area will work for me," she said, raising her glass toward her two daughters. She wasn't sure how they'd gotten there. Lori might have followed her from the office and Catherine had appeared a few minutes later. No doubt Lori had called her, wanting reinforcements.

Barbara had no idea for what. She was sitting by herself, drinking. She was hardly going to burn down the place, so why fuss. But she didn't say that, because it didn't matter, either.

"What do you mean?" Catherine asked, looking ridiculous as always in tie-dyed overalls. Dear God, tie-dye? Hadn't that gone out in the 1960s? "Who won't work for you?"

"Any decent winemaker in the area. We're looking in California. We're going to end up with some loser, but what choice is there?" She swallowed about half of her margarita. It was her third, she thought. Or maybe her fourth.

"Everything is ruined," Barbara continued. "First Mackenzie leaving, then Stephanie. I miss them both. They were so fun to talk to." She glared at her remaining daughters, wondering why they couldn't be more sparkling conversationalists.

"And the lawyer was a disaster. He refused to even consider suing Mackenzie for custody. Why not? I raised four children. She has no experience and she's an orphan."

Lori looked confused. "What does her being an orphan have to do with anything?"

"She has no family, no support system."

"But it's her baby, Mom," Lori said, her voice tentative. "You can't take it away from her."

"So people keep telling me," Barbara snapped, wondering why her middle daughter was so tiresome.

"Let's change the subject," Catherine suggested.

"Talk about happy things. Lori, tell Barbara about Owen."

Barbara turned sharply to stare at Lori. "Who's Owen?"

Lori looked flustered, then blushed, which was always a disaster for her. She went blotchy. It was so unattractive.

"He's an assistant manager at a winery. We've been going out for a while now."

Lori dating? "Since when?"

"A few weeks." Her daughter looked past her. "I didn't think you'd want to talk about it, what with everything else going on."

While that was true, Barbara resented someone else deciding things for her. "You should have told me."

"I'm sorry. You're right."

"I am." Barbara finished her drink. "I'm glad he doesn't care that you're fat. That's something, I suppose."

Lori's eyes widened the way they always did before she burst into tears. Barbara held in a sigh and braced herself for the onslaught. Seconds later, her daughter raced from the room.

"Really?" Catherine shook her head. "Do you have to be mean all the time? Can't we limit it to odd-numbered days?"

"She's weak."

Catherine pressed her lips together. "You know, a lot of research says that overeating is the result of a bad childhood, so technically her weight issues are your fault."

Barbara raised her eyebrows. "Yes, it's very trendy to blame the mother, isn't it?"

Rather than respond, Catherine pulled out her cell phone and sent a quick text. She smiled at her mother.

"Are you happy?"

The unexpected question unsettled Barbara. She dropped her gaze to her glass, not wanting to respond.

"I am," Catherine added, her tone cheerful. "Every day. I have Jaguar and my children. My art fills my soul and I live in a beautiful house surrounded by my family. I'm blessed."

"You certainly don't require much from life," Barbara snapped.

Catherine's calm smile was annoying.

"I require what's important to me."

"Oh, please. Jaguar is a mechanic. He's never going to get into management. Your bits and pieces that you call art don't sell for very much."

"Happiness isn't about money or position. It's about feeling fulfilled by your life. Jaguar enjoys his job and doesn't want to move up in the company. He would rather have time with his family."

"What a shock. You married a man with no ambition."

Catherine, as per usual, ignored her. "We don't need much money, thanks to the family trust. I sell my art when it pleases me. The amount isn't important. I like knowing my pieces make people happy. I'm connected to the earth and creatures around me. My children thrive. What else could I possibly want?"

"A brain?"

Catherine laughed. "I know you're not trying to be funny, but sometimes you are." Her smile faded. "I wish you could be happy. You have so much and you never bother to appreciate it."

"What do I have? Betrayal? Abandonment? A failing company?"

"You have good health and family and a man who loves you."

As if on cue, Giorgio walked into the room. Barbara was surprised to see him, then he and Catherine exchanged a knowing look and she realized the text her daughter had sent earlier had been a request for him to come by. They were plotting against her, she thought grimly. She shouldn't even be surprised.

Giorgio sat next to her and took her hand in hers. "How are you, my sweet?"

"Angry. Depressed. Fearful about the future."

Old, she thought, but didn't say that. Why state the obvious?

"You should have a little faith," he told her, his tone chiding. "It will all work out."

"Will it? How wonderful. While you're prognosticating, when will the new winemaker show up? That would be helpful information."

Giorgio frowned. "Why are you angry with me?"

"Because you're making ridiculous statements. You don't know that everything is going to work out. In your mind, you say it's fine and it is, but that's not reality. If I don't stay on top of everything, then it will all fall apart."

He released her hand and moved to the sofa opposite. "If you hang on too tight, you'll strangle everyone."

"Am I hanging on too tight?" she asked, her voice stiff. "Do you want to tell me what else I'm doing wrong? How this is all my fault, from Mackenzie leav-

ing to Lori's weight problem? I seem to be the villain
of the day. Feel free to pile on."

She was both furious and close to tears. The former
was fine, the latter only added to her anger. She was
done with crying. It made her feel small and alone and
accomplished nothing.

"Barbara, why are we fighting?"

"Because you're unreasonable." She glanced around
and saw that Catherine had slipped out of the room.
"Stop telling me everything is going to work out. You
don't know that it is."

"You don't know that it's not. Why do you have to
look for the dark cloud?"

"Because it's raining trouble every single day."

They glared at each other. Barbara couldn't remember ever fighting with Giorgio before—not like this.
He'd always been supportive and understanding, but
lately, it felt like all he'd done was criticize her.

"Maybe we should change the subject," he said quietly. "Talk about something more pleasant."

She had a lot of energy and would have been fine
yelling for another hour, but saw the sense in his suggestion. Although on second thought, she hoped he
wasn't going to suggest they go upstairs. Right now
sex was the last thing on her mind.

"We have to make our travel plans for Rosemary's
birthday. I suspect you have no interest in going to
Bermuda right now."

"That's perceptive," she said sarcastically, then
wished she hadn't.

Giorgio leaned back in his seat and studied her.
She felt herself flush and wanted to apologize, only

she couldn't seem to get the words past the tightness in her throat.

He glanced away. "As I was saying, we're not going to Bermuda, so let's firm up our dates for New York."

"I'm not going."

"It's her fortieth birthday. She's having a big party with all her friends and family. You need to be there."

"She's not a child. She's a grown-up. She'll understand. It's just a birthday."

He tilted his head. "This isn't about her, Barbara. It's about us. This trip is important to me and I want you to go with me. Whatever is happening with the winery will still be happening when we return. It's one week. I don't think my request is unreasonable."

"It is to me. I don't want to go. Not now. My business needs me."

She wished she had another drink. She wished he would stop looking at her with a combination of surprise and disappointment that made her feel so small.

"Not everything in this relationship is about you," he said quietly.

"That's not fair. I'm in a crisis here. Why can't you understand that? I'm not making this about me, you're making it about you."

"Is that what you really think?"

"Of course. It's what's happening."

"I see." He rose. "Then there doesn't seem to be anything else to say."

She stood. "So you're going to leave? Just like that? No more discussion, no talking about it? Just throw your cape over your shoulder and walk out?"

His dark gaze was steady. "Is there anything I can say to change your mind about New York?"

"No."

"Then staying has no purpose. With Bel Après in crisis, you must be needed back at the office. Don't let me get in the way."

He walked out of the room. Seconds later, she heard the front door close. She collapsed back onto the sofa and covered her face with her hands. She'd gotten what she wanted from him, but somehow it didn't feel like a win at all. In fact, her stomach was churning as if she was going to be sick, and she honestly couldn't say why.

twenty-eight

Saturday afternoon Mackenzie let Stephanie into her bedroom. "Don't judge," she said, pausing in the hallway. "I did the best I could."

Stephanie laughed, then pushed past her. "It's shopping, not repairing the economy of a third-world nation. It's not supposed to be hard."

"And yet it is. But I have to do something." Mackenzie held up the front of her T-shirt to show that she'd been unable to zip her jeans. She had been forced to loop string through the buttonhole and then tie it to the button.

"Oh, honey, that's just sad."

"I know. I might not feel connected to my baby, but I'm getting bigger by the day."

Stephanie walked into the bedroom. "We'll deal with your emotional fragility later. Right now, clothes. What have you got?"

"Nothing that fits. It's all too big." She motioned to the open boxes she'd put on her bed.

As per Stephanie's advice, she'd ordered a bunch

of stuff online, but none of it worked for her. She held up a T-shirt she'd tried on.

"It's huge. The shoulders fit, but I'm swimming in this. Why can't I find maternity clothes that fit? And don't get me started on pants. Mine don't fit but the ones I've bought online are too big."

Stephanie grinned. "You know that the baby is about the size of a lima bean, right? And in five months, it's going to be the size of a baby. You'll grow into the shirt."

Mackenzie didn't look convinced. "I can't picture that happening."

"You don't have to. It's going to happen all on its own."

Stephanie crossed over to the bed and pulled out a pair of jeans and a pair of leggings.

"The jeans will be less baggy right now because of how they're made and the fact that their tummy panel isn't as big as the ones on the leggings. You'll wear the leggings as the baby grows. Get four pairs of each, along with a couple of pairs of dressier pants for when you have a business event."

"How will I know if they're going to fit?"

"If they're your usual size and the legs fit, then just go with it. The same with the shirts. They should fit through the shoulders and arms. You wear T-shirts and sweatshirts for work. Buy those, along with a couple of nice blouses for when you have to dress up. That will get you started. In a couple of months, you and I will drive into Tri-Cities to do some more shopping."

"I'm not sure I can do this," Mackenzie said, staring at the clothes on the bed. "And I'm not sure about the whole baby thing."

Stephanie grinned. "Gee, I wonder why. Look at all you've been through. Having a baby has to be the last thing on your mind."

She crossed to the bed and quickly sorted through the clothes Mackenzie had ordered. She pulled out all the long-sleeved T-shirts, the sweatshirts and two sweaters and put them in a pile, then held up two blouses.

"These are hideous prints. What were you thinking?"

"I was feeling desperate and they were on sale."

"They go back. Find something you at least sort of like." She pointed to the pile. "Try those on, and if the shoulders and sleeves fit, keep them."

She crossed to the closet. It didn't take long to pull out every top that was fitted.

"These go into storage, making room for the maternity stuff." She pointed at the clear bins she'd brought with her. "You'll have to go through your bras and panties, as well. For a while you can make do with bikini underwear but eventually we all give in to the granny panties. Don't worry. We'll buy those when we go shopping. Are you still fitting in your bras?"

Mackenzie nodded. "I have a bunch of stretchy sports bras that will fit for a long time." She glanced at her chest. "I hate my boobs getting bigger. It's weird."

"It is so going to get worse."

Mackenzie sighed. "I couldn't get through this without you. I mean that. I'm totally lost, which isn't like me at all."

"I'm here for you and so is Four. Now let's go downstairs and have some of the muffins I brought over."

"I love your muffins. We're lucky it's Saturday and

Bruno isn't here, otherwise he would have eaten them all. Four brought by cookies the other day and it turns out the man has a thing for homemade baked goods."

They went downstairs. Mackenzie knew she would have to deal with the clothes later, but for now she was grateful to hang out with her friend.

She poured them each a cup of coffee.

"Decaf," she said. "I don't have any real coffee here. Sorry."

"Decaf is fine." Stephanie pushed the plate of blueberry muffins across the table. "You have to save me from these. I already ate two this morning. Bruno isn't the only one with a fondness for homemade baked goods. The difference is he's a guy so it's harder for him to gain weight."

"He's a fairly healthy eater. He's always insisting we have salads for lunch. I want to say that's all about the baby, but I think some of it is him."

Stephanie raised her eyebrows. "You're having lunch together. Do tell."

"It's nothing." Mackenzie waved away the comment. "We're sharing very close quarters while the offices are being remodeled, so we eat lunch together."

"I'm not convinced. He's a good-looking guy, you're newly single. Are you saying there's not sparkage?"

"I've never heard you say sparkage before. I'm a little afraid."

"One of us should have a love life."

"Not me." Mackenzie thought about seeing Rhys having lunch with that woman. He'd been so quick to move on, but she wasn't the least bit ready. "It's too soon."

"Are you missing my brother?"

SUSAN MALLERY

"Not exactly. I miss the us we could have been."

"Were you ever that us?"

She wanted to say of course they had been, but if she was honest, she knew the truth. "No, not even on our best day."

"Do you want that?"

"Do you?"

Stephanie reached for a muffin. "Eventually. I'd like to have a normal adult relationship with a man who isn't my ex-husband."

"You could meet someone online."

"Or I couldn't." She tore off a piece of the muffin and ate it. "What about you? How long do you think you're going to wait to find someone?"

"I have no idea. As you mentioned earlier, there's a lot going on. The last thing I need is a guy."

"What about a baby?"

"So we're circling back to that?"

"We don't have to." Stephanie smiled. "It's okay not to feel bonded to your kid. Right now it's a medical condition, not a person. You're doing all the right things. You're eating right, you're taking your vitamins, spitting after you drink wine. You have time to get used to the idea of being a mom."

"I don't know how to do that," she admitted. "Be a mom. I never had one."

"Love them with all your heart and don't let them drown in the tub. Four and I will be here for you. You know that."

"I do. Even with all the drama, you've been here. You're a good friend."

"If we ignore my initial screwup."

Mackenzie smiled. "I have no recollection of that

event. So enough about me and my issues. What's new with you?"

Stephanie smiled brightly. "I'm moving forward with the job search. I have a few leads."

"What happened with Elias? You said he was going to get back to you."

Stephanie got up and poured more coffee. "He gave the job to someone else."

"Oh, no. You didn't tell me. I'm sorry."

"It's okay." Stephanie returned to the table. "I didn't do very well with the interview. But I did learn a lot. It turns out I wasn't a great employee at my last job."

"How can you say that? You were great. Retail sales were up every single year. Plus you had excellent ideas for expanding the retail base. And the café was brilliant. Barbara refused to see it, but it added a whole new element to what Bel Après offered. It was a chance to be a destination."

She held her hands palm up. "I hope you take this in the spirit I mean it, but I've been stealing your best ideas when I talk to Bruno about what we're going to do at Painted Moon. He's perfectly comfortable with our lack of income, but I hyperventilate on a regular basis."

"You're sweet. Thank you for stealing my ideas. Maybe I'll get some more and share them with you."

"I'll take anything." Mackenzie hesitated. "Bruno's in charge of hiring people, but I'm happy to talk to him if you want."

"No." Stephanie's voice was firm. "No and no. I want to get my next job on my own. I'm already doing a lot of research and coming up with a plan. Let me work it my own way."

Mackenzie knew all about wanting to prove herself. "I won't say anything."

"Thank you. Now I have gossip." Stephanie's eyes lit up. "Mom's been day drinking and by day drinking I mean tequila. Four was over there a couple of weeks ago and she was drunk at three in the afternoon."

Mackenzie smiled because she knew that was what Stephanie expected her to do, but there was no joy inside her. Despite everything, she felt badly for what Barbara was going through. Dumb on her part, but there it was.

"Is there a new winemaker?"

"Not yet, but I understand there will be interviews soon."

"I hope whoever she hires is careful with the Syrah. They can be tricky to work with."

Stephanie leaned toward her. "Mackenzie, not your rock."

"I know, but—"

"No buts. You have to let it go. You have Painted Moon now. Worry about those Syrah grapes."

"I do. It's just hard to let go."

Stephanie picked up her coffee. "Tell me about it."

The remodel of the Painted Moon workspace finished exactly on time—something Mackenzie had never experienced before. She supposed overseeing the construction was just another of Bruno's many talents. It took only a couple of trips to move her things into her new office. While the space was much nicer than what she'd had at Bel Après, it was nothing like the original plans.

Bruno had wanted to give her double the square

footage, with a fancy attached bathroom. She'd explained she did most of her work much closer to grapes and wine, and that she didn't need anything other than a desk and a few files. He'd given her more than that, including lovely built-in bookcases and a small sofa against the far wall.

By nine thirty, she was settled, her computer hooked up to the new Wi-Fi. She had a fancy new phone with way too many buttons. Her cell she could handle, but a landline with two rows of buttons made her nervous. She was staring at it when Bruno appeared in her open doorway.

"Is someone going to explain all this to me?" she asked, waving to the phone.

"There's a hold button, a speaker button and one that has my name on it."

"What about the rest of them?"

"They're for when we start growing. I'm interviewing office managers in the morning. Any requests?"

"Don't make me participate."

He grinned as he walked into her office and settled on the sofa. "I promise. I'm taking care of all the office staffing. The bookkeeper is staying, as are both warehouse guys. The vineyard manager wants to retire."

"He told me yesterday. He's in his seventies and looks like he's a hundred and five, so he's earned it."

"He'll be hard to replace."

"I know."

"Know anyone who might be interested?"

"You mean poach from another winery?" she asked, trying not to sound scandalized.

The smile returned. He had a great smile, one that almost made her forget her train of thought. He wore a long-sleeved shirt tucked into dark jeans, and loafers. A little fancy, but still, he was an attractive package. She, on the other hand, had on the stretchiest yoga pants Target sold, and an oversize blouse she hated but that covered her stomach. Mackenzie didn't usually care about clothes, but dressed as she was, she felt frumpy.

"We make them a better offer," he told her, reminding her of their conversation. "It's just business. Let me put together a list of potential replacements."

"Is one of them going to be Rhys?"

His eyebrows rose. "Do you want it to be?"

"No." She hesitated. "He's very good at his job. Am I wrong to say I don't want to work with him?"

"No. You're handling the divorce better than most, but why make things awkward when they don't have to be?"

"Thank you."

"You're welcome. We need to figure out what to do with the bottled wine. I have some feelers out with distributors in the restaurant business. We put on a house label and, voilà, it's special."

"That would work." They had a lot of inventory and she would feel better knowing cash was coming in.

"We'll do the same with the barrels," he added. "Once you know what you want to do with all that, we can start making plans. We can sell some under the Painted Moon label here domestically, bottle some for house wines for restaurants and see if there's a market for the rest of it elsewhere."

While her first instinct was to dump the barrels and start over, that wasn't feasible—at least not financially. He was right—she had to let go of her quest for perfection. These weren't her wines and keeping the business making money was important.

"I'll be done tasting in the next couple of weeks," she told him. "I'm sticking to a schedule and it's slow going. I'm being careful like the doctor said to be."

"I wish I could do the tasting for you."

She smiled. "No offense, but I don't trust your palate."

"None taken, and you're right not to. Are you feeling all right?"

She nodded. "I've been really lucky to not have morning sickness. I feel fine. There are the physical changes, of course, but you don't want to know about them." She grinned. "Let's just say my jeans aren't fitting anymore and leave it at that."

"I appreciate the lack of detail."

She laughed. "I'm reading the pregnancy book Stephanie gave me, along with a couple of others my doctor recommended. They're kind of scary. Apparently having a baby is a whole thing."

"Are you overwhelmed?"

"Not if I don't think about it too much."

"I'm here if you need me. I can go with you to the doctor or get you pickles." He cleared his throat. "And when I say go with you to the doctor, I mean I'd wait outside. I think the exam part would be awkward for both of us."

She laughed. "It would be. Regardless, I appreciate the offer. I don't have any pickle cravings, but if that changes, I'll let you know."

"I'm looking forward to the baby. I like kids."

"If I bring him or her to the office, you're going to get to know this one really well."

"I think that's a plus."

He would be good with a child. He was patient and he understood people. There was something solid about him, but not in a boring way.

Her gaze drifted to his mouth and she had the craziest thought that she would like to know how he kissed. Did he just go for it or was he looking for a shared experience? He was powerful and used to getting his way and—

"I'm going to head back to my office," he said, coming to his feet. "I have calls to make and I know you'll want to spend some quality time getting to know your phone."

His statement drew her back to real life. Yikes, where had that weird kissing thought come from? Kiss Bruno? They were business partners. Sure, she liked him, but she liked lots of people and she never thought about kissing them.

Pregnancy hormones, she told herself as he left. Her body was becoming an alien being. She was going to have to ignore the weirdness and wait for things to return to normal in a few months. Kissing Bruno. As if!

Barbara waited for the ibuprofen to take effect. She'd awakened with a headache nearly every morning for the past week. She was tired of starting her day with painful throbbing in her head.

There were multiple causes—her nightly half bottle of tequila for starters, the stress of everything going on. She hadn't seen Giorgio since their fight about his daughter's stupid birthday party and Lori was keeping late hours, sometimes not coming home at all, no doubt staying with her loser boyfriend. Well, let her,

Barbara thought, collecting her handbag and briefcase before stepping out into the morning.

She paused to take in the deep blue sky and the perfect fall temperature. Harvest was done, the wines were being transferred into barrels and the hard work for the year was finished. Or it would have been if Mackenzie hadn't left, ruining them all.

She drove over to work in her golf cart. After climbing the stairs, her head pounding in time with her footfalls, she made her way to her office. She clicked on lights and walked toward her desk, fighting a sense of dread and helplessness.

How would Bel Après survive? This was a critical time and they had no winemaker. Worse, no one would come to them now—at least no one decent. So what were they going to do?

There was no good answer, she thought grimly. She checked her email before heading into the break room. By now one of the staff would have started the coffee. The caffeine would make her feel better, she told herself. Once her head stopped hurting, she could think.

But when she returned, mug in hand, she found Rhys pacing in front of her desk.

"Oh dear God, either sit down or get out," she snapped. "This morning I have no patience for you or your moods."

He waited until she was seated, then slapped both hands on her desk and loomed over her. His eyes flashed with anger.

"How dare you?" he growled.

"You forget I've been dealing with your tantrums since you were two. You can't intimidate me. Sit down or get out."

Their gazes locked. She saw indecision in his, and the second before he settled in the chair, she knew that she had already won.

"You talked to a lawyer about suing Mackenzie for custody of the baby."

Catherine, Barbara thought, not even surprised that her youngest had been talking behind her back. There was no loyalty there.

"You won't do it, so one of us has to."

"I don't want custody. I'm still trying to figure out my obligations and I sure as hell don't need you getting in the way of that. Don't mess things up like you always do. For once, just act like a normal person."

"I'm the most normal of anyone in this family," she told him pointedly. "You're less than useless on this matter. If you'd just challenge her for the baby, I could stay out of it."

"That's not going to happen."

Because he didn't care, she thought grimly, surprised to feel a flicker of compassion on Mackenzie's behalf. James had been thrilled with each of her pregnancies. He'd been a wonderful, doting husband and a good father.

"Getting out of your marriage at any price?" she asked, her tone bitter. "You're going to let her get away with anything so long as you get your freedom?"

"If necessary, yes."

"How you disappoint me."

"The feeling is mutual, Mom."

They were at an impasse.

"I wish she wasn't pregnant," she said with a sigh.

"Me, too, but we are where we are. I'm tired of fighting."

"So you'll do whatever it takes to get along with me, as well?" she asked tartly.

"As long as it doesn't involve custody of the baby, yes."

How disheartening to realize he wasn't going to push back. He wasn't going to take the high ground and quit the way his sister had.

She and Stephanie had never gotten along very well, but Barbara had to admit at least her oldest daughter had principles and a spine. She was willing to walk away to prove her point, while Rhys was not.

She supposed his life was too comfortable. He had a lovely house, food delivered to his refrigerator, and even after paying off Mackenzie, he'd have plenty of money. No doubt he was very popular with all the single women in town. He was going to turn into a dilettante and throw away any opportunity for greatness. Why had she never seen it before?

Because of Mackenzie, she thought. He'd been swept along by her passion and work ethic. Mackenzie had been the driving force, loving her work and Bel Après with every fiber of her being. She'd brought a sense of purpose to them all and now she was gone.

Barbara's eyes burned and she knew the sensation had nothing to do with her hangover. Disillusionment, bitter and tinged with regret, flavored her tongue. She allowed herself a few seconds of emotional indulgence, then shook off the feelings.

"Are the barrels ready for the wine?" she asked, sitting straighter in her chair and picking up her mug of coffee. "Did you order enough?"

"I did. Everything is in place." He paused. "She

would come back and help us for a few days. It would make things easier."

Barbara glared at him. "I'm not interested in easy, Rhys. I would have thought you would know that by now. Get it done and get it done right. What's happening with the winemakers in California?"

"I have interviews lined up with a couple. If I think they're all right, I'll send them along to you."

"Have you ever interviewed anyone for a job before?" she asked.

"Plenty of times." But he looked uncomfortable as he spoke.

"You might want to do a little research online. Otherwise you're likely to make a fool out of yourself."

He stood up. "Anything else?" he asked, his voice tight.

"No. Keep me informed about the interviews."

He nodded and walked out. She leaned back in her chair and wondered why he couldn't have been the one to leave instead of Mackenzie. Or any of her children, or all of them. Mackenzie was the only one worth anything. The rest of them were simply deadweight.

twenty-nine

Stephanie couldn't remember being this sick to her stomach since her pregnancies. Unlike Mackenzie, she'd spent most of the first three months unable to keep down anything but crackers. She could say for certain that her current state of nausea had nothing to do with hormones and everything to do with nerves. She was scared. No. Terrified.

Kyle's unexpected proposal and her realization that she was willing to take the easy way out had been what she'd needed to get off her butt and find the job of her dreams. Ignoring the top five producers in the area, she'd focused on the middle twenty or so who would appreciate her experience and skills. From there she'd done her best to figure out who might want to hire her and, of all of them, there was only one who was for sure looking for staff. Painted Moon.

Which presented a dilemma, she thought as she sipped coffee at the kitchen island. She wanted to be hired because of what she brought to the job and not because she was best friends with one of the two owners. To that end, she hadn't said anything to Mackenzie, and when she'd phoned Bruno to set up the meeting, she'd asked him not to say anything, either.

"Oh, the lies we tell," she murmured to herself as she reviewed her notes for the thousandth time.

Carson ambled into the kitchen, pulling a Seahawks sweatshirt over a long-sleeved T-shirt. His cast was gone and he was back playing sports, as if his arm had never been broken.

"Hey, Mom."

He walked over and gave her a brief hug, followed by a kiss on the top of her head.

"Hey, I know you're a lot taller than me," she said in mock outrage. "Stop rubbing it in."

He flashed her a grin as he opened the refrigerator and pulled out the breakfast burrito she'd defrosted for him. She made them in batches and froze them individually so the kids could have them for breakfast.

After popping it in the microwave, he poured himself a glass of milk.

"You ready for your interview?" he asked.

"I hope so. I may have studied too much."

"You can never be too prepared. You ran the drills, Mom. You're going to do great."

"Thanks."

The microwave beeped. Carson collected his breakfast, then sat at the island where she'd put fresh fruit. He'd just started eating when Avery sailed into the kitchen.

"My hair wouldn't cooperate," she said, dumping her backpack on the floor, then crossing to Stephanie and hugging her. "Why does it have days like that?"

"It just does, sweetie."

"My hair always cooperates," Carson said.

Avery pulled out protein powder and almond milk. "Your hair is an inch long. You don't know if it cooperates or not."

"You should try it."

Avery drew in a breath. "Carson, you're not normal."

"I'm more normal than you."

The bantering had always been a part of their morning routine. Stephanie knew she was lucky when it came to her kids. She and Avery had gone through a rough patch in the summer, but now they were friends again. She was going to focus on the good in her life and let the rest of it take care of itself. As for her interview—she would do her best. This time she was prepared. If things didn't go well, she would come up with another plan, because no matter what, she wasn't taking the easy way out.

Stephanie had known Bruno Provencio for several years and always thought of him as impressive, but she'd never actually trembled in his presence before. Of course he'd never had any power over her life before, and that certainly made a difference.

"The remodel came out great," she said as she sat across from him in his large office. "There's lots of functional space."

"Mackenzie's office is smaller than the original plan," he said with a chuckle. "She refused the extra square footage and the private bathroom."

"She's not one for frills."

"I agree. She's not here right now. She's having lunch with your sister, I believe. Your doing?"

Stephanie nodded. She'd confided in Four, asking

that she arrange lunch at the same time Stephanie had her interview.

"I didn't want her to know. She's a full partner in the business and her opinion would influence yours."

His gaze was unreadable. "Good to know. Tell me what you want to talk about."

Her stomach sank, her heart rate increased and her mouth went dry. At least she didn't feel like she was going to pass out. Fainting would not make her look capable.

"You're in a unique position. Painted Moon is well established and yet you're starting over. From my perspective, you need to remodel the tasting room, design and stock a retail space, revamp your digital presence, start a wine club, entice tourists, and sell your library wines."

"That's a big list."

"It is, so there need to be priorities. The digital aspect is out of my area of expertise." She smiled. "So that's on you."

One corner of his mouth lifted. "Passing the buck so soon?"

"Absolutely. As for the rest of it, the tasting room needs to be open by early spring for tourist season. The retail space falls in line with that. The other priority should be the library wines. From what I've calculated, you have over a million dollars' worth of wine tied up in that. Let's get it out there."

"You want to start a wine club?"

"Not yet. That should be a year-two endeavor. Right now you don't have wines to sell. The library wines are a separate project."

"How would we sell them without a wine club?"

And here it was, she thought, opening the folder she'd set on the conference table in his office.

"By letting the wines tell a story. Mackenzie had no part in them, so we can't use her. By the way, I have ideas on how to make her the star when it comes to the wines you're going to start producing. But for the library wines, I thought the focus should be on Herman and his family."

She opened the folder to show him the first of the labels she'd designed. "The oldest bottles are twelve years old."

"How do you know that?"

She felt herself relax. "You have very poor security. The last time I visited Mackenzie, I went into the production area and walked into the cellar. No one stopped me or asked me why I was there. I took a quick inventory."

"Interesting." He made a note on a pad. "Go on."

She explained how the new labels would feature pictures of the winery dating back to when it had been a farm and how it had changed. Four had drawn the pictures in her whimsical style.

She flipped to another page. "See how we can do a boxed collection, featuring three years and five years? The presentation would be lovely and it's something we could offer in the retail space next year."

"How would we get customers?"

"Painted Moon used to have a wine club. You would have all those names and addresses. We do a mailing, talking about what's happened at the winery and what they can expect in the future. Herman said the list was nearly ten thousand people."

"Let me guess," Bruno said dryly. "You called him and asked."

"I did. He's so sweet. I've known him forever."

"Apparently."

She smiled. "Small-town living, Bruno. You need to get used to that."

"So Mackenzie tells me."

"Now, about the tasting room," she said, setting a second folder in front of him. "There are two stars of this particular show. The wines and the bar. Rumor has it, the bar started in a San Francisco brothel during the gold rush. Whether or not that's true doesn't matter—it's a great story and one that should be played up in all the materials."

She opened the folder to a picture of the bar.

"Let me guess," he said, looking from the picture to her. "You wandered around the old tasting room, as well."

"Of course I did."

An hour later, she'd gone through all her material. The last folder she handed him was about sales to China.

"Not my area of expertise," she admitted. "So these are just random thoughts. It's a huge market. There are already wine tours for Chinese tourists in California and Oregon. Why not do that here? There are plenty of wineries to tour, and if Painted Moon initiates the idea, you can be one of the star attractions."

"I've been thinking the same thing myself," he said, taking the folder. "You've done your research."

"I think you're in a unique position to grow over the next few years. I know how Mackenzie works, so having great wines is a given. I have retail experience from my time at Bel Après and I've learned a lot about the business simply by osmosis. I'd like to put those skills to use here."

He looked at her, his expression just as unreadable as it had been for the entire interview. But instead of being scared by that, she felt good. She'd worked hard and it showed. She'd studied Painted Moon and she'd had suggestions that were specific to them. Something she should have done the first time around, but at least she'd learned from her mistakes.

"I do the hiring here," he said, "but not without running the senior positions by Mackenzie."

Senior positions? Her heart fluttered in a very happy way. "Of course."

"Give me a few days to take all this in and I'll get back to you."

"Thank you."

She rose and they shook hands. Stephanie managed to get all the way to her car before pride made her pump her fist in the air. She'd done it. She'd worked hard and she'd had a great interview. That wasn't a guarantee of a job, but at least she knew she had it in herself. Whatever happened, she could tell herself she'd done everything right and that made today a very good day.

Mackenzie stood in the doorway to what would be the baby's room and stared at the furniture pushed together at one end. At some point, she was going to have to figure out what she wanted to do in here. The walls needed painting and she needed a rug for the hardwood floors, along with curtains for the windows.

Based on the books she was reading, she was going to need a bunch of supplies before the baby was born. Diapers and stuff. Clothes maybe. Sheets. She wasn't sure about toys. Newborns mostly ate and slept, so she could wait on those. It was a lot to think about, and realizing that made her uncomfortable, which was why she tried not to think about the postpregnancy part of her life. At some point she was going to have to ask Stephanie and Four to talk her through the baby-prep thing, just not today.

She glanced at her watch and knew she had to get moving. She'd come home to shower and change after a day of walking the vineyards. But they had a meeting with a Chinese wine distributor at three and professional dress was required.

She'd chosen the least baggy pair of black maternity pants she could find and a floaty, sleeveless top. In honor of the meeting, she'd put on a little makeup and had replaced her work boots with cute flats.

Knowing she couldn't distract herself any longer, she went downstairs, then drove the short distance to the offices. She saw an unfamiliar rental car parked in front and realized their potential clients had arrived early.

"What happened to just being punctual?" She hurried to the conference room.

Bruno was there, along with three men Mackenzie had never seen before. Bruno saw her first. She mouthed a quick "Sorry" before turning to their guests.

"Hello, everyone."

All three men looked at her. Mackenzie gave a broad smile as she approached.

"I was out in the vineyards. Now that we're finished with harvest, I'm thinking about what changes I want to make. I know I could do that from my office, but

I find it easier to think about the vines when I'm out among them."

For a second, no one said anything. Mackenzie had just enough time to wonder if she'd somehow put her foot in her mouth when the three men rushed toward her.

The tallest of the visitors reached for her hand. "Mackenzie Dienes. An honor. Your reputation precedes you."

The other two also praised her abilities, speaking in amazing English.

Mackenzie shook hands with them all, trying to put names with faces and willing herself not to say anything stupid. Around her grapes, she was absolutely in charge. It was the whole doing a business deal with people that she found intimidating.

Bruno saved her by taking charge of the meeting.

"Gentlemen," he said, directing them to the table. "Let me show you what we've been working on."

He passed around different label options. The three men spoke in Chinese before Mr. Lin pointed to the simple dark blue label with a plain font reading Painted Moon Presents.

"Next time we'll have your name on the wine," he said, looking at Mackenzie. "That will bring us top dollar."

Mackenzie smiled rather than speak. She didn't want to inadvertently make a commitment.

Once the labels were chosen, they went into the barrel room. Earlier Mackenzie had set up a tasting with a few wines from the library and the equipment necessary to taste directly from the barrel. She had a pad of paper and a pen, so she could keep track of their thoughts on the various options.

Mackenzie had already tasted everything, careful to spit the samples once she'd determined what she thought about them. For this tasting, she would talk about the wines without drinking. She and Bruno had decided that spitting in front of prospective clients wasn't a selling strategy.

"There are three wines from the Painted Moon library that I think are special enough for you to consider," she began. "All three are blends, combining the very best of what the vineyard had to offer that year. The wines are smooth, ready to drink and, if you bought the entire inventory, would be exclusive to you."

Bruno handed her a bottle. Mackenzie expertly cut through the foil, then pulled out the cork. After pouring the liquid into five glasses, Mackenzie passed them out. She held up her glass.

"Let's start with the color. This one is a beautiful deep purple color. It looks as luscious as it drinks." She swirled the wine in the glass. "You can see there's a high alcohol content."

She inhaled the scent of the wine and smiled. "Very fruit forward, which I believe is your preference. You can smell the freshness, the health of the grapes, plus a hint of spice and chocolate that's unique to our area."

Everyone else sniffed their glasses. Their guests smiled, then looked at her.

"Now we taste?" Mr. Meng asked.

She laughed. "Now we taste."

"How did you get the restaurant to deliver?" Mackenzie asked Bruno as she pulled out to-go boxes on her dining room table.

"They just made the food. I had someone else bring it here."

Her stomach rumbled as the delicious smells tempted her. After a long afternoon of entertaining their Chinese visitors, she was starving.

She'd already set out a wineglass for him. She had her lovely carafe of water to chug. Yum. But rather than think about what she couldn't have, she looked at the bounty spread out in front of her. Mushroom ravioli with a brown butter sauce, two different salads, a pork tenderloin and summer squash pancakes with feta.

"I love Whitehouse-Crawford," she said. "Rhys and I went there maybe once a month for dinner. Good food, a fun atmosphere. We preferred it off-season, but even dining with the tourists was fun."

"I enjoy their food, as well."

She looked at Bruno. "Should I not mention Rhys when I talk about my old life?"

"Why? He's a part of who you are. You're still friends."

"We are," she said automatically, although she wasn't sure that was actually true. They hadn't spoken since she'd told him she was pregnant. Their only contact had been through her lawyer, setting up a meeting to discuss a proposed parenting plan.

"Are you happy with how the meeting went?" she asked.

Bruno smiled as he served her ravioli. "I ordered this for us for dinner, didn't I? It's a celebration meal."

"You ordered this before the meeting. Our visitors only left a half hour ago."

His dark eyes brightened with amusement. "You're right. I ordered the dinner a couple of days ago. I had a feeling we were going to have something to party about. And if the meeting had gone badly, we would have used the food to get over our disappointment."

Instead they would be toasting the very large order Mr. Hsia and his coworkers had placed. They'd taken the entire inventory of all three of the library wines Mackenzie had suggested, along with a thousand cases of wine still in the barrel.

"We're going to have to make some decisions about the Chinese market," Bruno said. "They'll want to buy for as long as we want to sell to them. How much of what we harvest do we want to commit to the overseas market?"

"I don't know how to answer that. I did research a few years ago, but when I tried to talk about China as a potential market, Barbara was never interested. I know there's a huge profit margin."

"We could expand capacity by buying grapes from other vineyards."

Mackenzie stared at him, hoping she didn't look as horrified as she felt. "Grapes over which I don't have any control?"

He smiled. "I thought that would be your answer. If we want to keep selling into the Chinese market, then we might have to buy more land."

"That I could get behind."

"Stephanie is going to be disappointed about our meeting today."

Mackenzie looked at him. "I'm so confused. Why would she care?"

"Because she had big plans for the library wines. They're taking the oldest three years of inventory, which still leaves her with three to work with." He picked up his wineglass. "She came to see me last week. About a job."

"What? Why didn't I know about this? She never said a word. What happened? Are you hiring her?"

Emotions piled on top of one another. How could her best friend not have said anything to her about the job interview? Yet even as she asked the question, she knew the answer. Stephanie wanted to earn her place.

"She blew me away," Bruno admitted. "She understood the problems we're facing and had a lot of solutions. She has great ideas for the tasting room and retail space. She also came up with a unique plan to sell the library wines. A plan that will have to be modified now that we've sold three years of them out from under her."

"Does that mean you want to hire her?"

He smiled. "I do, if you have no objection."

"None at all. I like working with her. She's local, she knows the business and she's very creative."

"Then I'll call her in the morning and make her an offer."

"This day is getting better and better."

She ate a few of the ravioli and tried not to moan at the delicious flavor. The pork was just as good.

"There's going to be a ton of leftovers," she said. "You should take it home."

"You keep it. I want you to have food in the house."

"I have plenty."

"Still, it would make me feel better. I worry about you getting enough to eat."

Which was sweet, but unnecessary. "I'm pregnant, not infirm."

"I believe the phrase is 'in a delicate condition.'"

"Not in this century."

"When I care about someone, I worry. It's a thing. Deal with it."

His tone was so casual, she knew she would be foolish to read anything into his words, but she couldn't help wondering about the "when I care about someone" part. What did that mean? *Get a grip!* She sent the instruction to her brain. She was not going to get weird about her relationship with Bruno. He was the best thing to ever happen to her and he was a genuinely nice man. Nothing more. Although she had to admit, she kind of liked the idea of Bruno caring about her.

"How are you settling into condo life?" she asked.

"It's fine. The neighbors are quiet. When the business is running more smoothly, I'm going to take up golf again."

"You play golf?"

"Yes. I like it."

"Why? The sport has never made sense to me."

He laughed. "What about a Sunday afternoon watching football?"

"Oh, I like that."

"Football makes sense but golf doesn't?"

"Of course. I like team sports. There's lots of action. Plus the food is great."

"Football has food?" His voice was teasing.

"Of course. People eat all kinds of things watching football that they would never eat in real life."

"They also drink beer."

"I'm okay with that. Not every event has to be wine-centric."

He laughed. "You continue to surprise me."

"Only good surprises, though, right?"

"Only good ones. How are you feeling about the baby these days?"

The change in subject surprised her. "I'm slightly more accepting. Just before our meeting today, I was thinking I need to paint the baby's room."

"You're not painting it yourself. I'll do it."

Her eyes widened as she took in his elegant suit. "You know how to paint?"

"Yes. You can't breathe in the fumes." He pulled out his phone and typed something. "Once you pick out the color, I'll prime and paint the room while you're at the office. We'll keep the door closed until the space airs out."

"That's kind of bossy of you."

He raised his eyebrows. "I believe what you meant to say was thank you."

She smiled. "Thank you."

"Have you thought about colors? And themes for decorations?"

"You're not supposed to know all that."

"I've been reading and looking online. You should find out the sex of the baby in the next few weeks. Unless you don't want to know."

"I want them to tell me. I think knowing will help me feel that the baby is real." She shook her head. "I know it's real, but it's still, I don't know, complicated."

"You have time to figure it out."

She nodded because saying she would never be ready sounded weak and sad.

Their conversation returned to the wine business.

"There's a rumor that Bel Après is bringing in a couple of guys from Northern California for your position," he said.

Mackenzie flinched. "Really? They couldn't get anyone local? Although maybe that's a better idea. Fresh eyes and all that." Not that she wanted to picture anyone dealing with her grapes. What if they did it wrong?

"What are you thinking?" Bruno asked.

"That letting go is hard."

"Regrets?"

She looked at him. "None. This is an amazing opportunity and I'm grateful to be a part of what we're building."

"Me, too."

About nine thirty, she walked him to the door. He insisted she keep the leftovers.

"Have them for breakfast," he told her. "I know you're hating your protein drink."

"It's disgusting. I can't believe people drink those on purpose."

Bruno stared into her eyes. "Still missing Rhys?"

"What? No." She shook her head. "There's nothing to miss. I'm even letting go of the lifestyle, although I will admit the meal service was fantastic. There's nothing like coming home and finding a home-cooked meal in the refrigerator."

"We could make that happen here."

She laughed. "I keep forgetting how you love to solve a problem. And while I appreciate the offer, no thank you. I'm going to take care of my meals the way regular people do. With a little planning and a pressure cooker."

"If you're sure."

"I am."

He gave her a brief hug. "Then I'll see you tomorrow."

She smiled at him. "Yes, you will."

thirty

Stephanie listened intently as Bruno detailed the offer. She made notes, asked questions and was fairly sure she'd said all the right things, including a very calm, "I would be delighted to accept your offer." But when she hung up the phone, she spun in her kitchen and let out a little scream.

She had a job! A really good one that paid well, offered benefits. She came to a stop and waited for the room to settle back in place before glancing at her notes to make sure she was remembering correctly.

She would be in charge of the retail space and the tasting room. Bruno was going to be hiring someone to handle digital content and the PR aspect of the business but hoped she would be available to consult on those topics, as well. Oh, and she would be managing the people who worked for her!

She spun again, laughing out loud, and she held her arms wide. She'd done it! She'd—

She came to a stop and opened her eyes. "I have to call Mackenzie." Because she wasn't sure what her friend knew or even if she was upset about not being told what was happening.

She reached for her phone, but before she could dial, she heard a knock at the front door, then a familiar voice calling, "It's me."

Stephanie ran to the front of the house and met Mackenzie in the hallway. They stared at each other for a second before rushing into a big hug with them both jumping up and down.

"I have a new job!" Stephanie shouted.

"I know. I drove over when Bruno called, and I was waiting for him to say you'd accepted." Mackenzie grinned. "We're going to be working together. I'm so excited. This makes me so happy."

"You're not mad that I didn't tell you I'd applied?"

"No. Of course not. I know why you wanted to do this on your own. Bruno didn't say anything, by the way. Not until he'd decided to hire you."

They walked back to the kitchen. Mackenzie took her usual place at the island while Stephanie heated water for tea. While the bags were steeping, she drew in a breath and confessed the truth.

"I didn't tell you everything about my interview with Elias," she said, looking at Mackenzie. "I was too embarrassed to want to talk about it."

Her friend leaned toward her. "What does that even mean? What else is there to share?"

Stephanie busied herself putting the used tea bag on a small plate and then stared at her mug. "He wasn't impressed with my work," she began before explaining how she hadn't noticed the duplicate flyers and that her own mother had been saying she was basically a pity hire.

Mackenzie listened until she'd finished, then reached for Stephanie's hand. "None of that is true. He's wrong about you."

"I wish I could agree with you, but I can't. I didn't do the job I should have. I was mad at my mom for dismissing my ideas, and the last couple of years, I wasn't even trying. That's on me. I didn't even do a good job of researching the winery."

"Okay, sure, you had one stumble, but Bruno was very impressed with you and how you handled yourself. He loved your ideas."

"I'm glad. I worked really hard to be dazzling."

"It worked." Mackenzie smiled at her. "I love you. There's nothing you can say or do to make that change. Now what else don't I know?"

Stephanie felt herself warm with gratitude. "You're a better friend than I deserve, but I'm going to accept the gift of your love. As for other secrets, sorry, but I don't have any. You already know that I quit my job and that my ex-husband proposed and currently isn't talking to me. Mom's still a bitch, so hey, no news there. It's been nearly two years since I've had sex." She paused, as if considering, then laughed. "Those are the highlights."

"They're good ones. Have you heard from Kyle?"

"No. He's in touch with the kids, but he's avoiding me."

"Probably because you broke his heart."

"I'm less sure about that," Stephanie admitted. "We've been getting along better than ever lately, and while that's nice, it's not love." She held up a hand. "That's not to say I wasn't tempted, because I was.

Getting back together with Kyle would have solved all my problems."

"Not if you don't love him."

"There is that." She picked up her mug. "You ever think about dating?"

"No." Mackenzie grimaced. "I was never very good at it when I was a teenager. I can't imagine meeting someone now and trying to make it work."

Stephanie understood the reluctance to make the effort, but if they didn't, they weren't ever going to find anyone.

"Do you want to be alone for the rest of your life?" she asked.

Mackenzie shrugged. "I don't know. Not really. I liked parts of being married. I just wasn't very good at it."

"Some of that is on Rhys."

"Yes, but a lot of it is on me." She bit her lower lip. "We didn't have much of a sex life. Or one at all." Color stained her cheeks. "I knew we'd grown apart, but I never much thought about the sex thing. Rhys did, though. He's mentioned it more than once, so I know I let him down."

"You didn't miss that part of things?" Stephanie asked, careful not to let on what her brother had told her.

"At first." She paused. "Okay, this is definitely TMI, but it wasn't ever that good. I never felt like your mother looked after a night with Giorgio."

"Ugh. You didn't just talk about sex with my brother and my mother doing it with Giorgio in the same sentence. No. Don't. It's too much."

Mackenzie grinned. "Sorry. I take it back."

"Too late." She paused. "I'm sorry things weren't great with Rhys."

"Me, too. Because I was a virgin when we met, so I have no way of knowing if it was because of me or because of him."

"Technically there *is* a way to find out."

Mackenzie looked at her. "I'm four and a half months pregnant. I'm not going to have sex with some guy just to figure out who was at fault."

"Fine. Wait until the baby's born."

"I'm going to have other things on my mind."

"Possibly. I, on the other hand, am going to start dating."

Mackenzie's eyes widened. "You are?"

"Yes. I'm giving myself six months to get settled into my new job and then I'm putting myself out there."

"I'm impressed."

"Let's wait on that to make sure I follow through."

Mackenzie smiled at her. "You will. Look at how far you've come."

Stephanie raised her mug of tea. "How far we've both come."

Barbara knew the man sitting in front of her was a third-rate winemaker at best. His resume was unimpressive, his appearance was run-down, and after tasting his wines, she wasn't the least bit excited about hiring him. Still, he was the best of the three she'd interviewed, and with fermentation finished and the wines about to go into the barrels, she was out of options. Beggars and all that, she thought, trying not to let herself fall into hopelessness.

The anger that had sustained her since Mackenzie's

defection had faded—no doubt overcome by the enormity of trying to carry on without her former daughter-in-law.

"When can you start?" Barbara asked.

"I can stay until the wine's in the barrels, then head back to California for a week to get things settled."

This was not what she wanted for Bel Après, she reminded herself. She and the winery both deserved better. But there was no "better" to be had and it was this man or someone worse.

"Excellent," she said, holding out her hand. "Once you've moved here permanently, the first task we need to take on is getting an assistant winemaker in place."

"I agree. It's something you should have done years ago."

Barbara glared at him, fighting all the sarcastic responses that came to mind. Knowing they wouldn't help and might, in fact, scare him away, she forced out a tight smile and only said, "So let's fix that, shall we?"

When he was gone, she closed her eyes against the horror of it all. She turned her chair away from her desk and told herself to breathe. That they had a winemaker now and that was one problem solved. But when she opened her eyes, she found herself staring at a picture of her and Mackenzie, their arms around each other's waists, standing in the Red Mountain vineyard, laughing in the bright sunshine.

It had been a perfect day, she thought sadly. Everything had been as it should be. Unlike her life now.

"Damn you," she said quickly, then repeated the statement more loudly. When that didn't make her feel better, she took off one of her pumps and threw it at the picture. The heel hit the glass, shattering it.

Shards fell onto the carpet. She saw a sharp gash over her own image.

But Mackenzie's half of the picture was untouched, and her smiling face seemed to turn mocking as Barbara looked away and let herself surrender to her tears.

Mackenzie tried to control her frustration. Taking time out of her own day was bad enough, but she'd also had to pay to have her attorney drive over from Seattle for a meeting with Rhys and *his* attorney. She had no idea why all this was required for what she had hoped would be a wrap-up meeting, finalizing the divorce settlement, child support agreement and parenting plan.

As per Rhys's recent request, she and Ramona had prepared a parenting plan for him to review. The amount of child support he had to pay was based on his salary, and she had no intention to ask for more, so there wasn't much to talk about there. Ramona had explained about the additional payments Mackenzie could request for things like private school or a college fund. Mackenzie had considered her options and had settled on asking him to set up a college fund such that he would put aside the equivalent of two years at WSU. She would do the same. If their kid wanted to go somewhere more expensive, she would figure that out herself.

Per Ramona's recommendation, there was also a clause about medical payments if their child be born with some kind of disability. Under those circumstances, Rhys would be expected to contribute more than the base amount. The rest of it—visitation and the like—had been pretty easy. She'd assumed Rhys would want every other weekend, alternating birthdays, Thanksgivings and Christmases. She'd offered him a month every summer, with a notation that deferring the month while the child was still young didn't take away his right to ask for it later.

Ramona had assured her that the parenting plan was fairly standard. There were mentions of who paid ordinary expenses. While the child support was meant to cover day-to-day costs, it was not unreasonable to ask Rhys to pay for an occasional haircut or new shoes.

As she pulled into Rhys's lawyer's parking lot, she told herself to breathe. That she would get through the meeting and then she and Rhys could be done with all this.

She met Ramona in the lobby of the small building. Her lawyer led the way to the receptionist, where she gave their names. They were immediately shown back to a large conference room with a table that easily seated thirty. Rhys and his lawyer were at one end. Ramona walked toward them and sat down, across from them. Mackenzie settled next to her.

As she greeted her soon-to-be ex-husband and his lawyer, she tried to remember the last time she'd seen Rhys. It had been several weeks ago, she thought, when she'd told him she was pregnant. Despite living in a small town, their paths rarely crossed.

She felt herself tense as she remembered she was wrong about the last time she'd seen him. It had been when she'd spotted him having lunch with a blonde woman.

Trying not to be obvious, she studied him. He was dressed in his usual jeans and a long-sleeved shirt. His hair was longer, and she thought maybe he'd lost weight. When his gaze met hers, he offered her a tight smile.

"How's it going?" he asked.

As she had no idea which "it" he meant—baby, winery, the divorce—she could only shrug and say, "Fine."

Mr. Norris, Rhys's attorney, slipped on his glasses. "Thank you all for coming," he began. "We only have a few items left to wrap up to finalize the paperwork for the divorce. My client and I are hoping we can get through them all today."

My client? Mackenzie frowned at the odd phrasing. The formalness made her uncomfortable and gave her a bad feeling in the pit of her stomach.

Ramona pulled a stack of paperwork from her briefcase. "I have the copies of the settlement agreement you emailed me and I've looked them over. My client has agreed to the changes noted."

They'd all been minor and more procedural than anything else.

"Do you have your changes on the parenting plan?" Ramona asked.

Mr. Norris glanced at Rhys, who nodded. The older man passed over two sets of documents. Ramona took one and handed the other to Mackenzie.

"The modifications might be greater than what you were expecting," Mr. Norris said.

Mackenzie glanced at the pages in front of her. The first paragraph stated that Rhys claimed paternity of the unborn child and would not require a DNA test for the parenting plan to go into effect, although he did request one after birth, on behalf of a family member.

She looked at him. "You believe it's your baby?"

For the first time since she'd walked into the room, he seemed to relax. "I know it is. I was there when it happened, and I know you haven't been seeing anyone else. But it would make things easier with Mom if we could get confirmation."

"Sure. I'm happy to do that."

The tension she hadn't acknowledged eased a little bit. Everything was going to be fine. She'd been silly to worry about the meeting. It was what Mr. Norris had said—a chance to get everything finalized so the divorce could move forward. Rhys was the man he'd always been—she should trust him to do the right thing.

Mackenzie continued to read the document. Two paragraphs later, she realized that there weren't changes to the parenting plan so much as a complete rewrite of what she'd offered. She read the proposed visitation schedule twice before she could understand what it all meant.

He didn't want every other weekend, or holidays or summers. Rhys was proposing seeing his child one afternoon a month for the first year, two afternoons a month from ages one year to four years. From then until age eighteen, he would see his child two days a month.

She flipped to the second page, looking for some hint that he wanted more than a cursory relationship with his own kid, but she couldn't find one. Because it *wasn't* what he wanted.

She looked at him, trying to understand what was happening, but he wouldn't meet her gaze. He carefully stared down at the papers in front of him, his expression giving nothing away.

Disappointment joined shock. He'd meant what he'd said when she'd told him she was pregnant. He didn't want a baby in his life. He wanted to be free. He would do the very minimum required and nothing more.

"I thought you were better than this," she said into the quiet.

He flinched but still didn't look at her. Mr. Norris cleared his throat.

"We've increased the amount of child support, as you can see. It's a very generous amount."

She supposed it was but didn't bother looking at it. Instinctively, she put a hand on her belly, as if to protect her unborn child. By whatever circumstances, they had created this life together. It was a part of both of them and yet that didn't mean anything to him.

Oh, she didn't think he should have warm fuzzies about her, but his child should mean something to him, and it didn't.

That truth jolted her more than anything that had happened over the past six months. It made her wonder if she'd ever known him at all. She hadn't been foolish enough to think he would jump for joy at the thought of being a father, but she had thought he would suck it up and do what was right. And she'd been wrong.

Mackenzie squared her shoulders and turned to Ramona. "Once you look it over and make sure everything is legal, I'll sign it."

Her attorney raised her eyebrows. "You're willing to accept this parenting plan?"

"I am." She turned to Rhys. "I'm not going to force you to see your child when it's obvious you don't want to. I want to say I hope you'll have regrets about what you're doing later, but somehow I don't think that's going to happen."

If she'd expected shame or embarrassment, she didn't get it. Rhys looked at his attorney. "Has any of this gotten in the way of finalizing the divorce?"

The parenting plan proposal had been a blow to the heart, but that last statement was a kick in the gut.

Mr. Norris looked vaguely uncomfortable as he said, "I shouldn't think so. Ramona and I will go over the paperwork one last time. After that, all that's left is for you each to sign and then we file it with the court."

Mackenzie glanced at her attorney. "Anything else?"

"No. You can go."

Mackenzie nodded and rose. She walked out of the conference room and momentarily got turned around. She started to backtrack to find the reception area and the way out, only to come to a stop when she saw a familiar-looking blonde in one of the private offices. As Mackenzie passed, the woman looked up and her eyes widened with recognition and shock.

Mackenzie forced herself to keep moving, heading directly for the glass door she could see in front of her. She got into her Jeep and started the engine, then drove directly back to Painted Moon.

She managed to keep every thought, every emotion carefully locked away until she burst into Bruno's office. Her business partner took one look at her and came to his feet.

"What happened?"

"He doesn't want the baby. I don't care about me but how am I supposed to explain that his or her father doesn't want to know his own child?"

Strong arms drew her against a warm, wide chest. She let her purse drop onto the floor and wrapped both arms around Bruno's waist. The tears came after that, quickly morphing to sobs that shook her whole body.

"I don't love him," she said, her voice shaking. "I

don't want to be with him. Whatever we had has been over for a long time. But he's not who I thought. He's not a good man. We're talking about a *baby*. Even people who don't like kids make an effort for their own."

Bruno didn't speak. Instead he continued to hold her tight. One hand moved up and down her back in a comforting, circular motion.

After what felt like hours but was probably ten or fifteen minutes, she managed to get control.

"I'm being very unprofessional."

He chuckled. "Pshaw."

She raised her head and sniffed. "What did you say? Pshaw? Are you like a hundred and twenty?"

He pulled a box of tissues off a bookshelf and guided her to the sofa in his office. He sat close to her, angled to face her.

"I'm sorry Rhys is being a dick."

"Me, too. And I'm surprised." She wiped her face and blew her nose. "I was so wrong about him. What else didn't I see? It's his own child. Possibly his only child. He's not some seventeen-year-old jock losing out on a college scholarship because he knocked up his girlfriend. He's a mature man. We were together sixteen years. This baby should matter and it doesn't."

"He's a fool, and years from now, he's going to have regrets."

She nodded. "You're right, and as you say that, I realize I don't care about his regrets. I don't want my child to suffer."

"She won't. You'll be a great mom, plus she'll have Stephanie and her family, Four and her family, and she'll have me."

She managed a smile. "Still hoping for a girl?"

"Yes, but I'll be equally thrilled with a boy. You have family, Mackenzie. Maybe not biological, but we're here all the same."

"You're very good to me."

His dark gaze was steady. "I care about you."

She nodded. "I care about you, too. And I got your shirt all wet."

"I'll wear it as a badge of honor."

She laughed and brushed at the soft cotton. "It will dry, but you'll be wrinkly. I'll try not to make a habit of crying on you, but you might want to keep a second shirt in the office, just the same."

"Tell me what else happened at the meeting."

She told him about the very pathetic visitation schedule. "Rhys is offering more in child support. Guilt money, I suppose. Ramona's going to go over everything one more time. Once it's finalized, I'll sign and he'll sign and then we get a divorce."

"How do you feel about that?"

"Sad. I was wrong about so much. Him, Barbara, my place at Bel Après. I feel as if I've been living a lie or something."

"You weren't the liar. They were."

He sat back on the sofa and pulled her with him so she was leaning against him. While the contact was unfamiliar, it felt nice. Comfortable and safe. Bruno always knew what to do and he was strong.

"You must work out," she said without thinking.

She felt his chest shake as he laughed. "Yes, I do. Most mornings."

She shifted so she was leaning against the sofa instead of him and drew her shirt tight across her belly. "I'm really starting to show."

"It's nice. Proof of life. Have you felt the baby move?"

"No. The books say it happens between sixteen and twenty weeks, with first-time mothers feeling it later. I'm almost at twenty weeks, so I'm kind of waiting, but so far, nothing. Oh, I have an ultrasound in a couple of weeks and we should find out the gender."

"I'm excited about that."

"Me, too." She sat up. "My breakdown is officially over. I married the wrong guy and I'll do better next time."

"Yes, you will." He smiled. "You know what would be great?"

"What?"

"If you picked out a paint color for the baby's room when you find out the gender."

She groaned at the thought of the little swatches he'd shown her. "Do I have to?"

"Yes. I insist."

"You're so bossy."

"Four needs the walls painted so she can get going on the mural. We're all trying to help and you're making that difficult. So in two weeks?"

She smiled at him. "How about if I don't even make you wait that long?"

She got up and walked over to his desk. She pulled out the second drawer on the right and removed the half-dozen swatches.

"This one," she said, pointing to the pale yellow. "It will be a good backdrop for the tropical jungle animals."

He smiled. "No unicorns?"

"I asked for toucans and monkeys, but knowing

Four, she'll squeeze in a unicorn or a dragon some-where."

"That's a good quality to have." He rose and moved toward her. "Come on. I'll buy you lunch. We'll go to that tacky Mexican place you like so much. Orla will fuss over you, bring you the healthy version of what you love, and you'll feel better afterward."

"That would be great. Just let me wash my face first. I'll meet you in the hall."

As she turned to leave, she had the thought that while Rhys was so much less than she'd thought he would be, Bruno was so much more. Nearly every day he showed her that he was a kind and honorable man, not to mention an excellent manager and a killer businessman. He also gave great hugs and didn't mind getting cried on. But she supposed the thing she liked about him best of all was the look in his eyes when he talked about her baby. Her girlfriends weren't the only ones on her side when it came to her pregnancy. Bruno was right there with them.

thirty-one

The big bar in the tasting area of Painted Moon had cleaned up better than Stephanie had hoped. Three weeks after starting her new job, she was knee-deep in the remodel, working long hours and loving every second.

She'd already designed a mailer to go to previous customers of Painted Moon, detailing the purchase and that Mackenzie was the new winemaker. Bruno and Mackenzie had approved the new labels for the remaining library wines, and they were getting started on that project. She felt energized by all she had to do in a day. Sometimes the work was hard, but a good kind of hard that challenged her.

She stood in the center of the construction zone, assessing what had been done for the week. Bruno liked her to do that on Fridays, then report back to him on the progress. She'd already gone over the plan for the coming week with the general contractor and was satisfied they were on time and on budget. A minor miracle.

Mackenzie walked through the layers of plastic around the construction site, Avery at her heels.

"Look who I found lurking around," Mackenzie said with a grin. "I like the looks of her. I think we should keep her."

Avery laughed. "You're stuck with me."

"Oh, good." Mackenzie glanced at Stephanie. "Homecoming's tomorrow night. I'll be at your place at, what, five? Is that too early?"

"Not if you want to be involved in the whole makeup ritual."

"I won't be involved," Mackenzie said, hugging Avery. "I'm nowhere near as good as your mom at the beauty stuff. But I do want to sit on the edge of the tub and tell you how pretty you are."

Mackenzie waved at them both before heading back to her office. Stephanie turned her attention to her daughter. Things were still good between them. Avery was going to Homecoming with a group of girlfriends. They'd rented a limo together and had an after-party planned at Stephanie's place. She and Avery had spent much of the week coming up with menu ideas and brainstorming movie possibilities. Carson would escape to Four's house, where he and Jaguar had a video game marathon planned once the younger kids went to bed.

"What can I do for you, girl child of mine?" Stephanie asked.

Avery looked around at the framed space. "It's going to look good in here, Mom."

"It is." Stephanie hesitated, not sure if she should point out that Avery had avoided the question. She sensed there was something on her daughter's mind and decided she would give her a little time to get it out.

"There's going to be a retail space, right?" Avery asked.

"Uh-huh. Similar to what you're used to at Bel Après, but with a slightly different vibe."

Avery sighed. "Vibe? Really?"

"I'm hip with the slang. Watch me get funky."

"Oh, Mom." Avery walked around the makeshift desk covered with floor plans. "When this is done, could I get a part-time job here instead of working at Bel Après?"

"Sure, sweetie, but why would you want to change jobs?"

"It's not fun anymore. Grandma's so intense. She keeps coming into the tasting room and yelling at the staff. She's even yelled at me a couple of times and all I was doing was stocking shelves. I need a job to pay for my gas, and I thought it might be more fun to be here. With you."

Stephanie tried not to let her pleasure show. "I'll be hiring people to staff the tasting room and the retail area in March. If you're interested, you're welcome to fill out an application."

Avery rolled her eyes. "Fine, but I'll point out I have experience and I can get a reference from Mackenzie."

"That would be helpful."

"You're not going to give me a break at all, are you?"

"Maybe a really small one."

But instead of smiling, Avery looked troubled. She looked at Stephanie, then away. Stephanie waited.

"Have you talked to Dad lately?" her daughter asked.

"Not really."

The more polite answer than the truth. She hadn't heard from Kyle since he'd proposed and she'd told him no. All their communication about visits and drop-offs had gone through the kids. Sometimes that happened, so as far as she knew, neither Avery nor Carson suspected anything was wrong.

She supposed at some point she was going to have to get in touch with him and force the issue. They had children together—they couldn't simply avoid each other forever.

"So he didn't say anything about Thanksgiving."

Ah, the holiday. It was his year to have the kids. Sometimes they were in Seattle, but as often as not, he spent the day in Walla Walla. It usually depended on whether or not he was covering the Apple Cup— the annual game between the cross-state rivals WSU and UW—and where it was being played.

"I'm going to Four's house," Stephanie said. "Does your dad want you in Seattle?" She would miss them both but was used to the occasional separations.

"Um, well, not exactly." Avery bit her lower lip. "You really haven't talked to him, have you? Dad's in New York. He's got an interview for a job there and he's going to be in New York for Thanksgiving."

She tried not to let her surprise show. "He's going national," she said, remembering how he'd thrown the possibility at her when they'd last spoken. "Good for him. He should have done it a long time ago."

"He said he didn't want to be that far from Carson and me, but we're older now."

An interesting twist on what he'd told her, Stephanie thought, then decided to be charitable and assume both could be true.

"I'm glad for him. So you'd like to go to New York for Thanksgiving?"

Avery avoided her gaze. "Kind of. I've never been and it's a cool city and Dad will know by then if he has the job, so if he does, we'll be apartment hunting with him. He's renting an Airbnb for us to stay in." She wrinkled her nose. "Carson and I have to share a room and a bathroom, which is so gross, but still, it's New York. What do you think?"

"That you're going to miss out on an amazing Thanksgiving here." Stephanie crossed to her daughter and hugged her. "But I want you to have a good time with your dad."

"You sure? You won't be too lonely?"

"I'll survive." Stephanie released her. "It's a big city, Avery. We're going to have to talk about staying safe."

"I know. And I'm responsible for Carson. He wants Dad to get the job, by the way, because then he can go to a Yankees game." She sighed. "Baseball. Why did it have to be baseball?"

They both laughed.

When Avery left, Stephanie pulled out her phone and sent a text to Kyle.

I hear you're in NYC. When were you going to tell me?

It took only a few seconds for his answer to appear.

I should have said something. Sorry. I was dealing with

our last conversation. I'd had different plans, but then this opportunity came up, so here I am.

Will you get the job?

Probably. Which means a move. It will complicate things with the kids.

In more ways than one, Stephanie thought. Visiting their dad on the East Coast increased the chances that one or both of them would want to go to college there. She hated the thought of her children being so far away but knew she had to be brave about it. They deserved the chance to follow their dreams.

We'll make it work, she told him. Avery told me about Thanksgiving. I would rather have heard it from you.

I should have said something. Is it okay?

It's fine, although your daughter isn't thrilled about sharing both a bedroom and a bathroom with her brother.

We all have to make sacrifices. You sure you're fine with it?

Yes. You can buy their tickets. Oh, and Avery will want to go shopping. Don't let her spend too much.

There was a long pause before he replied.

I miss you.

Now it was her turn to hesitate.

To be honest, she really hadn't been thinking much about Kyle lately. She'd been focused on her new job and the kids. For her, the marriage was long over. But it would be cruel to say that.

This is the best thing for both of us. I know it is. I'll see you soon.

C U

Barbara could feel the heat of the flames as they rose higher and higher in the sky. They moved so fast, consuming row after row of vines, burning them down to nothing. The wall of fire roared past her, leaving nothing but dry, burnt earth behind.

She ran back and forth, not sure what to do. She couldn't find water, or anyone to help her. She screamed, but the wind swallowed up the sound. The temperature rose until she was afraid she would disintegrate into dust and blow away.

She ran closer to the vines only to realize that the fire was turning back, chasing her. She tried to escape but suddenly couldn't move and woke herself with her screams.

She sat up in the cool, dark bedroom, desperate to catch her breath as her heart raced and her body dripped with sweat. The nightmare was familiar— she'd had it often when she and James had first been married and things had been so tough—but it had been years since she'd had it.

Still shaking, she collapsed back on the bed. She went from hot to cold and quickly pulled up the covers. The bed seemed large and empty with no Giorgio to keep her company. He was back east for his daughter's birthday, she thought, then glanced at her clock.

Five o'clock. That meant it was, what, eight where he was?

She reached for her phone and pushed the button to call him. Three rings later she heard his voice.

"Yes?"

"Giorgio, thank goodness. I had the most horrible dream. I dreamed that Bel Après was on fire and there was nothing I could do." She shuddered at the memory. "It was awful. I used to have it all the time, when James and I were struggling. I'd forgotten what it was like. I'm still shaking."

Instead of comforting her or asking questions, he didn't say anything.

"Giorgio? Are you still there?"

"I'm here."

He sounded impatient or upset.

"What's wrong? I haven't talked to you in a few days. What have you been doing?"

"That's the question?" he asked, his voice low and cold. "What have I been doing?"

"Why are you angry with me?" She sat up again. "You're in a mood this morning."

"Last night was Rosemary's birthday party. You were supposed to be here with me. You didn't call, you didn't send a gift or flowers. In fact, you forgot completely."

"I didn't," she said, telling the lie automatically. "I couldn't call last night. By the time I got home, it was too late. I didn't want to wake up everyone."

"We both know that's not true. It's taken me a while

to see the truth, Barbara, but now I have. You don't care about anyone but yourself. You put on a good act, but that's all it is. An act."

Her breath caught. "Giorgio, no! Don't say that. You don't mean it. I love you. I'm sorry about Rosemary, I am. Desperately sorry. Let me make it up to you. When you get home, we'll go away together. Maybe to Portland. We'll stay at that hotel you like, just the two of us."

The long silence that followed frightened her more than his anger. Her heart sped up again.

"I won't be coming back."

"What does that mean?"

"I'm moving back here to be with my family."

She felt herself go cold as his words sank in.

"No! You can't. You're not leaving me. Darling, no. Please." Tears formed and fell. Her voice thickened. "Giorgio, I love you. You're the world to me."

"If that were true, we wouldn't be having this conversation. You were my princess, but I was never your prince. I don't know what you saw in me. I wasn't even a means to an end because I have nothing you want. I guess the problem is Bel Après is your one true love and I'll always come in second. Maybe that's enough for you, but not for me."

"Giorgio, stop." She found it difficult to talk but forced herself to keep trying. "Don't leave me. I love you."

"I don't think you're capable of love. You can keep the ring."

"Giorgio. Giorgio, don't. Please, I—"

The silence of her phone told her the call had been

disconnected. He wasn't on the line anymore—he'd hung up on her.

She dropped the phone onto the bed and pulled a pillow over her face to muffle her screams. She screamed until her throat was raw and she couldn't make a sound, then she rolled on her side and cried.

With the wine in barrels, Mackenzie allowed herself to take a little breath. In theory there was nothing she could do but hover while science and nature did their thing. Still, when it came to wine, she was a worrier, so she preferred to stay close—as if her presence would make a difference.

"I'm crabby," she said, climbing into Bruno's elegant Mercedes. "I don't want to go."

He looked at her, amusement crinkling his eyes. "You sound like a two-year-old."

"Good. I feel like stomping my feet. I need to be here. It's not a good time to leave."

"The wine is in barrels. What are you going to do for it?"

"I provide an encouraging spirit."

"This is the first event for winemakers since harvest. You and I are the new owners of Painted Moon. We need to make an appearance."

She knew he was right, but she still resisted. "It's going to be weird."

"Are you nervous?"

"Yes. I won't know what to say to anyone. I've always been a part of Bel Après. Now I'm not."

He reached across the console and lightly squeezed her hand. "You'll do fine. Everyone will be excited to talk to you. Barbara isn't going to be there."

Her mood brightened. "Are you sure?"

"When I RSVP'd for us, I asked. The coordinator said Rhys and Lori would be representing Bel Après."

Mackenzie wasn't sure how she felt about seeing her ex so soon after their lawyer meeting. Not that it mattered. They lived in the same town and worked in the same industry. They were going to run into each other on a regular basis. Better to get that first awkward professional meeting out of the way.

"You all right facing Rhys?" Bruno asked.

"Why are you reading my mind?"

"I was guessing."

"I suppose it's the obvious question." She thought for a second. "I don't care about seeing him. I'm disappointed in him as a person and I'm questioning our relationship and I feel as if I wasted too much time on him, but I'm not angry. And my general dissatisfaction is more about the baby than him."

"Sounds reasonable. And on the Barbara front?"

She smiled. "Did you anticipate the emotional element of our partnership when you signed on to this?"

He grinned. "I knew there were would be baggage. At least yours is interesting."

"I hope it gets boring really, really soon. Okay, Barbara." She briefly closed her eyes. "It's not that I'm afraid to confront her, it's that I'd rather not. I'm not comfortable making a scene. Or screaming at someone."

"No scenes today," he promised. "We'll go in, say hello to everyone, stay a polite half hour or so, then duck out."

"You have a plan."

"Always."

"I like your ability to anticipate things. It makes me feel like I can relax."

He glanced at her. "Good. Some people find my planning annoying."

She smiled. "Not the ever-perfect Gloria."

He grinned at her. "She thought I was too much of a planner."

"She has a flaw! I'm so happy. I was worried your past was too perfect, which wouldn't be fair. You're dealing with mine nearly every day."

"You're worth it."

She told herself he meant that in a business-partner way and not personally, but that didn't stop a little happy warmth from filling her chest.

She leaned back in her seat and tried not to think about the upcoming event. "I'm wearing fake yoga pants," she grumbled. "It's horrible."

"How are they fake and why is it horrible?"

"They're weird looking. They're supposed to look like dress pants, but they're not. Soon I'm going to have to wear actual maternity pants and I don't want to. The whole having-a-baby thing is messy. What was nature thinking?"

"You would prefer children appear fully formed? Maybe left under a tree?"

"Not a tree. A bush. Or some kind of plant. Something pretty like a lily or an orchid."

"Climate-wise, that could be a problem. Orchids don't grow everywhere."

"That's true. Okay, so the current system is probably best, but still. Maternity pants suck. And I hate my shirt."

"You look nice. Stop fussing. I know you're nervous

but in a couple of hours we'll be done and you can go back to hovering outside the barrel room."

"Promise?"

"Yes."

He pulled into the hotel parking lot. The meet and greet was in one of the large meeting rooms. The association put them on several times a year, allowing those in the industry to get together and catch up.

Mackenzie and Bruno walked inside. She was trying not to wonder if she looked pregnant or worry about what people would say. The last time she'd seen most of these people had been at the Summer Solstice Party when she'd been married to Rhys and working for Barbara. Five plus months later, everything was different.

They walked into the already crowded room. Mackenzie resisted the urge to cling to Bruno's arm or hide behind him. She would be fine, she told herself. She knew how to work a room and she was proud of what she'd accomplished.

She walked up to a group of men she knew and smiled.

"Hi, everyone."

"Mackenzie! Good to see you."

"Hey, Mackenzie. Who's the new guy?"

She introduced Bruno. They all knew he was her business partner and immediately started asking him questions.

Paul, a manager of a large winery at the other end of the valley, leaned close. "How was harvest? You went a hundred percent mechanical?"

"Because of the timing, we weren't able to hire anyone to handpick." She smiled. "I went in kicking and screaming, but it was actually a really smooth process. I was happy with how it turned out. Next year we'll handpick a little, but now that I've seen it in action, I'm going to stick with a lot of mechanical harvesting."

"I'm shocked."

"Me, too, but I can't argue with the results. It's going to be a good year."

"We got lucky," Paul said. "If the heat had stayed with us until the end, we would have been screwed."

"But it didn't."

Paul started to ask a question, then paused before shifting his weight. "Okay, this is uncomfortable. Rhys and Lori just walked in."

"Would you rather be talking to them?"

He relaxed. "You know I wouldn't. Rhys has no vision and Lori never has anything to say. It's just you two used to be married."

"I remember that." She did her best to look calm and relaxed. "It's fine, Paul. Rhys and I are working our way through the divorce. We're about to sign the final paperwork and then we'll be consciously uncoupled, as the young people like to say."

"And you're good with that?" He sounded worried.

She thought about all that had happened so quickly. How different things were these days, how different she was. The journey had been painful, but, she supposed, she'd taken the right path.

"I'm doing well and I'm very happy. Next spring come out to Painted Moon and see what we're doing. It's pretty magical stuff."

Bruno and the winemakers he'd been talking to joined the conversation. Mackenzie tried to pay attention to what they were saying, all the while aware that Rhys was somewhere in the room.

Would he come over and speak to her? Should she try to speak to him? Was this ever going to be easy?

She shook off the questions and focused on the conversation. She and Bruno chatted for a few more minutes, then went to circulate. Mackenzie introduced him to people he didn't know and reacquainted herself with the winemakers and owners she'd known for years.

Jack, a grizzled old guy who had been growing grapes since the 1980s, pulled her aside.

"Good for you," he told her. "Leaving all that Bel Après crap behind. You're better off with Painted Moon. Put your mark on it. Barbara was always going to do her best to trim your wings. She didn't want anyone being the star and you can't help shining wherever you are."

The unexpected compliment surprised her. "That's so nice."

"It's true. We all knew you were talented. Lucky her, grabbing you first."

She smiled. "Rhys had a piece of that."

"True, but the rest of us wanted to make you a job offer. We'd heard about you from the folks at WSU. We all knew you had something. She got there first."

"I didn't know that," she admitted, surprised to find out anyone had even known who she was back then. How would everything have been different if she hadn't gone to work for Bel Après? There was no way to know.

She excused herself and got a glass of water. She glanced longingly at the various bottles of wine. Events like these were a chance to taste what everyone was doing. She had always enjoyed sampling, but not today.

"You came."

She turned and saw Lori standing behind her.

"I did." Mackenzie looked around. "Are you with Owen?"

Lori glared at her. "Who told you about that?"

"Stephanie mentioned you were dating him. I'm glad. He's a great guy."

She was going to say more, but Lori's expression tightened.

"Do you think I care what you think about him or anything? I don't. I can't believe you showed your face here, after what you did."

While Lori's vitriol was not as vicious as her mother's, there was a familiar theme. Mackenzie knew she had a choice—she could respond in kind or she could try to get through to the woman she'd always thought of as part of her family.

"Lori, please. I don't want to fight with you. I know things are different, but I never wanted to hurt anyone and I still care about you. Can't we please at least be friends?"

Lori stared at her for a long time. "We were never friends. I accepted you because I had to, but I always knew what you were. No matter what happens with the winery, I'm glad you're gone and I don't have to pretend anymore."

She walked away. Mackenzie stared after her, trying not to react. Her face heated and her legs felt a little shaky, but she refused to let herself be cowed.

Bruno appeared at her side. "What happened?"

"Nothing."

He looked at her. "I was watching both of you. It wasn't a friendly exchange."

"Oh. In that case, I thought Lori and I liked each other, and she made sure I knew that had never been true."

"You okay?"

"I will be."

"Want to leave?"

She smiled at him. "I don't retreat."

"Good. There are a couple more people I'd like to meet. In the meantime, let me say that I'm looking forward to seeing you in maternity pants."

The random comment was so startling, she couldn't help laughing. "You can't mean that, and if you do, you're just plain weird."

"I'll accept weird, if it's important to you."

"Thank you. So why are you looking forward to seeing me in maternity pants? I don't think they're an especially flattering look on anyone."

"You'll rock them."

She looked at him. "You're always nice to me."

"You're my business partner. What else would I be? Besides, you're not upset about Lori anymore, are you?"

She realized he was right. "You're trying to distract me."

"Not trying, Mackenzie. Doing. There's a difference."

"So there is. I'll have to remember that."

thirty-two

Stephanie arrived at her mother's house, a sweet potato casserole in hand. The family dinner tonight was a potluck, at least that was what Lori's text had said. An odd choice, Stephanie thought, letting herself inside. Her mother usually wouldn't trust anyone else to simply show up with food. What if the flavors didn't match or the colors were off? But she'd been asked to bring a potato dish that would go with pork, so she had.

She passed Four's kids playing a card game with Owen and Jaguar, then joined her sisters and mom in the kitchen.

"Hi, all," she said as she set the casserole dish on the counter. "This is just out of the oven, so it shouldn't need to be reheated."

Four hugged her. "You look so happy."

"I feel good."

"It shows."

Stephanie shrugged out of her coat and hung it on the rack just inside the mudroom. "Hi, Lori. Owen looks pretty comfortable out there with all the kids. You found a good one in him."

Lori gave her a suspicious look before offering a slight smile. "I think so."

Stephanie drew in a breath for courage before tentatively hugging her mother. "Hey, Mom. How are things?"

Her mother didn't return the hug, nor did she look the least bit pleased about anything.

"Hunky-dory. Now can we please get on with dinner? Did anyone check the table? Is it set correctly? Lori, that was your job. Let's go examine all the ways you failed."

She swept out of the room, Lori at her heels. Stephanie turned to Four.

"She's in a mood."

Four pulled a large pork roast out of the oven and set it on an unused portion of the stove, then grabbed Stephanie's hand and pulled her into the walk-in pantry.

"Giorgio dumped Barbara," Four said in a whisper. "I can't get more details than that. It happened a few days ago. I didn't know they were fighting, but I guess they were. Lori says it's been bad around here. The only thing I can figure is he got fed up with her selfishness. She wouldn't go back east with him for his daughter's birthday."

"Mom wouldn't think that was important. Not with everything going on."

"I know that and you know that, but I think it was a wake-up call for him." Four's mouth twisted. "It makes me sad. He was her one shot at happiness and now he's gone. She's going to get meaner and meaner until no one wants to be around her. It's very upsetting."

They heard talking in the kitchen and quickly moved out of the pantry. Their mother glared at them.

"If you two are done whispering like schoolgirls, we can work at getting dinner on the table."

Stephanie ignored the glower and the sharp words, crossing to her mom and taking one of her hands.

"I'm so sorry about what happened with Giorgio. I wish you'd told me. I could have come over to be with you."

Her mother snatched back her hand, her brown eyes cold and empty. "And do what? I'm perfectly fine. Giorgio was a ridiculous man who made impossible demands. He had no understanding of my responsibilities or expectations. He was a waste of my time. Good riddance."

Stephanie shook her head. "Mom, you don't mean that. You loved him. He made you happy. I'm sorry he's gone, and if there's anything I can do to—"

"What could you possibly do for me? You quit your job and walked out on my wedding planning. I don't need any more 'help.'" She made air quotes. "From you."

For a moment, time seemed to freeze. She saw Lori's look of relief at having someone else getting the brunt of Barbara's temper, and Four's genuine compassion for another human in pain. She saw the smallness of her mother's action and knew Barbara would rather die alone than ever admit to what she perceived as a weakness. She also saw herself—stronger now. Going in the right direction. There would be challenges, but she'd worked through the hardest part. She'd been brave, and as long as she kept being brave, then she was going to be just fine.

She thought of all the things she could say to her mother. All the cutting words, the sarcastic comments, and then she told herself it wasn't worth it. Barbara would be who she had always been. She wouldn't change until she wanted to.

"I'm here if you need me," Stephanie repeated. "Either way, I'm really sorry."

Her mother looked at the roast. "This is done. Get Jaguar in here to cut it and start putting the food on the table. Assuming you're all capable of those minor tasks."

With that, she walked into the dining room. Stephanie watched her go. "It must be hard to be her."

Four smiled. "And that, sister of mine, is the lesson to be learned."

Mackenzie stared at the blurry image that was, in theory, her daughter. According to the doctor, her weight was good, her blood pressure and blood sugar were perfect, and the baby was doing her baby-growing thing.

"Five months down, four to go," she told herself as she drove back to Painted Moon. And she was having a girl.

She let that information sink in. Bruno had teased her about wanting a girl, so the news would delight him. As for her feelings, she thought maybe a girl would be easier for her as a mom. She'd been a girl. She knew a few girl things.

"A girl," she whispered. "I'm going to have to come up with a name. Maybe Amy, after my mom."

She touched her belly. "Hi, Amy. I'm *your* mom." She grinned. "That is the strangest thing I've ever said, but it's true. I'm your mom."

She let the words settle on her, wondering when she would know they were true. She was pregnant and she was having a daughter.

She felt herself smile at the news and thought about everyone she wanted to tell. Bruno, for sure, and Stephanie. Four. She wondered about letting Rhys know. Would he care about the gender of the child? He'd never asked and she didn't know if she should offer.

"I'll deal with that next week," she told herself as she drove through the large gates at Painted Moon. Today was for her and the people she loved. She was having a girl!

She parked and hurried to the office. Before she got there, Bruno walked out of the building, as if he'd been waiting for her.

"You're back," he said, his voice tense.

"I am." She hadn't told him she had a doctor's appointment today, instead saying she was going to run errands. She'd known about the ultrasound and hadn't been sure she would want to discuss it when she got back. A silly thing, now that she'd been through it.

"We have to talk."

The edge to his voice brought her to a stop. Whatever he was going to say, it wasn't good. Had there been a fire? Was he calling the bridge loan? No, it couldn't be that. She was weeks away from the divorce being final and getting her payout. He wouldn't call the loan. Then what?

"I bought you something," he added, motioning for

her to go with him to the production area. "It was supposed to be a surprise, but now that it's here, I'm not sure I did the right thing. If you're angry, I'll understand. I can always sell them somewhere else. I just thought for the Pepper Bridge vineyards you'd wanted to do something different and then this opportunity came up."

"This is about the winery?" she asked.

He came to a stop. "Yes. Why?"

"You scared me."

His expression softened. "Did I? I'm sorry. I didn't mean to. It's about—" He cleared his throat. "I bought some vines."

What did that mean? "You bought plants?"

Why would he do that? Ignoring the time it would take to have them grow from seedlings into mature vines, that just wasn't how they did things these days. Painted Moon had excellent rootstock. If she wanted to make changes, all she had to do was buy what she wanted and graft it in. That way she would lose only a year of production.

They stepped into the big, open building. There was a package about the size of a shoebox sitting on a workbench.

"No, not vines. I bought these." He pointed to the box. "Through a friend of a friend, I know a guy in the Bordeaux region of France. He's had some financial trouble and I helped him out. In return, he's going to send us these."

He lifted the lid. Inside was wet newspaper wrapped around what looked like fat sticks. Mackenzie felt the breath leave her body as she walked closer.

"Scions," she said, her voice a reverent whisper. "He sent you scions."

"Just a few. He'll send the bulk of them after the first of the year. It's better to cut them while the vines are dormant." He gave her a lopsided grin. "But you know that."

She carefully unwrapped the newspaper and stared at the beautiful thick sections of vine. They were healthy, about ten inches long. Grafted into rootstock, they would produce grapes within two seasons.

She looked at him. "What are they?"

"Cabernet sauvignon, merlot, petit verdot. He's sending enough for fifty acres. I have the particulars on the vineyards. His family has been making wine there for about six hundred years."

French grapes. He was offering her beautiful, vibrant, elegant French grapes.

"Do you know what I can do with these?" she asked, feeling as if she was close to touching the face of God. "Do you? We can go traditional. We can have estate-grown wines unlike any others in the state." She quickly put down the scion and held up her hands. "I'm shaking. Oh, Bruno, I don't know how you did this, but thank you so much."

"You're not mad?"

"Why would I be mad?"

"I'm kind of stepping on your toes here. You do wines, I do everything else. It's just when he made the offer, I thought you'd be happy."

"I am."

She was about to throw herself at him when she felt the oddest sensation in her belly. Sort of a fluttering, bumping, shifting that she'd never felt before. Almost as if—

"The baby," she breathed, instinctively grabbing his hand and pressing it to her stomach. "She's moving. Can you feel it?"

They both stood there for a second and then it happened again. His eyes widened until he looked as dazed and terrified as she felt.

"That's the baby?" he asked.

She nodded. "Or I have serious gas issues and will probably need a bathroom."

"You don't have gas." He smiled. "You said she."

"It's a girl. You got your wish."

"Are you happy?"

"Yes. I'm going to call her Amy, after my mom."

"That's a beautiful name."

They stood like that, close together, his hand on her stomach, for a few more minutes, but there wasn't any more movement. Slowly, Mackenzie became aware of their close proximity and the oddly intimate nature of their contact. She released his hand and took a step back.

"Sorry. I didn't mean to make you uncomfortable. I just thought you might like to feel her move."

"I did. Thank you."

She looked away. "Good. I won't make a habit of throwing myself at you like that or putting your hands on me because—" She told herself to be quiet because she definitely wasn't making the situation any more comfortable for either of them.

She cleared her throat. "What I meant was, um—"

Bruno stepped in front of her. "Stop talking."

"I really should."

"It wasn't awkward."

She raised her gaze to his. "It wasn't?"

"No. I liked it."

Feeling the baby move or touching her? Before she could figure out how to ask, he moved closer and slowly, carefully cupped her face in his hands.

His fingers were warm and held her gently. She supposed she could have pulled away if she wanted to, only she didn't. When he lowered his head, she knew exactly what he was going to do. Anticipation battled caution. Was she willing to take the risk of what a kiss could mean? What if everything changed and it was—

His mouth brushed against hers. The barely there contact made her breath catch and the world fall away. She felt heat and tingles and need and a thousand other wonderful things that she couldn't explain beyond the fact that she *knew* everything about this moment was right.

He drew back, still cupping her face, and stared into her eyes. She saw a matching desire, but also questions. He wanted her to be sure.

She smiled. "We should do that more."

"I like how you think."

He kissed her again, this time with more intensity. She wrapped her arms around his neck as she pulled him against her. They touched everywhere and she reveled in all of it. Her breasts nestling against his chest, their thighs pressing against each other, his lips on hers in a way that offered and took and made her want it all.

This, she thought happily. Unexpected and sexy and just plain right.

When he drew back a second time, they were both breathing a little hard.

"It's been a day," she said, her voice a little unsteady. "I find out I'm having a girl, we feel the baby move, you buy me grapes from France and now we're kissing. It's a lot to take in."

"Too much?"

"Just right."

One corner of his mouth turned up. "Dinner tonight?"

"Yes, please."

"I'll bring takeout."

She laughed. "One of us is going to have to learn how to cook."

He put his arm around her and they started back to the office. "Don't worry about it. I'll hire a chef."

"Of course you will." She was still laughing when they went inside.

Mackenzie carefully spit the wine into a pitcher, then rinsed her mouth with water. She was working her way through Herman's barrels on the schedule she'd created for herself, but it was slow going. Life would be much easier if she could just taste the wine like a regular person.

"Not that I'm complaining," she told Amy. "I want you to be healthy."

She made several notations on the pad on her clipboard. She wanted to start blending in the next few weeks. The response to Stephanie's first mailing to the Painted Moon customers had been overwhelmingly positive. If everyone who said they were interested in library wines and whatever blends Mackenzie created made a purchase, they would sell out in minutes.

She felt good, she thought happily. Physically, emotionally. She loved her work, she had finally wrapped her head around being pregnant and she was less than two weeks away from not owing Bruno two million dollars.

She had an appointment to sign the paperwork to finalize her divorce, and Rhys had put the payout into an escrow account. As soon as the courts did their thing, she would be single and momentarily flush with cash. Ten minutes later, she would wire the money to Bruno, but still. It was heady to think about.

She was still chuckling at the thought when she heard rapid footsteps on the concrete floor. She turned and saw Barbara rushing toward her. The other woman was pale and wide-eyed, her expression menacing and an odd contrast to her tailored suit and pearls.

"You have ruined me!" Barbara said, her voice tight as she approached.

Mackenzie wasn't afraid, exactly, but she was feeling cautious. She shifted to her right, putting a row of barrels between her and her former mother-in-law.

"Why are you here?" she asked, careful to keep her voice calm.

"To confront you once and for all. You stole everything from me and you're going to have to pay."

"I didn't take anything from you. You're the one who fired me and tried to get me thrown out of my house. You're the one who wanted me to sell off my child's inheritance."

"Why wouldn't I? You're nothing to me. Nothing!" She pressed a hand to her throat. "You took the China deal."

"What?" Mackenzie came out from behind the barrels and slapped her clipboard on a table. "You wait a minute. You never wanted to do anything with China. We talked about it and you said no every time. Just like you said no to buying land in Oregon so we could make great pinots and you said no to every other suggestion. The China thing is not on me."

They glared at each other. Mackenzie recovered first.

"Barbara, I'm sorry it's come to this. You were so much to me. I never wanted to hurt you. You were like a mother to me."

"I was never your mother. I wouldn't want a child like you. You came from nothing and you deserve nothing. I trusted you with Bel Après and you walked away." She narrowed her gaze. "I wish you were dead."

The words hurt but not as much as they would have three months ago. Mackenzie supposed that in addition to a bigger belly she was getting a thicker skin.

She took a second to collect herself. "You're going to leave now. If you come back again, I'll get a restraining order against you. As it is, I'm going to talk to Rhys about making sure you don't have any unsupervised time with the baby. I'll put it in the parenting plan. Unlike you, Barbara, I protect what's mine. Now get out."

She pointed to the open doorway for emphasis, only then noticing Bruno standing in the shadows. She was grateful for his presence and even more thankful that he was letting her handle the situation.

"I'll hate you forever," Barbara said in a low voice.

Mackenzie felt a rush of sadness. "I'm not going to say the same back to you. You're not worth the energy."

She picked up her clipboard and studied the notes, pretending she could read them, even with all the emotions pulsing through her. Several seconds later, she heard retreating footsteps, then silence. Barbara was gone.

Bruno walked over to her. "We're getting security."

"No, we're going to wait and see what happens. If she shows up again, we'll go talk to a judge."

"Did you mean what you said about making sure she can't be alone with Amy?"

"Every word. I'm not trusting her with my child, although she would probably tell me she would rather eat glass than spend time with my daughter." She gave him a humorless smile. "Regardless, I'm supposed to sign the final documents tomorrow. Do you think Rhys won't agree to the change? The man wants to be divorced. At this point he'll do anything to be free. I'm going to take advantage of that." She shrugged. "It's not as if I'm asking for anything outrageous. He'll agree."

"You have a ruthless streak," Bruno teased. "I like it."

"I'm kind of impressed myself."

thirty-three

Thanksgiving morning dawned cold and clear. Mackenzie woke at her usual time, a little after six. After pulling on yoga pants and a T-shirt, she drank an entire glass of water, then did her stupid pregnancy yoga video for twenty minutes before heading downstairs for her disgusting protein shake.

Technically she could have a real breakfast if she wanted, but it was too much trouble to cook. She needed to have protein and the right kind of carbs and fiber. A protein shake was easy.

Halfway down the stairs, she heard a noise in the kitchen, followed by the smell of bacon. She ran the rest of the way and found Bruno at the stove, bacon simmering and the table set.

He was intent on his task and didn't see her at first. A white "Kiss the Cook" apron covered his jeans and the front of his long-sleeved shirt.

The old fan above the stove was loud enough to cover the sound of her approaching. She walked up behind him and slid her arms around his waist.

"You're a surprise," she said, leaning against him. "Happy Thanksgiving."

He turned toward her and smiled. "Happy Thanksgiving. It's a holiday, so I thought I'd slip in early and save you from your protein drink."

"That's very thoughtful. Thank you."

"You're welcome. Now go sit down and I'll get going on the eggs."

She sipped the juice he'd poured while he finished cooking. When the toast popped in the toaster, she carried it over to the table. He put down the plates and they sat across from each other.

"You're okay with me using the key you gave me?" he asked. "I won't make a habit of it."

"I gave you the key so you could use it."

Not that he'd had reason to. It had been only a couple of weeks since their first kiss. They'd gone out to dinner a few times and continued with the kissing, but nothing more. She sensed he was taking things slow for her.

She took a bite of her eggs, moaned slightly at the deliciousness, then excused herself to go get her phone. When she was back at the table, she turned it so he could see the picture Lori had forwarded. It showed Rhys on a beach, the blonde from the café and the lawyer's office at his side.

"I'm sure Lori thought she was hurting me," Mackenzie said, picking up her fork. "But I'm fine with it. We've both moved on."

He set down her phone. "If you're sure."

"I am. Oh, and I sent you a wire transfer yesterday. You should have a notification first thing tomorrow."

One eyebrow rose. "You paid off the bridge loan."

"I did." She grinned. "It was freeing and yet painful."

"Want the money back?"

"No. Stop. Don't even kid about that. I owed you and I've paid you back. Thank you for the loan. And for buying Painted Moon with me."

"You're welcome." He put down his fork and met her gaze. "You're officially divorced."

"I am. Single. Pregnant, but single."

"I like the pregnant part. It's sexy."

"Hardly, but thank you for saying that."

As they stared at each other, she felt a familiar heat blossoming low in her belly. Her already sensitive breasts began to tingle. According to the books she'd read and the slightly embarrassing conversation with her doctor, sex was perfectly fine. She wasn't supposed to go in a hot tub, but if she wanted to do the wild thing, that was allowed. Wasn't pregnancy the funniest thing ever?

He glanced at the clock. "We're supposed to be at Four's house around one."

"That's what she said."

They would be spending Thanksgiving with her family. Rhys was in Mexico, Barbara had said she wouldn't be attending any celebration with anyone this year, and Lori was off with Owen's family, so it was just going to be the fun half of the Barcellona clan.

"Did you, ah, have any plans for the rest of the morning?" he asked, his voice thick, his gaze sharp with arousal. "After breakfast, I mean."

She walked around the table, then drew him to his feet. "Breakfast can wait."

epilogue

Three years later...

"You have completely blown me away," Mackenzie said, looking at the outdoor area by the tasting room at Painted Moon.

Massive awnings provided shade for fifty round tables, each seating ten people. To the east was the dance floor, and to the west was the huge buffet line. Servers would circulate with appetizers and several bars offered wines as well as mixed drinks to their guests. Twinkle lights were strung and the DJ was already setting up.

"The party's going to be epic," Stephanie said with a laugh.

"Don't let Avery hear you say that," Mackenzie teased. "You know how she feels about people our age trying to use slang."

They linked arms as they toured the area. Big fans, tucked in with plants, would provide a nice breeze. Thankfully, the weather had cooperated and it would only be in the low eighties when the evening began.

"I'm glad you and Bruno are doing this," Stephanie said. "It's a great tradition. It deserves to continue."

"I felt a little weird about it," Mackenzie admitted. "But you're right about the tradition."

For the past two years, Barbara had chosen not to have the Summer Solstice Party at Bel Après. Last January, Stephanie had come to Mackenzie and Bruno to discuss the possibility of starting up the parties at Painted Moon. They'd given her the go-ahead to start planning it.

"I was afraid no one would come," Mackenzie admitted.

Stephanie laughed. "Why? Everyone wants to be here. We sent out five hundred invitations and we had four hundred and ninety-eight people say yes."

"That still surprises me."

"You're so weird."

Mackenzie laughed. "That is probably true." She looked around at what they'd all created together. "This is really good. I'm happy."

"Me, too."

Mackenzie stepped back and pointed at her. "That's because you have a shiny new boyfriend."

Stephanie blushed. "Liam does make the day more sparkly."

Liam was a professor at the local college. Handsome as a movie star and five years younger, he'd swept Stephanie off her feet last fall. Things were getting serious and Mackenzie had a feeling there would be an announcement in a few months.

"All right, you," Stephanie said with mock sternness. "I have last-minute details to check on and you have to get changed. Don't you dare be late to your own party."

"I'll be on time," Mackenzie promised.

She made her way to the farmhouse, thinking about how far they'd all come since the last Solstice Party. Avery was in college, studying at Georgetown. Carson was a senior in high school and still trying to decide between college and going pro. Four, Jaguar and their children were who they always had been—loving, content and unique. Rhys had yet another woman in his life. His relationship with Amy was distant at best. He rarely saw her, and while that made Mackenzie sad, she wasn't going to push him. Amy was surrounded by people who loved her and Bruno was father enough for ten children.

Lori had married Owen and gotten pregnant right away. Mackenzie had reached out a few times, but Lori really wasn't interested in being friends. Even more disappointing, Barbara had become something of a recluse. She was rarely seen in public, and from what Stephanie occasionally mentioned, the other woman was more bitter and mean-spirited by the day.

As for herself, Mackenzie was happy—happier than she'd ever been. She had work she loved, a winery that filled her with joy and a husband who made her feel like the most cherished woman alive.

She paused in the driveway to admire the new addition to the farmhouse. Last year they'd added a big family room, along with a larger office for her and Bruno to share. The one upstairs had been turned into a playroom for Amy. They'd also remodeled the kitchen and bathrooms but hadn't added any bedrooms. Mackenzie had learned her lesson—this house wasn't big enough for her and Bruno to live separate lives. Their daily routines were completely intertwined and that was how they both wanted it.

Once inside, she called out that she was back.

"We're upstairs."

She hurried to join Bruno and found him putting flower clips in their daughter's bright red hair.

"Mommy," her two-year-old said, smiling and holding out her arms. "I'm wearing pink."

Mackenzie took in the frilly dress and matching shoes. "I can see that. You're beautiful."

"You are, too."

"Thank you. Now I'm going to put on my own party dress."

Bruno, handsome as ever in black pants and a dark gray shirt, raised his eyebrows. "Need some help?"

"I know exactly where your 'help' would lead and we don't have time."

Although the thought of what he wanted to do made her a little weak at the knees. Even after nearly three years together, they couldn't get enough of each other. Just last week, while walking the Pepper Bridge vineyard, things had gotten a little out of hand and they'd ended up making love in the truck. A memory that still made her smile.

"Give me fifteen minutes," she said as she hurried toward the master bedroom.

"Don't rush," Bruno called after her. "We have plenty of time. It's our party—we get to arrive when we want."

Mackenzie showered and then blew out her hair. After putting on mascara, she pulled on the dress she'd picked out earlier. Given that she would be on her feet for hours, she chose flats rather than heels, then opened her jewelry box to choose something to wear that night.

One of the things she'd learned in the past couple of years was that Bruno liked to buy her jewelry. Just as surprising, she liked to wear it. She put on an emerald choker and slid on several gold bangles. She always wore her wedding ring and added a pretty diamond cocktail ring to her right hand.

"Donna's here," Bruno said, walking into the closet and pulling her close.

Donna, their full-time nanny-slash-housekeeper, was a godsend. She loved Amy nearly as much as they did and helped keep their busy lives running smoothly.

"She's coming to the party, isn't she?" Mackenzie asked, gazing up into his eyes.

"Yes. She'll stay until Amy's ready to come home."

They went downstairs and collected Donna and Amy before heading to the party. People had already started to arrive. The valet service they'd hired was parking cars and music spilled into the night.

Bruno walked with her, Amy in his arms. The little girl leaned against her father, her soft pink dress a contrast to his darker shirt. A couple of years ago, Mackenzie would have said owning Painted Moon was the best thing that had ever happened to her, but now she knew that was wrong. It was the love that was the true gift in her life. The family she'd built over the years, the daughter she'd given birth to, and the wonderful man who loved her with all his heart. That was what mattered, and tonight was a celebration of all of that. On the best day of the year.

* * * * *

the vineyard *at* painted moon

BOOK CLUB DISCUSSION GUIDE

SUSAN MALLERY'S
WINE PAIRINGS

Let me begin by saying there is no right or wrong way to drink wine. Drink what you like with whatever foods you like, but be open to trying something different. The lone exception being please don't put ice in your wine, I beg you! ☺ It dilutes the flavor, and the impurities in the water totally change the balance of the wine. If you don't like your wine getting warm, try using a thermal glass.

Okay—basic wine pairings. The rule of thumb is to balance the flavors and intensity. So, a lighter wine is paired with lighter-tasting foods. A heavy wine will crush the flavors of a light-tasting food and a heavy, spicy dish will make a light wine tasteless. Also, know that food can completely change the flavor of wine and vice versa. Don't believe me? Taste a dessert wine like an ice wine. Too sweet? Too thick? Try it with a tart lemon bar. Suddenly the dessert wine makes sense. The tartness balances the sweetness.

There are dozens of types of wines, so I'm going to stick with a few basics that are easy to find pretty much anywhere in the country. My suggestions are simply that—my suggestions. They will give you a starting point. If you enjoy wine, then playing with food and wine pairings can be so much fun, and so delicious!

SAUVIGNON BLANC

This is a lighter, fruitier white wine. It's best served chilled and is very drinkable. Try it with goat cheese, either plain or lightly flavored. It pairs well with salads made with a light vinaigrette and summer fruits. Honestly, a glass of sauvignon blanc and a ripe nectarine is pretty amazing.

CHARDONNAY

Chardonnay has changed over the years. Most winemakers are aging chardonnay in stainless-steel barrels rather than in oak, so the flavor is brighter, without the butteriness. I personally love an oaky, buttery chardonnay, but they aren't everyone's taste. Either chardonnay is great with a light-flavored fish, especially if there is a delicious cream or butter sauce. Shrimp scampi is a classic. For a good cheese pairing, try Brie on a piece of French baguette with a glass of chardonnay. And you're welcome!

PINOT NOIR

Try to find one from Oregon. They have the best climate for growing pinot. There are a few good ones in Northern California, but if you see one from Oregon, give it a taste. Pinot noir is a lighter red wine, but often with a hint of sweetness. Nothing overpowering, but that sweet edge gives it the ability to pair with some unexpected foods. What you want is a sweet/savory combination. Pork is perfect, but one of the best pairings is Thai food. Seriously. Try it. For a cheese pairing, either burrata or mozzarella would be great. Add basil, a little tomato and olive oil, and you have something magical.

CABERNET SAUVIGNON

I'll admit, this is a personal favorite for me. I love a wine with a lot of body and flavor. Cabs and cab blends often make their way to the dinner table at my house. Pair your cabernet sauvignon with beef, salmon and heavier chicken dishes. Also tomato-based pasta dishes. I speak from experience when I say cab and a burger are delightful. For a cheese pairing, try Gouda or blue cheese. Last but not least…dark chocolate and cabernet sauvignon. So good and the perfect way to end a meal.

SYRAH

If you can find a Washington State Syrah, please try it. They're really good here. Syrah is a heavier red wine, so it goes well with heavily spiced and braised meats. If you're not sure if you like red wines, don't start here. There's a lot of flavor. For a cheese pairing, try a nice sharp cheddar or a blue or Stilton cheese.

CHAMPAGNE

I know you already know this, but a sparkling wine can be called champagne only if it comes from the Champagne region of France. Otherwise it's sparkling wine. To open a bottle without "popping" the cork, hold the cork in one hand and the base of the bottle in the other. Rotate the base rather than the cork. I know the pop sounds fun, but the flying cork is dangerous.

Plus, you lose a lot of champagne and about half the carbonation! Champagne is a magical wine that literally goes with everything. Really! Having something greasy? The champagne will cut through the grease and bring out the best flavors. Fast food? Tacos? Crab puffs? Champagne works. Brunch—well, we already know that one. Birthday cake? Best with champagne.

So those are my suggestions for pairing food and wine. It all comes down to what you like. Don't be afraid to experiment. If you want to know more, see if there's a wine store nearby. They often have tastings on the weekends. Once you've explored the basic wines, you can branch out to other wines and different countries. Cheers!

QUINOA SALAD
YOUR WAY

Here are two delicious variations on a basic quinoa salad, completely adaptable to your tastes. Use whichever ingredients you like, and omit any you don't. And hey—if you don't like quinoa, use three cups of cooked and cooled pasta instead.

THAI-INSPIRED QUINOA SALAD WITH PEANUT DRESSING

INGREDIENTS:

1 ½ cups dry quinoa
1 large carrot, peeled and diced
2 stalks celery, diced
1 red bell pepper, diced
2 green onions with tops, sliced
¼ cup cucumber, diced
½ cup peanuts
½ cup fresh cilantro, minced
½ tsp sea salt

PEANUT DRESSING:

¼ cup creamy peanut butter
¼ cup + 2 tbsp mild rice vinegar
½ tsp toasted sesame oil
½ tsp fresh minced ginger
¼ cup vegetable oil

DIRECTIONS:

Cook the quinoa using your favorite method. I use my Instant Pot pressure cooker. I use 1 ½ cups of dry quinoa to 1 ¾ cups water, cook at high pressure for

3 minutes and allow 8 minutes of natural release. Allow to cool.

Whisk together the dressing ingredients. Add all ingredients to a bowl and stir well. Allow flavors to marinate. Serve cold or warm.

ITALIAN-INSPIRED QUINOA SALAD WITH VINAIGRETTE

INGREDIENTS:

1 ½ cups dry quinoa
1 large carrot, peeled and diced
2 stalks celery, diced
½ cup cauliflower, diced
¼ cup frozen peas, thawed
¼ cup frozen corn, thawed
½ cup cherry tomatoes, quartered
4 oz mozzarella cheese, diced
¼ cup pine nuts
¼ cup fresh parsley, minced

VINAIGRETTE:

This is a simple and delicious dressing made from ingredients most of us usually have on hand. Alternatively, you can use about ¾ cup of your favorite ready-made Italian salad dressing.

¼ cup apple cider vinegar
½ cup olive oil
1 tsp honey
1 clove garlic, minced
⅛ tsp each of salt and pepper

DIRECTIONS:

Cook the quinoa using your favorite method. I use my Instant Pot pressure cooker. I use 1 ½ cups of dry quinoa to 1 ¾ cups water, cook at high pressure for 3 minutes and allow 8 minutes of natural release. Allow to cool.

Whisk together the dressing ingredients. Add all ingredients to a bowl and stir well. Allow flavors to marinate. Serve cold or room temperature.

QUESTIONS
FOR DISCUSSION

Please note, these questions contain spoilers about the story. We recommend you finish
The Vineyard at Painted Moon
before reading any of the questions below.

1. At the Summer Solstice Party at the beginning of the book, Giorgio's proposal made several characters reassess their own lives. What was it about this moment that made such an impact? Discuss how this propelled both Mackenzie's story line and Stephanie's. (In fiction writing terms, this is known as the "inciting incident.")

2. What did you think of Mackenzie and Rhys's marriage when the book began? What was your first clue that all was not well?

3. Barbara and Mackenzie shared a love of the land of Bel Après. Discuss how this influenced their decisions.

4. Mackenzie doesn't have to leave Bel Après. When she and Rhys decide to divorce, she doesn't have to lose anything but her marriage. No one would care if she got a divorce and then stuck around. In light of all that, why do you think she walked away? What price was she willing to pay for her decision? Did she ultimately pay as severe a price as she feared she would?

5. What did you think of the way Rhys's behavior changed after he learned that Mackenzie was pregnant? How did his reaction contrast with Bruno's? Were you surprised when Mackenzie realized she was pregnant, or did you pick up on some foreshadowing that gave you a clue?

6. Susan Mallery promises readers that her books will have a satisfying ending. Were you satisfied with the ending of *The Vineyard at Painted Moon*? Why or why not? Would your answer change if Mallery hadn't written the epilogue? The wrap-up of Barbara's story line certainly couldn't be described as happy, but did it satisfy your sense of justice? Do you think the book would have worked if Barbara had gotten a happy ending? Why or why not?

7. Four was the youngest of Barbara's children, but the wisest. What do you think made her so wise?

8. Discuss Stephanie's journey. In what ways did she change as the book progressed? What moments motivated her to change?

9. What are the themes of this book? How does each story line—Mackenzie's, Stephanie's and Barbara's—reinforce these themes?

10. How did you feel about the setting of *The Vineyard at Painted Moon*? Were you surprised that Washington State has such a robust wine-making community, or did you already know? Did the book make you want to visit that part of the country?

11. If you were going to name your dream vineyard, what would you call it?

12. Share a wine-related memory with the group.

Keep reading for a special preview of
The Happiness Plan
a brand-new story from
#1 New York Times *bestselling author*
Susan Mallery!

Three women search for joy in this new novel of
hope, heartache, and the power of friendship.

1

"Is it possible you're overcommitting in your personal life because you don't want to feel your emotions?" Tori Rocha asked, her tone more concerned than judgy. "Kittens? Really? Because you needed one more thing?"

Heather Sitterly glanced down at the three sleeping two-week-old kittens she'd just agreed to foster, thought about the client she'd signed that morning and the kitchen remodel she was considering.

"Possible?" she repeated, grinning as she spoke. "No. Not possible. I think we can agree it's likely. Very likely."

Tori's mouth twitched, as if trying not to smile. "Admitting you have a problem is half the battle. How can I help?"

Heather shifted her wrist so her friend and the head graphic designer at 206 Marketing Group could see her smart watch.

"In forty-two minutes these little guys will need feeding."

"The conference room in forty-two minutes. I'll be there."

So would the rest of the senior staff, Heather thought, because forty-two minutes from now was the weekly update meeting.

"Thanks."

Heather walked to her large corner office where she had an oversize executive desk, a small conference table and a seating area. The traditional furniture contrasted with the soft-sided playpen in the back corner.

She set the box of kittens on the coffee table and pulled a couple of soft blankets from the closet, along with a large heating pad. She set the heating pad on the lowest setting and covered it with one of the blankets, then used the second one to make a little nest. Carefully, she transferred the sleeping kittens to the playpen where they mewed for a few seconds before falling back to sleep.

"I'll take good care of you," she whispered. "In a few weeks you'll be old enough to go to your forever homes. You'll have a great life."

Between now and adoption day, Heather would be their surrogate mother. While time consuming, the task wasn't a stretch. She fostered on a regular basis. Once she got the kittens back to her place, she would be aided by her crabby, mistrustful cat, LC, who loathed her but was an amazing foster dad to all the kittens she brought home.

Heather crossed to her desk and uploaded the signed contracts from Mountain Goat Northwest, their newest client. She'd been courting them for eighteen months, so having them sign on the dotted line was a sweet victory. MGNW specialized in outerwear for various sports but emphasized sustainable fabrics and bright colors, often decorated with faux fur. Many of their jackets and pants could be custom ordered with personalized details such as patterns and trim.

She'd sold MGNW on an experiential marketing campaign—one that would help form a relationship with their customers to create brand loyalty for a lifetime.

Once she'd sent the contracts to accounting, she answered her email briefly, fingers flying over the keyboard. She'd nearly finished when a new email appeared with a familiar subject line.

More detailed DNA results. See who else might be related to you.

"I already know who's related to me," Heather murmured, clicking on the link. She logged in to her Ancestry account and stared at the familiar information.

Potential blood relatives included a few distant cousins, some old lady in Belarus and a married man with two daughters living about forty-five minutes north of Seattle. Her gaze lingered on the last entry.

Fletcher Causey, age fifty-two. From what she'd learned in a cursory online search, he was a high school history teacher, had never been in prison and according to his Facebook page, which for reasons not clear to her wasn't private, was a devoted dad to two girls. He liked sports, grew his own vegetables and had been married to his wife for fifteen years. More compelling than all that was the fact that according to Ancestry, there was a 97.5 percent chance he was also Heather's father. The result of a one-night stand when he and her mother had been eighteen.

She'd learned about the possible DNA match six months ago but had yet to reach out. Her mother was enough of a pain—Heather wasn't interested in another clingy relative. Only Fletcher seemed like a good guy and she'd always wondered about her father and...

"Is it true? Are there kittens?"

She looked up and smiled at Sam, her head of market research. Sam was a genius when it came to understanding demographics and trends, often creating his own algorithms to dig down into the numbers. Heather didn't understand the how of what he did, but she appreciated the results.

"Three of them and you're the first one here."

"I washed my hands," he said as he crossed to the playpen. He slowly removed one kitten, getting a mew of protest as he carefully turned it over before putting it back.

There were two black-and-white kittens and one gray one. The second kitten barely stirred as he lifted it. Once he'd determined the gender, he sat down on the sofa and carefully put a tiny blue collar around its neck.

"Let me guess," she said drily. "Russell Wilson?"

"My hero."

"You know he's no longer a Seahawk. He left the team and our beautiful city."

Sam shook his head. "Don't care. Ten years after he's retired, he'll still be my man."

Heather's watch beeped a five-minute warning for the meeting.

"Time to heat the formula," she said.

"I'll bring these guys." Sam put Russell Wilson into the box and collected the other two kittens.

Heather walked to the break room where she found Tori collecting towels, feeding syringes and cotton balls. A can of formula was on the counter along with a cup of water.

"I warmed the water already," Tori told her. "But check the temperature."

"Thanks. Sam's already claimed his kitten. Did you want to name one?"

Her friend grinned. "Unlike Sam, I'm not comfortable giving kittens the same name over and over again and I've run out of creative options. I'll let someone else give it a shot."

The house rule was the first to help with a kitten got to name it—at least until its adoption.

Heather mixed the formula and tested the temperature before carrying it into the conference room. Her director of digital marketing had already claimed the gray girl. Tori passed out supplies while Heather filled each syringe.

"I hear we're due for a celebration," Elliot Young, her mentor and business partner, said as he walked into the conference room. "Someone signed Mountain Goat Northwest this morning."

He was followed by one of the marketing staff pushing a cart piled high with cupcakes, sparkling water and coffee.

Elliot sat next to her and reached for the kitten she held. "You worked hard for that account. You deserve to celebrate."

Everyone not holding a kitten applauded. Heather felt a flush of pride and gratitude.

"It was a team effort," she told them. "We're going to be good for them and they're going to be good for us."

Elliot set the kitten on the towel and picked up the syringe filled with formula. Like everyone at 206 Marketing Group, he was well practiced in feeding and caring for motherless kittens. It came with the job. During the interview process, all prospective employees were warned that there were nearly always cats in the building, along with Tori's dog. Those with a severe pet allergy might want to think about working elsewhere.

Once everyone had their cupcakes and drinks, Heather took control of the meeting.

"We'll start with experiential marketing," she said, glancing to her left.

As she listened to the update, Heather thought about how fortunate she was in her work life. With Elliot's wise counsel, she'd avoided many of the pitfalls that came with starting a new business. She'd been well funded and had been able to lure away top talent and clients. Four years after opening its doors, the company was thriving and so was she. At least professionally. The rest of her life was a disaster.

Well, not all of it—just the romantic part, driven by her inability to commit. Or say the L word. Okay, and she had trust issues. There was also the confusion of equally wanting and not wanting to meet her birth father. Plus, her mother. Other than that, she was the picture of mental health.

And while most of those problems could be solved—

with the exception of her mother—dealing with them made her uncomfortable. Which was why she had a new batch of foster kittens with which to distract herself.

Better kittens than emotional self-exploration, she thought. Maybe, at the end of the day, business success was enough and the relationship stuff wasn't necessary. A lie, of course, but one she thought she could embrace fully. At least for now.

Can't wait to find out what happens next?
Check out The Happiness Plan *today!*

Available soon from Canary Street Press!

Copyright © 2023 by Susan Mallery, Inc.